"You little wildcat, you haven't changed!"

Judd Prescott jeered. "Seven years may have given you a certain amount of sophistication, but underneath you're as passionate and untamed as ever. You want me to make love to you as much as I do."

"No!" Valerie rushed to deny his words vigorously.

His green eyes flashed at her. "I know you've been hurt and badly used. But I'm positive that I can make you forget the man who made you pregnant and ran off."

"Forget?" Valerie's laugh was strained and bitter. Judd Prescott *was* that man! If she told him, he would have one more reason to force her to resume their long-ago affair. She had fallen victim to her desire for him once—with dire consequences. She was not about to fall again.

Other titles by

JANET DAILEY

IN HARLEQUIN PRESENTS

JANET DAILEY

bed of grass

Harlequin Books

TORONTO • LONDON • NEW YORK • AMSTERDAM
SYDNEY • HAMBURG • PARIS • STOCKHOLM

Harlequin Presents edition published March 1980
ISBN 0-373-10343-3

Original hardcover edition published in 1979
by Mills & Boon Limited

Printed in U.S.A.

CHAPTER ONE

WITH EFFICIENT, PRECISE MOTIONS, Valerie Wentworth folded the lingerie and laid it in the suitcase. Tucking a strand of toffee-colored hair behind her ear, she walked back to the open drawer of the dresser for more. There was a determined line to the sensuous curve of her lips and a glint of purpose in her light brown eyes. Her complexion had a hint of shocked pallor under its pale gold tan.

A woman stood in the room watching Valerie pack. Her expression was not altogether approving of what she saw. She was in her forties; her figure had the solid build of middle age and her brown hair was beginning to become frosted with gray. Her mouth was pinched into lines that discouraged smiles.

"I still say you're a fool, Valerie Wentworth, to go tearing off to Maryland like this." The acerbic tongue of the older woman repeated an earlier claim.

"He was my grandfather." Valerie didn't pause in her packing as she walked to the closet and began stripping clothes from the hangers. "He didn't have any other family but me."

"Elias Wentworth didn't want you around when he was alive. What makes you think he'd want you at his funeral?" came the challenging retort.

"He isn't in a position to say what he wants, is

he?" A trace of anger was in Valerie's voice, an anger caused by the reference to the estrangement between herself and her grandfather. "And nothing you can say is going to make me change my mind, Clara," she warned.

"That sanctimonious old man turned his back on you seven years ago, at a time when you needed him most," Clara Simons reminded her sternly. "Him and his self-righteous ways," she murmured under her breath with a sniff of contempt. "Despite all the letters you wrote him, you haven't so much as received a Christmas card from him in all this time. He disowned you. Blood ties meant nothing to him. After the way he treated you, I wouldn't think they'd mean anything to you, either."

A tailored suit in a rich dark blue fabric was the closest Valerie came to a mourning outfit; her stringent budget couldn't absorb the cost of a new dress. She was inwardly grateful that changing customs no longer made black mandatory at family funerals.

"Granddad took me in and raised me after my parents died," she replied to Clara's comment. "I owe him something for that."

"What utter and complete nonsense!" the woman scoffed at her logic. "How can you feel obligated to that heartless, straight-laced coot? Anyone with an ounce of compassion would have stood beside you seven years ago. They might not have approved of what you'd done, but they would have stood with you and not turned a scared girl like you were out in the cold to fend for herself with no money and no place to go."

"You didn't know me when I was a young girl, Clara," stated Valerie. "I was a wild, irresponsible thing, always into trouble. My escapades would have grayed any young man's head. When I was thirteen, I started smoking cigarettes—I used to sneak off to the stables to smoke. Once I almost set the whole place on fire. I heard granddad coming and threw a burning cigarette away, and it landed in some hay. If granddad hadn't spotted it, the stable would have gone up in flames and the horses with it. Granddad had every right to be enraged with me. It scared me when I realized what I'd almost done, but despite the spanking I got, it didn't stop me."

"All youngster's experiment with cigarettes at some time in their lives." Her friend attempted to rationalize Valerie's behavior. "In your case, I wouldn't be surprised if you got into trouble just to gain that insensitive man's attention."

"You don't understand." Valerie sighed and turned to face the woman who had become her friend, her family and her surrogate mother over the last seven years. "It wasn't just the smoking. I drank his drink until he finally had to lock it up in the safe. I'd take one of his thoroughbred horses and go night-riding. I don't know how many times I led a lame horse home after a midnight gallop. They were valuable animals, his livelihood, and I treated them like toys."

"Children can be thoughtless at times," Clara admitted. Her defense of Valerie was not quite as vigorous as before, but she was still steadfast in her loyalty.

"There was more." She was driven to make a full confession, needing to expose her guilt. "I used to steal money from him to hitchhike into Baltimore and go to movies or just buy things. Sometimes I'd be gone all weekend, but I never told him where I'd been. Can you imagine what I put him through?"

"You're being too hard on yourself," was the stubborn reply. "Don't forget that I know what a frightened, love-starved girl you were when I met you."

"Love-starved," Valerie repeated thoughtfully. An ache that still hadn't receded after seven years flickered in her tawny eyes. "Perhaps," she conceded, since it was the easiest explanation. "But I'll never forget the anguish that was in granddad's face the day I told him I was pregnant." In her mind's eye she could still see the look of knife-stabbing pain he had given her. "He was such a moral, upright man that he felt shamed and disgraced by what I'd done. When he demanded to know who the father was and I beligerently refused to tell him, it was the last straw that broke him."

Tears burned her eyes at the memory of that stormy scene. She hid them in a flurry of activity, hurriedly folding the blouse to her blue suit and laying it in the suitcase.

"But to throw you out!" Clara refused to consider her grandfather's actions as justified.

"For a long time I resented him for abandoning me, even hated him," Valerie admitted. "But I was eighteen. Turning me out was probably the best punishment he could have given, because it made me responsible for myself. Now I know the heartache of worrying over a child, and I only regret that I never had the courage to go back and tell granddad how sorry I was for the anguish he suffered because of me."

"And that's your reason for going to his funeral," Clara concluded, crossing her arms in front of her in a stance that suggested disapproval and challenge. "It's an empty gesture, don't you think? And a costly one, too, considering the wages you'll lose."

"Mr. Hanover has given me the time off and I'm entitled to two days of compassionate pay." She tried to dodge the issue as she closed the suitcase and locked it with a decisive snap.

"What about the other three days you'll be taking off?" The pointed reminder pinned Valerie to the spot. "You won't be getting paid for them. And there's the cost of driving all the way to Maryland, too."

"I'll just have to cut back on a few things." She was determined not to consider the financial ramifications of her decision to attend her grandfather's funeral. Somehow she'd weather it.

"Humph!" Clara breathed out the sound. "You're barely making ends meet now."

"That's my problem." Valerie opened a second, smaller suitcase and set it on the bed. "You can't talk me out of going, Clara. You're just wasting your breath."

Walking to the dressing table, she opened a different drawer and took out half a dozen sets of little-boy-sized underpants and socks. When they were in the second suitcase, she began adding pajamas and slacks and shirts.

Clara watched in silence for several seconds, her expression growing more disgruntled. "If you must go, there's no sense in carting Tadd along with you."

"He'll think it's a vacation like all his school friends take in the summer," Valerie reasoned.

"Well, you won't think it's a vacation while you're driving there and back with that bundle of energy bouncing all over the car seats," her friend declared. "What will you do with him when you get there? A six-year-old boy isn't going to understand about funerals . . . or sit through one."

"I don't have much choice." Valerie glanced at the second single bed in the room, a twin to her own, except for the worn, stuffed teddy bear resting against the pillow. She was aware of the validity of Clara's argument.

"I'll look after him," Clara volunteered. There was a grudging quality to her voice, an impatience that she hadn't been able to persuade Valerie not to go.

She glanced at her friend, her strained features softening as she looked at the stern-faced woman. For all her gruffness, Clara had become her rock. She had been the cook in a restaurant Valerie had stumbled into a week after leaving her grandfather's home. She had been frightened, broke and hungry, looking for any kind of job that would put food in her stomach. Clara had taken pity on her, paid for the meal Valerie couldn't afford, persuaded the owner to hire Valerie as a waitress, and taken her to her apartment to live until she could afford a place of her own, which wasn't until after Tadd was born.

"If school weren't over for the summer, Clara, I might accept your offer," Valerie replied, and shook her head in refusal, pale brown curls swinging loosely around her shoulders. "As it is, you've barely recovered from your bout with pneumonia. The doctor insisted you had to rest for a month before going back to work at the restaurant. Looking after Tadd twenty-four hours a day could never be classified as a rest."

"What about Tadd's father? Will you be seeing him when you go back?" A pair of shrewd blue eyes were watching her closely.

A chill of premonition shivered over Valerie's shoulders. Her hands faltered slightly in the act of folding one of Tadd's shirts. The moment of hesitation passed as quickly as it had come and she was once again poised and sure of her decision.

"Probably," Valerie admitted with a show of indifference. "Meadow Farms adjoins granddad's property, so some member of the Prescott family is bound to put in an appearance at the funeral. I don't know whether it will be Judd or not. He runs the farm now so he may not consider the funeral of an insignificant horse breeder to be worthy of his time, neighbor or not. He may deputize someone else to represent the family."

"No woman ever completely forgets the man who takes her virginity, especially if she eventually bears his child. Do you still care about him, Valerie?" came the quiet but piercing question.

A wound that had never completely healed twisted Valerie's heart, squeezing out a bitter hatred that coated her reply. "I wouldn't have married Judd Prescott if he'd begged me—though he's never begged for anything in his life. He takes what he wants without ever giving a damn about anybody's feelings. He's ruthless, hard and arrogant. I was a fool ever to think I was anything more to him than a means to satisfy his lust," she coldly berated herself. "That's why I never told granddad who the father of my baby was. I knew he'd go over to Meadow Farms with a shotgun in his hand, ranting and raving about family honor and scandal, and I would rather have been stoned than see Judd Prescott's derisive amusement at the thought of being forced to marry me."

The suppressed violence in Valerie's denial and rejection of Tadd's father brought a troubled light to Clara's eyes. Her expression was uneasy, but Valerie was too caught up in her own turmoil to notice the gathering silence that met her denunciation. She continued folding and packing her son's clothes into the suitcase.

"Do you know, I believe there's a sensible solution to our problem?" Clara said after the long pause.

"What problem?" Valerie glanced briefly at her friend. There was none as far as she was concerned.

"I'm going crazy sitting around my apartment doing nothing and you're going to have your hands full trying to cope with Tadd on this trip." It was more of a statement than an explanation. "A change of scenery would do me good, so I'll ride along with you to Maryland. Naturally I'll pay my share of the expenses."

"I can't let you do that," Valerie protested. "I'd love to have you come with me—you know that. But you've done so much for me already that I couldn't take any money from you for the trip."

Clara shrugged her wide shoulders, her gaze running over Valerie's shapely, petite figure. "You aren't big enough to stop me." Turning toward the door, she added over her shoulder, "I'll go pack and fix some sandwiches to take along on the trip. I'll be ready in less than an hour."

Before Valerie's lips could form an objection, Clara was gone. A half smile tilted the corners of her mouth when she heard her apartment door closing. Arguing with Clara was useless: once she had made up her mind about something, not even dynamite could budge her.

Valerie didn't like to contemplate what her life might have been like if she hadn't met the other woman. It hadn't simply been food, a place to live or a job that Clara had given her. She had encouraged Valerie to take night courses in secretarial work, to acquire skills that would help her to obtain a better-paying job so she could take care of herself and Tadd.

Many times Valerie had thanked God for guiding her to this woman who was both friend and adviser, supporter and confidante. This gesture of accompanying her made her doubly grateful. Although she hadn't admitted it, she was apprehensive about going back for the funeral. There were a lot of people to be faced, including Judd Prescott.

Walking to the single bed in the corner, Valerie picked up the teddy bear to put in the suitcase. A combination of things made her hold the toy in her arms—the notification a few hours earlier of her grandfather's death, her hurried decision to attend his funeral, her discussion with Clara and the memories attached to her departure from Maryland seven years ago.

Those last were impossible to think about without Judd Prescott becoming entangled with them. Her interest in him had been sparked by a remark she'd overheard her grandfather make condemning the eldest Prescott son for his rakehell reputation. Prior to that Valerie had no interest in the wealthy occupants of Meadow Farms, dismissing them as stiff-necked snobs.

Meadow Farms was a renowned name in race-horse circles, famous for consistently breeding stakes-class thoroughbreds. The farm itself was a showcase, a standard of measure for other horse breeders. Few had ever matched its size or the quality of horses that were bred and raised there.

Her grandfather's low opinion of Judd Prescott had aroused her curiosity. She had ridden onto Meadow Farms land with the express purpose of meeting him. One glimpse of the tall, hard-featured man with ebony hair and devil green eyes had fascinated her. A dangerous excitement seemed to pound through her veins when he looked at her.

In the beginning, Valerie pursued him boldly, almost brazenly, arranging chance encounters that had nothing to do with chance at all. The glint in his eyes seemed to tell her he was aware they weren't, too. It angered her, the way he had silently mocked her initial attempts to flirt with him.

The first few times Judd kissed her, it was with the indulgent air of an adult giving candy to a beguiling child. It didn't take Valerie long to discover that her responses disturbed him and the warm ardency of their kisses became less one-sided.

Her previous experiences with the male sex had been with boys her own age or a year or two older, never with anyone more than ten years her senior. She had kissed many boys, necked with a few, but enough to know that the sensations Judd aroused were not common in an embrace. Also, he was skilled. His mouth knew how to excite her and his hands how to caress her.

What had started out as a lark became something more, and Valerie fell in love with him. Aware that he was a man with experience, she realized that her kisses wouldn't hold his interest for long, and her fear of losing him outweighed her fear of the unknown.

One afternoon Valerie noticed him riding alone through a wooded pasture adjoining her grandfather's land. Saddling a horse, she swallowed her nervousness and her pride and rode out to meet him. They rode only a short distance together before pausing to dismount under the shade of a tree. An embrace followed naturally. When Valerie demanded that he make love to her, Judd's hesitation was brief, his affirmative response given in a burning kiss.

Afterward he was oddly uncommunicative, an expressionless glitter in his green eyes whenever they were directed at her. Valerie suspected it was because he was the first to know her. Secretly she wanted him to be disturbed by the fact, to feel a little obligated, perhaps even guilty. Because she loved him so intensely, she had subconsciously attempted to blackmail him emotionally, making him the seducer and herself the innocent victim. When they parted he had said nothing, but Valerie was unconcerned.

Days went by without her seeing him before she finally realized that Judd was avoiding her. Hurt grew into indignation and finally a smoldering anger. Her injured pride demanded revenge. She began haunting the edges of the Meadow Farms stable yard, hoping to catch Judd alone.

At the sight of the luxury sports car that Judd usually drove coming slowly up the paddocked driveway to the stable, Valerie set her fleet-footed horse on a route that would intersect the car's path before it reached its destination. Jumping her mount over a paddock fence, she halted it in the middle of the road to block the way. The car's brakes were applied sharply to bring it to a skidding stop before hitting her.

Judd came storming out of the driver's side of the car, his features stone-cold with rage. "What the hell were you trying to do? Get yourself killed?" His icy gaze flicked to the lathered horse, dancing nervously under her tight rein. "And if you don't give a damn about yourself, you have no business abusing blooded animals that way. His mouth will be raw if you don't quit sawing on those reins."

"Don't tell me how to ride a horse! And what do you care what happens to me anyway!" Valerie had flamed. "At least I know what kind of a low, contemptible man you are! You take a girl's virginity, then drop her cold!!"

"I didn't want it." Judd drew out the denial through clenched teeth. "Considering the reputation you have, I thought you'd lost it years ago."

Valerie went white with rage at his insulting remark. She jabbed her heels into the sides of her hunter, sending it lunging toward the tall, insolent man. He stepped to the side and she began striking at him with her riding crop. Catching hold of the end, Judd pulled her from the saddle. Her horse then bolted for home pastures.

After he had twisted the riding quirt out of her grip, he crushed her twisting, kicking body against him. "You little she-cat, I should use this on you!" His savagely muttered threat made Valerie struggle all the more wildly, cursing and swearing at him, calling him every name she could think of. He laughed cruelly. "Your language would put a stablehand to shame!"

An animallike scream of frustration sounded in her throat, but immediately his mouth bruised her lips to punish them into silence. The dominating quality of his kiss subdued the rest of her until the only twisting Valerie did was to get closer to his leanly muscled frame.

When his mouth ended its possession of hers, she whispered, "Make love to me again, Judd."

"You damned little temptress," But his voice was husky with passion, the smoldering light in his green eyes fanning her trembling desire.

Valerie received the answer she wanted when he swept her off her feet into his arms and carried her to a secluded bed of grass that was to become their meeting place during the following months.

What Valerie lacked in experience, she made up for in willingness. Under the guidance of a master in the art of love, she learned rapidly. Over the course of time it became evident to her that Judd desired her as much as she desired him. Secure in this knowledge, it never bothered her that he didn't take her out anywhere. Besides, there was her grandfather's wrath to be considered if he should find out about the two of them.

Even when she first suspected she was pregnant, she wasn't worried. Nor later, when she hitched a ride to Baltimore to a medical clinic for confirmation of her condition, was she apprehensive. She was certain Judd would be as pleased as she was about the news and would be moved to propose.

She was saddling a horse to ride over to Meadow Farms when her grandfather walked up. "Where you going?" he demanded.

Valerie responded with a half-truth, patting the sleek neck of the bay horse. "I thought I'd take Sandal out for a canter, maybe over toward Meadow

Farms." Just in case he would see her heading in that direction.

"The place will probably be bustling with activity, what with the party and all," he commented in a disapproving way.

"What party?" It had been the first Valerie had heard about one.

"The Prescotts are having one of their lavish society affairs tonight." His eyes narrowed on her in accusing speculation. "And don't you be getting any ideas about crashing it. No granddaughter of mine is going to get involved with such carrying-on."

"Yes, granddad." Despite the feigned meekness of her tone, a vision had already begun to form of Judd possessively holding her hand while he introduced her to friends and family at the party.

Wrapped in her romantic imaginings, Valerie rode off to the secluded place in the wooded pasture where they always met, but Judd wasn't there. Even though the meeting hadn't been prearranged, she was positive he would appear. Within minutes after she had dismounted, he rode into the clearing.

There were so many things she wanted to tell him in that instant: how ruggedly handsome he was, how much she loved him, about the baby—their baby—and how ecstatically happy she was. But something made her keep all that inside. She even turned away when he dismounted and plucked a green leaf from a low-hanging branch.

"It's a beautiful day, isn't it?" she observed instead.

"Beautiful," came his husky agreement from directly behind her.

When his hands circled her waist to cup her breasts and draw her shoulders against his chest, Valerie breathed in sharply and exhaled in a sigh of pure pleasure. Her head lolled backward against his chest while his mouth moved against the windblown waves of her caramel hair.

"How do you always know when I come here?" she murmured, the wonder of it something she had never questioned before.

"A fire starts burning inside of me, here." His hand slid low on her stomach to indicate the location, his mouth moving against her hair as he spoke.

Valerie turned in his arms, in answer to the flames he had started within her. Hungrily he began devouring her lips and she felt herself begin to surrender to his appetite. But she wanted to talk. Finally she dragged her lips from the domination of his, letting his mouth wander over her cheek and ear and nibble sensuously at her throat.

"I thought you wouldn't come today," she said weakly.

"Why?" Judd sounded amused.

"Because of the party." Her limbs were turning to water.

"That isn't until tonight." He dismissed its importance, but made no suggestion that she should attend.

Valerie understood why no invitation had been given to her grandfather. He was not in the Prescotts' social or financial sphere. Besides, he was morally opposed to drinking and dancing. He would have considered it an offense to be invited, not a courtesy.

"I've never been to a party like that before." Valerie tried not to be too open about seeking an invitation. "It must be grand. I suppose the women will be wearing diamonds and beautiful gowns."

"In all their clothes, none of them will look lovelier than you do without any." Even as he spoke, his hands were unbuttoning her blouse.

Valerie attempted to gently forestall his efforts. "Why didn't you invite me?" Her question was light, not betraying how much she wanted to know.

"You wouldn't like it." His mouth worked its way to the hollow of her throat, tipping her head back to allow greater access.

"How do you know?" She strained slightly against his hold.

Judd lifted his head, ebony hair gleaming in the sunlight. Impatience was written behind his lazy regard. A firmness strengthened the line of his mouth.

"Because it isn't your kind of party," he replied in a tone that said the discussion was at an end.

At that moment fear began to gnaw at Valerie's confidence. Proud defiance was present in the way she returned his look.

"Maybe you aren't inviting me because you've made arrangements to take somebody else," she challenged.

"It isn't any of your business." A cold smile

touched his mouth as it began to descend toward hers.

Hurt by his attitude as much as his words, Valerie tried to draw out of his arms. Her blouse gaped open in the front and his gaze roamed downward to observe the creamy globes of her breasts nearly spilling free of her lacy bra. His hand moved to help them, but she managed to stop it.

"Please, I want to talk, Judd," she insisted.

"Why waste energy with words when it can be put to more pleasurable use?" he argued, and pressed her hips against his so she could feel his urgent need for her.

With a sickening rush of despair, she realized that they seldom talked when they met. They made love, rested and went their separate ways. Their past communications had always been physical, never verbal. Valerie suddenly saw what a fool she had been to think otherwise.

"Let me go!" She pushed angrily at his chest, the yellow lights in her pale brown eyes flashing warning signals of temper.

"What's this little display of outrage about?" Judd eyed her with cynical amusement, holding her but no longer forcing her close to him. "After as many times as we've made love together, it's a little late to be playing hard to get."

Her temper flared, adrenalin surging through her muscles to give them strength, and she broke out of his encircling arms.

"That's all I mean to you, isn't it?" she accused. "I'm just someone to roll around on the grass with, someone to satisfy your lusts. To you, I'm nothing but a cheap little tramp. I'm not good enough for you to be seen in public with!"

"You'd better sheathe your claws, tigress. You're the one who invited me into your bed of grass," Judd reminded her with deadly calm.

A couple of long jerky strides carried Valerie to the place where her horse was tethered. She gathered up the reins and mounted before turning to face him.

"I hope you go to hell, Judd Prescott." Her voice had begun to tremble. "And I hope it's a long, hot trip!"

Putting her heels to her mount, she turned and galloped the horse toward her grandfather's farm. Tears drenched her cheeks with hot, salty moisture. All her rosy dreams were shattered that day when she realized Judd had never felt more than desire for her.

An hour later she informed her grandfather that she was pregnant, immune to his wrath when she refused to tell him it was Judd who had fathered the life she carried. It was almost a relief when he ordered her out of the house. She put as much distance between herself and Maryland as possible.

That was how she had ended up here in Cincinnati, Ohio, living in the same apartment complex as Clara, with an illegitimate six-year-old son, and a job as secretary to an industrial plant executive.

Her cheeks felt hot and wet. She lifted the hand that had been clutching the teddy bear and touched her fingers to her face. They came away wet with tears. The wound inside her was as raw and fresh as it had been seven years ago. She scrubbed her cheeks dry with the back of her hands and blinked her eyes to ease the stinging sensation.

"Mom!"

A three-foot-tall whirlwind came racing into the bedroom. It stopped its motion long enough for her to gaze into a pair of hazel eyes predominantly shaded with olive green. Hair a darker shade of brown than her own fell across his forehead, crowding into his eyes.

"Clara said I was to come into the house. You said I could play outside until you called me," he declared in a breathless rush, already edging toward the door again. "Can I go back out? It's my turn after Tommy's to ride Mike's Big Wheels. What are you doing with Toby?" He saw the teddy bear in her arms.

"I was just packing him in your suitcase," she explained. "We're going on a trip, remember?"

Tadd momentarily forgot his turn on the Big Wheels. "Where's Maryland?"

"It's a long way from here. We'll have to drive all day." Valerie laid the teddy bear on top of his suitcase. "We'll be ready to go soon, so you'd better wash your face and hands and change into those clean clothes." She pointed to the colored T-shirt and jeans lying on the bed.

Tadd made a face when she told him he had to wash. "Why are we going to Maryland?"

"Because your great-grandfather died and I want to go to his funeral," she answered patiently.

"Why?"

Valerie concealed a sigh. She was never certain whether his questions were asked out of genuine interest or as an excuse to postpone something he didn't want to do.

"When I was your age, I didn't have a mommy, so your great-grandfather took care of me. I cared about him the way you care about me. That's why I want to go to his funeral."

"Did I know him?" Tadd tilted his head to one side, his expression showing only innocent curiosity.

"No." Valerie shook her head.

Her teeth nibbled at the inside of her lower lip. She had written to her grandfather about Tadd's birth, but had never received any form of acknowledgement. None of the letters she had regularly sent had ever been answered.

"Do I have a grandfather?" He altered the subject slightly.

Valerie hesitated. The only relatives Tadd had that were still living were on the Prescott side. But for the time being it was better if he didn't know about them. The time would come soon enough for him to learn about his heritage.

"No." Not legally, she defended her lie.

"If you died, there wouldn't be anybody to take care of me, would there? I'd be an orphan," he stated with a round-eyed look.

"Clara would look after you," Valerie reassured him, bending to kiss his forehead before he could dodge away. "Go and wash." She administered a playful spank to his backside as he scampered toward the bathroom. "You'd better hurry, too," she called the warning after him. "Clara's coming with us and you know how upset she gets if people aren't ready on time."

CHAPTER TWO

VALERIE HAD DONE most of the driving, with Clara spelling her for an hour every so often to give her a rest. They had traveled well into the night before stopping at an inexpensive motel along the highway for a few hours' sleep. The morning sun was in their faces, its light shining on the countryside of Maryland.

"How long before we get there, mom?" Tadd piped the question from the back seat and leaned over the middle armrest to hear her answer.

"To save the wear and tear on your vocal cords, Tadd, we should have tape-recorded that question when we started out." Behind the searing dryness of Clara's voice, there was a hint of amused tolerance. "You must have asked it a thousand times."

"How long, mom?" he repeated.

"Not long. We'll be seeing the lane to the farm any minute now." Valerie discovered her hands were gripping the steering wheel until her knuckles were white.

Seven years had brought some changes to the area where she had once lived, but they had just driven past the entrance gates to Meadow Farms. Charcoal black fences marked off its paddocks. Just over that far hill near that stand of trees was the place where she used to meet Judd. It was one place she would have preferred to forget.

"That's a fancy-looking place," Clara observed, but her eyes were on her companion when Valerie shot her a startled look.

"Yes," she agreed nervously. "It's the Prescott place." She knew she was confirming what Clara had already guessed.

"Look at all the horses!" Tadd breathed, pressing his face against a side window. "Did they ever let you ride them when you were a kid, mom?"

"I didn't ride any of those, but your grandfather owned horses. He raised them," Valerie explained, shifting the subject away from the breeding farm they were passing. "I used to ride his."

"You can ride?" There was a squeak of disbelief in his voice. "Gee, I wish I had a horse."

"Where would you keep it?" Clara wanted to know. "It's too big for the apartment. Besides, you're not allowed to have pets."

"When I get big, I'm going to move out of there and get me a horse," Tadd stated, his tone bordering on a challenge.

"When you get big, you'll want a car," Clara retorted.

"No, I won't." After the confinement of the car for almost twelve hours, Tadd was beginning to get irritable. Usually he enjoyed arguing with Clara, but he was starting to sound mutinous.

"Here's granddad's place." Valerie distracted his attention as she turned the car onto a narrow dirt lane.

A sign hung from a post on the left-hand side. The paint had faded, but enough of the letters were still distinguishable to make out the name Worth Farms, a shortened appellation of Wentworth. Board fences flanked the lane. Once they had been painted white, but the sun had blistered the paint away, leaving the wood grayed and weathered. Half a dozen mares with foals could be seen grazing in the green carpet of grass in the pasture.

"Look, Tadd." Valerie pointed to the opposite side of the car from where he was sitting. "There are horses here, too."

But not for long, she thought to herself. With her grandfather gone, they would be sold off, and the farm, too. It was difficult to accept that the place she had always regarded as home would soon belong to someone else. It was a sorrow, a resigned regret. Valerie had no hard feelings against her grandfather for disinheriting her; she had given him ample cause as a teenager.

"Can we stop and see the horses, mom?" Tadd bounced anxiously in the back seat, not satisfied with the slowed pace of the car that gave him a long time to watch the sleek, glistening animals.

"Later," Valerie qualified her refusal.

"Promise?" he demanded.

"I promise," she agreed, and let her gaze slide to Clara, whose shrewd eyes were inspecting the property. "The house and barns are just ahead." The roofs and part of the structures were in view.

"Are you sure there'll be somebody there?" Clara questioned with dry skepticism.

"Mickey Flanners will be there. I know he'll let us stay long enough to wash and clean up. We can find out from him the details about the funeral arrangements and all," she explained, and smiled briefly. "You'll like Mickey," she told her friend. "He's an ex-jockey. He's worked for granddad for years, taking care of the horses and doing odd jobs around the place. He's probably looking after things now until all the legal matters are settled and the farm . . . is sold." Again she felt the twinge of regret that this was no longer her home, not when her grandfather was alive nor now. She covered the pause with a quick, "Mickey is a lovable character."

"Which means he's short and fat, I suppose." The cutting edge of Clara's statement was blunted by her droll brand of humor.

"Short and pudgy," Valerie corrected with a twinkling look.

As they entered the yard of the horse farm, the barns and stables were the first to catch her eye. Although they were in need of a coat of paint, they were in good repair. Valerie hadn't expected differently. Her grandfather had never allowed anything to become run-down. The two-story house was in the same shape, needing paint but well kept. The lawn was overgrown with weeds in dire need of mowing.

Her sweeping inspection of the premises ended as her gaze was caught by a luxury-model car parked in front of the house. A film of dust coated the sides, picked up from dirt roads. A tingling sensation danced over her nerve ends. Her mouth felt dry and she swallowed convulsively.

"Did you really used to live here, mom?" Tadd's eager voice seemed to come from a great distance.

"Yes." Her answer was absent.

"I wish I did," was his wistful response.

Automatically Valerie parked beside the other car. It could belong to any number of people, she told herself, a lawyer, a banker, someone from the funeral home, just anyone. But somehow she knew better.

The car's engine had barely stopped turning before Tadd was opening the back door and scrambling out. Valerie followed his lead, but in a somewhat dazed fashion. A small hand grabbed hold of hers and tugged to pull her away from the house.

"Let's go see the horses, mom," Tadd demanded. "You promised we would."

"Later." But she was hardly conscious of answering him. An invisible magnet was pulling her toward the house, its compelling force stronger than the pleadings of her son.

"I want to go now!" His angry declaration fell on deaf ears.

The screen door onto the front porch opened and a man stepped onto the painted board floor. The top buttons of his white shirt were unfastened, exposing the bronze skin of his hair-roughened chest. Long sleeves had been rolled back, revealing the corded muscles of his forearms. The white of his shirt tapered to male hips, dark trousers stretching the length of his supple, muscled legs.

But it was the unblinking stare of green eyes that held Valerie in their thrall. Fine lines fanned out from the corners of them. Harsh grooves were etched on either side of his mouth, carved into sun-browned skin stretched leanly from cheekbone to jawline. His jet black hair was in casual disorder that was somehow sensuous.

Her heart had stopped beating at the sight of Judd, only to start up again at racing speed to send the blood pounding hotly through her veins. The seven years melted away until they were no longer ago than yesterday. Untold pleasures were no farther away than the short distance that separated them. That chiseled mouth had only to take possession of hers to transport her to the world of secret delights.

The compulsion was strong to take the last few steps to reach that hard male body. Valerie would have succumbed to it if the small hand holding hers hadn't tugged her arm to demand her attention. Reluctantly she dragged her gaze from Judd and glanced down to the small boy at her side. Only a few seconds had passed instead of years.

"Who's that man?" Tadd frowned, eyeing Judd with a look that was both puzzled and wary.

Valerie couldn't help wondering what would happen if she told him Judd was his father. But of course she couldn't, and didn't. Tadd's question had succeeded in bringing her to her senses. Valerie realized the painful truth that the aching rawness of her desire for Judd hadn't diminished over the years of separation, but she was equally determined not to become enslaved by that love as she had been seven years ago.

Her gaze swung back to Judd, her amber-flecked eyes masked. "It's a neighbor, Judd Prescott." Her voice sounded remarkably calm.

A muttered sigh came from Clara, issued low for Valerie's ears alone. "I didn't think it was your lovable Mickey." Her comment implied that she had guessed Judd's identity the minute he stepped out of the house.

Valerie didn't have time to acknowledge her friend's remark, for Judd was walking down the porch steps to greet her. He extended a hand toward her.

"Welcome home, Valerie." His low-pitched voice carried little other expression than courtesy. "I'm sorry your return is under these circumstances."

His words of sympathy were just that—words. They carried no sincerity. A bitter surge of resentment made her want to hurl them back in his face. One look at his hard features cast in bronze told her he was incapable of feelings, except the baser kind.

Valerie swallowed the impulse and murmured a stiff, "I'm sorry, too."

Unconsciously she placed her hand in his. When she felt the strong grip of his fingers closing over her own, she was struck by the irony of the situation. She was politely and impersonally shaking hands with a man who knew her more intimately than anyone ever had, a man who was the father of her child. There wasn't any part of her that the hand she held hadn't explored many times and with devastating thoroughness. She felt the beginnings of a trembling desire and withdrew her hand from his before she betrayed it.

"I'm Tadd." Her son demanded his share of the attention.

Her hand drifted to his small shoulder. "This is my son," she told Judd, and watched his reaction.

He didn't seem surprised by her announcement, nor was there any suspicion in his expression that he was looking into the face of his child. Valerie supposed that she saw the faint resemblance between the two because she knew and was looking for it.

"Hello, Tadd." Judd bent slightly at the waist to shake hands with the boy. It was a gesture minus the warmth of affection or friendliness, prompted only by courtesy.

At first Tadd seemed slightly overwhelmed by the action. Then a smile of importance widened his mouth. "Hello," he replied.

Valerie realized it was the first time an adult had ever shaken hands with him; usually they rumpled his hair and tweaked his chin. No wonder he was looking so proud and important! She was almost angry with Judd for being the one to treat Tadd as something other than a pet, because she knew he meant nothing by it. She stifled the rush of antagonism and turned to introduce him to Clara.

"Clara, this is Judd Prescott. He owns the land that adjoins my grandfather's." The explanation was unnecessary, but Valerie made it to show Judd that she hadn't found him important enough to discuss with her friend prior to their arrival. "This is my friend Mrs. Clara Simons."

"I'm pleased to meet you, Mrs. Simons." Judd issued the polite phrase and shook Clara's hand.

"Likewise, I'm sure." Clara returned the polite phrasing, while the two of them eyed each other like a pair of opponents taking the measure of one another's strengths and weaknesses. Tension seemed to crackle in the air.

"I didn't expect to see you here when we arrived, Judd." Valerie's brittle comment was a challenge to explain his presence on the farm. "I thought we'd find Mickey instead."

"Did you?" The gleam in his eyes seemed to taunt her statement, but Judd went on smoothly without waiting for a reply. "Mick is here. I just stopped by to check on things and see if there was any way I could be of assistance."

"A neighborly call, hmm?" Clara's sharp voice questioned his motive with mockery.

But he remained unscathed by the jibe, his cat green gaze swinging to the stoutly built woman unperturbed. "Something like that," he agreed. Turning to one side, he called toward the house, "Mick? Valerie has arrived."

"You don't say!" came the muffled exclamation in a lilting tenor voice that Valerie remembered well, and seconds later a short squat figure came bustling out of the house. Mickey looked older and wasn't as agile as she remembered. The wispy crop of hair on his head still reminded her of straw, but it was thinner. "As I live and breathe, it's Valerie!"

"Hello, Mickey." She smiled, unaware of the warmth and affection her expression held or the way Judd's eyes narrowed into green slits at the unconsciously alluring transformation.

With slightly bowed legs, Mickey Flanners was built so close to the ground that he appeared to tumble down the steps to greet her. A head shorter than she was, he clasped one of her hands in the powerful grip of both of his. She realized that his hands still had the strength to control the most fractious of horses.

"I got word yesterday afternoon that you was coming for the funeral, but I didn't know how soon you'd get here." His knowledge was of horses, not subjects like grammar, but his brand of reckless Irish charm made it easy to overlook.

"We drove practically straight through," Valerie explained. "We stopped here before going into town to rest and find out the details about the funeral arrangements. I thought you would know about them."

"Of course I do. You—" Mickey began, only to be interrupted by Tadd.

"You aren't even as tall as my mom. When are you going to grow up?" he wanted to know.

"Mind your tongue, Tadd!" It was Clara who snapped out the reproval, but Valerie just smiled and Mickey laughed, never having been sensitive about his size, and Judd's green eyes simply observed.

"To tell you the truth, me lad—" Mick adopted a poor imitation of an Irish brogue and winked at Valerie "—I don't intend to ever grow up," he confided to Tadd in a loud whisper. "Wouldn't you like to stay little like me all your life?"

Without hesitation, Tadd made a negative shake of his head. "No, I want to grow tall like him." He pointed at Judd.

Valerie caught her breath at the amused twitch of Judd's mouth. But he didn't know it was his son who wanted to grow up like him. At the rate Tadd was growing out of his clothes, she guessed he probably would top the six-foot mark like Judd.

"Well, if that's the way you feel about it, there's nothing I can do." Mickey looked properly crestfallen, but laughter danced in the eyes as he turned toward Valerie. "Where's your luggage? I'll carry it in the house for you."

"We were planning to stay at a motel in town." Valerie's instinctive response was a protest.

"A motel?" Mickey stepped back. "Eli would have my hide if I let you and the boy stay at a motel! I mean—if he was alive," he corrected with a sobering look. "You're the only family he had. There's no sense in sleeping in a strange place when your old bedroom is empty."

"Our luggage is in the trunk of the car and the keys are in the ignition." Clara offered this information while Valerie was still absorbing Mickey's reply.

He had made it sound as if her grandfather would have wanted her back. And he had known about Tadd, and obviously hadn't kept it a secret or Mickey would not have taken his presence for granted. For that reason alone Valerie wasn't going to argue about staying, discounting the fact that she could ill afford the cost of the motel room.

Mickey's ebullient spirits could never be battened down for long. They surfaced again as he obtained the key from the ignition and walked to the rear of the car to unlock the trunk. He began unloading the suitcases, chattering continuously.

"When you left here, Valerie, old Eli seemed to lose heart. He didn't quit or anything like that—he'd never give up his horses—but he just didn't seem to have the enthusiasm anymore." Mickey paused to glance around the place. "For the last three years he'd been talking about painting everything, but he never got around to it. The truth is I don't think he had the money to hire it done and neither one of us was spry enough to paint it ourselves. And you know your grandfather: if he couldn't pay cash for what he wanted, he did without." He set the last suitcase on the ground. "Is this all of them?"

"Yes," Valerie nodded.

He glanced down at them. "Guess I'll have to make two trips."

"I'll help you carry them inside, Mick," Judd volunteered, as the ex-jockey had expected him to do. Judd was aware of Mickey's tactics, but appeared tolerant.

"Thanks, Judd." Mickey picked out the heaviest suitcases and handed them to him.

That was when Valerie noticed that Tadd had tagged along after Judd. He tipped his dark head way back to look up at him, a determinedly adult look on his childish face.

"I can carry one," he insisted.

"Do you think so?" Judd's glance was indulgent and tolerant, but indifferent. He nodded toward Valerie's makeup case. "That one looks about your size. Can you handle it?"

"Sure." Tadd picked it up with both hands. It bounced against his knees as he walked behind Judd toward the house.

"I'll tell you one thing, Valerie," Mickey was saying as he led the way up the porch steps and into the house. "Your granddad sure perked up when he found out he had a great-grandchild. Proud as a peacock, he was, passing out cigars to anybody that came within hailing distance."

A lump entered Valerie's throat. Her grandfather had been proud; he hadn't been ashamed when he learned of Tadd's birth. Why hadn't he let her know? She would have brought Tadd for him to see. Hadn't he realized that she had expected her reception to be a door slamming in her face?

"Ain't got no coffee made," Mick added. "But I guess you could make a pot while we take the luggage to your rooms. Ain't nothing been changed since you left, so the fixings are where they always were. You know what old Eli said: 'a place for everything and everything in its place,' " he quoted the old adage that her grandfather had recited many times.

"A cup of coffee is just what I need," Clara stated briskly. "You go and fix some, Valerie, while I see to our luggage and hang our clothes up before they're permanently wrinkled."

Valerie was left downstairs to make her way to the kitchen while the rest of them climbed the steps to the second-floor bedrooms. She hadn't realized how tense she had been in Judd's presence until she was away from him. Her severely controlled nerves seemed to almost shudder in relief when she stood alone in the simple farm kitchen. She had wanted that fiery attraction between them to be dead, but it wasn't—not for her.

She heard footsteps approaching the kitchen, more than one set, and began filling the coffeepot with water. She turned off the taps as Judd entered the kitchen, followed closely by Tadd and Mickey.

"I saw the bedroom where you slept as a little kid, mom," Tadd announced, bouncing over to the counter and standing on tiptoe to see what she was doing. "Mickey showed it to me. He said it was the same bed you used to sleep in. Can I sleep in it, mom?"

"Yes, you may sleep in my bed if you want to," she agreed, and turned to open the cupboard on her left.

Her gaze encountered Judd's. She had the disturbing sensation that she had just given permission to him instead of her son. The canister of coffee was where it had always been kept. Her shaking hands lifted it down to the counter top as she turned to avoid the glitter of his eyes.

"When can we go see the horses?" Tadd reverted to his previous theme.

"Later on. I told you that before," Valerie replied with a hint of impatience creeping through.

"But it is later," he reasoned." And you promised."

"Tadd, I'm making coffee." She shot him a warning look not to pursue the issue and his lower lip jutted out in a pout.

"So it's horses you're wanting to see, is it, lad?" Mickey's lilting voice brought the light of hope back into Tadd's hazel green eyes.

"Yes, would you take me?" he asked unashamedly.

"First I have to find out how bad you want to see them," Mick cautioned, and walked over to open a cupboard drawer. "You can either have a piece of candy—" he held up a chocolate bar "—or you can come with me to see the horses. Which will it be?"

Except to glance at the candy, Tadd didn't hesitate. "The horses."

Mickey tossed him the chocolate bar. "Spoken like a true horseman! Your great-granddaddy would have been proud to hear you say that."

Tadd stared at the candy. "Aren't you going to take me to see the horses?"

"Of course, lad." Mickey reassured him with a wink. "But you'll be needin" some energy for the walk, won't you?"

"You mean I can have both?" Tadd wanted to be sure before he tore off the paper wrapping around the bar.

"Isn't that what I just said?" Mick teased, and moved toward the back door. "Come along, lad. And don't you be worrying about him, Valerie. I'll watch over him the same as I watched over you."

Valerie had enjoyed watching Mickey work his Irish charm on her son. It wasn't until the door shut that she realized she had been left alone in the kitchen with Judd. What was keeping Clara, she wondered desperately, but was determined not to lose her composure.

"Mickey has always had a way with children," she said into the silence, not risking a glance at Judd as she spooned the coffee grounds into the percolator basket.

"That's because there's a little bit of truth in the fact that he's never grown up." Judd had moved closer. Valerie was fully aware of his disconcerting gaze watching her. He leaned a hip against the counter a few feet from where she worked and entered her line of vision. "I knew you were coming," he said with studied quietness.

She glanced up, the implication of his words jolting through her. Judd had meant that he had known she was coming the same way he had always known when she would be at their meeting place, and she didn't want to know that.

Deliberately she pretended she was unaware of a hidden meaning in his comment. "Word gets around fast, doesn't it? I did tell the hospital when they called that I'd be coming as soon as I could. I suppose everyone in the area knows it by now." She put the lid on the coffeepot and plugged the cord into a socket. Out the kitchen window she could see Tadd skipping alongside Mickey on their way to the barns. "I suppose you're finally married and have a family of your own now." She turned away, trying not to picture Judd in the arms of some beautiful debutante.

"No, to both of those." An aloofness had entered his chiseled features when she glanced at him. "You've matured into a beautiful woman, Valerie." It was a statement, flatly issued, yet with the power to stir her senses as only Judd could.

"Thank you." She tried to accept his words as merely a compliment, but she didn't know how successful she had been.

"I'm sorry your husband wasn't able to accompany you. I would have liked to meet him," he said.

"My husband? Who told you I was married?" Except for startled surprise, there was little expression in her face.

"Your grandfather, of course." He tilted his head to one side, black hair gleaming in a shaft of sunlight.

Valerie realized that she should have guessed her grandfather would come up with a story like that in order to claim his great-grandson without feeling shame.

"That was rather a foolish question for me to ask, wasn't it?" she commented dryly.

Judd didn't make any comment to that. "I suppose he wasn't able to get time off from his job."

Valerie was toying with the idea of revealing her grandfather's lie and correcting Judd's impression that she wasn't married. When she had decided, shortly after Tadd was born, to keep him rather than give him up for adoption, she had accepted the fact that she would have to live with the illegitimacy of his birth, and refused to hide behind a phony wedding ring.

Before she could tell Judd that she had no husband and never did, Clara walked into the kitchen. She glanced from Valerie to Judd and back to Valerie.

"Where's Tadd?" she asked.

"Mickey took him out to see the horses," Valerie explained.

"Is the coffee done?" Clara sat down in one of the kitchen chairs, making it clear that she wasn't budging. "Will you be staying for coffee, Mr. Prescott?" Behind the question was a challenge to explain the reason he was still here.

"No, I don't believe so." Amusement glinted in his green eyes at the belligerently protective attitude of the older woman. His attention returned to Valerie. "The funeral home will be open from six until eight this evening so your grandfather's friends can come to pay their respects. You're welcome to ride in with me if you wish."

"It's kind of you to offer, but we'll find our own way." Valerie refused in the politest of tones.

He inclined his head in silent acceptance of her decision. Bidding them both an impersonal goodbye, Judd left. Neither woman spoke until they heard the roar of a powerful engine starting up at the front of the house.

"Well?" Clara prompted.

"Well, what?" Valerie was deliberately obtuse.

"Well, what did he have to say?" Clara demanded in gruffly autocratic tones.

"Nothing, really, if you mean any reference to our former . . . relationship." Valerie removed two cups from the cabinet above the stove.

"Did he say anything to you about Tadd?"

"No. Judd thinks I'm married. It's a story granddad cooked up."

"Did you tell him differently?" Clara wanted to know, an eyebrow lifting.

"I started to when you walked in," admitted Valerie, and shrugged. "I suppose it's just as well I didn't. Whether I'm supposedly married or single, it doesn't change anything."

"Are you going to tell him that Tadd is his son?"

"If he asks me, I will. What difference does it make?" Valerie said diffidently. "He has no legal right to Tadd—I've seen to that. There isn't anything he could do if he wanted to, which I doubt."

"But he still gets to you, doesn't he?" Clara's voice was understanding and vaguely sad.

"Yes," Valerie sighed. "After all this time, I'm still not immune to him. He's a rotten, insensitive brute, but he would only have to hold me to make me forget that."

"Don't let him hurt you again, honey." It was almost a plea.

Shaking the honey-dark mane of her hair, Valerie curved her mouth into a weak smile. "I'm not going to give him the chance!"

CHAPTER THREE

AT A QUARTER PAST SIX that evening Valerie slowed the car to park it in front of the funeral home of the small Maryland community. A few cars were already in the lot.

"Is this where we're going?" Tadd was draped half in the front seat and half in the back.

"Yes." Valerie glanced at him briefly. His little bow tie was already askew and his shirt was coming loose from the waistband of his trousers. "Clara, would you mind tucking his shirt in and straightening his tie?"

"Hold still!" Clara ordered when the boy tried to squirm away. "I don't know if it's a good idea to bring him along."

"He's old enough to understand what's going on," Valerie replied calmly.

"Are we going to a funeral?" Tadd asked.

"No, granddad's funeral is tomorrow," she answered patiently.

"What's a funeral?" At his question, Clara sniffed, a sound that indicated Valerie was wrong to believe Tadd knew what was going on.

"A funeral is when a person dies and all his friends and family come to say goodbye to him. Do you remember when your turtle died? We put him

"I should have guessed," he murmured dryly, shared amusement glittering briefly in his look.

More friends of the family arrived. Judd made no attempt to remain at her side as Valerie greeted them. Almost immediately he drifted to one side, although Valerie was aware that he was never very far away from her.

It wasn't long before the newness of Tadd's surroundings wore off. He became increasingly restless and impatient with the subdued conversations. He fidgeted in the folding chair beside Valerie's and began violently swinging his feet back and forth to kick at his chair rung. The clatter of his shoes against the metal was loud, like a galloping horse.

"Don't do that, Tadd," Valerie told him quietly, putting a hand on his knee to end the motion.

He flashed her a defiant look that said "I want to" and continued swinging his feet without letup.

"Stop it, Tadd," she repeated.

"No!" he retorted in open belligerence, and found himself looking into a pair of cold green eyes that wouldn't put up with such rebellion.

"Do as your mother tells you, Tadd," Judd warned, "or you'll find yourself sitting alone in your mother's car."

Tadd pushed his mutinous face close to Judd's. "Good." Olive green eyes glared into a brilliant jade green pair. "I want to sit in the car," Tadd declared. "I don't want to stay here in this dumb old place."

"Very well." Judd straightened, taking one of Tadd's hands and pulling him from the chair.

"No, wait." Valerie rushed out the halting words.

"Tadd is tired and irritable after that long trip," she explained to excuse her son's behavior, and glanced anxiously at Clara. "Maybe you'd better take him back and put him to bed, Clara." She opened her bag and took out the car keys. "Here."

"And how will you get back?" her friend challenged in a meaningful voice.

It didn't seem proper to Valerie to leave yet. Mickey Flanners was standing only a few feet away, chatting with a horse trainer.

"Mickey?" When he turned, Valerie asked, "Is it all right if I ride back to the farm with you?"

For an instant she thought Mickey glanced at Judd before answering, but she decided she had been mistaken. "Sure," he agreed immediately.

Judd released Tadd's hand as Clara walked over to take him with her. Tadd glanced at Valerie. "I'll be there soon," she promised.

It was more than an hour later when Mickey asked if she was ready to leave. Valerie agreed and was required to say no more as Mickey began relating a steady stream of racehorse gossip while they walked out of the funeral home. Only one car was parked in the area that Mickey was heading toward, and Judd was behind the wheel.

"Where are you parked?" Valerie interrupted Mickey with the question.

"I thought you knew." His startled glance was strictly innocent of deception. "I rode in with Judd."

"No, I wasn't aware of that." There was a hint of grimness in her voice, but she didn't protest.

Mickey opened the front door on the passenger

side for her. She had barely slid in when he was asking her to move over. She found herself sitting in the middle, pressed close to Judd. For such a small man, Mickey Flanners seemed to take up a lot of room.

Judd appeared indifferent to the way her shoulder kept brushing against his as he reversed the car into the street. It was impossible to avoid the accidental contact with him unless she hunched her shoulders forward and held herself as stiffly as an old woman, and she refused to do that.

The expensive scent of male cologne filled her lungs and interfered with her breathing. Mickey continued his nonstop banter, which was a source of relief to Valerie, for without it she was certain Judd would have been able to hear the erratic pounding of her heart.

When Judd had to swerve the car to avoid a pothole, Valerie was thrown against him. Her hand clutched at the nearest solid object to regain her balance. It turned out to be his thigh. His muscles contracted into living steel beneath her hand. She heard him sharply inhale a curse and jerked her hand away as if she had suddenly been burned.

She recovered enough of her poise to offer a cool, "I'm sorry."

His bland, "That's quite all right," made her wonder if she had only imagined that he had been disturbed by her unconsciously intimate touch.

Her grandfather's house was a welcome sight when Judd slowed the car to a stop in front of it.

Mickey didn't immediately climb out. Instead he leaned forward to take a look at Judd.

"There's some of Eli's good brandy in the house. Will you come in, Judd, and we'll have one last drink to old Eli?" A second after he had issued the invitation he glanced at Valerie. "That is, if you don't mind. After all, it is your grandfather's house and his brandy."

"It's as much your house as it is mine," Valerie insisted. What else could she say? Mickey had worked for her grandfather long before she was born. His years' of loyalty far outweighed her less than exemplary relationship with her grandfather, regardless of the blood ties.

"In that case, will you come in for a little while, Judd?" Mickey repeated his invitation.

There was an instant's hesitation from Judd. Valerie felt his gaze skim her profile, but she pretended obliviousness to the look. She hadn't seconded the invitation because she didn't want to give him the impression that she desired his company. Neither did she seek to avoid it because she didn't want him to know he still exerted a powerful attraction over her.

"Thank you, Mick, I'd like that," he agreed finally. "But I'll only be able to stay a little while. I've got a sick colt to check on."

"Oh? What's wrong with it?" Mick opened his car door and stepped out.

As Valerie partially turned to slide out the passenger side, the skirt of her grape-colored dress failed to move with her, exposing a sheer nylon-covered thigh and knee. She reached hastily to pull the skirt down, but Judd's hand was there to do it for her. In the confusion of his touch against her virtually bare leg, Valerie didn't hear his explanation of the colt's problem. She managed to push his hand away, an action that was at odds with her sensual reaction.

The warmth that was in her cheeks when she stepped out of the car wasn't visible in the fading sunset of the summer evening. It was a languid night, heavily scented with the smell of horses and hay and a sprinkling of roses that grew next to the house.

Mickey waited for Judd to continue his discussion of horses and their ailments. Valerie started immediately toward the house, not rushing her pace as one would in fleeing, although that was what she wanted to do. In consequence, Judd was there to reach around her and open the porch door.

Hearing them return, Clara appeared from the living room. She had already changed into her nightgown, its hem peeping out from the folds of her quilted robe. A pair of furry slippers covered her feet. At the sight of the two men following Valerie inside, Clara stopped and scowled. Only Valerie, who knew her, was aware it was a self-conscious and defensive expression for being caught in that state of dress.

"What are you staring at?" Clara demanded of Mickey in her most rasping and abrasive voice. "Haven't you ever seen a woman in a bathrobe before?"

"Not in a good many years." Mickey recovered

from his initial shock, his cheeks dimpling with mischief. "I'd forgotten what a tempting sight it could be."

"Watch your tongue!" Clara snapped, reddening under his sweeping look.

Hiding a grin, Mickey turned aside from the bristling woman. "I'll get some glasses from the kitchen. Why don't you go on into Eli's office, Judd? I'll be along directly."

"Don't rush on my account," Judd replied.

Valerie felt his glance swing to her when Mickey left the room, but she didn't volunteer to show him to her grandfather's office/study. Instead she walked into the living room to speak to Clara, denying any interest in where he went or when.

"Is Tadd asleep?" she asked Clara.

"Finally, after throwing a holy fit to see the horses again," was the gruff response.

"I'll go and look in on him." Her sensitive radar knew the instant Judd turned and walked toward the study.

"Leave him be for now," Clara insisted. "You might wake him, and I don't care to hear him whining again about those horses." She shot a look in the direction Judd had taken and whispered angrily, "You could have warned me you'd be inviting them in when you got back. I wouldn't have been traipsing around the place in my robe if I'd known."

"I had no intention of inviting them in," Valerie corrected. "In fact, Mickey was the one who invited Judd, not me."

"It's neither here nor there now," Clara muttered.

"I'm going up to my room where I can have some privacy."

Valerie was about to say that she'd come along with her when Mickey appeared at the living room entrance. Clara scurried toward the staircase under his dancing look.

"I'll be up shortly," she called after Clara, then asked Mickey, "Did you want something?"

"I know you're tired and will be wanting to turn in, but will you have one small drink with us to the old man?" He wore his most beguiling expression as he raised an arm to show her he carried three glasses.

The haunting loneliness in his blue eyes told Valerie that he truly missed her grandfather and wanted to share his sense of loss with someone who had been close to Elias Wentworth. Her glance flickered uncertainly toward the study where Judd waited.

"Very well," she agreed, and wondered whether she was a sentimental fool or a masochist.

Judd's back was to the door, his attention focused on the framed pictures of thoroughbred horses that covered one paneled wall of the study. Valerie tried not to notice the way he pivoted sharply when she and Mickey entered, or the almost physical thrust of his gaze on her. She walked to the leather-covered armchair, its dark brown color worn to patches of tan on the seat and arms.

"I've got the glasses," Mickey announced. "All we need is the brandy." He walked to the stained oak desk and opened a bottom drawer. "Up until a few years ago Eli used to keep his liquor locked up in the safe."

Valerie's fingers curved into the leather armrest at Mickey's unwitting reminder of her past misdeeds. Her grandfather had kept it locked away to prevent her from drinking it. To this day, she didn't understand why she had done it. She hadn't liked the taste of alcohol and had usually ended up getting sick.

"Eli never touched a drop himself," Mickey went on as he held the bottle up to see how much was in it. "He was an alcoholic when he was younger. He told me once that it wasn't until after his wife died that he gave up drinking for good." He poured a healthy amount of brandy into the first water glass.

"Only a little for me," said Valerie, understanding at last why her grandfather had been so violently opposed to drinking.

"Eli swore he kept liquor in the house purely for medicinal reasons." When he reached the third glass, Mickey poured only enough brandy in to cover the bottom. "Personally, I think he kept it on hand to befuddle the brains of whoever came to buy a horse from him."

Picking up two of the glasses, Mickey carried the one with the smallest portion to Valerie and handed the other to Judd. Judd took a seat on the worn leather-covered sofa that was a match to her chair. Mickey completed the triangle by hoisting himself onto the desk top, his short legs dangling against the side.

"To Eli." Judd lifted his glass in a toast.

"May he rest in peace," Mickey added, and drank

from his glass. Valerie sipped her brandy, the fiery liquid burning her tongue and throat, conscious that Judd's gaze seldom wavered from her. "Yeah, old Eli never smoked or drank," Mickey sighed, and stared at his glass. "They say a reformed hellion is stricter—and he sure was with you, Valerie. I remember the time he caught you with a pack of cigarettes. I thought he was going to beat the livin' tar out of you."

"I caused him a lot of grief when I was growing up." She lifted her shoulders in a dismissing shrug.

"You were a chip off the old block," the ex-jockey insisted with a smile, countering her self-criticism. "Besides, you gave him a lot of pleasure these last years." His comment warmed her. "Remember how Eli was, Judd, whenever he got a letter from her?"

"Yes," Judd answered quietly.

At his affirmative reply, her gaze swung curiously to him. "Did you visit granddad? I don't remember that you came over when I was still living here."

He rotated his glass in a circle, swirling the brandy inside. He seemed to be pretending an interest in the liquor while choosing how to word his answer.

"Your grandfather had a yearling filly that I liked the looks of a few years ago. Her bloodline wasn't bad, so I offered to buy her," Judd explained with a touch of diffidence. "After a week of haggling back and forth, we finally came to an agreement on the price. It was the first time I really became acquainted with Eli. I like to think that we had a mutual respect for each other."

"After that, Judd began stopping by once or twice a month," Mickey elaborated. "Your granddad would get out his letters from you and tell anybody who would listen how you were."

Apprehension quivered through Valerie that Judd might have seen what she wrote. Of course, she had never told her grandfather the identity of Tadd's father, not even in the letters. Not that she cared whether Judd knew, but she didn't like the idea that he might have read the personal letters intended only for her grandfather. Mickey's next statement put that apprehension to rest.

"He never actually read your letters aloud, but he'd tell what you said. All the time he'd be talking, he'd be holding the envelope with your letter inside it and stroking it like it was one of his horses."

"I wish . . . I could have seen him before he died." But she hadn't thought she would be welcomed.

"I wanted to call you when he was in the hospital," Mickey told her. "But Eli told me that in your last letter you'd said you and your husband were going to take a Caribbean cruise. I didn't know he was so sick or I would have got in touch with you anyway."

"On a cruise?" Valerie frowned.

"That's what he said," Mickey repeated.

"I didn't go on any cruise," she denied before she realized that it was another story her grandfather had made up.

"Maybe he got your letters confused," he suggested. "He kept them all, every one of them. He hoarded them like they were gold. He carried them around with him until they stuck out of the pockets of his old green plaid jacket like straw out of a scarecrow."

"He did?" Valerie was bemused by the thought. The idea that he treasured her letters that much made her forgive him for making up those stories about her.

"He sure did. As a matter of fact, they're all still in his jacket." Mickey hopped down from his perch on the desk and walked to the old armoire used as a storage cabinet for the farm records. The green plaid jacket hung on a hook inside the wooden door. "Here it is, letters and all."

As he walked over to her, Mickey began gathering the letters from the various pockets, not stopping until there were several handfuls on her lap. Some of the envelopes had the yellow tinge of age, but all of them were worn from numerous handlings.

Setting her brandy glass down, Valerie picked up one envelope that was postmarked five years ago. She turned it over, curious to read the letter inside, but the flap of the envelope was still sealed. A cold chill raced through her.

"No!" Her cry was a sobbing protest of angry and hurt disbelief. She raced frantically through the rest of the envelopes. All were sealed. None of the letters had ever been read. "No! No! No!" She sobbed out bitter, futile denials of a truth too painful to accept.

"What is it?" Mickey was plainly confused.

"What's wrong?" Judd was standing beside her chair. He reached down and took one of the envelopes.

"Look at it!" Valerie challenged through her tears.

When he turned it over and saw the sealed flap that had no marks of ever having been opened, his darkly green, questing gaze sliced back to her. In each of her hands she held envelopes in the same unopened condition. Her fingers curled into them, crumpling them into her palms. In agitation she rose from the chair, letting the letters in her lap fall to the floor. She stared at the ones in her hands.

"It isn't fair!" In a mixture of rage and pain, Valerie cast away the envelopes in her hands. She began shaking uncontrollably, her fingers still curled into fists. "It isn't fair!"

Scalding tears burned hot trails down her cheeks. The emotion-charged feelings and tempers maturity had taught her to control broke free of the restraints to erupt in a stormy display.

"Valerie!" Judd's quieting voice had the opposite effect.

The instant his hands gripped her shoulders and turned her around, she began pummeling his shoulders with her fists. Sobbing in earnest, she was like the tigress he had once called her, with tawny hair and topaz eyes, wounded and lashing out from the hurt.

"He never opened them. He never read any of my letters," she sobbed in frustration and anguish.

Indifferent to the hands on her waist, she pounded Judd's shoulders, hitting out at the only solid object in the vicinity. Her crying face was buried in his shirtfront, moistening it and the lapel of his jacket.

Somewhere on the edge of her consciousness she was aware of concerned voices, Mickey's and Clara's. Only one penetrated and it came from Judd.

"Let her cry. She needs the release."

After that, there was only silence and the heart-tearing sounds of her own sobbing. When the violence within subsided, she cried softly for several minutes more. Her hands stopped beating at the indestructible wall of muscle and clutched the expensive material of Judd's jacket instead. His arms were around her, holding her closely in silent comfort. Gradually she began to regain her senses, but there were still things that needed to come out.

Lifting her head far enough from his chest to see the buttons of his shirt, she sniffed, "He hated me." Her voice was hoarse and broken as she wiped the wetness from her cheek with a scrubbing motion of her hand.

"I'm sure he didn't," Judd denied.

"Yes, he did." Valerie bobbed her head, a caramel curtain of rippling hair falling forward to hide her face. "He couldn't stand the thought of having me as a granddaughter, so he made up a fictitious one, complete with stories about marriage and vacation cruises. It was all lies!"

His hand raked the hair from one cheek and tilted her face up for his glittering study. "What are you saying?" he demanded with tight-lipped grimness.

Golden defiance flashed in her eyes, a defiance for convention and her grandfather. "I work for a living. I couldn't afford a trip on a rowboat. I'm not married—I never have been. Tadd is his great-grandchild, but without the legitimacy of a marriage license."

"Damn you!" His head came down, his mouth roughly brushing across a tear-dampened cheek to reach her lips. "I've been going through hell wondering how I was going to keep my hands off somebody else's wife." He breathed the savagely issued words into her mouth. "And all the time you weren't even married!"

The hungry ferocity of his kiss claimed her lips, devouring their fullness. Her battered emotions had no defenses against his rapacious assault and he fed on her weakness. She was dragged into the powerful undercurrent of his passion, then swept high by the response of her own senses. The flames of carnal longing licked through her veins to heat her flesh. This consuming fire fused her melting curves to the iron contours of his male form. Not content with the domination of her lips, Judd ravaged her throat and the sensitive hollows below her ears.

His hand moved slowly down her back, unzipping her dress, but when the room's air touched the exposed skin, it was the cool breath of sanity that she had needed. She pushed out of his arms and took a quick step away, stopping with her back to him. She was trembling from the force of the passion he had so easily aroused.

At the touch of his hand on her hair, Valerie stiffened. Judd brushed the long toffee mane of hair aside. His warm breath caressed her skin as he bent to kiss the ultrasensitive spot at the back of her neck, and desire quivered through her.

"You're right, Valerie." His fingers teased her spine as he zipped up her dress. "This isn't the time nor the place, not with your grandfather's funeral tomorrow."

"As if you give a damn!" Her voice wavered under the burning weight of resentment and bitterness. She dredged up the parting phrase she had used seven years ago. "Go to hell, Judd Prescott!"

She closed her eyes tightly as she heard his footsteps recede from her. When she opened them they were dry of tears and she was alone. A few minutes later Clara came slopping into the room in her furry slippers.

"Are you all right now?" she questioned.

Valerie turned, breathing in deeply and nodding a curt, "Yes, I'm fine." The letters were still scattered on the linoleum floor, and she stooped to pick them up. "Granddad never opened them, Clara."

"That doesn't mean anything. He kept them, didn't he? So he must have felt something for you," her friend reasoned, "otherwise he would have burned them."

"Maybe." But Valerie was no longer sure.

"What did Prescott have to say?" Clara bent awkwardly down on her knees to help Valerie collect the scattered envelopes.

"Nothing really. I told him I wasn't married and that Tadd was illegitimate, so he knows granddad was lying all this time," she replied with almost frightening calm.

"Did you tell him he was Tadd's father? Is that why he left in such a freezing silence?"

"No. He never asked who Tadd's father was. I'm just a tramp to him. I doubt if he even believes I know who the father is," she said, releasing a short bitter laugh. The postmark of one of the envelopes in her hand caught her eye. It was dated two days after Tadd's birth, unopened like the rest of them. "If granddad never opened any of my letters, how did he know about Tadd?"

Clara stood up, making a show of straightening the stack of envelopes she held. "I phoned him a couple hours after Tadd was born. I thought he should know he had a great-grandson."

"What . . . did he say?" Valerie unconsciously held her breath.

Clara hesitated, then looked her in the eye. "He didn't say anything. He just hung up." The flickering light of hope went out of Valerie's eyes. "I was talking to Mickey today," Clara went on. "It wasn't until a year after Tadd was born that he told everybody he had a great-grandchild."

"I suppose so there was a decent interval between the time I supposedly was married and Tadd was born," Valerie concluded acidly. "Damn!" she swore softly and with pain. "Now all of them think Tadd is five years old instead of six."

"I know it hurts." Clara's brisk voice tried to offer comfort. "But, in his way, I think your grandfather was trying to keep people from talking bad about you."

"I'm not going to live his lies!" Valerie flashed.

"You don't have to, but I wouldn't suggest going around broadcasting the truth, either," the other woman cautioned. "You might be able to thumb your nose at the gossip you'd start, but there's Tadd to consider."

Valerie released a long breath in silent acknowledgement of her logic. "Where's Mickey?" she asked.

"He went out to the barn, said there was a place for him to sleep there where he could be close to the horses," Clara answered.

"I'm tired, too." Valerie felt emotionally drained, her energy sapped. Exhaustion was stealing through her limbs. She handed the letters to Clara, not caring what she did with them, and walked toward the stairs.

CHAPTER FOUR

A BEE BUZZED LAZILY around the wreath of flowers lying on the coffin and a green canopy shaded the mourners from the glare of the sun. Valerie absently watched the bee's wanderings. Her attention had strayed from the intoning voice of the minister.

At the "Amen," she lifted her gaze and encountered Judd's steady regard. Her pulse altered its regular tempo before she glanced away. The graveside service was over and the minister was approaching her. Valerie smiled politely and thanked him, words and gestures that she repeated to several others until she was facing Judd.

"It was good of you to come." She offered him the same stilted phrase.

His carved bronze features were expressionless as he inclined his head in smooth acknowledgement. A dancing breeze combed its fingers through his black hair as he drew her attention to the woman at his side, ushering her forward.

"I don't believe you've met my mother, Valerie," he said. "This is Valerie Wentworth." An inbred old-world courtesy prompted him to introduce the younger to the elder first. "My mother, Maureen Prescott."

"How do you do, Mrs. Prescott." Valerie shook

the white-gloved hand, her gaze curiously skimming the woman who had given birth to this man.

Petitely built, she had black hair with startling wings of silver at the temples. Her eyes were an unusual shade of turquoise green, not as brilliant as her son's nor as disconcerting. She was attractive, her face generally unlined. She conveyed warmth where her son revealed cynicism. Valerie decided that Maureen Prescott was a genteel woman made of flexible steel.

"Judd was better acquainted with your grandfather than I, but please accept my sincere sympathies," the woman offered in a pleasant, gentle voice.

"Thank you." Valerie thawed slightly.

"If there's anything you need, please remember that we're your neighbors." A smile curved the perfectly shaped lips.

"I will, Mrs. Prescott," she nodded, knowing it was the last place she would go for assistance.

Others were waiting to speak to her and Judd didn't attempt to prolong the exchange with her. As he walked his mother toward the line of cars parked along the cemetery gates, Valerie's gaze strayed after them, following their progress.

When the last of those waiting approached her, Valerie almost sighed aloud. The strain of hearing the same words and repeating the same phrases in answer was beginning to wear on her nerves.

She offered the man her hand. "It was kind of you to come," she recited.

"I'm Jefferson Burrows," he said, as if the name was supposed to mean something to her. Valerie looked at him without recognition. He was of medium height, in his early fifties, and carried himself with a certain air of authority. "I was your grandfather's attorney," he explained.

"I'm pleased to meet you, Mr. Burrows." She kept hold of her fraying patience.

"This is not perhaps the proper time, but I was wondering if I might arrange to see you tomorrow," he said.

"I'll probably be fairly busy tomorrow. You see, I stored many of my personal things at my grandfather's, childhood mementoes, et cetera," she explained coolly. "I planned to sort through them tomorrow and I'll be leaving the day after to return to Cincinnati. Was it important?"

"I do need to go over your grandfather's will with you before you leave." There was a hint of pomposity that she had implied he had made a request that was not important.

"There's a provision for me in his will?" Her response was incredulous and skeptical.

"Naturally, as his only living relative, you are one of the beneficiaries of his estate." His tone was reprimanding. "May I call in the morning? Around ten o'clock, perhaps?"

"Yes. Yes, that will be fine." Valerie felt a bit dazed.

As she and Mickey drove away from the cemetery a short time later, she saw the attorney standing beside the Prescott car talking to Judd. After having previously been convinced that she would be disinherited, Valerie had difficulty adjusting to the fact that her grandfather had left a bequest for her in his will.

It was even more difficult for her to accept the next morning after Jefferson Burrows read her the will. She stared at the paper listing assets and liabilities belonging to her grandfather and the approximate net worth of the estate. All of it, except for a cash amount to Mickey, had been left to her.

"You do understand," the attorney said, "that the values on the breeding stock and the farm are approximate market prices, but I've been conservative in fixing them. Also, this figure doesn't take into account the amount of tax you'll have to pay. Do you have any questions?"

"No." How could she tell him she was overwhelmed just at the thought of inheriting?

"You're fortunate that your grandfather wasn't one to incur a lot of debts. The only sizable one is the mortgage on the farm."

"Yes, I am." Valerie tried to answer with some degree of poise.

"I know this inheritance doesn't represent a large sum of money," he said, and she wondered what he used as a standard of measure. There was money for Tadd's education and enough left over that she wouldn't have to work for a year if she didn't want to. "But I'm sure you'll want to discuss it with your husband before you make any decision about possibly disposing of the property."

"I'm not married, Mr. Burrows." She corrected his misconception immediately.

He raised an eyebrow at that, but made no direct

comment. "In that case, perhaps I should go over some of the alternatives with you. Deducting taxes and the bequest to Mr. Flanners, there isn't sufficient working capital to keep the farm running. Of course, you could borrow against your assets to obtain the capital, but in doing so, you would be jeopardizing all of what you inherited."

"Yes, I can see that," Valerie agreed, and she didn't like the idea of risking Tadd's future education.

"I would advise that you auction all the horses to eliminate an immediate drain on your limited resources and to either lease or sell the land." He began going into more detail, discussing the pros and cons of each possibility until Valerie's mind was spinning in confusion. It was a relief when he began shoving the legal papers into his briefcase. "It isn't necessary that you make an immediate decision. In fact, I recommend that you think about it for a week or two before letting me know which course of action you would like to pursue."

"Yes, I'll do that." She would need that much time to sort through all the advice he had given her.

After he had gone, she broke the good news to Clara, but even then it didn't really sink in. It wasn't until after lunch when the dishes were done and she and Tadd and Clara had walked outside that the full import of it struck her.

Valerie looked out over the pastures, the grazing mares and colts, the stables and barns, and the house, and she was dazzled by what she saw.

"It's mine, Clara," she murmured. "I inherited all of this. It's really and truly mine."

"Do you mean it's yours like the car is?" Tadd asked, sensing the importance of her statement, but not understanding its implications.

"The car belongs to me and the bank," Valerie corrected him with a bright smile. "I guess the bank has a piece of this, too, but I have a bigger one."

"Does that mean we can live here?" His eyes rounded at the thought.

"We could live here if we wanted to," she agreed without thinking, since it was one of the choices.

"You're forgetting you have a job to go to in Cincinnati," Clara inserted dryly.

"I'm not forgetting." Valerie shook her head, then turned her bright gaze on the older woman. "Don't you see, Clara, I have enough money that I could quit my job?"

"Now you're beginning to sound like some heiress," observed Clara in a puncturing tone.

"I wouldn't be able to quit working forever," Valerie conceded, "but there's enough money here for Tadd to have a college education and to support us for a whole year besides."

"Are we really going to live here, mommy?" Tadd was almost dancing with excitement.

"I don't know yet, honey," she told him.

"I want to. Please, can we live here?" he asked breathlessly.

"We'll talk about it later," Valerie stalled. "You run off and play now. Don't go near the horses, though, unless Mickey is with you," she called as he went dashing off.

"You shouldn't be raising the boy's hopes up," Clara reprimanded. "You know you can't live here permanently."

"Maybe not permanently, but we could stay here through the summer." At the scoffing sound, Valerie outlined the idea that had been germinating in her mind. "It would be a vacation, the first time I'd be able to be with Tadd for more than just nights and weekends. And I'd like him to know the freedom of country life."

"What would you do with yourself out here?" Clara wanted to know.

"There's a lot that could be done. First, the horses would all have to be auctioned. And Mr. Burrows suggested that I might get a better price for the farm if I invested some money in painting the buildings and fences. The lawn would need to be cleaned up and maintained. There's something to be gained from staying the summer. Besides, it would take time to sell or lease the place," she reasoned. "What are we talking about anyway? Just two and a half or three months."

"What about your job? You are supposed to be back to work on Friday," Clara reminded her.

"I know," Valerie admitted. "I'll just have to see if Mr. Hanover will give me leave of absence until the fall."

"And if he won't?"

"Then I'll have to find another job." Valerie refused to regard this point as an obstacle. "This time I'll have enough money to support myself until I find a good one."

"It seems to me you have your mind all made up," Clara sniffed, as if offended that her counsel hadn't been sought.

"The more I think about it, the more I like it," Valerie admitted. "You could stay, too, Clara. The doctor said you had to rest for a month. Why not here in the fresh air and sunshine?"

"If you're set on staying here, I might, too." There was something grudging in the reply. "I'm just not sure in my mind that you're doing the right thing."

"Give me one good reason for not staying the summer," Valerie demanded with a challenging smile.

"Judd Prescott." The answer was quick and sure.

The smile was wiped from Valerie's face as if it had never been there. "He has nothing to do with my decision!" she snapped, her eyes flashing yellow sparks.

"Maybe he doesn't, but he's someone you're going to have to contend with," Clara retorted. "And soon, it appears." Her eyes narrowed, gazing in the direction of the pasture beyond Valerie.

Hearing the drum of galloping hooves, Valerie turned to see a big gray hunter approaching the yard. The rider was instantly recognizable as Judd. Alertness splintered through her senses, putting her instantly on guard.

Tossing its head, the gray horse was reined in at the board fence. Judd dismounted and looped the reins around the upright post. He crossed the board fence and walked toward the two women with ease that said it was a commonplace thing for him to be stopping by. His arrogant assumption that he would be welcomed rankled Valerie.

"What do you want, Mr. Prescott?" She coldly attempted to put him in his place as an uninvited trespasser.

His hard mouth curved into a smile that lacked both humor and warmth as he stopped before her. "I have some business that I want to discuss with you, *Miss* Wentworth." Sardonically he mocked her formality.

"What business would that be?" she challenged, her chin lifting.

His gaze skimmed her once over, taking in the crisp Levi's and the light blue print of her cotton blouse. His look belied his previous statement that his purpose was business, not personal.

"I understand that Mr. Burrows was here to see you this morning," he replied without answering her question.

"And where did you get that piece of information?" Valerie demanded.

"From Mr. Burrows," Judd answered complacently. His mouth twisted briefly at the flash of indignation in her look. "I asked him to call me after he'd informed you of your inheritance."

"Just what do you know about my inheritance?" She was practically seething at the attorney's lack of confidentiality.

"That your grandfather left everything to you."

"I suppose Mr. Burrows supplied you with that

information, too." Irritation put a razor-sharp edge to her tightly controlled voice.

"No, your grandfather did," Judd smoothly corrected her assumption.

"I see," she said stiffly. "Now that we have that straightened out, what did you want?"

"As I said, I have some business to discuss with you regarding your inheritance." His gaze flicked to the onlooking Clara. "In private."

"There isn't anything you have to say to me that I would object to having Clara hear," Valerie stated.

"But *I* object," Judd countered. "If you want to discuss my proposal with Clara after I'm gone, that's your business, Valerie. But my business is with you and you alone, with no third party listening in."

Valerie held her breath and counted to ten. Was it really business he wanted to discuss or was it some trick to get her alone? There was nothing in his expression to tell her the answer.

"Very well," she agreed, however ungraciously. "Shall we walk, Mr. Prescott? Then you won't have to worry about anyone eavesdropping on your so very private business conversation."

"By all means let's walk." Amusement glittered in his eyes at her sarcasm.

Valerie started off in the direction of the pasture fence where the gray hunter was tied. When they had traveled what she considered a sufficient distance, she glanced at him.

"Is this far enough?" she questioned.

He glanced over his shoulder at Clara, a taunting

light in his eyes when their gaze returned to Valerie. "For the time being," he agreed.

"Then perhaps you would be good enough to state your business." Her nerves felt as tight as a drum and the pounding of her heart increased the sensation.

"I don't know if you have had time to decide what you want to do about the farm, whether you're going to keep it or sell it," Judd began without hesitation. "I'm willing to pay whatever the market price is for the farm if you decide to sell."

So it was business, she realized, and was angered by the disappointment she felt. "I see." She couldn't think of anything else to say.

"I offered to buy the place from your grandfather, but he wouldn't sell. It isn't a money-making concern, Valerie," he warned. "Your grandfather has a good stallion in Sunnybrook, but his mares are less than desirable. I tried to convince him that he should be more selective in the mares he bred to the stallion, but he needed the stud fees and couldn't afford to buy better-bred mares."

But Valerie's thoughts had strayed to another area. "Why did granddad tell you he was leaving all this to me?"

His gaze narrowed with wicked suggestion. "Do you mean did he know that you and I were once lovers?" She hadn't expected him to word her suspicion so bluntly. The uncomfortable rush of color to her cheeks angered her. Turning her back on Judd, she walked to the pasture fence, closing her hands over the edge of the top rail.

"Did he guess?" she demanded, letting him know that she had never told her grandfather.

"No. If he had, he'd probably have chased me off his land with a load of buckshot," he answered.

"I . . . wondered," Valerie offered in a weak explanation for her question.

"You look more like the Valerie I remember, standing there with your lion's mane of shiny hair around your shoulders and those tight-fitting jeans that show off your perfectly rounded bottom."

If he had stripped her on the spot, Valerie couldn't have felt more naked. She pivoted around to face him, hiding the area he had described with such knowledge from his roaming gaze. Leaning against the fence, she hooked the heel of one boot on the lowest rail.

"I think you said it was business you wanted to discuss," she reminded him with flashing temper.

He looked amused. "Have you given any thought to selling?"

Despite his compliance with her challenge, Valerie didn't feel much safer. "I'm considering it . . . as well as several other possibilities."

"Such as staying on here permanently?" he suggested.

"I don't think that's possible," she said, rejecting that idea with a brief shake of her head. "As you mentioned, the horses barely pay for themselves, so it would be difficult for me to earn a living from the farm."

"You could always sell the horses and lease all the land except the house." Judd took a step toward the fence, but he was angled away from her, posing no threat.

"I could," Valerie conceded, "but the income from a lease wouldn't be enough to support us. I'd need a job and there aren't many openings for a secretary in this community, especially well-paying ones. It's too far to commute to Baltimore. For that reason leasing practically cancels itself out."

"Don't be too certain that you wouldn't have enough money from a lease," he cautioned. "The right party might be willing to pay what you need."

He began wandering along the fence row, gazing out over the land as if appraising its worth. Valerie watched him, confused by the possibility he had raised. She didn't know whether he was telling her the truth or dangling a carrot under her nose to lead her into a trap. Or had there been a hidden suggestion in his words that she hadn't caught?

Before she could puzzle it out, Judd was asking, "Do you mind if we walk on a little farther?" His sideways look of question held a bemused light. "I'd like to get out from underneath the eagle eye of that battle-ax."

"Do you mean Clara?" Valerie was startled but not offended by his mocking reference to her friend. Without being aware of moving she began following him, matching his strolling pace.

"Yes," he admitted. "She reminds me of one of those buxom warrior maids in a German opera. All she lacks are pigtails, a spear and an armored breastplate."

Valerie visualized Clara in such a costume and

couldn't help smiling at the image and the aptness of his description. "Does she make you uncomfortable?" she asked.

Judd stopped, his level gaze swinging to her with a force that rooted her to the ground. "You make me uncomfortable, Valerie."

His hand lifted, the back of his fingers stroking the line of her jaw before she could elude them. The light touch was destroying. When his fingertips traced the length of the sensitive cord in her neck all the way to the hollow of her throat, her breath was stolen by the traitorous awakening of her senses. She sank her white teeth into the softness of her lower lip to hold back the words trembling on her tongue, unsure whether they would come out a protest or an invitation.

Taking her silence as acceptance, Judd moved closer. He hooked a finger under the collar of her blouse and followed its line to the lowest point where a button blocked his way, but not for long. A languorous warmth spread over her skin when his hand slid inside her blouse to climb and claim the rosy mountain of her breast. He bent his head to kiss the lip her teeth held captive, and they abandoned it to his sensual inspection. Her heart throbbed with aching force under his sweet mastery. Inflamed by his slow burning fire, Valerie trembled with passion.

Satisfied with her initial response, Judd began nuzzling her cheek and eye, his tongue sending shivers of raw desire through her as it licked her ear. The heady male smell of him stimulated her already churning emotions. Of their own free will, her lips were nibbling and kissing the strong, smooth line of his jaw.

"I'll lease the place from you, Valerie," Judd muttered against her cheek, "and pay you whatever you need to live on."

His offer stopped her heartbeat. "Would you visit me?" she whispered, wanting to be sure she hadn't misunderstood.

"Regularly." His massaging hand tightened possessively on her breast as he gathered her more fully into his encircling hold. He sought the corner of her lips, his warm breath mingling with hers. "Night and day."

With shattering clarity, his true proposition was brought home to her. Leasing the land was only a means to give her money—money that would oblige her to be available whenever he felt the urge for her company. She inwardly reeled from the thought with pain and bitterness.

Her lips escaped his smothering kiss long enough to ask chokingly, "Would the lease be . . . long-term or . . . short?"

"Any terms, I don't care." Impatience edged his voice. "After seven years, I want to make love to you very slowly, but you drive me to the edge of control," he muttered thickly, his mouth making another foray to her neck.

Sickened by the weakness that made her thrill to his admission, Valerie lowered her head to escape his insatiable kisses and strained her hands against his chest to gain breathing room. Judd didn't object. It was as if he knew how easily he could subdue any major show of resistance from her. This arrogance was the whip to flog her into a cold anger.

"I'll tell you what my terms are, Judd." She lifted her head slowly, keeping her lashes lowered to conceal the hard, topaz glitter in her eyes until she was ready for him to see it. "My terms are—" she paused, taking one last look at her fingers spread across his powerful chest before lifting her gaze to his face "—no terms."

As his green eyes began to narrow at her expression, she struck with feline swiftness. Her open palm lashed across his cheek in a stinging report, to be immediately caught in the viselike grip of his fingers.

"I won't lease you the land, the buildings, or my body," she hissed. "I will not become your consort!"

She tried twisting her wrist out of his hold, but Judd wrapped it behind her back. Her other hand met the same fate and she was completely trapped in the steel circle of his arms. Deliberately he ground her hips against his, making her aware of his aroused state, which had nothing to do with the anger blazing in his expression.

"You spitting little hellcat," he jeered. "You haven't changed. Seven years may have given you a certain amount of poise and sophistication, but underneath you're the same passionate and untamed she-devil. You want me to make love to you as much as I do."

"No!" Valerie rushed the vigorous denial.

His upper lip curled into a taunting smile as if he knew how hollow her denial was. "Yes, you do," he insisted with infuriating complacency, and let her go. "Sooner or later you'll admit it."

Turning away smoothly, he began walking toward his horse, leaving Valerie standing there with a mouthful of angry words. She ran after him, trembling with rage.

"You'll rot in hell before I do," she told him in a voice shaking with violence.

His green eyes flashed her a lazy, mocking look before he slipped between the rails of the board fence with an ease that belied his six-foot frame and muscled build. The tall gray horse whickered as he approached. Valerie stopped, staying on the opposite side of the fence, her hands doubled into impotent fists.

Unhooking the reins from the post, Judd looped them around the horse's neck and swung into the saddle with an expert grace. The big gray bunched its hindquarters, eager to be off at the first command from its rider, but none came. Judd looked down at Valerie from his high vantage point in the saddle.

"I meant it when I said I wanted to buy this place," he said flatly. "If you decide to sell, I want you to know my interest in purchasing it is purely a business one. No other consideration will enter into the negotiations for the price."

"I'm glad to hear it." She struggled to control her temper and sounded cold as a result. "Because any offer from you with strings attached will be rejected out of hand!"

His half smile implied that he believed differently. If there had been anything within reach, Valerie would have thrown it at him. Before she could issue a withering comment to his look, her attention was distracted by the sound of someone running through the tall pasture grass.

It was Tadd, racing as fast as his short legs could carry him straight toward Judd. A breathless excitement glowed in his face, the mop of brown hair swept away from his forehead by the wind he generated with his running.

"Is that your horse?" The shrill pitch of his voice and his headlong flight toward the horse spooked the big gray. It plunged under Judd's rein, but its dancing hooves and big size didn't slow Tadd down. "Can I have a ride?"

"Tadd, look out!" Valerie shouted the warning as the gray horse reared and it looked as if Tadd was going to run right under those pawing hooves.

In the next second he was scooped off the ground and lifted into the saddle, Judd's arms around his waist. Her knees went weak with relief.

"Hasn't your mother taught you that you don't run up to a horse like that?" Judd reprimanded the boy he held, but Valerie noticed the glint of admiration in his look that Tadd had not been afraid. "It scares a horse. You have to let them know you're near and walk up slowly."

"I'll remember," Tadd promised, but with a reckless smile that reminded Valerie of Judd. "Will you give me a ride? I've never been on a horse before."

"You're on one now," Judd pointed out. "What do you think of it?"

Tadd leaned to one side to peer at the ground, his

eyes slightly rounded as he straightened. "It's kind of a long way down, isn't it?"

"You'll get used to it." Judd lifted his gaze from the dark-haired boy to glance at Valerie. "I'll give him a short ride around the pasture."

"You don't have to," she replied stiffly, and tried to figure out why she resented that Tadd was having his first ride with Judd, his father, and not her. "Worming your way into Tadd's favor won't get you anywhere with me."

A dangerous glint appeared in his look. "Until this moment that hadn't occurred to me. I have a whole flock of nieces and nephews who are always begging for rides, and I lumped your son into their category. I know you're disappointed that I can't admit to a more ulterior and devious motive."

Their exchange was sailing over Tadd's head. He couldn't follow it, but he had caught one of the things Judd had said. "Are you going to really give me a ride?" he asked.

"If your mother gives her permission," Judd told him in silent challenge to Valerie.

At the beseeching look from her son, she nodded her head curtly. "You have my permission."

"Thank you," Judd said mockingly as he reined the spirited gray away from the fence.

At a walk, they started across the grassy field. Tadd laughed and nearly bounced out of the saddle when the horse went into a trot, but he didn't sound or look the least bit frightened. After making a sweeping arc into the pasture, Judd turned the horse toward the fence and cantered him back to where Valerie was waiting.

With one hand, he swung Tadd to the ground. "Remember what I told you. From now on, you'll *walk* up to a horse." Tadd gave him a solemn nod of agreement. With a last impersonal glance at Valerie, Judd backed his mount away from the small boy before turning it toward its home stables.

"Come on, Tadd," Valerie called to him. "Let's go to the house and have something cold to drink."

He lingered for a minute in the pasture watching Judd ride away, a sight that pulled at Valerie, too, but she resisted it. Finally he ran toward her and Valerie wondered if he knew any other speed. He ducked under the fence as if he had been doing it all his life. He skipped along beside her, chattering endlessly about the ride.

"Where did you two disappear to?" Clara asked when Valerie reached the houseyard. Her question bordered on an accusation.

"I went for a ride," Tadd chimed out an answer, unaware he wasn't the second person Clara had meant.

"We just walked along the fence," Valerie answered, realizing a bushy shade tree had blocked her and Judd from Clara's sight.

"What was his business?" The tone was skeptical that there had been any such reason.

"He offered to buy the place," Valerie answered, and murmured to herself, "among other things!"

CHAPTER FIVE

AFTER MUCH DISCUSSION and debate, Valerie persuaded Clara that the three of them should spend the summer on her grandfather's farm. She refused to be intimidated by Judd's proximity as a neighbor. This was the only chance she would ever have to show her son what it had been like for her to grow up in this house. And perhaps it would be the only time she would have to devote solely to Tadd while he was in his formative years.

Eventually she swayed Clara into going along with her. Once the agreement had been reached, they had to tackle the problem of arranging things in Cincinnati to be absent for possibly three months.

Clara's married sister agreed to send both of them more clothes from the apartments, forward their mail, and see that everything was locked up. Valerie's telephoned request to her employer for an extended leave of absence received a notification of her dismissal, as Clara had warned. But all in all, the arrangements were made with minimal complications.

Amid all this was the decision of what to do about the farm and consultation with Jefferson Burrows, the attorney. At the end of the following week Valerie came to the decision she had known all along she would have to make. After confiding in Clara, she sought out Mickey at the stables.

Valerie came straight to the point. "I wanted to let you know, Mick, that I've decided to sell the farm."

Sitting in the shade of the building, cleaning some leather tack, the retired jockey didn't even glance up when she made the announcement. He spat on the leather and polished some more.

"Then you'll be selling the horses?" he asked.

"Yes, I'll have to," she nodded.

"Since you're not keeping the place, you'll be better off to sell them soon," Mickey advised. "Were you going to have an auction?"

"Yes. Mr. Burrows, the lawyer, said if I decided to sell the horses, an auction could be scheduled within two weeks," she explained.

"It won't give you much time to do very much advertising," he shrugged, "but word has a way of getting around fast among horsemen. I'm sure you'll have a good turnout. As soon as you set the date, I'll call some of my friends in the business and start spreading the word."

"Thanks, Mick."

"It's the least I can do. There is one thing, though." He put the halter aside and stood up. "You see that bay mare grazing off by herself?"

Valerie glanced toward the paddock he faced and saw the bay mare he meant, a sleek, long-legged animal with a chestnut brown coat with black points.

"She's a beauty," Valerie commented in admiration.

"Don't put Ginger in the auction," Mickey said, and explained, "She's the best get out of old Donnybrook, but she's barren, no good for breeding at all. She's got no speed, but she's a good hack, might even make it as a show jumper. But you'd never get your money's worth out of her in a breeding sale. If I was you, I'd advertise her as a hunter and try to sell her that way."

"Thanks, I'll do that," she promised. His thoughtfulness and ready acceptance of her decision made her feel a little guilty. This farm and these horses were practically like his own. He had lived here and taken care of all the animals here, many of them since birth. Now they were being sold and he was out of a job and a place to live. "What will you do, Mickey? Where will you go?"

"Don't worry about me, Valerie," he laughed. "I've had a standing offer from Judd for years to come to work for him taking care of his young colts. He claims that I'm the best he's ever seen at handling the young ones."

The mention of Judd's name made her glance toward the paddock again to conceal her expression. "Judd wants to buy this," she said.

"Are you going to sell it to him?" he asked, not surprised by her statement.

"It depends on whether or not I get an offer better than the one he makes." Common sense made her insist that it didn't matter who ultimately purchased the property. She wouldn't be here when they took possession.

"If Judd has set his mind on buying it, he'll top any reasonable offer you get," Mickey grinned. " 'Cause once he makes up his mind he wants somethin', he seldom lets anything stand in his way till he gets it."

It was a statement that came echoing back a week later. Valerie was walking out of the bank in town just as Judd was coming in. Courtesy demanded that she speak to him, at least briefly.

"Hello, Judd." She nodded with forced pleasantness, and would have walked on by him, but he stopped.

"Hello, Valerie. I saw the auction notice." His tone sounded only conversational.

"For the horses? Yes, in less than two weeks from now," she admitted. His gaze was inspecting her in a most bemused fashion. Valerie had the feeling a strap was showing or something, and her hand moved protectively to the elastic neckline of the peasant-styled knit top. "Is something wrong?" she queried a bit sharply.

"You look very cool and proper with your hair fixed like that," Judd answered. It was pulled away from her face into a loose chignon at the back of her head.

"It's a very warm day. I feel cooler if my hair is away from my neck," Valerie replied as if her change of hairstyle required an explanation.

"It's attractive, but it isn't exactly you," he commented in a knowing voice. Without skipping a beat, he continued, "I suppose once all the legal arrangements are completed after the auction you'll be leaving?"

"We're staying a little longer." She didn't see the need to tell him she would be there for the summer. He would discover it soon enough, so there was no point in informing him in advance.

"We?" A jet-dark brow lifted at the plural.

"Yes—Tadd, Clara and myself," Valerie admitted.

"The old battle-ax isn't leaving, either, huh?" But the way he spoke the word was oddly respectful. Then his manner became withdrawn. "I must be keeping you from your errands. Will you be at the auction?"

"Yes." She was a bit puzzled by his behavior and curious as to why he hadn't mentioned anything about buying her land.

"I'll probably see you there," he said.

Valerie had the feeling she was being brushed off. "Probably," she answered with a cool smile, her chin lifted stiffly, then walked away.

Between that brief meeting in town and the auction, she didn't see Judd. She ignored the knotting ache in her stomach and told herself she was glad she had finally convinced him that she wanted nothing to do with him. She was positive Judd had only pursued her at the beginning of her return because he had thought she would be easy. Now he knew differently. She wasn't easy and she wasn't available.

But the way her heart catapulted at the sight of his familiar figure in the auction crowd made a mockery of her silent disclaimers of interest in him. It was a bitter admission to recognize that she was still half in love with him.

The stable and house yard was littered with cars, trucks and horse trailers. There seemed to be an ocean of buyers, lookers and breeders. Around the makeshift auction ring was an encircling cluster of people jostling to get a look at the brood mare up for bids.

Valerie looked for Tadd and saw him firmly holding on to Mickey's hand, as if concerned he might get separated from his friend in the shuffle of people. Another look found Judd working his way through the crowd toward the trailer being used as the auctioneer's office.

A horse neighed behind her, a nervous sound that betrayed its agitation at the unusual commotion going on around it. Valerie turned to watch a groom walking the horse in a slow circle to calm it, crooning softly. All the horses looked sleek and in excellent condition, thanks to Mickey's unstinting efforts.

She glanced back to the auction ring where in a rhythmic droning voice the auctioneer was making his pitch. She walked in the opposite direction to the relative peace and quiet of the stables. Here the fever pitch of activity was reduced to a low hum as the grooms Mick had handpicked for the day prepared the brood mares and colts for the sale.

The warm air was pungent with the smell of horses. Straw rustled beneath shifting feet. Valerie wandered down the row of stalls, pausing to stroke the velvet nose thrust out toward her. She stopped at the paddock entrance to the barns and gazed out over empty pastures.

"It looks strange, doesn't it, not to see any mares grazing out there with their foals," Judd commented with an accurate piece of mind reading.

Valerie jumped at the sound of his voice directly behind her. "You startled me," she said in accusing explanation.

"Sorry," he offered, but she doubted that he meant it. "Is the auction going well?"

"So far," she answered with a shrug, and turned to look out the half door to the pasture. "It's bedlam out there," she said to explain her reason for escaping to the barns.

"A lot of buyers is what sends the prices up," Judd reminded her. "And, from the sound of the bidding on the number-fourteen mare, Misty's Delight, she's going to bring top dollar."

"Misty's Delight," Valerie repeated, and released a short, throaty laugh. "When I saw the names on the sale catalogue, I didn't know any of the horses. Granddad called that mare Misty's Delight by the name of Maude. As far as I'm concerned, they aren't selling Black Stockings. They're auctioning Rosie, or Sally or Polly."

"Yes, I'm glad your grandfather isn't here. Those mares were his pets, and the stallion, Donnybrook, was the most precious to him of them all," Judd admitted.

"If granddad were here, there wouldn't be a sale. There wouldn't be any need for one," Valerie sighed, and turned away from the empty paddocks. "But there is. And I'm selling. And I'm not going to have any regrets," she finished on a note of determination.

"Have you listed the farm for sale yet?" he asked, taking it for granted that she was selling it.

Since it was true, she didn't see any point in going into that side issue. "In a way," she answered, and explained that indecisive response. "It won't officially be listed for another couple of weeks."

"Why the delay?" He studied her curiously.

"I had a couple of appraisals from two local real estate agents," Valerie began.

"Yes, I know," Judd interrupted. "I saw them, and I'm prepared to buy it for two thousand more than the highest price they gave you."

She took a deep breath at his handsome offer and nibbled at her lip, but didn't comment on his statement. "They suggested I'd be able to get about five thousand more if I painted all the buildings. So I'm going to take some of the profits from the horse sale and have everything painted."

"I'll match that, and you can forget about the painting," he countered. "I'd just have to do it all over again in the Meadow Farms' colors."

Leaning back against a wooden support post, Valerie eyed him warily, unable to trust him. She knew how vulnerable she was; she had only to check her racing pulse to be reminded of that. So she was doubly cautious about becoming involved in any dealings with him.

"Tell me the truth, Judd, why are you so determined to buy Worth Farms?" she demanded, her mouth thinning into a firm line.

A brow arched at her challenge as he tipped his head to one side, an indefinable glint in his eyes. "Why are you so determined to believe that I have some reason other than business?"

"Don't forget that I know you, Judd Prescott," she countered.

The corners of his mouth deepened. "You know me as intimately as any woman ever has, considerably more so than most." He taunted her with the memory of their affair.

Her cheeks flamed hotly as conflicting emotions churned inside of her. "I meant that I know you as a man."

"I should hope so," Judd drawled, deliberately misinterpreting her meaning.

"In the general sense," she corrected in anger.

"That's a pity." He rested a hand on the post she was leaning against, but didn't move closer. "Meadow Farms needs your grandfather's acreage, the pastures, the grass, the hay fields. The stables and barns can be used for the weanlings and the yearlings. The house can be living quarters for any of my married help who might need it. If the old battle-ax had inherited it, I would still want to buy it. Have you got that clear, Valerie?" His level gaze was serious.

"Yes," she nodded, a stiff gesture that held a hint of resentment.

"Good." Judd straightened, taking his hand from the post and offering it to her to seal their bargain. "Have we got a deal?"

"Yes." Wary, Valerie hesitated before placing her

hand in his and added the qualification, "On purely a business level."

"Strictly business." He gripped her hand and let it go, a faint taunting smile on his lips. "The matter is in the hands of our respective attorneys. We've agreed on the price, so the only thing left is for me to pay you the money for your signature deeding the land to me."

"There's just one thing," Valerie added.

"Oh? What's that?" Judd asked with distant curiosity.

"I'm not giving you possession of the house until the first of September. The barns, the stables, the pastures, everything else you can have when we sign the papers, except the house," she told him.

"And why is that?" He seemed only mildly interested.

"Because that's how long we'll be staying. I want to have this summer with Tadd," Valerie explained with a trace of defensiveness. "With working and all, I haven't been able to spend much time with him up until now. He's been growing up with babysitters. I've decided to devote this summer to him and begin working again this fall when he goes back to school."

"In that case, the house is yours until the first of September," Judd agreed with an indifferent shrug. "Are there any other conditions?"

"No." She shook her head, her long toffee hair swinging freely around her shoulders.

"Then everything is all settled," he concluded.

"I guess it is."

IT ALL WORKED AS SMOOTHLY as Judd had said it would. The matter was turned over to their attorneys. There wasn't even a need for Valerie to see Judd. When all the estate, mortgage and legal matters were completed, Jefferson Burrows brought out to the house the papers she needed to sign and gave her a check. The property became Judd's without any further communication between them and the documents gave her possession of the house until the first of September. It was all strictly business.

Something jumped on her bed, but the mattress didn't give much under its weight. "Mom? You'd better get up," Tadd insisted.

Valerie opened one sleepy eye to identify her son and rolled onto her stomach to bury her head under a pillow. "It's early. Go back to sleep, Tadd."

His small hand shook her bare shoulder in determined persistence. "Mom, what's that man doing on a ladder outside your window?" he demanded to know.

"A ladder?" she repeated sleepily, and lifted her head from under the pillow to frown at the pajama-clad boy sitting on her bed. "What are you talking about, Tadd?"

His attention was riveted on her bedroom window. A scraping sound drew her bleary gaze, as well. The sleep was banished from her eyes at the sight of a strange man wearing paint-splattered white overalls standing on a ladder next to her window.

"What's he doing there, mom?" Tadd frowned at her.

There wasn't a shade at the window, nothing to

prevent the man from looking in and seeing her. Valerie was angered by the embarrassing situation she was in. She tugged the end of the bedspread from the foot of the bed and pulled it with her. It was white chenille with a pink rose design woven in the center. She sat up on the side of her bed with her back to the window.

She picked up the alarm clock on the small table. Its hands pointed to seven o'clock. She began wrapping the bedspread around her sarong-fashion, fighting its length as her temper mounted. Pushing her sleep-rumpled hair away from one side of her face and tucking it behind her ear, she rose from the bed.

Tadd followed. "What's he doing there?" he repeated.

"That's what I'm about to find out!" she snapped, flinging a corner of the bedspread over her shoulder in a gesture unconsciously reminiscent of a caped crusader.

She stalked to the staircase and hitched the bedspread up around her ankles to negotiate the steps. Part of the white bedspread trailed behind her like a train and she had to keep yanking it along to prevent Tadd from tripping on it.

As she slammed out of the screen door onto the porch, another white-clad stranger was walking by carrying a stepladder. At the sight of Valerie, he stopped and stared.

"Would you mind telling me what's going on here?" she demanded, ignoring his incredulous and slightly ogling look. "And where are you going with that ladder?"

"Don't look at me, ma'am." The man backed away, absolving himself of any blame. "I just do what I'm told. The boss said I was to come here and I'm here."

"Where is your boss? I want to speak to him." Valerie forgot to hitch up the spread before starting down the porch steps and nearly tripped.

"He . . . he's on the other side of the house," the man stuttered as one side of the spread slipped, revealing the initial curving swell of one breast before Valerie tucked the material back in place.

She had taken one step in the direction the flustered man had indicated when she heard the cantering beat of horse's hooves and looked around to see Judd riding up on the big gray. She stopped and glanced back at the man.

"You can go on about your business now," she snapped.

"Yes, ma'am!" He scurried off as if he had been shot.

Tadd stood on the porch, one bare foot resting on top of the other. He was watching the proceedings with innocent interest, curious and wide-eyed. Like his mother, his attention had become focused on Judd, who was dismounting to walk to the house. Valerie stepped forward to confront him.

"Would you like to explain to me what these men are doing here at this hour of the morning?" she demanded, her nostrils distending slightly in temper.

"I came by to let you know I'd hired a contractor to paint the place. I think I'm a little late." As he spoke, his gaze was making a leisurely inspection from her tousled mane of honey-dark hair down her bedspread-wrapped length and returning for an overall view of her alluring dishabille.

At the touch of his green-eyed gaze on her bare shoulder and its lingering interest on the point where the white material jutted out to cover her breasts, Valerie tugged the spread more tightly around her. She realized he was very much aware that she was naked beneath it.

"A little late is an understatement," she fumed. "I woke up this morning to find a man outside my bedroom window on a ladder!"

"If I'd known you slept in the altogether, I would have been the man on the ladder outside your window," Judd drawled with soft suggestiveness.

An irritated sound of exasperation came from her throat. "It's impossible talking to you. I'll speak to the contractor myself and tell him to come back at a decent hour!" As she started to take a step, her leg became tangled in the folds of the bedspread.

Judd reached out with a steadying hand on her arm. "I think you'd better go back into the house before you trip and reveal more of your considerable charms than you'd like." He lifted her off her feet and into his arms before she could suspect his intention. The bedspread swaddled her into a cocoon that didn't lend itself to movement.

"Put me down!" Valerie raged in fiery embarrassment.

A lazy smile curved his mouth as he looked down at her. "I hired house painters, not nude artists. Not that I wouldn't object to having a private portrait of you."

She caught sight of Tadd staring at them with open-mouthed amazement. "Will you stop it?" she hissed at Judd, and he just chuckled, knowing she was at his mercy.

"Will you open the door for me, Tadd," he requested in an amused voice as he carried Valerie onto the porch.

Tadd scampered forward in his bare feet to comply, staring at Valerie's reddened face as Judd carried her past him. He followed them inside, letting the screen door close with a resounding bang. In the entry hall, Judd stopped.

"Now will you put me down?" Valerie demanded through clenched teeth, burning with mortification and a searing awareness of her predicament.

"Of course," he agreed with mocking compliance.

The arm at the back of her legs relaxed its hold, letting her feet slide to the floor while his other hand retained a light, steadying grip around her waist. Having both feet on the floor didn't give Valerie any feeling of advantage. Without shoes, the top of her head barely reached past his chin. To see his face, she had to tip her head back, a much too vulnerable position. She chose instead to glare upward through the sweep of her lashes.

"I think it would be wise if you put some clothes on," he suggested dryly as his gaze swung downward from her face, "or at least rearrange your sarong so that pink rose adorns a less eye-catching spot."

His finger traced the outline of a rosebud design on the chenille bedspread. In doing so, he drew a circle around the hard button of her breast. Heat raced over her skin as Valerie jerked the bedspread higher, pulling the rose design almost to her collarbone. Judd chuckled for the second time, knowing how deeply he had disturbed her.

Spinning away from him, Valerie lifted the folds of the material up around her knees and bolted for the staircase. On the second step she stopped, remembering the predicament that awaited her upstairs. She sent an angry look over her shoulder.

"You go out there and tell that painter to get away from my window!" she ordered in an emotion-choked voice.

"I'll have him on the ground at once." Judd grinned at her, laughter dancing wickedly in his eyes.

Valerie glanced at the boy standing beside him. "Tadd, you come with me," she commanded. "It's time you were dressed, too."

Reluctantly Tadd moved toward the stairs. As Judd started toward the door, Valerie began climbing the steps to the second floor. Clara met her at the head of the stairs, her nightgown ruffling out from beneath the hem of her quilted robe.

"What's all the commotion about?" Clara ran a frowning look over Valerie's attire. "And what are you doing dressed like that?"

"Mr. Prescott neglected to inform us that he'd

hired some painters to come out to the farm," was the short-tempered reply. "I woke up to find one outside my window on a ladder." Bunching the spread more tightly around her hips, Valerie started toward her bedroom.

"I've told you about going to bed like that," Clara's reproving voice followed her. "Haven't I warned you that someday there'd be a fire or something and you'd be caught!"

Valerie stopped abruptly to make a sharp retort and Tadd, who was following close behind her, bumped into her. Her hand gripped his shoulder to steady him and remained there as she sent Clara a look that would have withered the leaves from a mighty oak, but Clara was made of stronger stuff.

Swallowing the remark she had intended to make, Valerie muttered, "You're a lot of comfort, Clara," and glanced at the small boy. "Come on, Tadd. Let's get you dressed first."

Altering her course, she pushed Tadd ahead of her to her old bedroom that Tadd now occupied. While she went to the dresser to get his clean clothes, Tadd padded to the window and peered out.

"I don't see those men anymore, mommy. Judd made them go away," he told her.

"Good. Now off with those pajamas and into these clothes," she ordered curtly.

When Tadd was dressed, Valerie sent him downstairs and went to her own room. She made certain there wasn't a painter anywhere near the vicinity of her window before getting dressed herself. When she came downstairs she walked to the kitchen where the aroma of fresh-perked coffee wafted invitingly in the air.

Tadd was sitting at the breakfast table. An elbow was resting on the top and a small hand supported his forehead, pushing his brown hair on end. A petulant scowl marked his expression.

"Mom, Clara says I have to drink some of my milk before I have another pancake." He glared at the stout woman standing at the stove. "Do I have to? Can't I drink it afterward, mom? Please?"

Valerie glanced at the glass of white liquid that hadn't been touched. "Drink your milk, Tadd."

"Aw, mom!" he grumbled, and reached for the glass.

"Don't fix any pancakes for me, Clara." Ignoring her son, Valerie walked to the cupboard and poured a cup of coffee. "I'm not hungry."

"You'd better eat something," the woman insisted.

Before Valerie could argue the point, there was a knock on the back door and a taunting voice asked, "Are you decent in there?"

"Yes!" Valerie shot the sharply affirmative retort at the wire mesh where Judd's dark figure was outlined, and carried her cup to the table.

The hinges creaked as the screen door opened and Judd walked in. "The coffee smells good," he remarked. After one dancing look at Valerie's still simmering expression, he addressed his next words to Clara. "Do you mind if I have a cup?"

"Help yourself," the woman agreed with an indifferent shrug.

As he walked to the counter on which the coffeepot sat, Valerie watched the easy way he moved. His broad shoulders and chest, his narrow male hips, and the muscled columns of his long legs moved in perfect harmony. His body was programmed and conditioned to perform every task well. An ache quivered through her as Valerie remembered how well.

Pausing at the stove, Judd observed, "Pancakes for breakfast. Buckwheat?"

"Yes." Clara expertly flipped one from the griddle.

"Help yourself, Judd," Valerie heard herself offering in a caustic tone born out of a sense of inevitability. In an agitated desire for movement she rose from her chair to add more coffee to her steaming cup. "Orange juice. Bacon. Toast." She listed the choices. "Just help yourself to anything."

"Anything?" The soft, lilting word crossed the room to taunt her. She pivoted and caught her breath as his gaze leisurely roamed over her shape to let her know his choice.

She felt as if her toes were curling from the heat spreading through her. She turned away from his disturbing look and breathed an emotionally charged, "You know very well what I meant." Adding a drop more coffee to her cup, Valerie silently acknowledged that she didn't have many defenses against him left, certainly none when the topic became intimate. She attempted to change it. "Did you straighten those painters out about starting work at such an hour?" she demanded.

"In a manner of speaking," Judd replied, casually accepting the change in subject matter. "They started early to avoid working in the heat of the day. Unfortunately, they were under the impression that all the buildings were vacant, including the house. They know better now," he added with faint suggestiveness.

Valerie didn't need to be reminded of the early-morning episode. The absence of a direct answer to her first question prompted her to ask, "You did arrange for them to begin work at a more respectable hour, didn't you?"

"No," he denied. "There isn't any reason to change their working hours—"

"No reason?" she began indignantly.

But Judd continued, "However, from now on they'll be working on the barns and stables in the mornings."

"I should hope so," Valerie retorted tightly.

"I drank some of my milk," Tadd piped up, a white moustache above his upper lip. "Can I have another pancake now?" Clara set another one in front of him. As Tadd reached for the syrup, he glanced at Judd. "They're very good. Do you want one?"

"No, thank you. I've already had my breakfast." Judd drained the last of the coffee from his cup. "It's time I was leaving. If the painters give you any trouble, Valerie, call me."

"I will," she agreed, but she could have told him that the only one who gave her trouble was himself. He troubled her mentally and emotionally, and there didn't seem to be any relief in sight.

CHAPTER SIX

A RESTLESSNESS RACED THROUGH VALERIE. She tried to contain it as she had for the last several days, but it wouldn't be suppressed. There had been too much time on her hands lately, she reasoned. She was accustomed to working eight hours, coming home and working eight hours more with meals, housework and wash. But here the workload of the house was shared with Clara and she had no job except to play with Tadd.

One of the painters had a radio blaring a raucous brand of music that scraped at her nerves. Of the half a dozen men painting the barns and stables, there always seemed to be one walking around, getting paint, moving ladders, doing something, which was more than Valerie could say for herself.

Sighing, she left the porch and entered the house. Clara was in the living room, watching her favorite soap opera on television. Her gaze was glued to the screen and she didn't even glance up when Valerie entered the room.

"Clara," Valerie began, only to be silenced by an upraised hand. A couple of minutes later a commercial came on and she was allowed to finish what she had started to say. "I'm going to take Ginger out for a ride. Tadd is upstairs having a nap. Will you keep an eye on him while I'm gone?"

"Sure. Go ahead," her friend agreed readily.

Outside, Valerie dodged the gauntlet of ladders and paint cans to retrieve the bridle and saddle from the tack room. Several people had been out to look at the bay mare Mickey Flanners had suggested she sell privately, but so far no one had bought her. Valerie didn't mind. One horse wasn't that difficult to take care of and Tadd enjoyed the rides she took him on.

The bay mare trotted eagerly to the pasture fence when she approached. Lonely without her former equine companionship, the mare readily sought human company. There was never any difficulty catching her and she accepted the bit between her teeth as if it were sugar.

Astride the animal, Valerie turned the brown head toward the rolling land of the empty pasture. The mare stepped out quickly, moving into a brisk canter at a slight touch from Valerie's heel. She had no destination in mind. Her only intention was to try to run off this restlessness that plagued her.

The long-legged thoroughbred mare seemed prepared to run forever, clearing pasture fences like the born jumper Mickey had claimed she was. Valerie rode without concentrating on anything but the rhythmic stride of the animal beneath her and the pointed ears of its bobbing head.

When the bay horse slowed to a walk, Valerie wasn't aware that it was responding to her pressure on the reins. They entered a stand of trees and she ducked her head to avoid a low-hanging branch. When she straightened, it was in a clearing. Her fingers tightened on the reins, stopping the bay, as the blood drained from her face.

Unconsciously she had guided the mare to the place where she and Judd had met. From a long-ago habit, she dismounted and wound the reins around the broken branch of a tree. The mare lowered her head, blew at the grass and began to graze.

Almost in a trance, Valerie looked around her. The place hadn't seemed to change very much. The grass looked taller and thicker, promising a softer bed. She tore her gaze from it and noticed that lightning had taken a large limb from the oak tree some time ago.

Wrapping her arms tightly around her stomach, she tried to assuage the hollow ache. There was a longing for Judd so intense that it seemed to eat away at her insides. She wanted to cry from the joy she had once known here and the heartache that had followed, but no tears came.

It was crazy—it was foolish—it was destroying to want him. She was so successful at stimulating his lusty appetite, why hadn't she ever been able to arouse his love, she wondered. She was so filled with love that she thought she would explode.

The bay mare lifted her head, her ears pricking. Her sides heaved with a long, questioning whicker. Then the soft swish of grass behind her made Valerie turn as a big gray horse stopped at the edge of the clearing and Judd dismounted. He walked toward her with smooth, unhurried strides like a page from the past. Her heart lodged somewhere in the vicinity of her throat. She was unable to speak, half-afraid that she might discover she was dreaming.

But his voice was no dream: "I knew you'd come here sooner or later." Neither was the smoldering light in his green eyes as he came closer.

The instant he touched her, Valerie was convinced it wasn't a dream and she knew she didn't dare stay. "It was an accident," she insisted, her breath quickening. "I didn't mean to come here."

She tried to push out of his arms and make her way past him, but a sinewed arm hooked her waist and pulled her against his side. A muscled thigh brushed her legs apart to rub against her, while the hand at the small of her back pressed her close to him. His fingers cupped the side of her face and lifted it for inspection.

"Ever since the day you returned, I knew you would eventually come here." His gaze roamed possessively over her features. "You can't fight it any more than I can. It's always been that way with us."

"Yes." Her whispered agreement carried the throb of admission.

As his mouth descended on hers, Valerie realized his persistence had finally eroded her resolve. The surroundings, her love, the feel of him were more than she could withstand and she surrendered to the pulsing fire of his embrace.

Her lips parted under the insistence of his. His practiced hands molded her more fully against his length, but this closeness only heightened their mutual dissatisfaction with their upright position.

Burying his face in the curve of her neck, Judd swept her into his arms and carried her the few feet to the grassy nest. Kneeling, he laid her upon it, lifting the heavy mass of tawny hair and fanning it above her head. Her hands were around his neck to pull him down beside her, part of his weight crushing her.

"I've waited a long time to see that honey cloud of hair on that green pillow." His husky voice vibrated with passion. "And to see that love-drugged look in your cat eyes."

His mouth kissed the hollow of her throat as his skilled fingers unbuttoned her blouse. His hand wandered over the bareness of her waist and taut stomach. Its leisurely pace sent a languorous feeling floating through her limbs. His mouth trailed a fiery path to intimately explore the rounded softness of her breast. Her nails dug into the rippling muscles of his back and Judd brought his hard lips back to hers. More of his weight moved onto her.

He rubbed his mouth against the outline of her lips. "There were times when I wondered whether I had the control or the patience to wait for you to come here," he admitted. "I knew you'd been hurt and used badly. But I was also positive that I could make you forget the man who got you pregnant and ran off."

"Forget?" Her breathless laugh was painful and bitter, because he had made her forget. With a twist, she rolled from beneath him and staggered to her feet, shakily buttoning her blouse. "How could I forget?" The questioning statement was issued to herself. "You are that man, Judd."

Stunned silence greeted her tautly spoken announcement. Then Valerie heard him rise and a steel claw hooked her elbow to spin her around. A pair of blazing green eyes burned into her face.

"What are you saying?" Judd ground out savagely.

"You're Tadd's father," she informed him with flashing defiance. "I was almost three months pregnant when I left here seven years ago. Granddad threw me out because I wouldn't tell him who the father was. It was you . . . you and your damned virility!"

"If it's true, why didn't you come to me seven years ago and tell me you were pregnant?" Judd demanded.

"If it's true?" Valerie repeated with a taunting laugh. "You just answered your own question, Judd. You're the one and only man who has ever made love to me. But to you, I was just a cheap little tramp."

"That isn't true," he denied.

"Isn't it?" she mocked. "Why should I have endured the humiliation of telling you and have you question whether you were responsible?"

"I would have helped you," Judd replied grimly.

"What would you have done?" Valerie challenged. "Given me money for an abortion? Or paid me hush money to keep quiet about your part in it? You made me feel small enough without taking money from you."

"I never guessed you felt that way." A muscle in his jaw was flexing.

"I don't think you ever considered the possibility that I had feelings," she retorted. "I'm a human being with feelings and a heart, Judd. I'm not made of stone like you. Look—I even bleed." She scratched her nails across the inside of her arm, tiny drops of red appearing in the welts.

He caught at the hand that had marked her. "You crazy little fool!" he growled, and yanked her into his arms, crushing her tightly against him, the point of his chin rubbing the top of her head.

For an instant Valerie let herself enjoy the hard comfort of his arms before she rebelled. "Let me go, Judd." She strained against his hold. "Haven't you done enough?"

He partially released her, keeping one arm firmly around her shoulders as he drew her along with him. "Come on."

"No!" She didn't know where he was taking her.

Stopping in front of the bay mare, Judd lifted her into the saddle. "I'm taking you back," he said, and handed her the reins.

"I can find my own way," she retorted. "I always did before."

His hand held the mare's bridle, preventing Valerie from reining her away. "This time I'm going with you," he stated.

"Why?" Valerie watched him with a wary eye when he walked to the big gray.

Judd didn't respond until he had mounted and

ridden the high-stepping gray over beside her. "I'd like to have another look at my son."

Her fingers tightened on the reins and the mare tossed her head in protest. "Tadd is mine. You merely fathered him. He's mine, Judd," she warned.

He didn't argue the point and instead gestured for her to lead the way to her grandfather's farm, one that Judd now owned. They cantered in silence, their horses skittish and nervous, picking up the tenseness of their riders.

Tadd had awakened from his nap when they arrived. He didn't rush out to greet Valerie, but remained sitting on the porch step, sulking because she had gone riding without him. Valerie was nervous as she walked to the house with Judd. Tadd was no longer just another little boy to him. He was his son, and Judd's green eyes were studying, inspecting and appraising the small boy.

"Did you have a good nap, Tadd?" Valerie asked with forced brightness.

"Why didn't you wait until I was up and take me for a ride?" he pouted.

"Because I wanted to go by myself," she answered, and promised, "You and I can go later this afternoon."

"Okay," Tadd sighed, accepting the alternative, and glanced at Judd. "Hello. How come you were riding if Mom wanted to be by herself?"

"We happened to meet each other while I was on my way here," Judd explained easily, his attention not wavering from Tadd's face.

"Were you coming over here to tell those men to

go away?" Tadd wondered. "There hasn't been any man outside Mommy's window since that other day. But one of them gave me a brush—I'll show you." In a flash, he was on his feet and darting to the far end of the porch.

Judd slid a brief glance in Valerie's direction. "Have you told him anything about . . . his father?" he asked quietly.

"No." She shook her head.

But his voice hadn't been pitched so softly that Tadd hadn't picked up a piece of the conversation. He came back, holding up a worn-out brush that had not been used in some time. The bristles were stiff and broken.

As he showed it to Judd, he glanced up. "I don't have a father. Do you?"

Judd's dark head lifted in faint surprise. Valerie couldn't tell whether it was from Tadd's directness or the acuteness of his hearing. Bemusement softened the corners of the hard male mouth.

"Yes, I had one, but he died a long time ago," Judd admitted, and tipped his head to one side to study Tadd more closely as he asked, "Did your father die?"

"No. I don't have a father," Tadd repeated with childlike patience. "Some kids don't, you know," he informed Judd with blinking innocence. "Three of the kids I go to school with don't have dads. Of course, Cindy Tomkins has two." He lost interest in that subject. "It's a pretty neat brush, isn't it?"

"It sure is," Judd agreed.

"I wanted to help them paint, but they said I

couldn't. They said I was too little." Tadd's mouth twisted, his expression indicating it was a statement he had heard many times before. "I'll be seven on my next birthday. That isn't too little, is it?"

"I think you have to be ten years old before you can be a painter," Judd told him.

Valerie's nerves were wearing thin. There wasn't much more of this conversation she could tolerate. Judd had seen Tadd again and talked to him. Surely that was enough?

"Tadd, why don't you run into the house and see if there's a carrot in the refrigerator for Ginger. I think she'd like one," she suggested.

"Okay." He started to turn and stopped. "Can I feed it to her?"

"Of course," she nodded, and he was off, slamming the screen door and tearing through the house to the kitchen. Feeling the scrutiny of Judd's eyes, her gaze slid from his direction.

"He isn't too familiar with the birds and the bees, is he?" Judd commented dryly. "Some children don't have a father," he repeated Tadd's statement. "Is that what you told him?"

"No, it's a conclusion he's reached all on his own. He has a general idea about the birds and the bees, but he hasn't comprehended the significance of it," Valerie admitted, a shade defensively.

"What are you going to do when he does?" His level gaze never wavered from her. "What will you tell him when he asks about his father?"

"When he's old enough to ask the question, he'll

be old enough to understand the truth," she retorted, knowing it was a day she didn't look forward to.

The sound of racing feet approached the porch in advance of the screen door banging open. "I got the carrot!" Tadd held it up. "Can I give it to Ginger now?"

At the nod from Valerie, Tadd started down the porch steps. As he went past Judd, he was cautioned, "Remember, Tadd, walk up to the horse."

With a carefree, "I will!" Tadd raced full speed halfway across the yard, then stopped to walk the rest of the way to the pasture fence where the bay mare was tied. Valerie watched him slowly feed the gentle mare.

"I feel that I owe you something for these last seven years," Judd said.

"You don't owe me anything." She shrugged away the suggestion, the idea stinging.

"I mean it, Valerie. I want to take care of you and Tadd," he stated in a firm tone.

The full fury of her sparkling eyes was directed at him. "I wouldn't take your money then, Judd, and I won't take it now."

Instead of being angry, Judd looked amused by her fiery display. His gaze ran over her upturned face, alight with temper and pride.

"Tigress," he murmured. "All this doesn't change anything."

Unable to hold that look, Valerie glanced away. She seemed incapable of resisting him, but she tried anyway. "Yes, it does."

"Valerie." His voice commanded her attention.

When she didn't obey, his fingers caught her chin and turned her to face him. "It isn't any use fighting it."

"I've made up my mind, Judd," she insisted stiffly. "I won't be your lover. Please! Just leave me alone."

His mouth slanted in amusement. "Do you think I haven't tried?" he mocked, and kissed her hard. When he straightened, he murmured, "And tell that battle-ax that it's impolite to eavesdrop." With that, he turned and walked across the yard to where the gray hunter was standing next to Valerie's mare.

The screen door opened and Clara stepped out. "Humph!" she snorted. "So it's impolite to eavesdrop, is it? What do you suppose they call what he was proposing?"

"You shouldn't have been listening," Valerie said, and continued to watch Judd, who had stopped to say goodbye to Tadd.

"You shouldn't carry on private conversations where people can overhear," Clara retorted. "So you decided to tell him he was the boy's father, did you?"

"Yes," Valerie admitted.

"What do you suppose he's going to do about it?"

"There isn't anything he can do. Tadd is mine. Judd knows that," Valerie insisted.

"Mark my words, he'll figure out a way to use it to his advantage. Judd Prescott is a tenacious man." There was a hint of admiration in Clara's voice as they both watched him ride away.

CHAPTER SEVEN

JUDD CAME OVER twice more that week, ostensibly to check on the progress of the painting crew, but that possessive light was in his eyes whenever his gaze met Valerie's. It held a warning or a promise, depending on her mood at the time. His attitude toward Tadd remained relatively casual, a little more interested and occasionally warmer at different moments.

Valerie was in the kitchen helping Clara wash the breakfast dishes when a car drove into the yard. The painting crew had finished the day before, so she knew it wasn't one of them. As she walked to the front door, she wiped her hands dry on the towel and wondered if the lawyer, Jefferson Burrows, had more papers for her to sign.

Judd's visits had always been made on horseback. It didn't occur to her that the car might be driven by him. Not until she saw him step out. Tadd was outside playing and immediately stopped what he was doing to rush forward to greet Judd.

After sending one green-eyed glance toward Valerie standing on the porch, Judd directed his attention to the boy skipping along beside him. His hair gleamed jet black in the sunlight, with Tadd's a lighter hue.

"Do you have anything planned to do today?" Judd asked him.

"Mom and me are going riding later on," Tadd answered after thinking for a minute.

"That's something you could do tomorrow if you have a place to visit today, isn't it?" Judd suggested, and Valerie felt a tiny leap of alarm.

"I guess so," Tadd agreed, then frowned. "But we don't have a place to visit." The frown lifted. "How come you drove a car? Are you going to take us someplace?"

"I might," was the smiling response.

"Tadd, come into the house and wash your hands!" Valerie called sharply.

With a gleeful expression, Tadd came bounding to the porch hopping excitedly from one foot to the other. "Mom, did you hear? Judd said he might take us someplace."

"Yes, I heard what he said." She sent Judd an angry look and attempted to smile at her son. "Go into the house and wash your hands as you were told."

"Find out where we're going!" Tadd called over his shoulder, and hurried into the house.

Descending the porch steps, Valerie walked out to confront Judd. "Why did you tell Tadd we might be going someplace with you?" she demanded angrily. "It isn't fair to raise a little boy's hopes up like that."

"Why?" He returned her look with feigned innocence. "I came over to ask you and Tadd to spend the day with me. There's a tobacco auction over by

Lothian, probably one of the last of the season. I thought Tadd might find it interesting."

"I'm sure he would find it very interesting, but we aren't going," she stated flatly. "And you shouldn't have let Tadd think we would."

"How did I know you'd refuse?" He smiled lazily. "I hadn't even asked you yet when I mentioned it to him."

"You knew very well I'd refuse!" she snapped.

"Temper, temper, little spitfire," Judd taunted.

"Of course I'm angry," Valerie argued defensively. "You've made me the villain as far as Tadd is concerned."

"You could always change your mind and agree to come with me," he reminded her.

"You know I won't."

"Yes, you will." His level gaze became deadly serious. "Otherwise I'll have to have a talk with Tadd and tell him who his father is."

Valerie paled. "You wouldn't do that!" she protested. "He wouldn't understand. He'd be hurt and confused. You wouldn't be that ruthless!"

"I'll have my way, Valerie." It wasn't an idle warning. "Will you come or shall I have a talk with Tadd?"

Tears burned the back of her eyes and she bit the inside of her lip to keep it from quivering. She had known he was hard, and not above using people to get what he wanted, and he'd already made it plain that he wanted her.

"If I agree to come, will you give me your word

to say nothing to Tadd about being his father?" she demanded tightly.

"You have my word," Judd agreed, "if you come."

"I . . . I'll need a few minutes to change my clothes," Valerie requested.

His skimming gaze conveyed the message that he preferred her without any, but he said, "Take all the time you need. I'll be waiting."

Frustrated, Valerie ground out, "You can wait until hell freezes over and it still won't do any good!" Pivoting on her heel, she rushed into the house.

Fifteen minutes later she emerged cool and composed in a yellow-flowered cotton sun dress. Tadd's face and hands had been scrubbed and inspected by Clara, his shirt and pants changed to a clean set. Valerie couldn't help thinking that the three of them probably looked like the ideal American family, leaving on a day's outing to a tobacco auction in Lothian, Maryland. It hurt to know that they would never be a family in the legal sense, but Tadd's steady stream of chatter didn't give Valerie any time to dwell on that.

The sights, sounds and smells of the tobacco auction proved to be as fascinating to Valerie as they were to Tadd. Various grades of Maryland tobacco were sold off in lots. The rhythmic cadence of the auctioneer's voice rang through the area, the slurring words punctuated by a clear "Sold!" at the end. The summer air was aromatically pungent with the smell of stacks of drying tobacco leaves. Colors varied from dark gold to brown.

They wandered around the auction area and strolled through the warehouse. Tadd saw most of the scene from Judd's shoulders. They had a cold drink beneath a shade tree.

Later, Judd drove to a park and they picnicked from a basket his mother had packed. Through it all, Judd was at his charming best and Valerie found herself succumbing to his spell as if she didn't have better sense.

She took his hand, accepted the arm that occasionally encircled her shoulders, smiled into the green eyes that glinted at her, and warmed under the feather kisses Judd would bestow on the inside of her wrist or her hair. In spite of her better judgment, she relaxed and enjoyed his company, flirting with him and feeling carelessly happy all the while.

As they lingered at the picnic area, Judd peeled an orange and began feeding her sections while Tadd played on the swings. Each time a bead of juice formed on her lips he kissed it away until Tadd demanded his share of the attention by handing Judd an orange to peel for him.

When they started back in the early afternoon, Valerie was too content to care that it would soon be over. She closed her eyes and listened to the mostly one-sided conversation between Tadd and Judd. A faint smile tugged at the corners of her mouth from Tadd's domination.

The miles sped away beneath the swiftly turning tires. Valerie guessed that they were almost home, but she didn't want to open her eyes to see how close they were. A large male hand took hold of one of hers. Her lashes slowly lifted to watch Judd carry it to his mouth, kissing the sensitive palm. His gaze left the road in front of him long enough to send one lazy, sweeping glance at her.

"Did you enjoy yourself today?" he asked softly.

"Yes, very much," she admitted.

Tadd, who couldn't be silent for long, cried, "Look at all the horses, mommy!"

Dragging her gaze from Judd's compelling profile, she glanced out of the window. The familiar black fences of Meadow Farms were on either side of the car. She sat up straighter, realizing Judd had turned off the road that would have taken them to her grandfather's farm.

"Where are we going?" she asked. There was only one destination possible at the end of this lane: the headquarters of Meadow Farms.

"Are we going to see the horses?" Tadd asked, leaning over the seat.

"There's someone who wants to see you," Judd answered, glancing in Tadd's direction.

"See me?" His voice almost squeaked in disbelief. "Who?"

"Who?" Valerie echoed the demand, a quiver of uncertainty racing through her.

"Mickey Flanners," Judd answered. "When I mentioned I'd be seeing you today, he asked me to bring you over if we had time."

"I haven't seen Mickey in a long time," Tadd declared in a tone that exaggerated the time span.

"That's what he said." Judd slowed the car as the lane split ahead of them.

In one direction were the stables and barns of the thoroughbred breeding farm; in the other direction was the main house in which the Prescotts lived. Judd made the turn in the latter direction. Valerie, who had relaxed upon learning it was Mickey Flanners they were going to see, felt her nerves stretching tense.

The lane curled into a circular driveway in front of a large pillared house, glistening white in the bright afternoon sunlight. To Valerie, it appeared the embodiment of gracious living, a sharp contrast to the simple farmhouse in which she was raised.

"Is *this* where Mickey lives?" Tadd asked in an awed voice.

"No, this is where I live," Judd explained, stopping the car in front of the main entrance to the house. He glanced at Valerie and saw the hesitation in her gold-flecked eyes. "I'll be on my mother's black list if I don't stop at the house first so she can say hello to you and Tadd."

"Judd, really. . . ." Valerie started to protest, but it was too late.

The front door of the house had opened and Judd's mother was coming out to greet them, petite and striking with those angel wings of silver in her dark hair. The white pleated skirt and the blue and white polka-dot top with a matching short-sleeved jacket in blue that Maureen Prescott wore was so casually elegant that Valerie felt self-conscious about her becoming but simple cotton sun dress.

"Here's mother now." Judd opened his door and stepped out.

It wasn't manners that kept Valerie inside the car. The magnificent house, the beautifully landscaped grounds, the status attached to the Prescott name, and the woman waiting on the portico warned her that she was out of her league.

Her door was opened and Judd stood waiting, a hand extended to help her out of the car. She turned her troubled and uncertain gaze to him. He seemed to study it with a trace of amusement that didn't make her feel any more comfortable.

"What happened to my tigress?" he chided softly. "You look like a shy little kitten. Come on." He reached in and took her hand to draw her out of the car.

Once she was standing beside him, Judd retained his hold of her hand. Valerie absorbed strength from his touch, but the twinges of unease didn't completely go away. It seemed a very long way from the car up the walk to the steps leading to the columned portico. To cover her nervousness, Valerie held herself more stiffly erect, her chin lifted a fraction of an inch higher than normal, her almond gold eyes wide and proud.

Tadd didn't appear to suffer from any of Valerie's pangs of self-consciousness. He skipped and hopped, turned and looked, and generally let his curious eyes take in everything there was to see. He exhibited no shyness at all when the unknown woman walked forward to meet them.

"Hello, Valerie. I'm so glad you were able to stop in," Judd's mother greeted her warmly, a smile of welcome curving her mouth.

"Thank you, Mrs. Prescott," Valerie answered, and suddenly wished that Judd would let go of her hand, but he didn't.

"Please, call me Maureen," the other woman insisted with such friendliness that Valerie was reminded her reputation as hostess was without equal.

This open acceptance of her only made Valerie more uneasy. "That's very kind of you . . . Maureen." She faltered stiffly over the name.

Maureen Prescott either didn't notice or overlooked Valerie's stilted tones as she turned to Tadd, bending slightly at the waist. "And you must be Tadd."

After an admitting bob of his head, he asked, "How did you know me?"

The woman's smile widened. "I've heard a lot about you."

"Who are you?" Tadd wanted to know.

"I'm . . . Judd's mother."

Did Valerie imagine it or had there been a pulse beat of hesitation before Maureen Prescott had explained her relationship? Then Valerie realized she was being ridiculously oversensitive to the situation.

"Say hello to Mrs. Prescott, Tadd," Valerie prompted her son.

Dutifully he extended a hand to the woman facing him and recited politely, "Hello, Mrs. Prescott."

"Mrs. Prescott is quite a mouthful, isn't it?" The teasing smile on Maureen's lips was warm with understanding. "Why don't you call me Reeny, Tadd?" she suggested.

"Reeny is what my nieces and nephews call her,"

Judd explained quietly to Valerie. "When they were little, they couldn't pronounce her given name so they shortened it."

Valerie was uncomfortably aware that Tadd had been given permission to use the same name that the other grandchildren called their grandmother. She felt the creeping warmth of embarrassment in her cheeks. Did Maureen Prescott know Tadd was her grandchild? Had Judd told her?

Almost in panic, she searched the woman's face for any indication of hidden knowledge. But the turquoise eyes were clear without a trace of cognition. A tremor of relief quaked through Valerie. She wasn't sure she could have handled the situation if this genteel woman had known the truth.

"Reeny is nice," Tadd agreed to the name.

"I'm glad you like it, Tadd." Maureen Prescott straightened and cast an apologetic smile at Judd. "Frank Andrews called and left a message for you to phone him the instant you came back." With a glance at Valerie, she added, "It seems every time a person tries to set aside a day strictly for pleasure, something urgent like this crops up."

Valerie's head moved in a rigid nod of understanding before a slight movement from Judd drew her attention. A grim resignation had thinned his mouth and added a glitter of impatience in his eyes.

"I'm sorry, Valerie," he said in apology for the intrusion of business. "But it'll only take a few minutes to phone him."

"That's all right. Go ahead," she insisted, and

untangled her fingers from the grip of his to clasp her hands nervously in front of her.

"While Judd is making his phone call, you and Tadd can come with me. After that long drive, I'm sure you're thirsty and I have a big pitcher of lemonade all made, as well as some cookies," Judd's mother invited.

"No, thank you, Mrs. Prescott . . . Maureen," Valerie refused quickly, and reached for Tadd's hand. "It's very kind of you, but Tadd and I will walk down to the stables and find Mickey."

"You'll do no such thing, Valerie." Judd's low voice rumbled through the air with ominous softness. Her sideways glance saw the hardened jaw and angry fire in his eyes. His look held a silent warning not to persist in her refusal of the invitation. "I'll be through in a few minutes to take you myself. In the meantime, I'm sure Tadd—" his gaze flicked to the boy "—would like to have some cookies and lemonade. Wouldn't you, Tadd?"

"Yes." The response was quick and without hesitation, followed by an uncertain glance at Valerie. "Please," Tadd added.

"Very well," Valerie agreed, smiling stiffly, and added a defensive, "If you are sure we aren't putting you to any trouble?"

"None at all," Judd's mother assured her, and turned to walk toward the front door.

Judd's fingers dug into the flesh of Valerie's arm in a punishing grip as he escorted her up the steps to the portico. At the wide double entrance to the house, he let her go to open the door for his mother, then waited for her and Tadd to precede him inside.

"Excuse me." Almost immediately upon entering, Judd took his leave from them. "I won't be long." His look warned Valerie that he expected to find her in the house when he was finished.

"We'll be on the veranda, Judd," his mother told him.

Valerie watched him walk away, skittishly becoming conscious of the expansive foyer dominated by a grand staircase rising to the second floor. The foyer was actually an enormously wide hallway splitting the house down the center with rooms branching off from it.

Furniture gleamed with the rich-grained luster of hardwood, adorned on top with vases of flowers and art objects. Valerie took a tighter grip on Tadd's hand, knowing she couldn't afford to replace anything he might accidentally break. It was a stunning, artfully decorated home, elegance and beauty blended to comfort, like something out of the pages of a magazine.

"We'll go this way." Maureen Prescott started forward to lead the way, the clicking sound of her heels on the white-tiled floor echoing through the massive house.

"You have a lovely home." Valerie felt obliged to make some comment, but her tone made the compliment sound uncertain.

"It's a bit intimidating, isn't it?" the woman laughed in gentle understanding. "I remember the first time Blane, Judd's father, brought me here to meet his parents. It was shortly after we'd become engaged, and the place terrified me. It was much more formal then. When Blane told me that we would live here after we were married, I wanted to break the engagement, but fortunately he talked me out of that."

Maureen Prescott's instinctive knowledge of Valerie's reaction allowed her to relax a little. It was comforting to know that someone else had been awed by this impressive home.

"The house is at its best when it's filled with people, especially children," Maureen continued in an affectionate voice. "It seems to come to life then. When my five were growing up, the house never seemed big enough—which sounds hard to believe, doesn't it?"

"A little," Valerie admitted.

"They seemed to fill every corner of it with their projects and pets and friends. That reminds me—" she glanced down at the brown-haired boy trotting along beside Valerie "—there's something outside that I want to show you."

"What is it?" Tadd asked, his olive brown eyes rounding.

"You'll see," Maureen promised mysteriously, and paused to open a set of French doors onto the veranda. As she stepped outside, she called, "Here, Sable!"

A female German shepherd with a coat as black and sleek as its name came loping across the yard, panting a happy grin, tail wagging. Ten roly-poly miniatures tumbled over themselves in an effort to match their mother's gait.

"Puppies!" Tadd squealed in delight and followed Maureen Prescott to the edge of the veranda. The female shepherd washed his face with a single lick before greeting her mistress. Tadd's interest was in the ten little puppies bringing up the rear. "Can I play with them?"

"Of course you may." The instant she gave permission he was racing out to meet the pups. When he knelt on the ground, he was immediately under siege. Valerie joined in with the older woman's laughter as Tadd began giggling in his attempts to elude ten licking tongues. "Puppies and children are made for each other," Maureen declared in a voice breathless from laughter. "Come on, let's sit down and have that drink I promised you. I don't believe Tadd will be interested in lemonade and cookies for a while."

"I'm sure he's forgotten all about it," Valerie agreed, and followed the woman to a white grillwork table with a glass top.

A pitcher of lemonade sat in the center, condensation beading moisture on the outside. Four glasses filled with ice surrounded it as well as a plate of chocolate drop cookies with frosting on the top. Valerie sat down in one of the white iron-lace chairs around the table, plump cushions of green softening the hard seats.

"Tadd is really enjoying himself. The apartment where we live in Cincinnati doesn't permit pets, so this is really a treat for him," Valerie explained, taking the glass of lemonade she was handed and thanking her.

"Misty, my second daughter, lives in a complex that doesn't allow animals, either, and her children are at an age when they want to bring home every stray cat and dog they find. She and her husband have had a time keeping them from sneaking one in. I think their love of animals is part of the reason they come home to Meadow Farms so often. There's Sable and her puppies, the horses, and cats at the barns. But I don't mind what their reason is," Maureen insisted. "I just enjoy having them come. Although it's quite a houseful when they're all here at once."

"Are all your children married?" Valerie asked politely.

"Yes, with the exception of Judd, of course," Maureen answered with a smiling sigh. "There have been times when I've wondered if my firstborn was ever going to get married, but I've never said anything to him."

"I'm sure there are any number of women who would like to be the one to put an end to your wondering." Valerie was careful not to make it sound as if she was one of them.

"That's the problem—there've been too many women," Maureen Prescott observed with a trace of sad resignation. "The Prescott name, the wealth and his own singular attractiveness—Judd has been the object of many a woman's matrimonial eye. I'm afraid it's made him feel very cynical about the opposite sex."

"I can imagine," Valerie agreed and sipped at the tart, cold liquid in her glass.

"Yes, I've often teased him that I don't know if he's more particular about matching the bloodlines of his thoroughbreds or finding a compatible bloodline for a wife. He always answers that if he ever finds a woman with breeding, spirit and staying power, he'll marry her. Of course, we're only joking," his mother qualified her statement with a dismissing laugh.

Perhaps she had been teasing, but Valerie wouldn't be surprised to discover that Judd wasn't. She knew how cold-blooded he could be about some things . . . and so hot-blooded about others.

Maureen's comment made her wonder whether Judd's mother was subtly trying to warn her that she wasn't good enough for her son. Not that it was needed. Valerie had long been aware of Judd's low opinion of her, an opinion she sometimes forgot, as she had earlier that day. That feeling of unease and a panic to get away came over her again. She had to change the subject away from the discussion of Judd.

Her glance swung over the lawn, including a glimpse of a swimming pool behind some concealing shrubbery. "You must enjoy living here, Mrs. Prescott. It's peaceful, yet with all the conveniences."

"Yes, I love it here," Maureen agreed. "But you must call me Maureen. I learned that there were two requirements to enjoy living here the first year I was married. You have to like country life and you have to *love* horses. Fortunately I managed to fulfill both.

The only objection I have is at weaning time when the mares and foals are separated. It tears at my heart to hear them calling back and forth from the pastures to each other. I usually arrange to visit my youngest son, Randall, and his family in Baltimore then. Judd insists that it's silly and impractical to be upset by it, but then he isn't a mother."

The veranda door behind Valerie opened. She glanced over her shoulder, her heart skipping madly against her ribs as Judd's gaze slid warmly over her. Damn, but she couldn't stop loving him, even when she had admitted to herself only a moment ago that it was no good.

Smiling crookedly, he walked to the table. "I told you I wouldn't be long." He glanced to the lawn where Tadd was still playing with the puppies, the black shepherd lying in the grass and looking on. "Tadd is enjoying himself. What have you two been doing?"

"Gossiping about you, of course," his mother replied.

"I didn't realize you gossiped, mother." His comment held a touch of dry mockery.

"I'm human," she said in explanation. "Would you like some lemonade?"

"Yes, I'll have a glass, mother. Thank you." Judd pulled one of the chairs closer to Valerie and sat down. His hand rested on the back of her chair, a finger absently stroking the bare skin of her shoulder. She felt that quivering ache to know the fullness of his caresses and had to move or betray that need.

"Tadd's been so busy playing with the puppies he

hasn't had time for lemonade," said Valerie, rising from her chair. "I think I'll see if he wants some now."

Avoiding the glitter of Judd's green eyes, she walked to the edge of the veranda. All but one of the puppies had grown tired of Tadd's games and had rolled into sleepy balls on the lawn.

"Let the puppies rest for a while, Tadd," she called. "Come and have some lemonade and cookies."

"Okay," he agreed, and stood up, hugging the last puppy in his arms as he started toward the veranda. The mother shepherd rose, made a counting glance at the sleeping litter, and pricked her ears toward Tadd.

"Leave the puppy there, Tadd," Valerie told him. "Its mother wants to keep them all together so they won't accidentally become lost."

Glancing over his shoulder, Tadd saw the anxious black dog looking at him and reluctantly put the puppy onto the grass. The puppy didn't seem sure what it was supposed to do, but its mother trotted over, washed its face and directed it toward the others. Tadd, who seemed to know only one speed, ran to the veranda. He stopped when he reached Valerie, his face aglow, happiness beaming from his expressive hazel green eyes.

"Did you see the puppy? He likes me, mom," he informed her with an eager smile.

"I'm sure he does." She tucked his shirt inside his pants and brushed at the grass stains on his clothes. Finished, she poked a playful finger at his stomach.

"How about some cookies and lemonade for that hole in your tummy?"

"Okay." Tadd skipped alongside of her to the table, hopping onto one of the chairs and resting his elbows on the glass-topped table. Maureen Prescott gave him a glass of lemonade and offered him a cookie. He took one from the plate. "Are all those puppies yours, Reeny?" He used the nickname without hesitation.

"I guess they are," she answered with a smile.

"You're lucky." Tadd took a swallow from the glass as Valerie sat down in her chair, moving it closer to the table to be out of Judd's reach, a fact he noted with a bemused twitch of his mouth. "I wish I could have one puppy," Tadd sighed, and licked at the frosting on the cookie.

"I'm afraid they aren't old enough to leave their mother yet," Maureen Prescott explained.

"Are you going to keep all of them?" His look said that would be greedy.

"No, we'll keep one or two and find good homes for the others," the woman admitted. "But not for another two or three weeks."

"We have a good home, don't we, mom?" Tadd seized on the phrase.

"No, we don't, Tadd," Valerie denied. "Those puppies are going to grow into big dogs like their mother. They need lots of room. Besides, you know that pets aren't allowed where we live."

"Your mother is right," Judd inserted as Tadd twisted his mouth into a grimace. "A puppy needs room to run. You really should live in the country to have a dog like Sable, somewhere like your grandfather's farm. Maybe then your mother would let you have one of the puppies."

Valerie shot him an angry look. She recognized Judd's ploy and resented his using Tadd's desire for a puppy as a wedge to get what he wanted. Tadd latched onto the idea as Judd had known he would.

"But we already live there." He turned an earnest, beseeching look on Valerie.

"Only until the end of the summer," she reminded him.

"Why can't we stay there forever and I could have my puppy," Tadd argued, forgetting the cookie he held.

"But we don't own it." She felt the lazy regard of Judd's green eyes and knew he was enjoying the awkward situation she was in. "Eat your cookie before you make a mess."

"We don't own the apartment in Cincinnati, either," Tadd argued. "So why can't we stay here?"

"Because I have to work. I have a job, remember?" Valerie tried to be patient and reasonable with his demands, knowing she shouldn't release her shortening temper on him.

"No, you don't. You got fired—I heard you tell Clara," he retorted.

"We'll discuss this later, Tadd," she said firmly. "Finish your cookie."

For a minute he opened his mouth to continue his stubborn argument, but the warning look Valerie gave him made him take a bite of the cookie. Tadd was wise enough to know that arousing his mother's temper would accomplish nothing.

"I'm sorry, Valerie," Maureen Prescott sympathized with her dilemma. "It isn't easy to say no to him."

"It isn't," she agreed, and flashed a look at Judd. "But it's a word you learn when you become an adult, sometimes the hard way."

A dark brow flickered upward in a faintly challenging gesture, but Judd gave no other sign that he had received her veiled message. Tadd washed his cookie down with lemonade and turned to Judd.

"Are we going to see Mickey?" he asked.

"Whenever you're ready," Judd conceded.

Tadd hopped off the chair, not even cookies and lemonade keeping him seated for long. "Maybe we can look at the horses, too?" he suggested.

"I think Mickey's planned to show you around and meet the new horses he's looking after." Judd rose from his chair when Valerie did. She avoided the hand that would have taken possession of her arm, and walked to Tadd.

"Thank you for the lemonade and cookies, Mrs. . . . Maureen," she said.

"Yes, thank you," Tadd piped his agreement.

"You're very welcome. And please, come any time," the other woman insisted generously.

"Maybe I could play with the puppies again," Tadd suggested, looking up at Valerie.

"We'll see," she responded stiffly and pushed him forward.

"It's shorter to cut across the lawn," said Judd

with a gesture of his hand to indicate the direction they would take.

Despite Valerie's efforts to keep Tadd at her side, he skipped into the lead and she was forced to walk with Judd. She was aware of the way he shortened his long strides to match hers. He made no attempt at conversation, letting his nearness wreak havoc on her senses.

At the barns, they had no trouble finding Mickey. He appeared from one of them as they arrived. He hurried toward them, his bowed legs giving a slight waddle to his walk. Tadd ran forward to meet him.

"Hello, Valerie. How have you been?" Mickey greeted her with his usual face-splitting grin.

"Fine," she responded, a little of her tension easing. "Tadd has missed you."

"I've missed him, too." Mickey glanced down at the boy holding his hand. "Come on, lad. I want you to see some of the finest-looking horseflesh there is in this part of the world. You've got to learn to know a great horse when you see one if you want to work with horses when you grow up."

"I do." Tadd trotted eagerly beside him as Mickey turned to retrace his path to the stable. "I'm going to have a lot of animals when I grow up—horses and dogs and everything."

Valerie followed them with Judd remaining at her side. She glanced at his jutting profile through the sweep of her gold-tipped lashes. The hard sensuality of his features attracted her despite her anger.

"It wasn't fair of you to tempt Tadd with the

prospect of a puppy," she protested in a low, agitated breath.

Judd's gaze slid lazily down to her face. "All's fair," he countered smoothly.

In the shade of the stable overhang, Valerie stopped. "The end does not justify the means," she said sharply.

Judd stopped, looking down at her in a way that heated her flesh. "You can justify any means if you want something badly enough—and you know what I want."

The message in his eyes seemed to cut off her breath. She could feel the powerful undertow of desire tugging at her, threatening to drag her under the control of his will. She seemed powerless to resist.

Farther down the stable row, Tadd glanced over his shoulder at the couple lagging behind. "Mom, are you coming?" he called.

Her breath came in a rush of self-consciousness. "Yes, Tadd," she answered, and turned to catch up with them.

"You can't run away from it," Judd's low voice mocked her disguised flight. He lingered for an instant, then leisurely moved to follow her.

CHAPTER EIGHT

THE QUARTET led by Mickey Flanners had made almost a full tour of the brood farm, impressive in its efficiency. Nothing had been overlooked, especially in the foaling barn, a facility that Valerie was sure had no equal.

The tour had paused at a paddock fence where Tadd had climbed to the top rail to watch a pair of galloping yearlings cavorting and kicking up their heels. From the stud barns came the piercing squeal of a stallion answered by the challenging scream of a second. Valerie glanced toward the sound, noticing Judd had done the same.

A frown flickered across his face, followed by a crooked smile of dismissal. "It sounds as if Battleground and King's Ruler are at it again. They're always feuding with each other across the way."

Valerie nodded in silent understanding. Stallions were often jealously competitive. The instinct within them to fight to protect their territory was strong, which was why they had to be kept separated by the strongest of fences. With Judd's explanation echoing in her mind, she ignored the angry exchange of whistles that had resumed.

A muffled shout of alarm pivoted Judd around. More shouts were followed by a flurry of activity around the stud barn. A grimness claimed his expression.

"I'll be back," he said without glancing at her.

His long, ground-eating strides were already covering the distance to the stallion pens before either Valerie or Mickey thought to move. Tadd followed curiously after them, sensing something different in the air.

When Valerie reached the barrier of the first stud pen, she felt the first sickening jolt of danger. The two stallions were locked in combat, rearing, jaws open and heads snaking for each other's jugular vein. The clang of pawing steel hooves striking against each other vibrated in the air amid the blowing snorts and rumbling neighs. Stable hands were warily trying to separate the pair. The blood drained from her face as she saw Judd wading into the thick of it.

"Stop him, Mickey!" she breathed to the ex-jockey beside her.

"Are you crazy?" he asked in disbelief. "Judd isn't going to stand by and watch his two prize stallions kill each other."

She could hear him snapping orders to coordinate the efforts. Fear for his safety overpowered her and she turned away. "I can't watch." Valerie knew what those murderous hooves could do. They were capable of tearing away hunks of human flesh, exposing the bones. "Tell me what happens, Mickey." She closed her eyes, but she couldn't shut her ears to the sounds. "No, I don't want to know," she groaned, and remembered Tadd.

She reached for him, trying to hide his face from the sight, but he tore out of her arms. "I want to see, mommy!" he cried fearlessly, and raced to Mickey's side.

Valerie felt sick with fear. The turmoil within the stud pen seemed to go on without end. Her eyes were tightly closed, her back to the scene as she prayed desperately that Judd would be unharmed. She hadn't the strength for anything else. Fear had turned her into jelly.

"Hot damn! He did it!" Mickey shouted, and danced a little jig, stopping at the sight of Valerie's ashen face as she collapsed weakly against a fence post. "Hey, Valerie—" his voice was anxious with concern "—it's over."

"Judd . . . ?" was all she could manage as a violent trembling seized her.

"He's fine." Mickey said it as though she shouldn't have thought otherwise. Tipping his head to one side, he looked up at her, smiling in gentle understanding. "You're still in love with him, aren't you?" he commented.

She nodded her head in a numbed, affirmative gesture before catching the phrasing of his question. "How . . ." she began, but her choked voice didn't seem to want to work.

"I noticed all those rides you were taking seven years ago and the look that was in your eyes when you came back. I knew a man put it there," Mickey explained softly. "And I happened to notice that Judd was taking rides the same time you were. I just put two and two together." At the apprehensive light in her eyes, he answered her unspoken question. "Your grandad didn't know and I didn't see where it was my place to enlighten him. There was enough grief around the place after you left without adding to it."

A shuddering sense of gratitude rippled through her and she smiled weakly. Her stomach had finally begun to stop its nauseous churning, but her legs were still treacherously weak. She gripped the fence tightly for support as Mickey turned away. She didn't guess why until she heard Judd's grim voice speaking as he approached them.

"I've fired that new man, Rathburn. The stupid fool had to clean King's paddock, so he put the stallion in the one next to Battleground and didn't check the gates," Judd said with ruthless scorn for the guilty man's incompetence. "Battleground has some wicked-looking cuts. The vet is on his way, but you'd better see if you can give Jim a hand, Mick."

"Right away." The ex-jockey moved off at a shuffling trot.

"That was really something!" Tadd breathed in excitement.

"Is that right?" Judd's mocking voice sounded tolerantly amused.

Valerie didn't find anything humorous about the near disaster that could have ultimately crippled horse and man. Glancing over her shoulder, she cast Judd an accusing look, her face still white as a sheet. His white shirt was stained with dirt and sweat, and a telltale scattering of animal hairs showed he had put himself in equal danger as his stable hands.

"You could have been killed or maimed!" A thin thread of her previous fear ran through her hoarse voice.

His gaze narrowed on her in sharp concern. "You look like a ghost, Valerie," Judd concluded in his own accusation. "Quick, Tadd, run and get your mother some water."

His hand gripped the boy's shoulder and sent him speeding on his way. Then he was walking to her. Valerie turned toward the fence, relieved that he had come away unscathed, frightened by what might have happened, and weak with her love for him. His hands spanned her waist to turn her from the fence and receive the complacent study of his gaze.

"As many times as you've wished me to hell, I would have thought you would relish the prospect of my death," Judd taunted her.

"No," Valerie denied, and protested painfully, "That's a cruel thing to say!"

"Why? Do you really care what happens to me?" His voice was dry and baiting.

"I do." What was the use in denying it? Her downcast gaze noticed the smear of red blood on the sleeve of his shirt. It was horse blood. At the sight of it, her hands spread across his chest to feel the steady beat of his heart. She swayed against him, the side of her cheek brushing against the hair-roughened chest where his shirt was unbuttoned. She wished she could absorb some of his indomitable strength. "I don't want to care, but I do," Valerie admitted in an aching breath.

His arms tightened around her in a crushing circle. The force of it tipped her head back and his mouth bruised her cheekbone. "You're mine, Valerie," he growled in possession. "You belong to me."

"Yes," she agreed to the inevitable.

"There'll be no more talk about you leaving in September," Judd warned.

"No." Valerie surrendered to his demand.

With that final acquiescence, his mouth sought and found her parted lips. He kissed her deeply, savoring this moment when she had yielded to his will and admitted what she couldn't hide. He stirred her to passion, creating a languorous flame that ravished her. She molded herself to his length, to fire his blood as he had hers. The sudden bruising demand of his mouth consoled her that he couldn't resist her, either.

"Mommy?" Tadd's anxious voice tore her lips from the satisfaction of Judd's kiss. Her dazed eyes focused slowly on the small boy running toward them. "Reeny's bringing the water. Is mommy all right?"

Judd's bulk was shielding Valerie from the view of both the boy and the woman hurrying behind him. With shuddering reluctance Judd relaxed his hold to let her feet rest firmly on the ground, instead of just her toes. His green eyes blazed over her face in promise and possession, letting her see he didn't welcome the interruption before he turned to meet it. A supporting arm remained curved across her back and waist, keeping her body in contact with his side.

"What's happened, Judd?" His mother hurried

forward, a glass of water in her hand. Her gaze flicked from her son to Valerie, and Valerie guessed that Maureen Prescott had recognized that embrace for what it had been. She flushed self-consciously. "I heard an uproar down around the stallion barns, then Tadd came running to the house talking about horses fighting and Valerie needing water. I didn't know whether to listen to him or call an ambulance."

Judd explained briefly about the stallion fight, glossing over his part in it, and concluded, "It left Valerie a little shaken, so I sent Tadd to the house as an excuse to get him away. I thought she was going to faint and I didn't want that scaring him." He took the glass from his mother's hand and offered it to Valerie. "You might want that drink now, though."

"Thank you." Nervously she took the glass and sipped from it, too self-conscious about the scene his mother had witnessed to draw attention to herself by refusing his suggestion.

"Do you feel all right now, Valerie?" Maureen asked with concern.

"Yes, I'm fine." But her voice sounded breathless and not altogether sure.

"You look a little pale," the other woman observed, frowning anxiously. "You'd better come up to the house and rest for a few minutes."

"No, really I——" Valerie tried to protest.

But Judd interrupted. "Do you want me to carry you?"

"No, I . . . I can walk," she stammered, and flashed a nervous glance at his mother.

Incapable of conversation, Valerie was relieved that no one seemed to expect any from her as they walked to the house. Judd's arm remained around her, his thigh brushing against hers. She kept wondering what his mother was thinking and whether she objected to what was apparently going on. But she guessed that Maureen Prescott was too polite and well-bred to let her feelings show.

As they crossed the lawn to the veranda, Tadd began his own description of the scene at the stud pens. "Mickey and I were watching it all, Reeny. You should have seen Judd when he—"

Judd must have felt the slight tremor that vibrated through her. "I think that's enough about that, Tadd," he silenced the boy. "We don't want to upset your mother again, do we?"

"No," Tadd agreed, darting an anxious look at Valerie.

"Why don't you play with the puppies, Tadd?" Maureen suggested, and he wandered toward the sleeping pile of black fur, but with some reluctance.

"I'm sorry." Valerie felt obliged to apologize for her behavior after she came under the scrutiny of Judd's mother, as well. "I'm not usually a fraidycat about such things."

"No, you're not," Judd agreed with a gently taunting smile, and escorted her to a cushioned lounge chair. "A spitting feline, maybe," he qualified.

"There's no need to apologize, Valerie," his mother inserted. "I saw a stallion fight once. It was a vicious thing, so I quite understand your reaction."

"Comfortable?" Judd inquired after seating her in the chair.

"Yes." But she was beginning to feel like a fraud.

"You relax for a little while," he ordered. "I'm going to wash up and change my shirt," he said, glancing down at his soiled front. "I won't be long."

When he had disappeared into the house via the veranda doors, his mother suggested, "There's some lemonade left if you'd like some."

"No, thank you," Valerie refused.

Tadd came wandering back onto the veranda, a sleepy-eyed puppy in his arms. He stopped at the lounge chair, studying Valerie with a troubled light in his eyes.

"Are you all right, mommy?"

His appealing concern drew a faint smile. "Yes, Tadd, I'm fine," she assured him.

"Maybe you'd feel better if you held the puppy." He offered her the soft ball of fur with enormous feet.

"Thanks, Tadd, but I think the puppy would like it better if you held it," Valerie refused, her heart warming at his touching gesture.

"It's sleepy anyway," he shrugged, and walked over to the grass to let it go. "Would you want to play a game, mom?"

"No, thanks."

He came back over to her chair. "What am I going to do while you're resting?" he wanted to know.

"Would you like some more cookies and lemonade?" Maureen Prescott suggested.

"No, thank you." He half turned to look at her. "Have you got any more animals for me to play with?"

"No, I don't believe so." The woman tried not to smile at the question. "But there's a sandbox over by those trees. If I'm not mistaken, there's a toy truck in that chest over there. You can take the truck and play with it in the sandbox."

"Great!" Tadd dashed to the toy chest she had indicated, retrieved the truck and headed for the sandbox.

"Tadd isn't used to entertaining himself," Valerie explained. "There are a lot of children his age in the apartment building where we live, so he's used to playing with them."

"It's good that he has children to play with," Maureen commented.

"Yes," Valerie agreed. "I think that's the only thing he's missed this summer. Mickey played with him at the farm a lot. Now that he's gone, Tadd gets lonely once in a while."

"Ellie, my eldest daughter, is coming this weekend with her husband and their six-year-old daughter. Meg is a regular tomboy. Why don't you bring Tadd over Sunday afternoon?" Maureen suggested. "They'll have fun playing together."

"I . . . I don't think so." Valerie hesitated before rejecting the invitation.

"Please try," the woman urged.

"Try what?" Judd appeared, catching the tail end of their conversation.

"I suggested to Valerie that she bring Tadd over on Sunday to play with Meg, but she doesn't think she'll be able to," his mother explained.

"Oh?" His gaze flicked curiously to Valerie. "Why?"

"I'm not sure it will be possible yet. I'll have to speak to Clara." Valerie couldn't explain the reason for her hesitation. She had the feeling it wouldn't be wise to become too closely involved with any more members of the Prescott family.

"Don't worry, mother," said Judd. "I can almost guarantee you that Tadd will be here. Valerie and I are having dinner together on Saturday night. I'll persuade her to change her mind."

Dinner together? It was the first she knew about it, but she tried not to let on. Things were happening at such a rapid pace that she couldn't keep up with them. She needed time to take stock of things and understand what was going on.

"I hope you will," his mother said. "Tadd is a wonderful boy. You must be very proud of him, Valerie."

"I am," Valerie admitted, feeling vaguely uncomfortable again.

"He has such an appealing face." Maureen was looking toward the sandbox in which Tadd was playing with the truck. "And those eyes of his are so expressive. There's something about him that makes him so very special, but those children generally are," she concluded.

"Those children?" Valerie stiffened.

A pair of turquoise eyes rounded in dismay as Maureen realized what she had said. She glanced quickly at Judd, an apology in her look. Valerie's questioning eyes were directed at him, as well.

Undaunted by either of them, he replied smoothly, "I believe mother means those children who are born out of wedlock."

"I'm sorry, Valerie," Maureen apologized. "I didn't mean to offend you by that remark—truly I didn't."

"It's quite all right." Valerie hid her embarrassment behind a proud look. "I've never attempted to hide the fact that Tadd is illegitimate. And I have heard it said that 'those children' tend to be more precious and appealing as a result. Tadd seems to be an example of that, but I doubt if it's always the case."

"I certainly didn't mean to hurt your feelings," Maureen insisted again. "It's just that I've been watching Tadd," she rushed her explanation, "and he's so like Judd in many ways that—Oh, dear, I've made it worse!" she exclaimed as she looked into Valerie's whitened face.

"No, no," Valerie denied with a tight, strained smile. "I understand perfectly."

A nauseous lump was rising in her throat as she truly began to understand. Maureen Prescott had known all along that her son was Tadd's father. Judd had obviously told his mother, but hadn't bothered to tell Valerie that he had. She hadn't thought it was possible to feel cheap and humiliated again, but she did.

"I didn't see any reason not to tell her," Judd explained, watching Valerie through narrowed eyes.

"Of course there isn't," she agreed, feeling her poise cracking and struggling inwardly to keep it from falling apart.

"I'm relieved." His mother smiled, somewhat nervously. "And I do hope it won't influence your decision about bringing Tadd here on Sunday. I would sincerely enjoy having him come."

"Don't worry about that, mother," Judd inserted. "I'm sure Valerie will agree."

"Your son can be very persuasive," Valerie commented, and felt a rising well of panic. "I don't mean to be rude, Mrs. Prescott—" she rose from the lounge chair "—but I'm really not feeling all that well. Would you mind if Judd took us home now? You've been very gracious to Tadd and me and I want to thank you for that."

"You're very welcome, of course," Maureen returned, hiding her confusion with a smile. "I'll call Tadd for you."

"Thank you." Valerie was aware of Judd standing beside her, examining the pallor in her face.

"What's wrong, Valerie?" he asked quietly.

"A headache—a nervous reaction, I suppose." Her temples were throbbing, so her excuse wasn't totally false.

He seemed to accept her surface explanation without delving further. When Tadd came racing to the veranda, Maureen Prescott walked them through the house to the front door and bid them goodbye. As they drove away, Tadd's face was pressed to the window glass to watch the horses in the pasture.

Valerie sat silently in the front seat. Judd slid her a questioning look. "Does it bother you that mother knows?" he asked, phrasing it so Tadd wouldn't attach any significance to it.

"No." She leaned her head against the seat rest. "Why should it?" she countered with forced nonchalance.

But it beat at her like a hammer. To realize that her relationship with Judd was out in the open was worse than if it had been a secret, clandestine affair. Kept woman, mistress, consort—all were terms for the same thing. She had agreed to it—in the stable yard in Judd's arms. There was no doubt about how deeply she loved him.

But she had more to think of than just herself. There was Tadd. Valerie closed her eyes in pain. Maureen Prescott was eager for him to visit on Sunday, but the invitation naturally hadn't included her. Was Tadd going to grow up on the fringes of the Prescott family, invited into the circle on their whim? He would be a Prescott without a right to the name. How would he feel when he discovered the truth? Would he become bitter and resentful that his mother was the mistress of the man who was his father?

Valerie was tormented by the love she felt for Judd and the life with him that she never could know. It gnawed at her until she thought she would be torn in two. It was a searing, raw ache that made her heart bleed.

"Valerie?" Judd's hand touched her shoulder.

She opened her eyes to discover the car was parked in front of the farmhouse. The screen door was already slamming behind Tadd, who was racing into the house to be the first to tell Clara of all that had happened that day.

"I . . . I didn't realize we were here already," Valerie began in painful confusion.

"I noticed," he responded dryly. His hand slid under her hair, discovering the tense muscles in her neck and massaging them. "You do know you're having dinner with me on Saturday night, tomorrow night," he told her.

"So you told me." She couldn't relax under his touch; if anything, she became stiffer.

"You're going." It was a statement that demanded her agreement.

"Yes," Valerie lied because it was easier.

Judd leaned over and rubbed his mouth against the corner of her lips. She breathed in sharply, filling her lungs with the scent of him. It was like a heady wine. Judd began nibbling the curve of her lip, teasing and tantalizing her with his kiss.

"Please, Judd, don't!" She turned her head away from his tempting mouth because she knew the power of his kiss could make her forget everything.

He hooked a hard finger around her chin and turned her to face him. His sharp gaze inspected her pale face and the carefully lowered lashes.

"What is it?" He sensed something was wrong and demanded to know the cause.

"I really do have a headache," Valerie insisted with a nervous smile. "It'll go away, but I need to lie down for a while."

"Alone?" His brow quirked suggestively, then he sighed, "Never mind. Forget I said that. I'll call you later to be sure you're all right."

"Make it this evening," Valerie asked quickly, and hurried to answer the question in his eyes. "By the time I rest for an hour or two, it'll be time to eat. Then there's the dishes to be done, and Tadd won't take a bath unless someone is standing over him. So I'll be busy until . . . ." His fingers touched her lips to silence them.

"I'll phone you later this evening," he agreed. "Or I'll come over if you can think of a way to get that battle-ax out of the house."

It was starting already, she thought in panic. "You'd better call first," she said.

"Very well, I will." He kissed her lightly.

CHAPTER NINE

VALERIE PAUSED on the porch to wave to Judd and stayed until he had driven out of sight down the lane. She felt the beginning of a sob in her throat and knew she didn't have time for tears. Lifting her chin, she turned and walked into the house.

"My gracious, it certainly sounds as if you've had a full day," Clara commented. "Tadd has been running nonstop for the last five minutes and doesn't give any indication of wearing down. What's all this about horses and puppies? I thought you were going to a tobacco auction. That's what you told me."

"We did go," Valerie admitted, "but that was earlier today. Then we went over to the Prescott place to see Mickey." She glanced down at her son. "Tadd, why don't you go outside and play for a while?"

"Aw, mom," he protested, "I wanted to tell Clara about the puppies."

"Later," she insisted. Reluctantly Tadd walked to the door, his feet dragging, and slammed the screen shut. Valerie turned to Clara. "How much gas is in the car?"

"I filled it up the other day when I was in town. Why?" Clara was startled by the question.

Valerie was already hurrying through the living room, picking up the odds and ends of personal items that had managed to become scattered around. She began stuffing them in a paper sack.

"What about the oil? Did you have it checked?" she asked.

"As a matter of fact, I did." A pair of hands moved to rest on broad hips. "Would you mind telling me why you're asking these questions?"

Valerie stopped in the center of the room, pressing a hand against her forehead. "I can't remember—did we put the suitcases in the empty bedroom upstairs or down in the basement?"

"Upstairs. And what do we need the suitcases for?" Clara followed as Valerie headed for the staircase.

"Because we're leaving. What other reason would I have for asking about the car and suitcases?" Valerie retorted sharply.

"Would you like to run that by me once more? Did I hear you say we were leaving?" repeated Clara.

"That's exactly what I said." Valerie opened the door to the empty bedroom, grabbed two of the suitcases in the corner, and walked to Tadd's room.

"I thought we were staying here until summer was over," her friend reminded her.

"I've changed my mind. Isn't it obvious?" Valerie opened drawers, taking out whole stacks of clothes regardless of their order or neatness, and jamming them into the opened suitcase.

"Suppose you give me three guesses as to why?" Clara challenged. "Judd Prescott, Judd Prescott, and Judd Prescott. What happened today?"

"I don't have time to go into it right now," Valerie stalled. "Would you mind helping me pack?" she demanded. "I don't want to take all night."

"I'll help," Clara replied, walking to the closet without any degree of haste. "But I doubt if what you're doing could be called packing. What's the big rush anyway? You surely aren't planning to leave tonight?" Shrewd blue eyes swept piercingly to Valerie.

"We're leaving tonight." The first suitcase was filled to the point of overflowing. Valerie had to sit on it to get it latched. "We'll never be able to put everything in these suitcases. Where are the boxes your sister used to send our things? We didn't throw them away, did we?"

But her friend was still concentrating on her first statement. "Tonight? You can't mean to leave tonight?" She frowned. "There's only a few hours of daylight left. The sensible thing is to leave first thing in the morning."

"No, it isn't," Valerie argued. "We're leaving tonight. Now where are the boxes?"

"Forget the boxes. I want to know why we have to leave tonight. And I'm not answering another question or lifting a hand until you tell me." Clara dropped the clothes in her hand on a chair.

"Clara, for heaven's sake, I don't have time for all this." Valerie hurried to the chair and grabbed the clothes to stuff them in the second suitcase. "Judd will be calling later on and I want to be gone before he does."

"And that's your reason?" Her friend sniffed in

scoffing challenge. "It seems mighty ridiculous to me!"

"Don't you understand?" Valerie whirled to face her. The conflicting emotions and raw pain that she had pushed aside now threatened to surface. Her chin quivered as she fought to hold them back. "If I don't leave tonight, I never will!"

"I think you'd better sit down and tell me what's happened," said Clara in a voice that would stand for no argument.

"No, I won't sit down." Valerie sniffed away a tear and shook back her caramel hair. "There's too much to do and not enough time." She walked to the chest of drawers and opened the last one to take out the balance of clothes.

"Well, you're going to tell me what happened," Clara insisted.

Another tear was forming in the corner of her eye and Valerie wiped it quickly away with a forefinger. "Judd's mother, Mrs. Prescott, knows about Tadd, that Judd is his father. She wants Tadd to come over on Sunday to play with another one of her grandchildren. It's all out in the open, and I can't handle it."

"What is Judd's reaction to this?" Clara gathered up Tadd's few toys and put them in a sack.

"He told his mother he would persuade me to bring Tadd."

"So? Don't let him persuade you," her friend suggested with a shrug.

Valerie's laugh held no humor. "All he has to do is hold me in his arms and I'll agree to anything. I did today. I promised I wouldn't leave here. I'm so in love with him I'm losing my pride and my self-respect."

"It isn't one-sided. Judd is absolutely besotted with you," Clara said. "I've seen the way he watches you. He never takes his eyes off you. He knows when you blink or take a breath."

"I know and it doesn't make it any easier. Clara, he wants me to become his. . . ." She broke off the sentence with a hurtful sigh. "I can't even say the word without thinking what it would ultimately do to Tadd."

"Maybe he'll marry you," Clara suggested in an effort to comfort her.

Valerie shook her head, pressing her lips tightly together for an instant. "I'm not good enough for a Prescott to marry. I lack breeding," she said bitterly. "I can't stay, Clara." Her hands absently wadded the bundle of clothes in her hand, her fingers digging into the material. "I can't stay."

There was silence. Then a detergent-roughened hand gently touched her shoulder. "The boxes are in my bedroom closet. I'll get them."

"Thank you, Clara," Valerie muttered in a voice tight and choked with emotion.

When the two suitcases were packed, she set them at the head of the stairs and took two more to her bedroom. With Clara's help, all her personal belongings were packed in either the luggage or the cardboard shipping crates. As soon as that room was cleared of their possessions they started on Clara's. No time was wasted on neatness or order.

"All that's left is to lug all this downstairs and out to the car," said Clara, taking a deep breath as she studied the pile of luggage and boxes in front of the staircase.

"And to check downstairs," Valerie added, picking up one case and juggling another under the same arm. "We'd better be sure to get everything because I'm not coming back no matter what we leave behind," she declared grimly, and reached for the third.

Leading the way, Valerie descended the stairs. Clara followed with one of the boxes. Tadd came bounding onto the porch as Valerie approached the door.

"Open the door for me, Tadd," she called through the wire mesh.

"I'm tired of playing, mom." He held the door open for her and stared curiously at the suitcase she carried. "What are you doing? Are you going somewhere?"

"Yes. Don't let go of the door; Clara is right behind me," Valerie rushed when she saw him take a step to follow her.

"Hurry up, Clara." Tadd waited impatiently for the stout woman to maneuver the box through the opening, then let the door slam and raced to catch up to Valerie. "Is Clara going, too?"

"We're all going," Valerie answered, and set the cases on the ground next to the car. "Where are the keys for the trunk, Clara? Are they in the ignition?"

"I'll bet they're in the house in my handbag," the

woman grumbled, and set the box beside the luggage. "Stay here. I'll go and get them."

"Where are we going, mom?" Tadd wanted to know, tugging at her skirt to get her attention.

"We're going home," she told him, only Cincinnati didn't seem like home anymore. This place was home.

"Home? To Cincinnati?" Tadd frowned.

"Yes. Back to our apartment," Valerie answered sharply.

"Is summer over already?" His expression was both puzzled and crestfallen, a sad light in his eyes.

"No, not quite," she admitted, and glanced to the house. What was keeping Clara? Valerie could have been bringing out more of the boxes herself instead of standing there.

"But I thought we were going to stay here until summer was over," Tadd reminded her. "That's what you said."

"I changed my mind." *Please,* Valerie thought desperately, *I don't want to argue with you.*

"Why are we leaving?" he asked. "If summer isn't over, why do we have to go back?"

"Because I said we are." She wasn't about to explain the reasons to him. In the first place, he wouldn't understand. And in the second, it would be too painful. The breeze whipped a strand of hair across her cheek and she pushed it away with an impatient gesture.

"But I don't want to go back," Tadd protested in a petulant tone.

"Yes, you do," Valerie insisted.

"No, I don't." His mouth was pulled into a mutinous pout.

"What about all your friends?" Valerie attempted to reason with him. "Wouldn't you like to go back and play with them? It's been quite a while since you've ridden on Mike's Big Wheels. That was a lot of fun, remember?"

"I don't care about Mike's dumb old Big Wheels," Tadd grumbled, the pouting mouth growing more pronounced. "It's not nearly as much fun as riding Ginger, anyway. I want to stay here."

"We're not going to stay here. We're leaving. We're going back to Cincinnati." Valerie stressed each sentence with decisive emphasis. "So you might as well get that straight right now."

"I don't want to go," he repeated, his voice raised in rebellious protest. "Judd said if we lived here, maybe I could have a puppy."

"I'm not going to listen to any more talk about puppies!" Valerie retorted, her nerves snapping under the strain of his persistent arguing. "We're leaving, and that's final!"

"Well, I'm not going!" Tadd shouted, backing away and breaking into angry tears.

"Tadd." Valerie immediately regretted her sharpness, but he was already turning away and running toward the pasture. She could hear his sobbing. "Tadd, come back here!"

But he ignored the command, his little legs churning faster. He was running into the lowering sun. Valerie shaded her eyes with her hand to shield out the glaring light. She waited for him to stop at the paddock fence, but instead he scooted under it and kept running.

"Tadd, come back here!" she called anxiously.

"I've got the keys." Clara came out of the house, dangling the car keys in front of her. "I couldn't remember where I had left my handbag. I finally found it underneath the kitchen table. If it were a snake, it would have bit me."

"Would you pack all this in the trunk?" Valerie motioned to the luggage as she started toward the pasture. "I'd better get Tadd."

"Where's he gone?" Frowning, Clara glanced around the yard, missing the small figure racing across the pasture.

"I lost my temper with him because he said he didn't want to go," Valerie explained. "Now he's run off."

"Let him be." Clara dismissed any urgency to the situation with a wave of her hand. "He's just going to sulk for a while. He'll be back. Meanwhile, he won't be underfoot."

"I don't know. . . ." Valerie answered hesitantly.

"He won't go far," the other woman assured her as she walked to the car to unlock the trunk and begin arranging the luggage and boxes inside.

"He was very upset." Gazing across, she could see Tadd had stopped running and was leaning against a tree to cry.

"Of course he was upset," Clara agreed in a voice that disdainfully dismissed any other thought. "All children get upset when they don't get their way. You go right ahead and handle the situation any way you want. I don't want to be telling you how you should raise your kid."

Valerie received her friend's subtle message that she was making a mountain out of a molehill and sighed, "You may be right."

"If you're not going after him, you could give me a hand with some of this stuff. You're the one who was in such an all-fired hurry to leave," came the gruff reminder. Then Clara muttered to herself, "I get the feeling we're making our getaway after robbing a bank."

When another glance at the pasture showed that Tadd was in the same place, Valerie hesitated an instant longer, then turned to help Clara with the luggage. A second trip into the house brought everything down from upstairs.

A search of the ground floor added a box of belongings. Valerie carried it to the car. Her gaze swung automatically to the paddock, but this time there was no sign of Tadd. She walked to the fence and called him. The bay mare lifted its head in answer, then went back to grazing.

What had been merely concern changed to worry as Valerie hesitantly retraced her steps to the house. The sounds coming from the kitchen located Clara for her. She walked quickly to that room.

"You haven't seen Tadd, have you?" she asked hopefully. "He isn't in the pasture anymore and I thought he might have slipped into the house."

"I haven't seen hide nor hair of him." Clara shook her wiry, frosted gray hair. "Would you look at all this food? It seems a shame to leave it."

"We don't have much choice. It would spoil if we tried to take it with us." Valerie's response was automatic. "Where do you suppose Tadd is?"

"Probably somewhere around the barns." The dismissing lift of Clara's wide shoulders indicated that she still believed he wasn't far away. "Since we haven't had any supper, I'll fix some sandwiches and snacks to take along with us. That way we'll get to use up some of this food and not leave so much behind."

"I'm going to check the barns to see if Tadd is there," Valerie said with an uneasy feeling growing inside her.

A walk through the barns proved fruitless and her calls went unanswered. She hurried back to the house to tell Clara.

"He wasn't there," she said with a trace of breathless panic.

"The little imp!" Clara wiped her hands on a towel. "He's probably off hiding somewhere."

"Well, we can't leave without him," Valerie said, as if Clara had foolishly implied that they would. "I'm going to walk out to the pasture where I saw him last."

"I'll check through the house to make sure he didn't sneak in here when we weren't looking." Clara put aside the food she was preparing for the trip and started toward the other rooms.

While Clara began a search of the house, Valerie hurried to the paddock. She ducked between the fence rails and walked swiftly through the tall grass to the tree on the far side of the pasture where she had last seen Tadd.

"Tadd!" She stopped when she reached the tree and used it as a pivot point to make a sweeping arc of the surrounding country. "Tadd, where are you?" A bird chattered loudly in the only response she received. "Tadd, answer me!" Her voice rose on a desperate note.

From the point of the tree there was a faint trail angling away from it, barely discernible by the tall, thick grass that had been pushed down by running feet. The vague path seemed to be heading in the opposite direction from the house. It was the only clue Valerie had and she followed it.

It lead her to the boundary fence with Meadow Farms and beyond. Halfway across the adjoining pasture, the grass thinned. Grazing horses had cropped the blades too close to the ground. She lost the trail that had taken her this far, and stopped, looking around for any hint that would tell her which direction Tadd had gone.

"Tadd, where are you going?" she muttered, wishing she could crawl inside her young son's mind and discover his intention.

Did he know he had crossed onto the home farm of the Prescotts? It didn't seem likely. Despite the time they had spent there, Tadd wasn't familiar with the area beyond the farm and its immediate pastures. Yet it was possible that he knew the general direction of Meadow Farms' main quarters.

But why would he go there? To see Judd and enlist his support to persuade her to stay? No, Valerie dismissed that idea. Tadd was too young to think in such terms. The idea of finding Judd wouldn't lead him to the Prescott house, but the puppies might.

Hoping that she was reading his mind, she set off in the general direction of the Meadow Farms' buildings. Her pace quickened with her growing desire to find Tadd before he reached his destination. The last thing her panicking heart wanted was a confrontation with Judd. She had to find Tadd before he found the puppies and Judd.

As she crossed the meadow, Valerie caught herself biting her lip. There was painful constriction in her chest and her breath was coming in half sobs. It did no good to try to calm her trembling nerves.

The ground rumbled with the pounding of galloping hooves and she glanced up to see Judd on the gray hunter riding toward her. She looked around for somewhere to hide, but it was too late. He had already seen her. Besides, she had to know if he had found Tadd, regardless of whether Judd had learned of her intention to leave. At the moment, finding Tadd was more important.

Judd didn't slow his horse until he was almost up to her. He dismounted before it came to a full stop. Then his long strides carried him swiftly toward her, holding the reins in his hand and leading the horse to her.

"Have you seen Tadd?" Her worried gaze searched his grimly set features. "He ran off and I can't find him."

"I know," said Judd, and explained tersely, "I

phoned the house a few minutes ago to find out how you were feeling and Clara told me Tadd was missing." His large hand took hold of her arm and started to pull her toward the horse. "Come on."

"No!" Valerie struggled in panic. "You don't understand. I have to find Tadd," she protested frantically.

If Judd hadn't seen Tadd, it meant he was still out there somewhere, possibly lost. The shadows cast by the sun were already long. Soon it would be dusk. She had to find him before darkness came, and there was a lot of ground yet to be covered. That knowledge made her resist Judd's attempt to take her with him all the more wildly.

"Dammit, Valerie. Stop it! You're coming with me," Judd snapped with savage insistence. Her arms became captured by the iron grip of his hands.

"No, I won't!" she protested violently. "I won't!"

A hard shake jarred her into silence. "Will you listen to me?" His angry face was close to hers, his eyes glittering into hers in hard demand. "I have a feeling," he said tightly. "I think I know where Tadd is. Now, will you come with me or do I have to throw you over my shoulder and take you with me?"

Tears of panic had begun to scorch her eyes. She blinked at them and nodded her head mutely. But Judd didn't alter his hold. He seemed determined to hear her voice an agreement before he believed her.

"I . . . I'll come with y-you." She managed to force out a shaky agreement.

His hands shifted their grip from her arms to her waist. He lifted her up to sit sideways on the front of the saddle. Then he swung up behind her, his arms circling her to hold the reins and guide the gray.

The horse lunged into a canter, throwing Valerie against Judd's chest. The arm around her waist tightened to offer support. The solidness of his chest offered comfort and strength. Valerie let herself relax against it. She hadn't realized how heavy the weight of concern had been for Tadd's whereabouts until Judd had taken on half of the burden.

Through the cotton skirt of her sundress she could feel the hard muscles of his thighs. Her gaze swept up to study his face through the curl of her gold-tipped lashes. The jutting angle of his jaw and the line of his mouth were set with grim purpose. He slowed the horse as they entered a grouping of trees and wound their way through them.

As if feeling her look, he glanced down and the light in his green eyes became softly mocking. "When you were spitting at me in all your fury, did you really believe I was going to try to keep you from finding our son?"

"I didn't know," Valerie answered, uncertain now as to what she had believed his intention was.

"I guess I have given you cause in the past to question my motives," Judd admitted.

"Sometimes," she agreed, but she didn't question them now.

His gaze was drawn beyond her and he reined in the gray. "Look," he instructed quietly.

Valerie turned and saw a familiar grassy clearing. They had stopped on the edge of it. In the middle of it, a small figure lay on his stomach, a position in which Tadd had cried himself to sleep.

Her gaze lifted in stunned wonderment to Judd's face. "How?" she whispered.

"I can't begin to explain it." He shook his head with a similar expression of awed confusion mixed with quiet acceptance of the fact. His gaze wandered gently back to hers. "Any more than I can explain how I knew Tadd would be here."

Valerie remembered stories of the salmon finding their way back to their spawning grounds and wondered if Tadd possessed that same mysterious instinct in order to be led here. It was a miracle that filled her with a glowing warmth.

Judd swung off the horse and reached up to lift her down. His look, as their eyes met, mirrored her marvelous feeling. When her feet were on the ground, her hands remained on his shoulders as she stood close to him, unmoving.

"It's right, isn't it?" Judd murmured. "It proves that what we shared here was something special."

"Yes," Valerie agreed, a throb of profound emotion in her answer.

His mouth came down on hers to seal the wonder of their blessing. The closeness they shared was marked by a spiritual union rather than mere physical contact. The beauty of it filled Valerie with a sublime sense of joy such as she had never experienced in his arms. It was nearly as awe-inspiring as the miracle they had witnessed.

When they parted, she was incapable of speech. Judd let her turn from his arms and followed silently as she made her way across the clearing to the place where their son lay. She knelt beside him, staring for a moment at his sleeping tear-streaked face.

"Tadd, darling." Her voice sounded husky and unbelievably loving. "Wake up! Mommy's here."

He struggled awake, blinking at her with the misty eyes of a child that had suffered a bad dream and still wasn't certain it had ended. She smoothed the rumpled mop of brown hair on his forehead and wiped his damp cheek with her thumb.

"Mommy?" His voice wavered.

"I'm here," she assured him.

"I didn't mean to run away." His lips quivered. "I was going to come back after I got a puppy. But I couldn't find Judd's house, and I . . . I couldn't find you."

"It doesn't matter," Valerie said to dismiss the remnants of his fear. "We found you."

She gathered him into her arms, letting his arms wind around her neck in a strangling hold as he began to cry again. Judd crouched down beside them, his hand reaching out to hold Tadd's shoulder.

"It's all right, son," he offered in comfort. "We're here. There's nothing to be frightened about anymore."

Tadd lifted his head to stare at Judd, sniffling back his tears. Almost immediately he turned away and buried his face against Valerie. Hurt flickered briefly in Judd's eyes at the rejection in Tadd's action.

"I think he's embarrassed to have you see him cry," Valerie whispered the explanation.

The stiffness went out of Judd's smile. "Everyone cries, Tadd, no matter how old he is," he assured the small boy, and was rewarded with a peeping look. Like Tadd, Valerie had difficulty in imagining that Judd had ever cried in his life, but his quiet words of assurance had eased the damage to a small boy's pride. "Come on," said Judd, rising to his feet, "it's almost dark. It's time we were getting you home."

Tadd's arms remained firmly entwined around her neck. At Judd's questioning look, Valerie responded, "I can carry him," and lifted her clinging son as she rose.

Judd mounted the gray horse and reached down for Valerie to hand him Tadd. When Tadd was positioned astride the gray behind him, Judd slipped his foot from the left stirrup and helped Valerie into the saddle in front of him. The gray pranced beneath the extra weight.

"Hang on, Tadd," Judd instructed, and a pair of small arms obediently tightened around his waist. Judd turned the gray horse toward the farmhouse.

CHAPTER TEN

TWILIGHT WAS PURPLING THE SKY as they approached the house. Judd reined the gray horse toward the paddock gate and leaned sideways to unlatch it, swinging it open and riding the horse through. Stopping in front of the porch, he reached behind him and swung Tadd to the ground, then dismounted to lift Valerie down.

"Thank the Lord, you found him!" Clara came bustling onto the porch as if she had been standing at the window watching for them.

"A little frightened, but safe and sound," said Judd, his hand resting lightly on Valerie's waist. He glanced down at her, smiling gently at the experience they had shared.

Tadd went racing onto the porch. "I was going to Judd's house to see the puppies and I got lost," he told Clara. Now that he was safely back, the episode had become an adventure to be recounted.

Clara's knees made a cracking sound as she bent to take hold of his shoulders and scold him. "You should be spanked for the way you made your mother and me worry!" But already she was pulling him into her arms to hug him tightly. Tadd squirmed in embarrassment when Clara kissed his cheek, and rubbed his hand over the spot when she straightened. "If you hadn't come back before dark, I was going to call the sheriff and have them send out a search party."

"I think we're all glad it wasn't necessary," Judd inserted, and started toward the porch with Valerie at his side.

"Isn't that the truth!" Clara agreed emphatically.

"If it hadn't been for Judd, I wouldn't have found him," Valerie stated, giving the credit for finding Tadd where it was due.

"Someone else had more to do with it than I did." Judd gave the responsibility to someone higher up.

As he took the first step onto the porch, Valerie felt his gaze slide past her to the car. The moment she had been dreading ever since the house had come into sight was there. The trunk of the car was open and all of the suitcases and boxes stuffed inside were in plain sight. Judd stiffened to a halt. As his arm dropped from her waist, Valerie continued up the porch steps, a tightness gripping her throat.

"What's going on here? Is someone leaving?" His low, slicing demand was initially met with pulsing silence.

She turned to face him. Leaving after what they had just shared was going to be a hundred times more difficult, but Valerie knew it was a decision she had to stand behind. The words of response were a long time in coming.

Finally it was Tadd who answered him. "We're going back to Cincinnati. That's why I ran away—'cause I wanted to stay here and have a puppy and mom said I couldn't."

At the cold fury gathering in Judd's gaze, Valerie

half turned her head, her eyes never leaving Judd's face. "Clara, will you take Tadd in the house? He hasn't had any supper. He's probably hungry."

"Of course," her friend agreed in a subdued voice. "Come with me, Tadd." Clara ushered him toward the door and into the house.

When the screen door closed behind them, Judd slowly mounted the steps to stand before Valerie. "Is it true what Tadd said? Are you leaving?" His voice rumbled out the questions from somewhere deep inside, like distant thunder.

She swallowed and forced out a calm answer. "Yes, it's true."

"You promised you'd stay," Judd reminded her in a savage breath.

"No, I promised there'd be no more talk about my leaving," she corrected, her jaw rigid with control.

"So you were going to leave without talking about it," he accused. "You knew I was going to call. You knew I wanted to see you tonight."

"And I wanted to be gone before you did," Valerie admitted. He grabbed her shoulders. "Don't touch me, Judd. Please don't touch me," she demanded in a voice that broke under the strain. If he held her, she knew she would give in, whether or not it was right or wrong.

He released her as abruptly as he had taken her. Turning away, he swung a fist at an upright post. The force of the blow shook the dust from the porch rafters.

"Why?" he demanded in a tortured voice and

spun around to face her. "Dammit to hell, Valerie! I've got a right to know why!"

For a choked moment she couldn't answer him. A welling of tears had turned his eyes into iridescent pools of anguish. She wanted to reach up and touch the sparkling drops to see if they were real or merely crocodile tears. The sight of them held her spellbound.

"When I discovered your mother knew about us . . . and Tadd, I realized I couldn't stay no matter how much I wanted to," she explained hesitantly. "Maybe if I hadn't learned that she knew, or maybe if I'd never met her, it would have been easier to stay. Now, it's impossible."

"Why is my mother to blame for your leaving?" Confusion and anger burned in his look as he searched her expression, trying to follow her logic.

"I don't really blame her." Valerie was having difficulty finding the right words. "I'm sure it's only natural that she wants to become acquainted with your son."

"You'd better explain to me what you're talking about, because you aren't making any sense," Judd warned. "In one breath you say you want to stay and in the next you're saying you can't because of my mother. Either you want to stay or you don't!"

"I can't," she stated. Her chin quivered with the pain her words were causing her. "Don't you see, Judd? What will Tadd think when he learns about us? Eventually he will. We can't keep it from him forever. I can't become your mistress. I can't put my wants above Tadd's needs."

"Then you do love me?" His hands recaptured her arms. "Valerie, I have to know," he demanded roughly.

"Yes, I love you," she choked out the admission, and averted her gaze. "But it doesn't change anything. Nothing at all, Judd." Relief trembled through her when he let her go. She closed her eyes and fought the attraction that made her want to go back into his arms.

"I wanted to see you tonight to give you this." A snapping sound opened her eyes. Judd was holding a small box. In a bed of green velvet was an engagement ring, set with an emerald flanked by diamonds. Valerie gasped at the sight of it. "And to ask you to marry me."

Her gaze flew to his as she took a step backward. "Don't joke about this," she pleaded.

"It isn't a joke," Judd assured her. "As a matter of fact, I bought the ring the day after you told me about Tadd. But I didn't give it to you before now because I didn't want you marrying me because of him."

"I don't understand," she murmured, afraid that Judd didn't mean what he was implying.

"I didn't want you marrying me in order to have a father for your child—our child," he corrected. "I didn't want you marrying me for the Prescott name or wealth. I wanted your reason to be that you loved me and wanted me as much as I love and want you."

A piercing joy flashed through her. She stared into the warm green fires of his eyes that seemed to echo the words he had just spoken. She was afraid to say anything in case she was dreaming.

"Until today I wasn't certain how much you really cared about me," Judd continued. "But when I saw the terror in your eyes at the thought that I might have been hurt by the stallions, I knew what you felt for me was real. My name and position meant nothing to you, not even the fact that I'm the father of your son."

Without waiting for an acceptance of his proposal, Judd took her left hand and slipped the ring on her finger. Valerie watched, slightly dazed, as he lifted her hand to his mouth and kissed the emerald stone that was the same vivid color as his eyes.

"You can't really want to marry me." She heard herself say. "I'm not good enough for you."

Anger flashed in his eyes. "Don't ever say that again!"

Valerie glowed under the violent dismissal of her statement, but she persisted, "Your mother told me you'd always said you wanted your wife to have classy breeding, spirit and staying power. My background is very common."

Judd's mouth thinned impatiently, but he responded to her argument. "Class has nothing to do with a person's social position. I became acquainted with your grandfather and know you come from fine stock. That untamed streak in you proves your spirit. And as for staying power, after seven years I believe that has answered itself."

"Judd . . ." she began.

"No more discussion," he interrupted. "You're going to marry me and that's the end of it."

"Yes!" She breathed the answer against his lips an instant before he claimed hers.

An involuntary moan escaped her throat at the completeness of her love. His kiss was thorough, his masterful technique without fault. Beneath her hands she could feel the thudding of his heart, racing as madly as her own. Yet her appetite seemed insatiable.

"I thought I loved you seven years ago, Judd," she murmured as he trailed kisses down to her neck, "but it's nothing compared to what I feel for you now."

"I was such a fool then, darling," he muttered against her skin. "A blind, arrogant fool."

"It doesn't matter that you didn't love me then," she told him softly. "It's enough that you love me now."

"I was obsessed with you seven years ago," Judd confessed, lifting his head to let his fingers stroke her cheek and trace the outline of her lips.

"I was just someone you made love to." Valerie denied his attempt to have her believe she had been special to him. The past was behind them. The way he felt toward her at this moment was all that counted.

"For every time I made love to you, there were a hundred times that I wanted to," Judd replied. "It irritated me that a fiery little kitten could sink her claws into me that way. All you had to do seven years ago was crook your little finger at me and I came running. Do you have any idea how deflating it was to my masculine pride to realize that I had no control where you were concerned?"

"No, I didn't know." She looked at him in surprise.

His green eyes were dark and smoldering. There was no mistake that he meant every word he was saying. His caressing thumb parted her lips and probed at the white barrier of her teeth. Unconsciously Valerie nibbled at its end, the tip of her tongue tasting the saltiness of his skin.

"God, you're beautiful, Valerie." He said it as reverently as a prayer and moved to let his mouth take the place of his thumb, which he let slide to her chin.

He fired her soul with his burning need for her. Valerie arched closer to him, pliantly molding herself to his hard length. His hands were crushing and caressing, fanning the flames that were threatening to burn out of control. Just in time, he pulled back, shuddering against her with the force of his emotion and rubbing his forehead against hers. He breathed in deeply to regain his sanity.

"Do you see what I mean?" he asked after several seconds. The rawness in his teasing voice vibrated in the air. "I never intended to make love to you that first time, but your kisses were like a drug that I'd become addicted to. After a while, they weren't enough. I needed something more potent. Even if you hadn't been willing, I would have taken you that first time. It isn't something I'm very proud to admit."

"But I did want you to make love to me, Judd," Valerie assured him, hearing the disturbed shakiness in her own voice. "Foolishly, I thought it was the only way to hold you. Also, I wasn't satisfied anymore, either. I wanted to be yours completely and I thought that was the way."

"If you hadn't, there are times when I think I might have crawled all the way to your grandfather to beg his permission to marry you. That's how completely you had me under your spell," Judd told her, and rubbed his mouth against her temple. "But it's something we'll never know for sure."

"No," Valerie agreed. "And I wouldn't want to turn back the clock to find out. Not now."

He couldn't seem to stop slowly trailing kisses over her face. His gentle adoration was almost worshipful, while Valerie felt like a supplicant begging for his caresses. This freedom to touch each other with no more self-imposed restraints was a heady elixir to both of them.

"When I made love to you that first time and realized no other man had ever touched you, I was filled with such a self-contempt and loathing that I swore I'd never come near you again," Judd murmured. "I felt like the lowest animal on earth. Then you confronted me with your justifiable accusations that I'd abused you for my pleasure and dropped you, and I was lost."

"I thought you were avoiding me because I was so inexperienced," Valerie remembered, her fingertips reaching up to explore his jaw and curl into his hair. "Because I hadn't satisfied you."

"It was never that," Judd denied. "You were a wonder to me. I wanted you to know the same feeling of fulfillment that you gave me."

"Judd, there's something I want to ask." Valerie hesitated, hating to ask the question, yet after his revelation it troubled her.

"Ask away," he insisted, lightly kissing her cheekbone.

Her hands slid down to his chest, her fingers spreading over the hard, pulsing flesh. Eluding his caressing mouth, she lifted her head to see his face, and the contentment mixed with desire that she saw reflected in his eyes almost made her dismiss the question as unimportant and as trivial as all that had gone before them.

"Why didn't you ever take me anywhere, ask me out on a date?" she finally asked the question, her look soft and curious.

Judd winced slightly, then smiled. "You were my private treasure," he explained. "I wanted to keep you all to myself. I wanted to be the only one who knew about you. I guess I was afraid if I took you somewhere someone might steal you from me. So I kept trying to hide you, but I ended up losing you anyway."

"Only for a time," she reminded him and sighed. "I thought it was because I was just Elias Wentworth's granddaughter, not worthy enough to be seen in the company of a Prescott."

"I know. Or at least, I realized it that last time we met," he qualified his statement. "I was angered by that. But I was more worried that someone at the party you were so anxious to attend might take you from me. And I suddenly questioned whether you hadn't been meeting me just to eventually obtain an invitation to one of the Prescotts' parties in order to meet someone else. I was enraged at the thought that you might be using me."

"Judd, you didn't!" Valerie protested incredulously, frowning.

"Jealousy is an ugly thing, darling," he admitted, "especially the obsessively possessive kind. Mine was almost a terminal case."

"You don't need to be jealous. Not now and not then," she told him, her throat aching from the love she felt. "There's never been anyone else but you. Oh, I've dated a few times these last seven years," she admitted in an offhand manner that said those dates had meant nothing. "But it seemed that if I couldn't have you, I didn't want to settle for second best."

Judd kissed her hard, as if grateful for the reassurance and angry that he had needed it. "The week after we argued and you stormed away, I practically haunted our place. Then I went into town and overheard someone mention that you'd gone away. For a while I told myself I was glad you'd left because I could finally be in control of my own life again. When I found myself missing you, I tried to make believe it was because you'd been such a satisfactory lover."

"And it wasn't that?" she whispered hopefully. Her hands felt the lifting of his chest as Judd took a deep breath before shaking his dark head.

"No, it wasn't that," he agreed. "After six months, I finally accepted the fact that mere lust wouldn't last that long. That's when I rode over to your grandfather's to find out where you were. Remember that filly I told you I bought from him?"

"Yes," Valerie remembered.

"That's the excuse I used." There was a rueful twist of his mouth. "It took me a week of visits to get the subject around to you. When he finally did mention you, it was to tell me you'd eloped with some man."

"But—"

"I know." Judd staved off her words. "It wasn't true, but at the time I didn't know it. I almost went out of my mind. Half the time I was calling myself every name in the book for letting you go. Or else I was congratulating myself on being rid of a woman who could forget me in six months. But mostly I was insane with jealousy for the man who now had you for himself."

"And I was trying so desperately to hate you all that time." Her voice cracked and she bit at her lip to hold back a sob. "Seven years." So much time had been wasted, unnecessarily.

"Everybody pays for his mistakes, Valerie," he reminded her. "What we did was wrong and we both had to pay. My price was seven years of visiting your grandfather and listening to him talk about your happy family and his grandchild and all the places your husband was taking you to see. I had seven years of endless torture picturing you in another man's arms. While you had to bear my child alone and face the world alone with him."

"In Tadd, I had a part of you. I loved him even more because of that." Valerie hugged him tightly to share the pain they had both known.

"When your grandfather died and Mickey told me you were coming for the funeral, I vowed I wouldn't come near you. I didn't think I could stand seeing you with your husband and child. But I couldn't stay away from the house."

His voice was partially muffled by the thickness of her tawny hair as his mouth moved over it, his chin rubbing her head in an absent caress. "I think I was trying to rid myself of your ghost. I was almost hoping that having a child had ruined your figure and being married would have turned you into a nagging shrew—anything to rid me of your haunting image. Instead you'd matured into a stunningly beautiful woman who made the woman-child I loved seem pale in comparison."

"When you walked out of that door, I nearly ran into your arms," Valerie admitted. "It was as if those seven years we were apart had never existed."

"If I hadn't believed you had a husband somewhere, that's exactly what would have happened," he said, and she felt his mouth curve into a smile against her hair. "It wasn't until that night that I found out you didn't have a husband. It was as if the heavens had just opened up and I tried to rush your surrender."

"Before I came back, I thought I'd got over you. All it took was seeing you again to realize I hadn't," she confessed. "I fought it because I knew how much you'd hurt me the last time and I didn't think I could stand it if that happened again. And I . . . I thought all you wanted was to have me back as your lover."

"My lover, my wife, my friend, my everything," Judd corrected fiercely. "It was after the funeral that I told my mother about our affair seven years ago and that this time I was going to marry you no matter how I had to make you agree. But first I had to try to convince you to stay."

"I thought you were trying to set me up as your mistress when you offered to lease the farm," Valerie remembered.

"I was," he admitted. "I knew you still felt a spark of desire for me."

"A spark?" she laughed. "It was a forest fire!"

"I didn't know that," Judd reminded her. "I was simply desperate to try anything that would reestablish what we once had. Later I could persuade you to marry me."

"But when you found out about Tadd . . ." Valerie began.

"Yes, I had the weapon," he nodded. "I knew that for his sake I could persuade you to marry me. That's when I realized that if you married me without loving me, the hell of the last seven years would be nothing compared to what the future would hold. I had to find out first whether you felt more than sexual attraction for me."

"Have I convinced you?" She gazed into his face, her eyes brimming with boundless love.

His mouth dented at the corners. "I'll be convinced when you stand in front of a minister with me and say, 'I do.' And if I can arrange it, that day will come tomorrow."

"The sooner the better," Valerie agreed, and couldn't resist murmuring the title, "Mrs. Judd Prescott . . . Valerie Prescott. It sounds beautiful, but I'm not sure it's me."

"You'd better get used to it," he warned. "Because it's going to be your name for the rest of your life."

"Are you very sure that's what you want?" Just for an instant, she let herself doubt it.

"Yes." Judd kissed her hard in punishment. "As sure as I am that our next child is going to be born on the right side of the blanket."

"What about Tadd?" Valerie began.

Only to be interrupted by Clara ordering, "Tadd! Come back here this minute!" from inside the house.

A pair of stampeding feet raced to the screen door and pushed it open as Tadd came rushing out, staring wide-eyed at the embracing pair. "Clara said we might not be leaving after all!" he declared. "Is it true, mom? Are we going to stay?"

"Yes," Valerie admitted, making no effort to move out of Judd's arms, not that he would have permitted it.

"Till summer's over?" he questioned further.

"No, you're going to live here," Judd answered him this time.

Clara came hustling to the door, scolding, "Tadd, I thought I told you not to come out here until I said you could." Her shrewd blue eyes glanced apologetically at Valerie. "He bolted out of the kitchen before I could stop him."

"It's all right," Valerie assured her, smiling into the twinkling eyes.

"Does that mean I can have a puppy?" Tadd breathed in excited anticipation.

"You not only can have a puppy, you're also going to have a father," Judd told him. "I'm going to marry your mother. Is that all right with you?"

"Sure." Tadd gave his permission and switched the subject back to a matter of more urgent interest. "When can I have my puppy?"

"In another couple of weeks," Judd promised. "As soon as it's old enough to leave its mother."

"That long?" Tadd grimaced in disappointment.

"It's better than seven years," Judd murmured to Valerie as his arm curved more tightly around her waist.

"It will go by fast, Tadd," Valerie told him. "In the meantime, you can choose the one you want and play with it so it will get to know you."

"Can I go over now? I know which one I want," he said eagerly.

A wicked light began to dance in Judd's green eyes. "Clara might be persuaded to take you," he suggested. "While you're playing with the puppies, she could be helping my mother make arrangements for the wedding reception tomorrow."

"And leave you here alone with Valerie?" Clara scoffed at the very idea of it. "As virile as you are,

Judd Prescott, there'd be a baby born eight months and twenty-nine days after the wedding!"

Judd chuckled and Valerie felt her cheeks grow warm at the thought. He glanced down at her, his gaze soft and loving.

"She's right," he said. "After seven years, I can wait one more night. Because it's the last night we're ever going to be apart. I promise you that, Valerie." Unmindful of the small boy and the older woman looking on, his dark head bent to meet the toffee gold of Valerie's.

the Bagthorpe Saga

Bagthorpes V The World

Also by Helen Cresswell

The Bagthorpe Saga
1. Ordinary Jack
2. Absolute Zero
3. Bagthorpes Unlimited
4. Bagthorpes V. the World
5. Bagthorpes Abroad
6. Bagthorpes Haunted
7. Bagthorpes Liberated
8. Bagthorpes Battered

Snatchers

For Younger Readers
The Little Sea Horse
A Game of Catch
The Sea Piper
Bag of Bones
The Little Grey Donkey

The Winklesea Trilogy:
A Gift From Winklesea
Whatever Happened in Winklesea
Mystery at Winklesea

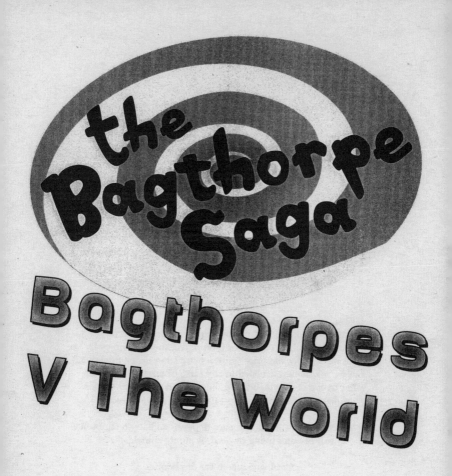

the Bagthorpe Saga

Bagthorpes V The World

HELEN CRESSWELL

Hodder Children's Books

A division of Hodder Headline Limited

First published in hardback in Great Britain in 1979
by Faber and Faber Limited

Published in paperback in Great Britain in 1998
by Hodder Children's Books

This paperback edition published in Great Britain in 2001
by Hodder Children's Books

10 9 8 7 6 5 4 3 2 1

A Catalogue record for this book is
available from the British Library

ISBN 0 340 72246 0

Typeset by Palimpsest Book Production Limited
Polmont, Stirlingshire

Printed and bound in Great Britain by
Clays Ltd, St Ives plc

Hodder Children's Books
A Division of Hodder Headline Limited
338 Euston Road
London NW1 3BH

For E.H. Rowe – without whom The Bagthorpes would never have been.

1

The Great Bagthorpe Daisy-chain was two weeks old and still the Bagthorpes were not assured of immortality. *The Guinness Book of Records* had been very interested, and had conceded that the Bagthorpes' chain was the longest yet.

'But the daisy Season is not yet over,' they wrote, 'and another, longer chain may be recorded before we go to press.'

'Rubbish!' snapped Grandma when she read this. She wrote back saying that if by some freak of nature such a chain were produced, she wished to be notified immediately, so that she could beat *that*, too. As yet no reply had been made to this, and the younger Bagthorpes, at least, were feeling restless and threatened.

'I know we're the *cleverest* family in England,' said Rosie, aged nine, 'but it doesn't necessarily mean we've got the fastest fingers.'

The others gloomily assented that this was so.

'Any fool can string daisies together,' said William, who at sixteen was the eldest, and felt marginally more obliged to prove himself than the rest. 'We should have gone in for a record that takes brains.'

'No one round here thinks we've got brains, any more,' Rosie told him. 'Not after that photo.'

The *Aysham Gazette* had devoted a full half-page to a photograph of the Bagthorpes sitting on the front lawn up to their ears in daisies and forking mutton stew into their mouths.

'Zero came out all right in it,' Jack said. 'He was just sitting and acting natural.'

'Which is hardly a picture of the epitome of luminous canine intelligence,' Tess told him.

'Mutton-brained pudding-footed hound,' added William for good measure. (This assessment of Zero's I.Q. and appearance was in fact Mr Bagthorpe's, but William tended to use it in his absence.)

'If our daisy-chain *doesn't* get in *The Guinness Book of Records*, there's not much point in saving it for *my* Records,' said Rosie dolefully. (Keeping Records was one of Rosie's Strings to her Bow.)

No one replied. Enough had already been said about the impractability, not to say downright lunacy, of attempting to preserve for posterity a daisy-chain four thousand seven hundred and fifty feet long and consisting of over twenty-two thousand daisies.

'It will be compost within the month,' Mr Bagthorpe told her. 'It will not even be *balanced* compost. Pray do not put it on *my* heap.'

'Archaeologists will be able to piece it together again,' Rosie said obstinately. 'They can piece *anything* together, even things millions of years old. They've got special techniques.'

To this Mr Bagthorpe had returned that even if anyone five hundred years hence did think it worth his while to resurrect a composted daisy-chain, the technique required would be of a supernatural, rather than scientific, order.

'It would require a Second Coming,' he declared. 'And do not leave those daisies where I can see them. And stop talking about daisies, the lot of you!'

Mr Bagthorpe was extremely bitter about the Great Bagthorpe daisy-chain. It had cost him the only chance he had ever had (or was indeed now likely to have) of being seriously interviewed by the *Sunday Times*, and commanding a quarter page in the Review section. Instead, a piece of what Mr Bagthorpe said was unparalleled idiocy had appeared in the Colour Supplement. The only allusion to Mr Bagthorpe and his work had been in parenthesis:

'The Bagthorpe family (the head of which is Henry Bagthorpe, the TV scriptwriter) were discovered by Gerald Pike on the lawn of their home, in pursuit of immortality via a daisy-chain . . .'

The accompanying photographs had come out in shaming detail, thanks to Grandma's having had floodlights looped around in branches, on the pretext that threading daisies was trying to her eyes. The only people who liked the photographs and article were Grandma herself, Aunt Celia, and Daisy.

Grandma liked to appear eccentric, and Aunt Celia thought how poetic and symbolic everybody looked, crouched under their dripping umbrellas and knitting daisies. She wrote several poems about it, and encouraged her daughter to do the same. (Daisy, aged four, often wrote poems, especially on walls.)

'If I catch that accursed infant writing any poems on *my* walls,' Mr Bagthorpe warned, 'she will herself be in immediate need of an elegy.' He further said that he would with the utmost pleasure compose one himself.

The Bagthorpes, then, while still unsure of the success of their bid for immortality, threw themselves with increased zeal into their everyday pursuits. They practised frenetically every String to their respective Bows. All the younger Bagthorpes were more or less genii and had several Strings to their Bows, with the exception of Jack, who had none. William (who, his father claimed, had clearly been a tribal warrior in a previous incarnation) beat out long and frenzied tattoos on his new drums. (His old ones had been pierced by Daisy with a knife and fork.) Also, between winning tennis tournaments and attempting to disprove the Theory of Relativity, he held long conversations over his radio with Anonymous, from Grimsby, a radio pirate with a gift for lugubrious pronouncements and forecasts.

'Anonymous from Grimsby reckons that a U.F.O. came down again last night,' William would announce. Or, 'Anonymous from Grimsby reckons there's an Alien Intelligence in Outer Space. He reckons it's sending out messages in code. He's trying to crack it.'

Nobody but William himself took any of this very seriously, especially Mr Bagthorpe, who would say that even if it were all true, it would still be the least of his problems.

'It's for the Government to worry about,' he would say. 'Let *them* worry. *Any* Alien Intelligence would make less of a mess of things than they do.'

Tess went round the house quoting whole passages in French, mainly from Voltaire, entered a National Judo Contest and spent hours holed up in her room either practising her oboe or endlessly playing Danish Linguaphone records.

Rosie practised the violin, tried to disprove Pythagoras' Theorem, and embarked on a full-scale mural, in oils, of the Great Bagthorpe daisy-chain Making.

'That's *bound* to be immortal,' she told everybody. 'Nobody's ever done that before.'

No one commented on this except Mr Bagthorpe, who contented himself with warning her to keep it out of his way. 'If I come across it,' he told her, 'I shall not be accountable for my actions. And stop *talking* about daisies, the lot of you!'

Rosie, despite her father's hostility to the project, was none the less experimenting with different techniques to preserve the daisy-chain intact. She tried painting it with colourless nail varnish, glazing it with a starch solution, and squirting it with the stuff used to spray on Christmas trees to keep the needles from falling. The latter worked best, but turned out to be unfeasible. In the first place, it made the chain so stiff that it could not be coiled up, and would have to stay starchly zig-zagged all round the garden of Unicorn House for ever. In the second, Rosie worked out that it would cost thirty-nine pounds fourteen pence in Christmas Tree Preserver. She invited the rest of the family to contribute towards this sum, but they declined to a man.

Rosie took a good yardage of the chain to her room and embalmed it, in sections, between pages of the *Children's Encyclopaedia Britannica*, while continuing her experiments to preserve the whole of the chain at a viable economic rate. (If you were a Bagthorpe you never, ever, gave up.)

Mrs Bagthorpe had been little affected one way or another by the daisy-chain episode.

'It will be lovely if you all achieve a record,' she told the family, 'and I shall be terribly proud of you. But I do not really believe that this achievement will constitute an extra String to anybody's Bow. I should try to forget the whole matter, for the time being, and concentrate on your *real Strings*' – as, indeed, they were doing.

Mrs Bagthorpe was pleased to note that her offspring had taken this sensible advice, and felt that she had, for once, acted as 'Stella Bright' to her own family. (Mrs Bagthorpe ran a monthly Agony Column in a woman's journal under the name of Stella Bright, but found that as a rule, any advice she might give in her capacity of wife and mother to her own family was rarely taken, let alone effective.)

Mr Bagthorpe tried to work his way through his current problems by battling with a new and unprecedentedly complex script which would, he assured everyone, be 'a breakthrough in the history of television'.

Jack, having no Strings to his Bow, found himself frequently thrown into the sole company of Zero – who belonged to the Bagthorpes in general, and Jack in particular. (He had just turned up in the garden, one day, and stayed.) The Bagthorpes were always running Zero down, and this despite the fact that he was now world-famous, and earned more money than anyone else in the house.

'You and me don't need Strings to our Bows, old chap,' Jack would tell him often. 'Only that lot. And take no notice of what they say. They're just jealous. Good old boy.'

Jack had to do a lot of this kind of praising even now Zero was famous, because he lacked self-confidence and was very easily undermined. When he was, his ears gave him away. They drooped.

Jack tried to bring Zero on during this period while the rest of the family were so obsessively engaged in their various pursuits. He failed, after a period of intensive training, to get Zero to bark up to five, like a dog Jack had once seen in a circus.

'Never mind, old chap,' Jack told him, when he finally gave up. 'It doesn't matter. You don't need to be able to count up to five. I just thought it would be an interest for you. Good old chap.'

Jack was reaching the stage of boredom when he was considering taking out the dowsing rods that had lain in his wardrobe since the Prophet days, and giving them another try, when the letter arrived from the Sainted Aunt.

Letters from Aunt Penelope had been thin on the ground since the Family Reunion débâcle at Easter. Indeed, most of the family had hoped that diplomatic relations would be cut off for a long time to come, if not for ever. Normally, only Mrs Bagthorpe would read her letters (possibly quoting the odd snippet to the rest) and answer them. On this occasion, however, she stopped the whole family in its tracks by reading out the whole thing. The Bagthorpes were all arguing noisily at the time, between mouthfuls of toast or cereal. (Mrs Bagthorpe believed that meals should be civilized occasions, with a brisk and lively interchange of views and opinions, even breakfast.)

'Hush, darlings!' she cried, brandishing the letter. 'You must listen to this!'

Grandma, who had just entered, took her seat, glanced at the missive, and remarked:

'It is from that dreadful woman who married my eldest and best-loved son, and is feeding her family on nuts and grass.'

None of this was true. Henry himself was her favourite son, because he had plenty of fight, and she could conduct frequent and truly stupendous rows with him. Aunt Penelope and Uncle Claud had certainly turned vegetarian but did not, so far as the others knew, eat grass. No one, however, argued. It was a whole lot of trouble to argue with Grandma, and on this occasion, definitely not worth it.

'Luke has already reached the semi-final of the Young Brain of Britain Contest,' Mrs Bagthorpe exclaimed, ignoring this interruption.

This intelligence met with stony silence from her offspring and a further speech from Grandma.

'She will never rear those children,' she said. 'If, indeed, they *are* children. Why do they never raise their voices? Why do they never shout? Their blood has been turned to water.'

'Their brains haven't,' said Rosie gloomily. 'Trust that revolting Luke. I bet he cheated.'

'Let me read you the whole letter,' said Mrs Bagthorpe. 'It is full of news.'

Mr Bagthorpe looked up from behind his newspaper.

'I shall not be required to listen, I hope,' he said. 'I am engaged in an extremely complex and demanding creative exercise, and the least thing will destroy my balance. If necessary, I shall cover my ears.'

He retreated behind his paper, and Mrs Bagthorpe took a deep breath and prepared to regale her unenthusiastic audience.

'"Dear Laura",' she read. '"We trust and pray that yourself, dear Henry, and the family are thriving and well, despite your corrupt diet."'

There came here a snort from behind Mr Bagthorpe's newspaper which seemed to indicate that he was not managing not to listen.

'"There is very little news to tell,"' Mrs Bagthorpe continued, '"other than that Claud and myself feel so blessed in our children, and are continually offering up thanks for them. I am sending under separate cover an inscribed copy of the volume in which four of little Esther's poems appear. And I know that you will all be thrilled to hear that dear Luke has now reached the semi-final of the radio Young Brain of Britain Contest. He is, indeed, the youngest child ever to do so."'

William muttered something under his breath and to Jack it sounded like 'Bloody *hell*!' It may have sounded like this to his mother, as well, because she frowned reprovingly over the top of the letter before continuing.

'"Claud and I are naturally exceedingly proud of them both, and I know that you will rejoice with us. 'And Solomon's wisdom exceeded the wisdom of all the children of the east country and all the wisdom of Egypt.' (I Kings, Chapter 4, verse 30.) You will be interested to know that tomorrow dear Great Aunt Lucy is coming to be our guest for several days."'

'What?' Here Mr Bagthorpe threw down his newspaper on the marmalade pot and abandoned all pretence of not listening.

'"We have always been so fond of her,"' continued his wife, '"and the dear children write to her almost every week. We shall do all possible to make her stay happy, and also to see the error of her ways and turn to a more natural and wholesome diet. Blessings on you all. God be with you. Penelope."'

'Hell's bells!' fumed Mr Bagthorpe. 'The woman's a – she's a whited sepulchre. A snake in the grass. She's a worm in the—'

'That is enough, Henry,' said Grandma, interrupting her son's flow of mixed metaphors. 'We all know perfectly well why you are in this childish tantrum. You do not deceive us for a moment. You care not a fig for Lucy.'

This was true. Mr Bagthorpe did, at rare intervals, make a fleeting visit to Great Aunt Lucy (a distant connection on his father's side), in Torquay. He did this partly to get away from his own family, and partly because Great Aunt Lucy had few surviving relatives and was extremely rich. The thought that Aunt Penelope was now also putting herself in the way of a hefty bequest was too much for him.

'She will be driven mad within the week by that bunch of Latter Day Saints!' Mr Bagthorpe fulminated, 'and as likely as not alter her will while the balance of her mind is disturbed by nuts and water.' He then rounded on his own offspring. 'Why don't you lot write letters every week?' he demanded. 'What's the matter with you? Have you *no* concept of which side your bread is buttered?'

'I don't think I ever really do anything Great Aunt Lucy would be interested in,' said Jack honestly. His siblings were all more concerned with Luke than the matter of bequests, and suchlike.

'She'll have to come here,' Mr Bagthorpe said. 'Invite her, Laura. Do it now.'

'But, Henry, darling, you are in the middle of such a difficult piece of work,' his wife protested.

'To hell with that,' he said tersely. 'Invite her. And you lot – you just keep yourselves within bounds while she's here. I warn you. I can hardly afford to keep you as it is. If I am now to be sold down the river for a mess of pottage, I shall certainly not be able to afford it.'

'You could always borrow off Zero,' suggested Jack helpfully. 'He'd lend you some, wouldn't you, old chap?'

Zero made a movement of his tail that could in no way be described as enthusiastic, and Mr Bagthorpe pushed back his chair and stood up.

'*That* piece of uncalled-for sarcasm is all I needed,' he said. 'The day I am reduced to borrowing money from a dog – and in particular a numb-skulled, pudding-footed, matted-up hound like—'

'Don't, Father!' pleaded Jack. 'I'm sorry. I didn't meant it like that. I didn't mean to be sarcastic.'

Jack did not even know how to be sarcastic. He often wished he did, so that he could keep his end up with the rest of the family. And he could see that Zero already seemed to be lying closer to the ground under Mr Bagthorpe's onslaught, his nose buried under his paws, his ears wilting.

Mr Bagthorpe flung out. He was muttering under his breath, but Jack could hear only the odd words, like 'bankruptcy' and 'last ditch' and 'penury'.

'What a pity Henry is so impulsive and so bad-tempered,' remarked Grandma, spooning up honey. 'He should have taken up the offer of a loan from the dog, which I should imagine would almost certainly have been interest-free. It was extremely clever of you, Jack, to think of such a thing, and I hope that if the contingency arises, the same offer will be made to myself.'

'Of course, Grandma,' Jack told her, warmed by the unaccustomed compliment. Like Zero, he hardly ever got praised.

'I'm off,' announced William bitterly, pushing back his own chair. 'I hope they all die of food poisoning.'

Everyone knew whom he meant.

'William, dear!' murmured his mother in shocked tones as the door slammed. 'Oh dear, perhaps I should not have read out the letter at all.'

A blight had certainly been cast over the entire household except Grandma, who scented trouble in large doses ahead, and had perked up considerably as the row had developed. Grandpa, who was almost deaf and probably had his hearing-aid switched off, beamed round at everyone and observed:

'Warmer, today. Not far off the wasp season.' He folded his napkin and rose.

As he made his exit the knob of the outer door to

the kitchen turned, and Mrs Fosdyke entered. (She came in daily to do for the Bagthorpes, but refused to live in.)

'Morning,' she said, whipping off her headscarf and coat. 'I'm late on account of the marge, you'll remember, Mrs Bagthorpe?'

'Marge?' repeated Mrs Bagthorpe, her mind elsewhere.

'What you asked for from the shop.' Mrs Fosdyke slapped down four packets of this commodity. 'And the shop not open till half eight, as you'll remember.'

'No – yes – of course. Thank you so much, Mrs Fosdyke.'

'You have some good news to impart to Mrs Fosdyke have you not, Laura?' said Grandma, seizing the chance to stir troubled waters. Mrs Fosdyke had by now exchanged her shoes for the fur-edged slippers she wore winter and summer alike to 'keep off the cramps', and was noisily rattling dishes in the sink. Mrs Fosdyke's tendency to equate noisiness with efficiency was one of her less endearing traits, and one that frequently drove Mr Bagthorpe to near-breaking point.

'Oh. Yes. Well.' Mrs Bagthorpe seemed nervous. 'I wonder, Mrs Fosdyke, if you are in a position to cater for a house guest some time in the near future? Only one person, and I should think very little trouble.'

At this Mrs Fosdyke turned and wiped her hands on her flowered overall.

'Not one of them vegitinarians, I hope?' she inquired suspiciously. 'I can't say I'm up to that, not at the minute. My nerves still ain't up to what they were.'

Mrs Fosdyke's nerves had been badly affected during the Family Reunion. She had been forced to grate endless carrots and apples for the Latter Day Saints, and had been showered with maggots on two separate occasions.

'The lady concerned is an elderly relation of Mr Bagthorpe's,' Mrs Bagthorpe now assured her, 'and I should think would find raw foods quite indigestible. I should imagine that a light, bland diet would be more suitable, with plenty of junkets and custards and—'

'Relative of Mr Bagthorpe's?' Mrs Fosdyke interrupted. 'Never that old woman from Torquay!'

'Great Aunt Lucy certainly does live in Torquay, Mrs Fosdyke,' said Mrs Bagthorpe rather coolly.

'Never her that's got that Pekingese and that parrot that's always fighting? There'll be no Pekingese and parrots, I hope?'

'Whether or not Wung Foo is still living I am not certain,' replied Mrs Bagthorpe, 'but the parrot is definitely dead.'

'Got killed, did it?' asked Mrs Fosdyke. 'By that dog?'

'I believe it did,' Mrs Bagthorpe told her. 'So I hope that will put your mind at rest, Mrs Fosdyke.'

The latter sniffed and turned back to the sink. During the past year, while so many family meals were taken in the kitchen because of the burned-out and unusable dining- and sitting-rooms, Mrs Fosdyke had heard more than the usual number of Bagthorpian rows and arguments. Her mind was by no means put at rest. As she swished the suds into the water she tried to remember some of the things Mr Bagthorpe had said about his Great Aunt after his last brief visit. She could not at the moment recall details, but definitely remembered that they had been unflattering, and had given herself, Mrs Fosdyke, the distinct impression that Great Aunt Lucy was at least as mad as the rest of the Bagthorpes and possibly madder.

By the time she *had* remembered the missing details, it would be too late either to stop Great Aunt Lucy coming or for Mrs Fosdyke to hand in her notice. The die would have been cast, and events plummeting out of the control of herself or anybody else. Another blood-freezing chapter in the Bagthorpe Saga had begun.

2

Within twenty-four hours of the arrival of the letter from the Sainted Aunt, the whole household was disorientated to a degree hardly ever before known. Everybody's feelings were divided. One and all of them could see that it would be a good thing if Great Aunt Lucy left most of her money to themselves, rather than to the hateful Dogcollar Brigade. Nobody, on the other hand, wished to entertain this relative. They had all heard the odd remark made about her by Mr Bagthorpe, and even making due allowance for his tendency to gross exaggeration, nobody much liked the sound of the old lady.

Mr Bagthorpe himself went unusually quiet, and kept to his study for most of the day. He did this because he did not wish to be cross-examined about Great Aunt Lucy, as he certainly would have been had he emerged. It was then possible that the invitation would be withdrawn. Mr Bagthorpe had told his family a few things about her, but by no means all. He alone was aware, for instance, that Great Aunt Lucy did not have Strings to her Bow, she had what in his experience was far more deadly – Bees in her Bonnet.

Each time Mr Bagthorpe visited her the old lady had done a complete turnabout in her view on practically everything, and he had in fact told the family that no one else he knew could change their stance on any given subject with such inconsequence and speed.

'Her mind revolves like a spinning top,' he had said. 'She can turn through three hundred and sixty degrees in ten minutes flat.'

He said that many politicians had this ability, and indeed needed it, but that it was extremely unsettling to live with. This was why his visits to Torquay had rarely lasted longer than two days. And it was certainly why he had been so shaken by the intelligence that she was to visit the Dogcollar Brigade. She was, he well knew, perfectly capable of being converted to vegetarianism within an hour of arrival. And if she were, there would, he also knew, be no half measures.

'She will probably even try to make that accursed Peke of hers eat grass,' he thought glumly, 'and will certainly require all of us to.'

He mentally resolved to look up a few books on nutrition during the days prior to Aunt Lucy's visit, so that he could put forward a sufficiently powerful argument in favour of a meat diet to send her weathercock of a mind round through one hundred and eighty degrees.

'In which case,' he thought fatalistically, 'she will probably wish to roast an ox whole on the front lawn, or have us all eating raw hedgehogs.'

Fortunately, Grandma was not aware of the full extent of Great Aunt Lucy's eccentricity. Had she been, she would certainly have managed to put some kind of a spoke in the wheel to prevent her coming. She had, as it was, misgivings, but at present she kept these to herself. She had met this relative only once, many years ago, at a wedding, and remembered that she had worn the largest hat and more jewellery than anyone else present. Grandma accordingly did a good deal of rummaging through her own drawers for articles of adornment that would ensure her keeping her own end up in this respect.

The visitor was incontrovertibly *older* than Grandma (she was eighty-seven – older than Grandpa, even) and this in itself seemed to threaten her own position. The Bagthorpes deferred a lot to Grandma because of her age, and she did not wish to appear relatively less august in their eyes. She was also aware that the other old lady had claims to oddness, though she did not yet know about the Bees in the Bonnet. Grandma comforted herself with the thought that she was on home ground, and had years of experience in manipulating the Bagthorpes, and that if it came to a showdown, she would probably win. The prospect of a showdown on a large scale in itself appealed strongly to Grandma.

The younger Bagthorpes had never met their Great Aunt before and were not looking forward to their roles as sycophants. They were even less used than the average person to flattering and pleasing other people.

They boasted a lot, but tended to ignore, or even decry, the achievements of others. Luke's meteoric rise towards becoming Young Brain of Britain was making them all feel threatened. William, indeed, was spending a lot of time up in his room on the top floor fiddling with his radio equipment, in the hope that he might find a way of sabotaging the programme when it went out.

'If I can jam it,' he told the others, 'I definitely shall. The BBC can take whatever action they like.'

Tess suggested that if by the date the radio programme went out William was still not able to jam it, they might try another method of bringing about Luke's downfall. She had been reading lately a good many books about ESP, and wanted the Bagthorpes to try blanketing Luke with thought waves. She said that if they all sat round in a circle holding hands and with their eyes shut, every time Luke was asked a question they could instantly send out powerful telepathic thoughts of the wrong answer.

'We all have powerful brains, except Jack,' she told them, 'and our combined thought waves will be exceedingly strong.'

This suggestion aroused extremely hostile reactions from the others, who wanted no part, they said, in anything so silly. In the end, however, after Tess had quoted some convincing instances from books by Jung and Arthur Koestler, they reluctantly agreed that they would, as a last resort, try this.

'Though we shall have to lock the door first,'

William said. 'None of us will be able to hold up our heads again if we're caught at it.'

The entire Bagthorpe household was, then, under threat of some kind or other, and none more so than Mr Bagthorpe himself. It needed only the slightest nudge, he felt, to topple the balance of his mind and send it plummeting into full-scale schizophrenia or paranoia.

This nudge, which could hardly be described as slight, came the following day, when his current bank statement arrived. Everybody saw the nudge, because it happened at breakfast. Rosie dropped his mail on to his plate and he snatched it up instantly, as he always did, to see if any cheques had arrived from the BBC. He sorted deftly through the pile, putting anything in a buff envelope into a separate pile. Mr Bagthorpe had the profoundest suspicion of anything in a buff envelope, and had once missed claiming a handsome prize in a sweepstake because he had left the communication relating to this lying with a pile of unopened bills for over three months.

Today, nothing in the *white* envelopes seemed to be giving Mr Bagthorpe much pleasure, and there was certainly no cheque from the BBC.

'Why the devil do they not pay me?' he demanded of the company at large, flinging his white correspondence aside. 'I am constantly meeting *their* deadlines, why cannot they meet mine? I shall almost certainly have to go on strike.'

He frequently threatened this kind of industrial

action, but never carried it out, because he was afraid that in the absence of himself another scriptwriter would step into his shoes, probably permanently.

'What's this?' His eye fell on the top buff envelope. 'Bank statement!'

He was well into his stride now and, knowing that the contents would provide him with further ammunition, took the unprecedented action of opening the envelope there and then. He picked up his marmalade-smeared knife and slit the top. The Bagthorpes watched, because they knew he would almost certainly be overdrawn, and would accordingly put on a full-scale performance. They were, however, by no means prepared for the reactions that followed.

The first thing that happened was that Mr Bagthorpe went perfectly white. Then his mouth opened soundlessly. Then his face flushed dark red. His eyes were glazed. Then he went white again and his mouth worked, but still no sound was emitted. The younger Bagthorpes were more fascinated than concerned by this performance, but Mrs Bagthorpe was moved to inquire sympathetically:

'Not bad news, I hope, darling?'

Mr Bagthorpe looked up at this, and his voice now came out with such force that everyone present jumped and Mrs Fosdyke dropped a saucer in the sink.

'Bad news?' he yelled. 'Bad news? Oh my God!'

'What? What is it?' Mrs Bagthorpe, though no stranger to her husband's histrionics, was alarmed.

‘We’re bankrupted! It’s happened! I knew it would, I knew it would!’ He was gabbling now, and clutching at his hair with the free hand that was not brandishing the bank statement. ‘Those infernal bureaucrats have smashed me! They’ve been after me for years, and now they’ve got me!’

He seemed well into a full-scale paranoia.

‘Calm yourself, Henry!’ said Mrs Bagthorpe helplessly. She rose and went down the table. ‘Let me see.’

She stretched out a hand, but he snatched the paper back.

‘All those noughts!’ he gibbered. ‘Hundreds, thousands – oh my God – millions! I haven’t counted them. I daren’t! I daren’t!’

‘Has he *really* gone mad, d’you think?’ Rosie whispered to Jack. ‘He often nearly does. Has he really, d’you think?’

Mr Bagthorpe began to laugh jerkily and spasmodically, as if sneezing.

‘Might’ve,’ Jack whispered back.

‘No, Henry.’ Mrs Bagthorpe was being firm and sensible now, being Stella Bright. ‘Give that to me.’

Mr Bagthorpe had the bank statement crushed against his chest. Now he slowly drew it out and held it at arm’s length. Quickly his eyes flickered over it.

‘It is, it is! It’s true! Rows of noughts!’

Mrs Bagthorpe took advantage of his renewed

gibbering to snatch the statement away. The young Bagthorpes watched as she straightened it out.

'Oh!' she gasped.

'You see! You see!' almost shrieked Mr Bagthorpe. 'They've got me! They've been out to get me for years!'

His audience knew, by and large, whom he meant by 'they'. He meant the Tax Inspector, the Customs and Excise, the G.P.O., the Local Council, the Electricity Board and now, it appeared, his own bank.

'It is a mistake,' said Mrs Bagthorpe firmly. 'Quite clearly. Do pull yourself together, Henry. No one can possibly be overdrawn by a figure containing that number of noughts.'

'How much is it?' inquired William, who was one of the family's walking computers – the other being Rosie.

'It's – it's – I don't know,' admitted Mrs Bagthorpe. 'I have never seen so many noughts.'

'There you are! I told you! I told you!' Mr Bagthorpe gibbered. 'I can't pay it, I can't! If I wrote a script a day for the next twenty years, I still couldn't! It's jail – I shall be put in jail!'

Mrs Fosdyke, later describing the scene to her cronies in the Fiddler's Arms, was inclined to agree with Mr Bagthorpe about this.

'The wonder is he wasn't put in jail years ago,' she told them. 'He's not right in the head. If I was Mrs Bagthorpe I should leave him, I should, and let him play his noughts and crosses by himself. That dog of theirs has got more sense than he has.'

'Henry, somewhere, somehow, a computer has gone wrong,' said Mrs Bagthorpe loudly and distinctly.

This served only to heighten his hysteria.

'Computer!' he shrieked. 'I knew it! I knew it!'

Mr Bagthorpe had this theory that the country was run not by politicians, as people supposed, but by computers. The politicians, he said, were only front men, the pawns of the computers, which explained why they were all so stupid. Grandma sometimes argued about this, when she felt like it, and would ask him who, in that case, was working the computers? To this he would reply that nobody did, because the computers themselves had now taken on a life of their own, and become autonomous.

'The last real politician this country had was Aneurin Bevan,' he would maintain. 'You are wasting your time arguing with me. I am convinced of it.'

There certainly seemed little use in arguing with him on this occasion, and the only person likely to do so was Grandma, who entered at this juncture, having heard her son's agonized bellowings from her room. She had not wasted time dressing for fear of missing a good scene, and her hair was uncombed.

'Good morning,' she greeted the family.

'Oh Mother, are you not well?' asked Mrs Bagthorpe anxiously.

'I am perfectly well, thank you, Laura,' she replied, 'and hope that you are all the same.'

Mr Bagthorpe groaned.

'Are *you* not well, Henry?' inquired his mother.

'Why cannot people opt out of society?' said Mr Bagthorpe, ignoring the question. 'I want to opt out.'

'I have no idea why you should wish to take such a step,' Grandma told him, 'and can only suppose you have read something in the paper that has upset you again. You should take no notice of the papers. As I have frequently told you, they are a tissue of lies. You yourself should know that words can be manipulated to mean anything at all.'

Mr Bagthorpe was in no mood for a lecture from Grandma about the perniciousness of the word, either written or spoken. He had heard it all before. She had a very carefully prepared and rehearsed speech on the subject which she trotted out whenever she saw the opportunity, to detract from the worth of his own calling.

'Any words you have to say to me are wasted, Mother,' he interrupted. 'I am not in my right mind. I think I am now schizophrenic.'

'Henry has had a rather upsetting bank statement,' Mrs Bagthorpe explained.

'Upsetting?' Mr Bagthorpe threatened to take right off again. 'Upsetting?'

'Henry, of course, is very easily upset,' observed Grandma. 'Might I have a coffee, Mrs Fosdyke, please? By how much are you overdrawn this time, Henry?'

'A few billion, at a rough guess,' William told her. 'Can *I* see the statement, Mother?'

'And me,' piped up Rosie. 'I'll work it out for you, Father.'

'Certainly not,' Mrs Bagthorpe said. 'I think we should now let the whole matter drop.'

'Whole matter drop,' repeated Mr Bagthorpe in hollow tones. 'I shall be in a debtor's prison for the remainder of my life, like that chap in *Little Dorrit*. And it's my luck that I can't make sure that you lot have to as well. No one is going to convince me that an overdraft that size was achieved single-handed. It resembles the National Debt. I am a man of moderate tastes and live most abstemiously. It is the wanton and reckless squandering of money by my dependants that—'

'That really will do, Henry.' Mrs Bagthorpe was now moderately cross, despite having determinedly taken several very deep breaths during the course of the incident. 'You had better go and telephone your bank manager immediately and ascertain the true extent of your overdraft. You are now being silly.'

'I have never been overdrawn in my entire life,' said Grandma piously. 'I was brought up to consider any sort of debt disgraceful.'

'And who brought *me* up?' demanded Mr Bagthorpe triumphantly.

'I freely admit that I made a failure of your upbringing,' she returned calmly. 'We are none of us perfect, even myself. I did as well with you as any mother possibly could. That I failed is one of my greatest sorrows, and I think it most insensitive, Henry, to throw it at me in this way.'

'You made a fair old mess of Celia, if it comes to that,' continued her son remorselessly. 'Spouting poetry, throwing clay, nibbling lettuces. And look what *she* produced by way of progeny.'

He was referring to Daisy Parker, Aunt Celia's four-year-old daughter. It was unusual for him to refer to her, because by and large he tried to pretend that she did not exist. He only did so now because a powerful friendship had recently sprung up between Daisy and Grandma. They were known within the family as The Unholy Alliance. (There was sometimes a third party to this, known as Arry Awk, invisible to the ordinary human eye, but apparently well known and loved by Daisy.)

'Daisy is a shining jewel of a child,' said Grandma, predictably rising to the defence of her favourite. 'The fact that she is flesh of my flesh and blood of my blood is a constant source of pride and joy to me. She is the solace of my old age. I am glad that you have reminded me of her, Henry. I shall telephone The Knoll directly after breakfast, and see whether Celia will allow her to come and stay for a few days.'

'That,' said Mr Bagthorpe, 'is all I need. In that case, I shall go and stay with Aunt L—'

He broke off sharply. Aunt Lucy was not in Torquay. She was staying with the Latter Day Saints. Mr Bagthorpe was desperate, but not sufficiently desperate to consider a visit to them. His unfeeling offspring, seeing his discomfiture, tittered.

Mr Bagthorpe stood up.

'I am a broken man,' he declared. He tossed down the crumpled bank statement, which was instantly seized upon by William and Rosie, and tore loudly in half. '*You* ring the bank, Laura,' he told his wife. 'You can then break the news gently to me later. I must go to my study and revise my entire philosophy of life. The kind of trauma I have suffered lately has left me a changed man.'

He went out to revise his world view, and left his family to sort out his finances.

3

Mr Bagthorpe's bank overdraft turned out to be only in three figures, as usual. He was not comforted by this.

'The damage has already been done,' he asserted. 'I have suffered an irreversible trauma, and shall never be the same again. I am either schizophrenic, or paranoic, or both. I am not certain. I shall have to consult my Laing. In either case, the roots of my malady certainly lie within the family itself.'

At first the family did not believe this, but when the widening rings of his schizophrenia began to impinge on their own lives, they were forced to take more serious note of his claim. There could be little doubt that Mr Bagthorpe, for whatever reasons, was now in the grip of a fully developed, all-out obsession.

The form this obsession took was what Tess described as a 'Scrooge Complex'.

'He has focused all his subconscious anxieties on to one,' she told the others. 'He has tried to simplify his personal neuroses by converting them into something with which he feels he can cope – money.'

'But Father *can't* cope with money,' Rosie pointed out. 'You know he can't.'

'But his anxieties have at least been *externalized*,' Tess explained.

Nobody had the least idea what she was talking about.

'If you read much more Jung and Laing, you will go the same way yourself,' William told her. 'I think that you have more inherited genes from Father than any of us. That is a poor look out.'

Mr Bagthorpe astounded everyone by telling Mrs Fosdyke, just before lunch, that she could go home.

'Take the afternoon off,' he told her.

'But I ain't poorly,' Mrs Fosdyke objected. 'And what about the washing-up? And what about the blancmange for tea?'

'We shall deal with the washing-up and the blancmange,' he told her.

She was clearly stumped. Nothing like this had ever happened before. Knowing Mr Bagthorpe as she did, Mrs Fosdyke viewed this gesture of apparent magnaminity with the darkest suspicion.

'He's up to something,' she told Mesdames Pye and Bates later over her Guinness. 'You mark my words. There's more in this than meets the eye.'

'Could be that he's unhinged by being bankrupted,' suggested Mrs Pye with relish. 'You did say he was bankrupted, didn't you, Glad?'

'Oh, definite,' Mrs Fosdyke assured her.

She went on to say that she believed Mr Bagthorpe was trying to ease her gradually into redundancy.

'Which you ain't allowed to do,' she said. 'Not

these days. And even if you do, you've got to give a Silver Handshake.'

Mrs Fosdyke was not far off the truth in her prognosis, except that Mr Bagthorpe was not intending to give her a Golden, Silver, or any other kind of Handshake on her departure – not even one of the ordinary variety, if he could avoid it. He had never made any secret of his dislike of Mrs Fosdyke, and if any cuts were to be made, then clearly her services must be dispensed with as soon as possible.

'We can no longer afford Mrs Fosdyke,' he told them all, after her departure in what seemed to them unreasonable dudgeon. 'She is a luxury. Not only do we have to pay her wages, but she is day after day wearing out my carpets with her perpetual hedgehogging about with the hoover, and moreover has inflated ideas about what kind of meals we can afford. We cannot afford beef. We cannot afford rich pastry and pork pies. Tess, you will kindly make the blancmange for tea. And use half milk and half water.'

'But I don't know how,' Tess protested.

'Then learn,' he told her tersely. 'Read the instructions on the packet. We are now beginning to find the chinks through which the winds of the world howl!'

No one could make anything of this latter obscure utterance, other than it did seem to indicate that Mr Bagthorpe's mind had indeed become, at least temporarily, deranged.

Mrs Bagthorpe tried to humour her husband by

agreeing that their diet was perhaps too rich, and that in the interests of both health and economy, it should possibly be simplified.

'But as to dispensing with the services of Mrs Fosdyke,' she said, 'I really cannot agree. You will remember, Henry, how disrupted the household became in her absence earlier this summer.'

'This household *is* going to be disrupted,' he told her. 'The four horsemen of the Apocalypse are going to drive a coach and pair right through it. And Mrs Fosdyke will be trampled down in the process.'

'I have not the least idea what you are talking about, Henry,' said his wife, becoming tight-lipped. 'If necessary, I shall pay for Mrs Fosdyke's services out of my own money. I, too, am a breadwinner, and must be allowed some say in the management of things.'

'You do as you like,' he told her, 'but I warn you – I shall cut off the electricity at the mains at eight o'clock each morning.'

An electrified silence followed this stark pronouncement.

'I do not think I quite heard you, Henry,' said his wife at length.

'I think you did,' he returned. 'There will be nothing to prevent people filling flasks with hot drinks if they feel that they cannot get through the day without them. And there are, of course, methods of cooking which require nothing more than a bag of straw or a sandpit, or something. We shall use these methods in future.'

At some time Mr Bagthorpe had evidently read articles on self-sufficiency, and was now drawing on confused memories of these.

'We could always have salad every day,' suggested William with an attempt at sarcasm, 'like the Sainted Aunt.'

'There is no way this family will eat salads, with tomatoes at the price they are,' said Mr Bagthorpe stringently. 'When we have grown our own salad stuff, then we shall eat it.'

'Oh *dear*!' Mrs Bagthorpe felt quite helpless.

'I already have a row of cos lettuce,' he continued, 'and one of spring onions. There is also, I believe, some beetroot and rhubarb. We shall have to exercise our ingenuity with these ingredients.'

The Bagthorpes sat and bleakly pondered the prospect of such a diet.

'Go and fetch your grandmother, dear,' said Mrs Bagthorpe to Rosie, sotto voce. Mr Bagthorpe heard.

'There is nothing Mother can do,' he told his wife. 'This is my household. If she prefers to go and live with Claud or Celia, then that is her affair. If she went to Celia's, she could live on caviare and gin.'

Grandma, when the situation had been outlined to her, did not in fact opt for either of these alternatives. She scented a good deal of excitement and conflict ahead.

'I shall simply have a hamper sent from Fortnum and Mason each week,' she announced. 'Will you commence this absurd policy before the visit of Lucy, or after?'

'We shall commence it forthwith,' he said. 'If there is one thing that can be said for Aunt Lucy, it is that she admires determination and strength of character. She will observe a good deal of both these qualities during her stay.'

'But what about being *immortal*?' Rosie wailed. 'What about getting famous before that horrible Luke does? If we're all washing pots and digging and sowing seeds how can we do our Strings to our Bows?'

'That is enough of that kind of talk,' her father told her sternly. 'What this family is now concerned with is Survival. The whole world is ranged up out there against us. We shall shore up our defences against it. We shall become, in fact, totally Self-Sufficient. Only when we have achieved that shall we become free.'

'But, Henry, I feel free already!' cried Mrs Bagthorpe desperately. 'Why do you not take the afternoon off and go for a nice long walk?'

'Because I never go for long walks,' he replied, 'as you know full well, Laura. I detest long walks. I shall spend the afternoon tilling the soil. And then, this evening I shall draw up a rota of duties for the whole household.'

'Pray do not put me down for anything,' Grandma requested. 'I am too old to be caught up in this sort of hocus pocus. Wisdom, I am happy to say, comes with age.'

'Bilge, Mother,' Mr Bagthorpe told her. 'You have

never been wise, nor are you now. Age has simply compounded your unreason. The day you get to be wise, will be the day cows fly. And we shall, of course, have to get one.'

'Why will we?' demanded Tess.

'Because,' he told her, 'we shall require milk. Milk is necessary for bones and teeth and so forth. We can have a cow, or we can have a goat. You can take your pick.'

'Who'll milk it?' Jack asked.

'You, probably,' replied Mr Bagthorpe. 'The time has come when you are going to have to pay the way of that mutton-headed hound of yours. What does he cost to feed? What contribution does he make to this benighted household? There is no room for drones in this hive.'

There was nothing much that Jack could say in reply to this, because Zero did not in fact do much about the house, not even frighten off burglars.

'He makes money,' Jack said stoutly, 'and he doesn't cost you anything, Father. He gets free Buried Bones, remember. Anyway, I don't mind milking a goat as long as somebody shows me how to do it.'

'And who will that be?' inquired Tess. 'Can *you* milk a goat, Father?'

'There is no doubt a perfectly good manual on the subject,' he told her, unperturbed, 'which is more than Robinson Crusoe had the benefit of. Where is your spirit of adventure?'

The spirit of adventure seemed at a very low ebb

throughout the household. The only person who appeared to have it to any marked degree was Mr Bagthorpe himself, who, being now gripped by the notion of Survival, was fast spiralling out of control.

'The summer house will be converted to a chicken house,' he informed everybody, the idea having just occurred to him. 'We shall thus have the benefit of free-range eggs.'

'But if the hens are roaming about free, they'll eat all the lettuce and salads,' objected Rosie.

'Do not bother me with irksome details,' Mr Bagthorpe told her. 'I am concerned with evolving a Master Plan for Survival. It will be up to you lot to see to the details. I read an article recently about how to generate electricity from sewage and dung. You, William, had better look into it. At last your expensive and heretofore pointless interest in electricity will pay off.'

'It's not electricity, it's electronics,' William protested. 'They're two separate things.'

Mr Bagthorpe could not be brought to see this. A man who will not carry a calculator, despite his lack of arithmetic, because he insists that it is giving off dangerous radioactive rays inside his pocket, is unlikely to appreciate any fine shades of meaning in the scientific field.

'Electricity – electronics – what's the difference?' he said. 'I am disappointed in the way you are all reacting. There will be no malingering. It is also possible to generate electricity from a windmill, and you had better look into that as well. We cannot afford to waste anything, even the wind.'

There now fell a silence – a rare occurrence at a Bagthorpe meal. Everyone present – with the exception of Grandma and Mr Bagthorpe himself – was now thoroughly frightened. It was becoming clearer by the minute that Mr Bagthorpe was in deadly earnest. There was not even any point in sending for Dr Winters. He had made it clear enough in the past that he considered Mr Bagthorpe mad, and that he was not interested in treating this condition. He probably thought it untreatable.

The silence was eventually broken by the sound of spurting gravel from the other side of the house. Mrs Bagthorpe instantly leapt up and hurried to greet the visitors.

'Russell – Celia – thank heaven you are here!' Jack heard her say. 'Do come and see if you can do anything with Henry!'

'He has not, I hope, been standing on his head again?' came Uncle Parker's voice.

'I can hear you!' yelled Mr Bagthorpe. 'Come on in here! It's no good hatching things up out there!'

Mrs Bagthorpe re-entered, followed by Uncle Parker, Aunt Celia and Daisy, the latter almost totally eclipsed by a large, beribboned parcel.

'Hallo, all!' Uncle Parker greeted them affably. 'Hallo, Grandma. Daisy's got something for you.'

Daisy advanced and plonked her parcel in front of

Grandma, dislodging a plate as she did so. It fell to the floor and shattered.

'Oh *dear*!' squealed Daisy.

'You will pay for that, Russell,' said Mr Bagthorpe. 'We can no longer afford to underwrite your daughter's destructive behaviour. Does she go *anywhere* without wreaking havoc?'

'Hush, Henry!' cried Aunt Celia. 'Daisy has an offering for Mother. Do not spoil the moment!'

'Here you are, Grandma Bag,' squeaked Daisy. 'It's for you and it's a surprise because the other one got broke.'

The Bagthorpes watched numbly as Grandma pulled off the wrappings. They knew well what to expect. Uncle Parker had obviously commissioned a second replica of the late and sainted Thomas, to replace the one that had crashed in a shower of maggots at the Family Reunion. As the final tissues fell aside their fears were confirmed. The present offering was if anything larger, gingerier and more malevolent-looking than its predecessor.

'It is beautiful!' cried Grandma predictably. 'Oh darling Daisy! The child is an angel!'

No one said anything to this, because the statement was not even debatable. Daisy was *not* an angel. She was on the contrary, as all the Bagthorpes knew to their cost, the inevitable harbinger and purveyor of doom. Her influence was such that Mr Bagthorpe had once suggested, in all seriousness, that what she really needed was exorcising. He had even offered to telephone the rector himself and arrange the ceremony.

'Desperate situations need desperate remedies,' he had asserted. 'Bell, book and candle is our last ditch.'

'It's from Arry Awk as well!' Daisy burbled, hopping from foot to foot, 'and we're going to look for a *real* Thomas for you, Daddy says.'

Grandma had no opportunity to voice her thanks to Arry Awk, even if she had been so disposed, because Mr Bagthorpe's oar was in in a flash.

'He is *what*?' he demanded.

'Thought it more or less my moral duty, d'you see,' explained Uncle Parker, who had been looking forward to observing Mr Bagthorpe's reaction to this news.

Uncle Parker's two main interests in life were driving round the countryside in a fast car like a bat out of hell, and goading Mr Bagthorpe. The former practice had resulted, some years previously, in the untimely death in the drive of Unicorn House of Thomas, a villainous ginger tom who had, Grandma maintained, been the light of her life. She also asserted that he was irreplaceable, which was why Uncle Parker had not immediately offered to replace him.

He had (after allowing a suitable period of mourning) cunningly commissioned a pot life-sized replica of the original Thomas as a gift to Grandma, with the intention of following this up by the real thing. Nothing, he knew, would enrage Mr Bagthorpe more – even though he did not yet know that the latter had now embarked on a Master Plan for Survival in which there would be no place for non-productive livestock.

'Moral duty?' echoed Mr Bagthorpe incredulously. 'Moral—? Do you even know the *meaning* of the words?'

'I will look them up the moment I return home,' Uncle Parker promised. 'What do you say, Grandma? What about another shining purring jewel of a cat?'

'Aha!' yelled Mr Bagthorpe. '*Now* I've got it! Now I know what you're up to!'

Mr Bagthorpe, in his state of acute paranoia, and being alerted by certain key words in Uncle Parker's offer, had smelled a plot.

'It is a plot! A diabolical, malicious, well-laid plot!' he yelled. 'Think you'll kill two birds with one stone, don't you?'

'Er – which two birds were those, Henry?' queried Uncle Parker, delicately adjusting his cravat.

'My mother,' said Mr Bagthorpe carefully, making a real effort to control his voice and achieve Uncle Parker's kind of air of careless ease, 'has transferred her affections from that horrible dead cat to your daughter. Oh yes! Don't bother to deny it. It is common knowledge in this household, and strikes the fear of God into us all. What I suggest is that you, Russell, and you, Celia, are yourselves becoming uneasy about the situation. Though I may as well say that in my opinion your fears are groundless. In my opinion, Mother is more likely to fall under the pernicious influence of your accursed daughter than vice versa.'

'Russell!' wailed Aunt Celia faintly. 'Do not let him slander darling Daisy thus!'

'You will hear me out,' continued Mr Bagthorpe grimly. 'You have, as I say, become alarmed by the effects of this Unholy Alliance between the pair of them – and with just cause. *We're* all alarmed – some of us are nearly out of our minds. So what you are patently trying to do is retransfer Mother's affection from your daughter back to another hell-ridden and malignant ginger tom. You will thus kill two birds with one stone. You will have put your own house in order, and at one and the same time thrown my own into purgatory.'

He paused for breath. His entire audience was listening fascinated to this laying bare of Uncle Parker's deepest motives. Jack was particularly interested in the way Mr Bagthorpe, whether consciously or not, avoided referring to Daisy by name. He did this with Zero as well. It helped him to pretend to himself that neither of them existed.

'Your scheme has failed,' Mr Bagthorpe then continued. 'It has been exposed. I am all for cutting off all relations between that pair, and indeed for your confining your daughter and her everlasting Arry Awk to your own premises in perpetuity. But if you seriously intend to acquire some non-productive, non-milk, egg-or cheese-producing beast to add to this menage, then I am telling you, here and now, that the whole thing will boomerang on you, like *The Monkey's Paw.*'

He paused again.

'Which is – er – which is to say?' prompted Uncle Parker.

'Which is to say,' said Mr Bagthorpe triumphantly, 'that Mother, along with her Fortnum and Mason hamper and her familiar, will depart hence. She will go, Russell, to yourself and Celia.'

The company sat and pondered this ultimatum. In the resulting silence Daisy's voice, from somewhere outside, was heard. It was saying:

'Poor fing. Poor fing. Dusters to dusters and ashes to ashes!'

Mr Bagthorpe groaned.

4

It later transpired that Daisy had now entered a new Phase. Uncle Parker called it a Morbid Phase, but Aunt Celia insisted that it was an Intimations of Mortality Phase. Under whatever label, what it meant, principally, was that Daisy was now holding funerals. Sometimes she held only one a day, at other times several. It depended mainly on what she could find to bury. She took these ceremonies very seriously, and tried as far as possible to dress for her part. On the present occasion, for instance, she had taken advantage of the disorganization in the kitchen to bear off a long Indian frock of Mrs Bagthorpe's that was airing on a rail, and a striped tea towel. She was swathed in the frock and wore the towel on her head. She said that she thought her outfit looked religious, and that vicars always wore long frocks.

What Daisy was burying no one thought to inquire at the time, as the ceremony was almost complete when they all rushed out to see what was happening. They stopped more or less in their tracks at the sight of Daisy in her borrowed vestments. She was scattering earth into a small hole and had real tears running down her face. There could be little doubt that this new Phase was a serious one.

'Goodbye, goodbye!' she wailed, flinging the last fistfuls of earth into the grave. 'Where are you gone now, poor little fing?'

This question struck her audience as rhetorical, and no one attempted to offer a reply.

'Darling child!' cried Aunt Celia, and she swayed forward to embrace her daughter, thereby collecting a good deal of damp soil on her own frock, and inciting Mr Bagthorpe's further wrath.

'Ye gods!' he exclaimed in disgust. 'What more must I endure? That child, Russell, is in urgent need of treatment. You are mad. She is mad.' Then, after a pause, 'They are mad.'

He was declining the verb to deaf ears.

'Come, Daisy,' Grandma said. 'You must not be upset. Come to my room, and you shall have some sugared almonds.'

Daisy instantly disengaged herself from her mother's embrace.

'I can't come, Grandma Bag,' she cried. 'I've got to do the *writing* yet.'

The writing was in fact one of the parts of her burials that Daisy enjoyed most. It meant composing a fitting epitaph for each of her various victims. She was very original in her choice of monuments, as the Bagthorpes were later to discover to their cost. Mr Bagthorpe said that the people who ran Highgate Cemetery could learn a lot from her. On this occasion she had appropriated a black non-stick baking sheet from Mrs Fosdyke's cupboard, and intended to chalk on it.

'You'll have to go away,' she told them all. 'I can't fink and write poems when there's people there.'

They all obediently trooped back indoors, and Mr Bagthorpe went straight into his study and banged the door.

'Poor Henry, he has no panache,' remarked Grandma. 'I shall accept the offer of a cat, Russell.'

'Really?' Uncle Parker was non-plussed. 'But do you *really* want to come and live at The Knoll?'

'I do not intend to,' she replied calmly, 'though I thank you for the invitation.'

'Correct me if I am wrong,' said Uncle Parker, 'but I was under the distinct impression that Henry laid down—'

'I care nothing for Henry and his idle threats,' Grandma told him. 'Next week, his Aunt Lucy is coming to visit. He is hoping, as you will know, to figure largely in her will. If he is seen as a man who drives helpless and ageing female relations out into the night, he will receive not a penny. Henry can be discounted. I shall have a cat, and I shall stop here.'

'But, Mother,' protested Mrs Bagthorpe weakly, 'you always said that Thomas was irreplaceable, and unique.'

She feared, as did her whole family, that Thomas had *not* been unique, and that a ginger tom quite as hateful and toothy would be produced.

'Time heals,' Grandma said sanctimoniously. 'I shall accept a substitute. I shall probably call him Thomas the Second. I shall establish a dynasty.'

'You'll have to train him to do something, Grandma,' Rosie told her. 'Father said we'd all got to do something.'

'Do I take it that Henry has gone off again at one of his unaccountable tangents?' asked Uncle Parker.

'Oh Russell, it is dreadful!' Mrs Bagthorpe told him. 'Henry has become quite unhinged at the sight of his latest bank statement, on which a large number of noughts had been printed in error. He has decided that we must become self-sufficient. He intends to till the soil and buy chickens and cook everything in straw. It is dreadful!'

'Cheer up, Laura. Ten to one the whole thing'll have blown over in a couple of days,' Uncle Parker inaccurately forecast. 'You know Henry. Who better? Where, by the way, is the ubiquitous Mrs Fosdyke?'

'Gone home,' William said glumly. 'Father told her to take the afternoon off.'

'And I've got to make a *blancmange*,' put in Tess disgustedly.

'And we've all got to live on rhubarb and beetroot until something else comes up,' wailed Rosie.

'Henry has said that we must dispense with Mrs Fosdyke's services,' Mrs Bagthorpe informed him. 'But I am absolutely against it. On this point I shall remain quite adamant. Without Mrs Fosdyke, there would be no Problems.'

'Well, well!' Uncle Parker was by now impressed by the way things were going. 'Henry is the last person on earth I should have thought of as self-sufficient. We must hope that the novelty will soon pall on him. In the meantime, Celia and myself will be delighted to slip you the odd food parcel, and so forth.'

They all thanked him fervently.

'We must now be on our way,' Uncle Parker said. 'We must find a second Thomas.'

Outside, Daisy seemed to be winding up her service. She was singing *All Things Bright and Beautiful.*

'But cannot darling Daisy stop with me?' asked Grandma. Aunt Celia was not in favour of this.

'I cannot abandon my only child to a man who is raving,' she declared. 'And to who knows what unwholesome diet.'

'Nonsense, Celia!' Grandma said sharply. 'Henry is not raving. He is merely temporarily deranged, as he often is. And I do not imagine that we shall be reduced to a diet of rhubarb and beetroot in the immediate future. Surely the deep freeze and the larder are adequately stocked, Laura?'

'Of course,' replied Mrs Bagthorpe. 'As a matter of fact, I removed a chicken from the deep freeze only this morning, and shall casserole it tomorrow.'

The younger Bagthorpes cheered up considerably at this intelligence.

'Daisy will enjoy Mother's company, Celia dearest,' Uncle Parker told her. He had been subjected to a continuous procession of funerals in the past few days, and was ready for a rest from it.

Daisy herself then trotted in. She quickly pulled off the borrowed frock and tea towel and seemed all at once business-like again.

'That was a lovely funeral,' she told everyone. 'Poor little fing.'

Had the Bagthorpes not been in so bemused a state, they might have made inquiries as to whom or what Daisy had in fact been interring. When they did make the discovery, they were unanimous in heartily wishing *her* dead. On being asked whether she would like to stop at Unicorn House for a few days, she assented vigorously.

'You can help me with my funerals, Grandma Bag,' she offered generously. 'You can even dig.'

She waved a large, mud-covered serving spoon she had evidently also abstracted while the rest were preoccupied and off their guard.

'You can help me sow seeds, Daisy,' said Rosie, who was jealous of Daisy's friendship with Grandma. 'Then, when they've grown, you can help me pick things.'

'Are you not being a little optimistic?' said Tess. 'I know of no seeds other than cress that can be sown and harvested within the week. However, I have a paranormal experiment I wish to conduct, and will use your seeds as guinea-pigs, so to speak.'

The Parkers then departed, and the Unholy Alliance went up to Grandma's room for a conference. Mr

Bagthorpe emerged from his study shortly afterwards, brandishing a rota he had drawn up. During his absence, Mrs Bagthorpe had told her offspring that she thought it best if, at any rate for the time being, they co-operated with him.

'Russell may well be right,' she said hopefully, 'and this will turn out to be a mere whim, or a Passing Phase.'

Mrs Bagthorpe had a strong tendency to Positive Thinking, and believed touchingly in its power. The thoroughness with which Mr Bagthorpe had already plotted his Plan for Survival did not strike any of the others as looking much like a whim. It bore all the hallmarks of an all-out Bagthorpian obsession.

William was despatched on a bus to Aysham with orders to return with every single library book he could lay his hands on related to market gardening, chicken rearing, pig keeping, household economics and so forth. Every member of the family had to send back his or her current loans, whether or not they had been read.

'We need every ticket we possess,' Mr Bagthorpe told them. 'And moreover, there will in future be no time for people to lie around reading library books. We shall be peasants. Peasants do not lie around reading library books.'

Rosie was dismissed with strict instructions to dispose forth-with of the Great Bagthorpe Daisy chain still draped about the garden. Her protests were useless.

'There will be no room for anything ornamental in this garden,' he announced. 'That chain is neither use nor ornament. The front lawn will be ploughed up.'

Mrs Bagthorpe opened her mouth to protest about this but closed it again, remembering that she was supposed to appear to co-operate. She sat breathing very deeply as her husband continued.

'You, Tess, can go and clear all the rubble out of the summer house. Hens do not require deckchairs and parasols, and nor shall we, from now on. You, Jack, can get a spade and dig up the strawberry bed.'

Mrs Bagthorpe opened her mouth again, and closed it.

'Strawberries are a luxury we can no longer afford,' he continued. 'A large area of ground is devoted to a crop that is unproductive for eleven months out of twelve. We shall now rotate crops. We shall plant potatoes there. Get started, the lot of you. I shall go back to my desk and work out further details.'

'What shall I do?' asked Mrs Bagthorpe faintly.

'Make some chutney,' he advised her. 'Pickle some beetroot. Anything.'

'Just a minute,' William said. 'What about Grandma and Grandpa? What're *they* doing?'

'The former will be worse than useless to us,' replied his father. 'The most we can hope for is eventually to starve her out. And I do not at present have time to explain to Father what is happening.'

Grandpa was deaf, but nobody was sure to quite

what degree. Uncle Parker maintained that he was S.D. – Selectively Deaf. This meant that he heard, in effect, what he wanted to hear. In that case, Jack thought, it was likely that Grandpa never would understand what was now going on. He would not *want* to know.

The family scattered on its respective missions. Jack found his own task depressing.

'I think it's really terrible, digging up strawberries,' he told Zero, who lay watching him. 'You wouldn't know, old chap, but they're really nice. Especially with cream. I wonder if goats have cream?'

Tess kept going past, staggering under armfuls of deckchairs and other garden furniture. She seemed to be carrying on a muttered, incomprehensible monologue. Jack thought it probable that she was swearing in French. Every now and then Rosie trundled mournfully by with a wheelbarrow full of rapidly decomposing daisies.

'I shall still do a mural anyway!' she yelled defiantly on one such trip. 'I don't need to *see* the daisies. I can imagine them.'

Jack felt sympathetic towards this project.

'The only thing is, Rosie,' he said, 'what about paints? I mean, how many have you got left?'

'Why?' she demanded, staring.

'Because,' Jack told her wisely, 'Father is never going to let you buy any. You can't eat them, you see. They're non-productive. What I think you ought to do is start looking for berries and barks and things, like the cavemen did. You ought to get some wood and stuff.'

Rosie seemed impressed by this advice, and was evidently acting on it, because after the final load of daisies had been wheeled by, Jack caught occasional glimpses of her squeezing flowers between her fingers, or piggling at the bark of trees. He felt quite pleased and flattered by this.

'P'raps you and me are going to be quite good at this Survival thing,' he told an apparently uninterested Zero. 'If I get really good at it, it'd count as a String to my Bow. I bet Father'd let me count it.'

Jack had never quite given up hoping that one day he would have Strings to his Bow, like the others. He knew that he was not, and never would be, outstandingly clever or talented, but it seemed to him that he might well be good at Surviving. He was no more attracted than anyone else by the prospect of living on lettuce and water, and working his fingers to the bone. But if the thing was inevitable, he thought he might as well throw himself into it wholeheartedly. He could at least be on level terms with his siblings. Survival, he could see, was a great equalizer.

When the Bagthorpes forgathered at tea-time, only Jack himself, Mr Bagthorpe and the Unholy Alliance could be described as anything near cheerful. Everyone else looked tired and sullen. (Grandpa had gone fishing with firm instructions from Mr Bagthorpe to catch as many as possible large, edible fish.) Tess said that she had almost certainly slipped a disc carrying deckchairs, and would never be able to perform a Judo fall again. Rosie's arms and hands were indelibly stained with murky shades of crimson and tan, and bore a network of scratches. Mrs Bagthorpe had been making chutney and the whole ground floor smelled of hot vinegar. The food itself was hardly appetising. Tess had forgotten about the blancmange until late afternoon, and it was still warm, as well as unmistakably watery. Even Mr Bagthorpe had to force it down.

'This will be a tonic to us all,' he informed his unconvinced audience. 'We have been taking in far too much cholesterol. We shall soon reap the benefits in increased mental alertness and bodily vigour. Our brains are all furred up with cholesterol.'

Mr Bagthorpe was not really very strong on dietetics, and never succeeded in acquiring any sort of mastery of the subject. He used the expression 'furring up' a lot, and said that most modern foods did this, ranging from white bread through tinned fruit to ice cream. The opposite of these, and therefore beneficial to the system, were commodities that 'thin your blood down'. According to him, dandelion leaves did this, and also beetroot, rhubarb, and neat whisky. He was almost as confused as Mrs Fosdyke herself about vitamins, and maintained that they were 'alive'. He said this was why fruit should be eaten fresh. It was no good eating it, he said, when the vitamins were 'dead'. It could even be harmful. 'You would not wish to digest the contents of a charnel house,' he told them, 'and that is what you do when you eat a wizened apple.'

He also immovably contended that tea and coffee both stained your insides brown, and were detrimental to health. When the others said that they did not care what colour their insides were, he launched into a long and stern lecture about the way England had started to go downhill after the introduction into the country of these enervating foreign beverages.

'The honest English yeoman quaffed only ale, in large quantities,' he declared. 'It is how the British character was formed.'

This was lucky for Mr Bagthorpe, since he was the only member of the family who enjoyed drinking beer. (He was later, and with disastrous consequences, to begin brewing his own.) He told them to drink at least a gallon a day of water, which was full of oxygen, and would invigorate them. When they voiced their doubts about this theory, he asked triumphantly how, in that case, fish managed to survive? As piscatology was a String to nobody's Bow, the family were for the time being unable to come up with a satisfactory answer to this, though they were convinced there was one.

During this first meal since the Plan for Survival had been put into operation, Mr Bagthorpe was not yet fully into his stride about food values, and even let Tess open a tin of peaches, saying that the sooner such tainted food was eaten and out of the way, the better. He was beginning, Jack thought, to sound dangerously like the Sainted Aunt. The only difference was that the latter really believed in vegetarianism, whereas Mr Bagthorpe was just out to save money.

As they were stolidly making their way through this depressing meal, the telephone rang. Mrs Bagthorpe went out into the hall to answer it, and returned quite soon.

'An exact date has been fixed for Aunt Lucy's visit,' she announced. 'She is to arrive the day after tomorrow. I said that you, Henry, would meet her at the station at twelve noon.'

Nobody brightened perceptibly at this news.

'She didn't say anything about grated carrots and nuts, and such, did she?' William asked hopefully. If great Aunt Lucy liked food of a rich and unwholesome sort, then with any luck, the whole family would benefit.

'Not a word,' his mother told him.

The younger Bagthorpes reverted to gloom.

'If you ask me,' said Rosie dolefully, more or less voicing the thoughts of them all, 'this family's got a curse on it. Nothing ever goes right.'

'I agree,' Mr Bagthorpe told her. 'I am glad that you can see this. I am not so paranoic as I first feared. The whole world is ranged up against us out there. But we shall defy it. We shall gird up our loins. We shall survive.'

5

The following day Mrs Bagthorpe made a point of rising and going downstairs early, to be sure of seeing Mrs Fosdyke and explaining the situation before Mr Bagthorpe himself came down. She was not at all certain how she was going to do this explaining, and spent longer than usual on her Yoga and Breathing in the hope that they would stand her in good stead during the forthcoming ordeal. It seemed to Mrs Bagthorpe that it was going to be no easy matter to explain the situation in such a way that it would not sound lunatic.

It was unfortunate that Mrs Fosdyke herself was in no mood for receiving news of a direful and unsettling nature. She had remembered, while tossing restlessly during the night, certain fragments of Mr Bagthorpe's description of life as lived by Aunt Lucy in Torquay. She *thought* she had remembered these, but turning them over in her mind as she scurried from the village in the cold light of day, she felt that she must have remembered wrongly.

'Nobody could be that downright mad,' she told herself, though without real conviction.

What Mr Bagthorpe had said was that Aunt Lucy did not believe in Time, and accordingly tried to sabotage it. One of her methods of doing this was to have several clocks in every room of her considerable mansion, all showing different times. The combined incessant ticking, chiming and ringing of these were, he had said, a refined form of the Chinese water torture. A further inconvenience occasioned by this particular Bee in Aunt Lucy's bonnet, was that there were no regular mealtimes. She tried to fool the Time by dodging about with these, and it was no unusual thing, he said, if she were in a particularly perky mood, to find oneself tucking into buttered crumpets and China tea at eleven thirty at night, after the test card on television had disappeared and given way to a high-pitched whine. He had also, he claimed, been served with grilled kippers and toast at three in the afternoon, following on the heels of a supper served only an hour previously. Whether she had Time on the hop he did not know, he said, but judging by his own disorientation, it seemed likely.

'When the final trump sounds,' he said, 'it will be centuries ahead of schedule, and brought on by Aunt Lucy.'

Mrs Fosdyke had further memories of accounts of Mr Bagthorpe's nocturnal battles with the clocks ranged about his own room. He had buried clocks in drawers, stuffed socks into the works, and attempted to bend the chimes. On one occasion he had returned home with two of Aunt Lucy's alarm clocks, which he had wrapped in his dressing-gown and stowed in his suitcase in an attempt to muffle their particularly penetrating ticks. Fortunately, such was the plethora of timepieces in the house, these had not been missed, and he had been able to smuggle them back (wound down) on a subsequent visit.

None of this was any comfort to Mrs Fosdyke. As she hedge-hogged along she prepared a speech to Mrs Bagthorpe in which she would make clear that in this matter there would be no co-operation forthcoming from herself.

'If they think I'm coming in to fry bacon at midnight and be serving roasts and three veg at dawn, then they'll have to look elsewhere,' she thought. '*And* I shall have to make inquiries about the full moon.'

Aunt Lucy, she definitely recalled, was affected by the moon, and knew it. Mr Bagthorpe had given descriptions of how she would roam about the house blocking out every chink of light, and stuffing dusters into cracks, and as often as not would sleep through the daytime during critical phases, so that she could be wide awake during the hours of darkness and able to fend off the sinister influences of the moon's rays. (This, of course, fooled the Time, too.)

Mrs Fosdyke was no expert on madness, despite her years with the Bagthorpes, but did know that lunacy was connected with the full moon. She was an addict of Dracula and Frankenstein films, but preferred her madness and horror on a screen, safely partitioned from life as actually lived. She harboured no ambitions to meet mad persons roaming about with hatchets and newly grown incisors.

'It's no part of my duties,' she told herself firmly. She knew she would have to stand her ground very firmly when she confronted the Bagthorpes.

Mrs Bagthorpe, then, was already in the kitchen making herself a fortifying cup of coffee when Mrs Fosdyke entered, her lately rehearsed speech still fresh in her mind.

'Ah, good morning, Mrs Fosdyke,' Mrs Bagthorpe greeted her with a determined smile, behind which, had she been a student of human nature, Mrs Fosdyke would have detected desperation.

'Good morning, I'm sure,' she parried, in tones that implied that it was not, of course, anything of the sort. She went scooting through her routine of whipping off coat and headscarf and exchanging shoes for slippers, and Mrs Bagthorpe waited apprehensively.

'Ah!' she exclaimed brightly, as Mrs Fosdyke approached the sink for the first skirmish of the day with the dishes. 'I was hoping to have a word with you, Mrs Fosdyke.'

'I was hoping to have one with you, as well, Mrs Bagthorpe,' countered Mrs Fosdyke. 'About that old woman at Torquay.'

'Ah, well, I think I can answer your query about that,' Mrs Bagthorpe told her smilingly. 'She is to arrive tomorrow, at noon, and will be here in good time for luncheon.'

'Time for lunch for some it might be,' said Mrs

Fosdyke ominously. 'Time for lunch for ordinary mortals, I dare say.'

'Why, whatever do you mean?' cried Mrs Bagthorpe. 'Surely we normally take luncheon at one?'

'*You* do,' Mrs Fosdyke told her. 'It's that old woman. Roast and three veg in the middle of the night, Mr Bagthorpe said. I heard him. Only last time he went there. And buttered crumpets in the—'

'Oh really!' exclaimed Mrs Bagthorpe, with an attempt at a gay laugh. 'Surely you did not take that seriously? Surely you know Mr Bagthorpe's little jokes by now?'

'Oh, I know them, all right,' Mrs Fosdyke agreed, 'and not funny, neither, most of 'em. I shall have to give notice, Mrs Bagthorpe, that I shall be putting meals on tables at the times I always have. I take a pride in my meals, Mrs Bagthorpe, as you know.'

'Indeed, yes!' said Mrs Bagthorpe fervently, her brow clouding a little as she thought of the news she had herself to impart regarding meals that were to be variations on a theme of spring onions, lettuce, beetroot and rhubarb. 'So that is quite settled, Mrs Fosdyke.'

'That's all right, then,' assented Mrs Fosdyke grudgingly. 'She won't be stopping long, will she?'

'Oh I am sure not,' Mrs Bagthorpe assured her. 'Just for a day or two. She is quite elderly, you know – eighty-seven – and at that age, of course, there is no place like home.'

She felt pleased with this last speech which sounded,

even to her own ears, reassuring and sensible in the manner of Stella Bright.

'Because there's a full moon on the eleventh,' continued Mrs Fosdyke in dark tones, and on what seemed to Mrs Bagthorpe a quite inconsequential tack.

'Really?' Mrs Bagthorpe replied politely. She then made a determined effort to steer the conversation into the channels she had herself intended. 'What I really wanted to have a word with you about, was one or two changes in household arrangements.'

'Oh yes?' said Mrs Fosdyke unhelpfully.

'The fact of the matter is,' began Mrs Bagthorpe delicately, 'that household expenses have been rather heavy of late. And what with inflation, and the cost of living, and one thing and another, my husband and I think it advisable to make certain changes.'

'Oh yes?' said Mrs Fosdyke again. If the foregoing had been the introduction to her own dismissal, she was certainly not going to help matters along.

'For one thing, we thought we should make more extensive use of garden produce,' said Mrs Bagthorpe brightly.

'And what would that be?' inquired Mrs Fosdyke, beginning to set out plates and cutlery in preparation for breakfast.

'Well, to begin with, there is a row of perfectly delicious cos lettuce,' commenced Mrs Bagthorpe.

'Oh yes?'

'And then . . . then there is some beetroot. Which, of course, can either be eaten in a salad, or pickled.'

On this Mrs Fosdyke made no comment. Encouraged, Mrs Bagthorpe went on.

'Then there are some spring onions, I believe. And a very large crop of rhubarb.'

Mrs Fosdyke turned and faced her employer.

'Is it salad you're wanting tonight, then?' she asked. 'And stewed rhubarb with custard?'

'Well – yes, certainly,' Mrs Bagthorpe floundered. 'But – not *only* tonight. Quite frequently, you understand. Until we have exhausted the supplies.'

In the silence that followed, Mrs Bagthorpe thought helplessly that she would have to postpone the matter of cooking everything in straw to a later occasion. There was clearly a limit to how much Mrs Fosdyke was going to take in at present.

'Often,' said Mrs Fosdyke at length. 'You mean you want 'em often?'

'That is quite right, Mrs Fosdyke,' affirmed Mrs Bagthorpe with relief. 'And of course we shall immediately begin to grow other crops, to make for a more varied and nutritious menu.'

She decided to stop short of the cow and chickens for the time being, too.

'There won't be a deal you can do with them,' Mrs Fosdyke observed with perfect truth. 'You can't do much ringing the changes with beetroot and rhubarb.'

'That I quite understand,' Mrs Bagthorpe agreed, 'and you will certainly not find us unappreciative of your efforts to do so.'

'Well, up to you, of course.' Mrs Fosdyke shrugged her shoulders. 'You'll not be going vegitinarian, I hope?'

'Oh, *indeed* not!' Mrs Bagthorpe was glad that she could wholeheartedly make this assurance at least. 'As a matter of fact, I took a chicken out of the deep freeze only yesterday, and thought we would casserole it for lunch.'

'Hmm. Best get started on that, then,' Mrs Fosdyke said.

She went into the pantry and began to rummage about for her ingredients, and Mrs Bagthorpe, with a sigh of relief, sank back and began to drink her coffee.

'Things will not be so bad, after all,' she told herself Positively. 'The worst is now over.'

It was not.

'Where did you say you'd put that chicken?' Mrs Fosdyke's voice broke into Mrs Bagthorpe's self-congratulatory reverie.

'What? Oh – the chicken. Surely – on the side, Mrs Fosdyke.'

She rose.

'At least, I think . . .' she eyed dubiously the empty work-top. 'I may have put it in the fridge, later . . . we had rather a trying day yesterday. Now where . . . ?'

She stooped to examine the contents of the refrigerator.

'Extraordinary . . .' she murmured. Mrs Fosdyke had gone back into the pantry.

'Not in 'ere!' she called. 'Found it, 'ave you?'

'No. No, I have not,' admitted Mrs Bagthorpe. 'But the whole thing is quite absurd. I removed the chicken from the deep freeze, I placed it – I placed it somewhere *here* . . . and then . . .' her voice trailed away. She really had no inkling of the bird's movements beyond this juncture.

Mr Bagthorpe then entered, followed closely by Jack and William.

'Ah, Henry!' his wife greeted him. 'Perhaps you can throw some light on the matter.'

'What matter?' he demanded ungraciously.

'Mrs Fosdyke and I have mislaid a chicken,' she told him.

'And what, Laura, in the name of all that is wonderful, do you suppose *I* would do with a chicken?' he asked her.

'Well – nothing, of course, dear,' she faltered. 'I simply thought . . .'

'Simply nothing,' came the terse rejoinder. 'In this house, nothing is simple.'

'No, dear, of course not. But it *is* all such a mystery. You see, I moved this chicken from the deep freeze, and I placed it—'

'When?' interrupted William. He, in company with Jack, was more interested in the whereabouts of the missing chicken than was their father. They had both dreamed of it, a gravied oasis in a desert of lettuce and beetroot.

'Yesterday morning.' She was becoming a little desperate. 'I remember it quite distinctly. You may have noticed it standing on the side yourself, Mrs Fosdyke?'

'I might've,' Mrs Fosdyke said non-committally. 'I can't say I remember.'

'But I did, I definitely did,' Mrs Bagthorpe insisted. 'I *mentioned* it, you may remember?'

'You mentioned it, all right,' Jack told her reassuringly. 'You said you were going to put it in a casserole.'

'That's right! There!' she cried gratefully.

Her husband favoured her with a cool stare.

'Then where *have* you put it, Laura?' he inquired. 'Could it be that you have casseroled it already, and forgotten?'

'Oh Henry, do be *serious*!' Mrs Bagthorpe tried at all times to keep her sense of perspective, but could feel it now blurring into virtual invisibility.

'Let's do a recap,' William intervened. 'Reconstruct the thing. You took the chicken out in the morning. Right?'

'Right,' his mother agreed.

'And Mrs Fosdyke did not witness this, so at present we have only your word for it. Mrs Fosdyke went home.'

'I never asked to!' Mrs Fosdyke put in loudly.

'We then had lunch. As we finished, Uncle Parker came.'

'And Aunt Celia. *And* Daisy.' Jack said.

There was a sudden chill pause.

'*And* Daisy,' Jack repeated.

'Who held a funeral,' William supplied in flat tones. He sat down suddenly.

'But *surely* . . . ?' Mrs Bagthorpe faltered. 'Oh – I'm sure you are wrong!'

Followed closely by Jack, she hurried to the outer door, to Mrs Fosdyke's extreme mystification.

Jack and his mother stood and stared at Daisy's epitaph, chalked on to a non-stick black baking sheet:

Higledy pigledy pore ded hen
Yore fethers will nevver cum back agen.
1763–1800

Jack read this inscription out loud, to convince himself.

'Oh my God!' Mr Bagthorpe was now behind them. 'Even unto the grave!'

William and Mrs Fosdyke had now joined them round the newly dug grave.

'Whatever . . . ? That's my best non-stick baking—!' Mrs Fosdyke snatched up the monument and began to wipe off the inscription with her wrap-around pinafore. Jack, oddly, found himself fleetingly shocked by this desecration.

'So our dinner is under there, we can take it?' said Mr Bagthorpe unnecessarily. There could be no escaping this conclusion.

'The bird was, after all, dead,' said Mrs Bagthorpe feebly, 'and to the child it must have seemed the most natural thing in the world to bury it. She was weeping, Henry.'

'*I* am almost weeping,' he informed her, unmoved by this reminder of his niece's tenderheartedness. 'I shall telephone Russell at once.'

He left the graveside, cursing under his breath. It occurred to Jack that while it had been his father's idea to follow a policy of eating spring onions and rhubarb, he could hardly have been looking forward to this, any more than anybody else. The casseroled chicken must have appeared to him, too, a welcome landmark in such a diet.

'You mean to say,' came the disbelieving voice of Mrs Fosdyke (who did not, after all, know that Daisy had gone into a new Phase of Intimations of Mortality), 'that that Daisy's dug that bird into the *soil*?'

'I – I fear so, Mrs Fosdyke,' Mrs Bagthorpe told her faintly. 'But we must try not to be too harsh in our judgement. The bird was, after all, dead, and must have appeared to her—'

'You've already said that Mother,' said William coldly. What he really wished was that the hen was in the casserole, and Daisy in the grave.

'I don't believe—!' came Mrs Fosdyke's voice

flatly. 'Here!' She bent, and began to scrabble at the earth with her fingers.

'Ugh!' she screeched, and fell back.

Gleaming through the disturbed soil was the nude, pale pink and mottled skin of what was, unmistakably, an oven-ready chicken.

Mrs Bagthorpe shuddered. Even Jack felt as if he would never be able to face a cooked chicken again. He had never thought of one as a *corpse* before. He, too, wished Daisy dead and buried.

Mrs Fosdyke stood stockstill, goggling with shock.

'I don't believe it!' she said at last. And then, genuinely mystified, 'That Daisy – wherever does she get her ideas?'

'I don't know, Mrs Fosdyke,' replied Mrs Bagthorpe truthfully. 'She is certainly a most original child.'

'Original!' Mrs Fosdyke was disgusted.

'Original *and* tiresome,' qualified Mrs Bagthorpe, though Jack could see that from Mrs Fosdyke's point of view, even this description came nowhere near doing justice to the case.

'It'll have to *stop* buried, that is certain,' remarked Mrs Fosdyke. 'And what'll you be having with the veg, Mrs Bagthorpe? And it's to be hoped that dog of yours don't go ferreting down there and dragging chickens with soil on into my kitchen.'

'He won't,' Jack promised. 'He doesn't like digging things up.'

When the news of Daisy's latest exercise in creativity spread to the rest of the household, feelings ran high. Only Grandma, possibly feeling secure in the prospect of a Fortnum and Mason hamper, seemed unmoved by it.

'Celia has unwittingly produced a genius,' she told the others. 'You had better look to your laurels.'

Daisy herself was very upset by the hostile reaction to her funeral, and about having her gravestone removed and wiped.

'Poor little dead fing!' she sobbed. 'He was all cold and pimply and no feathers. Nobody cares!'

This was not strictly true. The Bagthorpes did care, deeply. Attitudes towards Daisy hardened further. To be ranged up against the whole world was in itself a considerable prospect, but now, it appeared, there was a saboteur within their very walls. The outlook ahead was bleak.

6

Before setting off to meet Aunt Lucy at the station, Mr Bagthorpe gathered his family together and gave them a thorough briefing.

'Have it clear in your minds,' he told them, 'that our whole future as a united family depends on this visit.'

'*Are* we united?' William asked.

'That is precisely the kind of unwarranted levity we can do without in the present crisis,' his father told him. 'We are united in the sense that we are, as yet, under one roof. Unless Aunt Lucy comes up with a fairly hefty contribution in the fairly near future, we shall be split up and sent to the four corners of the earth. We shall have to throw our lives upon the State.'

'Oh *Henry*!' his wife protested. 'Surely you are exaggerating!'

'Your trouble, Laura,' he told her, 'is that you have a congenital predisposition to look on the bright side of things. It is lucky that you have me to redress the balance. Furthermore, you will all show signs of determination and strength of character, whether or not you possess them.'

Jack wondered exactly how one should behave in order to be seen to possess these qualities, but did not like to ask.

'As for you,' Mr Bagthorpe addressed himself to Grandma now, 'you will forthwith desist from perpetually throwing spanners into the works. You will be polite and gracious to someone who is, after all, a full ten years older than yourself, and a lady to boot.'

'I do not require advice from you on how to conduct myself,' she replied coldly. 'I, of course, do not stand to benefit from behaving in a slavish and ingratiating fashion. It is fortunate, therefore, that I am possessed of naturally impeccable taste and manners.'

'And as for your protégée,' he continued, meaning Daisy, 'try to get through to her that this is not a public cemetery. Aunt Lucy, at her age, will not be entertained by a continual procession of funerals. Or cremations,' he added as a wise afterthought.

'I do not propose to fetter Daisy's creative urges,' Grandma returned. 'I would not want the responsibility. If *I* can contemplate the enactment of a funeral with equanimity, then so should this other person be able to.'

Mr Bagthorpe, knowing the futility of arguing the point further, stomped out of the house, leaving his already battered family to put themselves together. No one was very clear what part they were supposed to be playing. They had been given to understand, on the one hand, that Great Aunt Lucy's every wish was to be pandered to. On the other, they had been told to display determination and strength of character – which meant, presumably, that they were to press on with the rhubarb and beetroot aspect of things. The two policies seemed irreconcilable – unless, of course, the old lady turned out to be a devotee of a diet of unalleviated salad and stewed rhubarb.

'I think we ought to have meals as usual while she's here,' William told his mother as soon as Mr Bagthorpe had driven off. 'Aunt Lucy'll never leave us anything if she has to eat all that muck.'

'I agree,' Tess said surprisingly. She never agreed with William about anything unless her back was truly to the wall. 'Gastronomic considerations should override all others. I can easily demonstrate my own strength of character by conversing with her in French and Danish, and by playing arpeggios on my oboe.'

'I think we should try to strike a balance,' said Mrs Bagthorpe sensibly. 'It is, after all, summer, and the season for salads.'

'Which don't have to be kept hot,' put in Mrs Fosdyke, who still had misgivings about the Time aspect of things.

'Exactly,' Mrs Bagthorpe agreed. 'And do remember, everybody, that we are *humouring* your father. The thing will burn itself out if we give it the least chance.'

She sounded a good deal more like Stella Bright than she felt. She alone had seen the sheaf of stamped addressed envelopes on her husband's desk. They had been addressed to bodies like the Milk Marketing Board, the Council for the Preservation of Rural England and the *Farmer and Stockbreeder*. Mr Bagthorpe was not in the habit of wasting stamps, even without benefit of an overdraft running, as he professed still to believe, into untold figures.

It was very unfortunate that one of Rosie's hamsters was found dead immediately after Mr Bagthorpe's departure. It was William had who made this discovery. He had gone into one of the disused stables in search of a length of cable, and his eye chanced to fall on the cages in which the hamsters were kept. He looked at them because at the time they were producing a noticeable degree of noise. Several of the hamsters were busy exercising themselves by running non-stop on their wheels. William, whose mind was then currently occupied with devising methods of producing free electricity, cast a thoughtful eye upon them.

'A treadmill,' he murmured to himself. 'A windmill generates electricity, and so could a treadmill. If we could devise a means of harnessing the energy expended by the hamsters in treading those wheels, then we—'

He was halted on the threshold of a scientific breakthrough by observing a limp and furry shape to the fore of one of the cages. He advanced to investigate.

His half-formed theory was nipped in the bud. Clearly hamsters were not up to treading treadmills on any full time, regular basis. This one had obviously died of a heart attack after its exertions.

'Better tell Rosie,' he decided.

He did so without taking due thought. He might have known, he told himself bitterly later, that Rosie would go straight to tell Daisy of the death by misadventure. Rosie truly loved Daisy, and thought her sweet and funny, and used every means in her power to lure her away from Grandma's side whenever possible.

The result was that Mr Bagthorpe, later in the morning, motoring sedately up the drive with Aunt Lucy beside him, came close to a head-on collision with a funeral procession. It consisted of Daisy wearing a trailing black crocheted shawl and felt hat of Grandma's, followed by Rosie and Grandma herself, both suitably attired in deep mourning, and carrying flowers. It had been Grandma's idea to inter the hamster in the front garden, rather than the back, because she had secretly hoped for the confrontation that in fact now took place. She was exceedingly pleased with this outcome. It established herself in the eyes of the visitor as dauntingly and possibly unbeatably eccentric, and it goaded Mr Bagthorpe into a towering rage. Round one, Grandma thought with satisfaction, had definitely gone to her.

Mr Bagthorpe had to pull up quite sharply to avoid a situation that would have involved at least one real funeral, if not three. Jack heard the gravel scatter, and approached cautiously behind the screen of laurels to observe the scene. He looked first, naturally, at Great Aunt Lucy, to see if she would be how he had imagined her. In fact, her face was the least noticeable thing about her, sandwiched as it was between a large beflowered hat, and a chest crowded with lace and a good number of shining ornaments. (These later turned out to be brooch watches, all set at different times.)

The most striking figure present was undoubtedly Grandma, who was wearing a black bonnet and veil that she had kept for nearly half a century in case she ever wanted to take up bee-keeping again. None of her features were even faintly discernible under this thick veil, and Jack wondered how she could see where she was going. Rosie had struck a more casual note in a black leotard and tights, but evidently thought the addition of a hat necessary to the solemnity of the occasion, and wore low over her eyes a greenish-black homburg, presumably the property of Grandpa.

The members of this procession were singing a kind of dirge, or even three separate dirges. When Mr Bagthorpe wound down his window and started shouting they were not deflected from their course. They appeared to give only the briefest of glances in his direction, and then made slowly off over the far lawn, presenting an eerie picture in the brilliant midday sun. Jack himself was torn between following the car to the house, and attending the funeral. He decided on the latter course. A funeral was less of an everyday occurrence than the spectacle of Mr Bagthorpe shouting.

He caught up with the cortège just as it halted by what was clearly to be the final resting place of Rosie's hamster. Daisy was carrying a chocolate box. She placed it reverently under a lilac bush, and Jack guessed that it contained the corpse. She then delved under her layers of shawl and skirts and produced a trowel.

'You better sing another verse while I'm digging,' she told the other mourners, and herself set to work in a business-like way with the trowel. A hole soon materialized.

'Now,' said Daisy with satisfaction. 'Now it's the proper part. Oh dear, poor little mouse!'

'Hamster,' Rosie told her, sniffing. 'His name was Truffles.'

Daisy held aloft the chocolate box for a moment, in the manner of a magician inviting an audience to inspect a receptacle from which he is about to produce a dozen white doves.

'Goodbye, Truffles!' she said. Tears were already beginning to roll down her cheeks. Evidently a long personal relationship with the deceased was not necessary in order for her to experience deep feelings of bereavement.

'There you go now, for ever and ever, down into the soil for ever and ever!'

She bent and placed the box in the hole.

'Ashes to ashes, dusters to dusters,' she cried loudly, scattering handfuls of soil over the coffin.

Jack was unable to judge the strength of Grandma's emotions behind her black curtain, but Rosie was by now sobbing in earnest. She herself moved in and threw some soil.

'Goodbye, Truffles,' she sobbed.

'Poor dead Truffles,' agreed Daisy. 'For ever and ever,' she added, evidently feeling that these words had a strong ecclesiastical ring.

The hole filled in, Daisy straightened up.

'Now we'll sing hymn four thousand and ninety-six,' she announced. '"We Plough The Fields and Scatter."'

Jack thought this choice curious, but supposed that Daisy had only a limited repertoire of hymns. Her congregation obediently struck up, and Jack thought how amazing it was that Grandma should be so docile and allow Daisy to take the leading role. Usually if Grandma was involved in anything, she insisted on running it.

The trio sang nearly half 'We Plough The Fields and Scatter' before they trailed off for lack of words.

'Amen,' Daisy said. 'That'll do. Now we've got to do the flowers and writing.'

She again delved into her robes and produced what looked like a large, slender volume, with a message printed on it in yellow. This she pushed at something of an angle into the soil at the head of the grave.

'I seen books in the graveyard,' Daisy told the others. 'Books are good. Now put the flowers on.'

Grandma and Rosie then advanced with their bunches of flowers and each in turn placed her tribute under the headstone.

'For ever and ever amen,' Daisy said, terminating the ceremony. 'We better go and have dinner now. Goodbye, poor dead mouse.'

'Hamster,' Rosie told her again.

Jack waited until the mourners had disappeared from sight, then advanced to inspect the grave. The headstone, he noted with misgivings, was Mr Bagthorpe's Road Atlas. It bore the inscription:

> Here lies a mous
> In a holey hous
> But the pore dad thing
> Will here the bels ring
> 1692–1792
> Forevver and evver.

'That's oil paint she's used,' Jack thought. 'It'll never come off. Father'll kill her.'

He was reminded by this that Mr Bagthorpe would at that moment almost certainly be in murderous mood, and hastened back to the house to witness this.

He was not disappointed. The funeral procession had arrived just before him, and was being introduced to Aunt Lucy by Mrs Bagthorpe. Her husband had his mouth so tightly closed that it was virtually invisible. Great Aunt Lucy herself was sitting like a ramrod, her eyes fixed on Grandma – the only person present in whom she appeared to have any interest. Anyone handing out a prize for fancy dress would have been bound to give it to Grandma.

'Charmed,' Great Aunt Lucy was saying. 'May I inquire how old you are?'

'I am seventy-five,' Grandma replied, 'although of course I am aware that I look twenty years younger.'

'I should have put you at eighty,' Aunt Lucy said. 'I myself am eighty-seven. Or rather, I would be, if I believed in Time, which I am happy to say I do not.'

'Nor, perhaps, shall I,' parried Grandma, 'when I reach your age.'

Mrs Bagthorpe helplessly watched this exchange, which by no means, even to a confirmed Positive Thinker, seemed to augur well.

'Why are you wearing that ugly bonnet?' Great Aunt Lucy then inquired, fingering her own chiffon roses.

'I do not normally wear hats,' replied Grandma imperturbably, 'which are these days considered vulgar and dated. Today, however, I have been attending a funeral, and naturally observed the niceties.'

'We been burying a mouse,' Daisy piped up. 'He was Truffles and now he's dusters to dusters and ashes to ashes. *That* hat's got a lot of flowers!'

Mr Bagthorpe now unclenched his facial muscles.

'That child, I am profoundly grateful to say, is not my own. It belongs to Celia and Russell. The only reason it is in this house at all is because Mother invited it. I advise you to give the pair of them a wide berth. They are—'

'And this is Rosie,' interrupted Mrs Bagthorpe hastily. 'She is eight, but already has Several Strings to her Bow, don't you, dear? Perhaps she will paint your Portrait while you are with us.'

'And who is that?' inquired the old lady, ignoring this suggestion.

'This is Jack,' Mrs Bagthorpe told her.

'And what does *he* do?'

'I don't do anything, Great Aunt Lucy,' Jack told her. 'I'm very pleased to meet you, and hope you will have a happy visit. Does your dog fight?'

He had left Zero up in his room, on Mr Bagthorpe's instructions.

'If that infernal hound eats that accursed Peke, we're finished,' he said.

Jack looked at the intruder and tried to hide his distaste.

'Wung Foo certainly fights if the contingency arises,' his owner replied. 'Don't you, my pretty?'

The Peke, which snuffed incessantly and wore a pink satin bow, seemed to blow out its cheeks and at the same time showed two rows of tiny, pointed teeth.

'Which of you is going to take him for a walkie? His little legs need stretching after the journey.'

Nobody spoke or moved. Mr Bagthorpe tried to catch the eyes of his offspring, and was making powerful grimaces. They all affected not to notice.

'*I* will!' he finally ground out. 'Give it here.'

He looked and felt extremely silly, as if he were leading a toy. Rosie giggled, and the minute he had left the room dashed out herself, presumably to fetch her camera.

'What time is breakfast?' inquired Great Aunt Lucy then. 'I am hungry.'

At this, Mrs Fosdyke made a choking sound. She had been staring at the arrival with ill-concealed curiosity and apprehension, while ostensibly polishing a brass plate.

'We thought in about half an hour,' interposed Mrs Bagthorpe swiftly, forestalling any comments Mrs Fosdyke might have to make. 'Tess, dear, take your Great Aunt up to her room, and be sure she has everything she wants.'

'It makes no matter what we *call* a meal,' Mrs Bagthorpe told an unco-operative Mrs Fosdyke, after the visitor had left the room. 'A rose by any other name would smell as sweet.'

'First time *I've* heard of pork chops and rhubarb dumplings for breakfast,' Mrs Fosdyke sniffed. 'Did you see all them watches pinned on her front? *None* of 'em the right time, as I could see. Broke, some of 'em looked. What kind of person goes round with dozens of broke watches pinned on their front?'

'It certainly looks extremely silly,' Grandma chipped in. She was already on her mettle. Great Aunt Lucy constituted a stronger threat than she had supposed. 'As does that ridiculous hat. Some people, of course, will wear anything in order to draw attention to themselves.'

Jack wondered how any lady in her seventies, kitted out in a bee-keeping bonnet and veil in the total absence of hives, could make such a remark with a straight face.

'I may take up bee-keeping again.' It was as if Grandma had divined his thoughts.

'How lovely, Mother!' Mrs Bagthorpe enthused. 'We can then have delicious pure honey. Henry *will* be pleased.'

'I shall not do it to please Henry,' Grandma told her unnecessarily. 'I have immortal longings in me.'

At the time nobody could make much of this remark, unless to assume that Grandma, in the absence of an asp, intended to invite a Cleopatrian death by bee stings. Quite the reverse, however, was the case. Grandma had read some article about the beneficial effects of royal jelly, and now had the unbudgeable conviction that if one ate a sufficient number of queen bees, one would become immortal and quite rejuvenated. This prospect appealed strongly to her, especially following certain remarks made earlier to her by Daisy.

It was an unfortunate aspect of Daisy's new Intimations of Mortality Phase, that she was led to speculate on the life-expectancy of everyone she now met. She tended to do this out loud.

'I don't fink you'll be alive very long, Grandma Bag,' she had said. 'You got a wrinkly face and blue hair and short legs.'

Grandma had reluctantly conceded the first two observations, but denied the last. She was very vain about her lower limbs, which were always set off in silk stockings and elegantly heeled shoes. It was, indeed, some time before the Bagthorpes cracked the mystery of short legs as a sign of impending demise. Daisy was taking into account only the portion of leg visible, and as elderly ladies tend to wear longer skirts than their younger counterparts, Daisy had concluded that shrinking of the legs was a sign of old age.

'If you *do* die,' Daisy had hastened to assure her, 'I'll have a lovely funeral for you, Grandma Bag. And I'll write a really long pome, and have about ten hymns, and everybody will cry.'

None of this was any real comfort to Grandma, who could see no joy in a funeral at which, in the nature of things, she would not be present.

'I shall keep bees,' she repeated. 'Henry shall go and procure hives immediately. I have forgotten most of what I knew, but the rest of you will surely help me.'

What Grandma really intended was that other people should look after the swarm, and she would consume the royal jelly and queen bees.

'Ah, Henry, there you are! I have decided that I shall—'

'Everybody out – quick!' ordered Mr Bagthorpe. He was panting hard. 'I let that accursed Peke off its lead and it's made off. Quick – the lot of you!'

Everyone moved, with the exception of Mrs Fosdyke and Grandma. The former made great play with basting the pork chops, the latter said coolly to anyone who might be listening:

'You had better make haste. That young man who murdered Thomas will be back soon, in his car, to bring my cat. We do not, I think, wish another victim.'

Mr Bagthorpe, who had meant to stay and regain his breath, groaned. He recognized the truth of this observation. He turned in his tracks, and lurched off out again, cursing.

7

The Bagthorpes scattered about the grounds, but were all within earshot when Mrs Fosdyke screamed. Some of them – notably Mr Bagthorpe and William – carried on their way regardless. The scream was a terrible one, but neither of them cared what was happening to Mrs Fosdyke, nor bothered to pretend he did. For this callousness they were rewarded by coming back eventually to find lunch almost over and Wung Foo curled up on a cushion by his owner. They had also missed a good scene.

What had happened was that Wung Foo had entered the kitchen trailing in his mouth the disinterred body of one of Daisy's corpses (the chicken, not the hamster). Judging by its mutilated state, Wung Foo had been hiding under a bush somewhere chewing at it for some time, and was now bringing it in so that he could have another go at it later. It was not an appealing sight and was, moreover, distinctly malodorous. Aunt Lucy, astonishingly, was not the least perturbed by this.

'Darling Wung Foo is a hunter,' she informed everybody. 'How clever of him!'

'He can't be a hunter,' Rosie objected. 'The chicken was already dead. To be a hunter, you have to *kill* things.'

They all scowled at her, but she appeared not to notice.

'Wung Foo is a *humane* hunter,' Aunt Lucy told her severely. 'I will have no part in blood sports. What a curious breakfast menu you favour, Laura. I had rather expected kippers.'

'It is not breakfasttime,' Grandma told her. 'It is luncheon. Do you have difficulty in telling the time?'

'As I have already intimated, I do not recognize the existence of Time,' Aunt Lucy replied stiffly, 'and will thank you not to refer to it. It may be listening.'

'Did you enjoy your stay with Claud and Penelope?' interrupted Mrs Bagthorpe at this juncture. Grandma did not stand to benefit by Aunt Lucy's will, and was patently out to provoke her. This, however, could only put everyone else's bequests in jeopardy.

'I did not,' replied Aunt Lucy. 'I thought them excessively tedious. I thought I should have died of boredom. Moreover, I have the strong impression that the only reason I was invited there was that they hope to figure in my will.'

At this, something of a silence fell. The Bagthorpes studiously attended to their rhubarb dumplings. None of them wished to risk catching the old lady's eye. She was evidently a good deal more astute than anyone had given her credit for being.

'They will, of course, be disappointed,' she continued.

'They will?' prompted Mrs Bagthorpe, rather too hopefully to be in good taste. She thought that if Aunt Lucy then and there announced her intention of favouring Mr Bagthorpe's branch of the family, he would be instantly reassured, and would drop his Plan for Survival as abruptly as he had taken it up.

'Certainly they will,' Great Aunt Lucy told her. 'Everyone with expectations in that direction will be disappointed. As there is no such thing as Time, I shall outlive all these persons by decades – possibly by centuries.'

Nobody liked the sound of this, and Grandma least of all. Having only that day herself embarked on a scheme to ensure her own rejuvenation, she was much put out to find herself forestalled by a rival. She was casting swiftly about for a cutting rejoinder to Aunt Lucy's pronouncement, when Daisy offered *her* opinion of it.

'Silly griffin!' she exclaimed. (This was an expression often used by Daisy, though nobody knew its source. Aunt Celia said it was a poetic metaphor.)

Aunt Lucy turned her attention toward the author of this remark just as Mr Bagthorpe, scarlet and breathless, appeared at the outer door.

'Silly griffin!' repeated Daisy. '*Everybody* dies, don't they, Grandma Bag? And then there's funerals. Even Grandma Bag's going to die one day, and she's my favourite of anybody. And you're older than her, *and* you've got shorter legs, *and* you're more wrinkly. You're really creased up and wrinkly. So you'll die first!'

Everyone sat appalled by this apparent destruction at a single blow of their hopes. Mr Bagthorpe clutched wordlessly at his hair. Grandma alone was undismayed – she was, indeed, enchanted.

'When you *do* die,' continued Daisy helpfully, 'jus' think, you might die while you're here! And if you do, I'll have a really nice funeral if you like and a lot of hymns and crying.'

Aunt Lucy looked far from taking up Daisy's offer (or at any rate, voluntarily). She had really led far too sheltered an existence to fit her for survival in such a household as the Bagthorpes'. Also, she was much used to being pandered to. The Bees in her Bonnet had always been kept slavishly supplied with nectar by those about her. (Even Aunt Penelope had conceded that Aunt Lucy's theories about time might be given some credence. 'A thousand ages in thy sight are but an evening gone,' she had mused.) It was years, then, since Great Aunt Lucy had been thus confronted with the stark truth. Never, possibly, had she been presented with a truth as stark as this.

The Bagthorpes waited with bated breath for her reaction. (The younger ones were torn between desiring the short-term benefits of her upping and leaving on the spot, and the longer term benefit of a sizeable bequest. Aunt Lucy sat gasping for quite a long time. She and Wung Foo were breathing in much the same way, Jack noted with interest.

In the end, Aunt Lucy disappointed nearly everyone by rising, still gasping, scooping Wung Foo under her arm, and making wordlessly for the door.

'Oh Lucy, dear!' protested Mrs Bagthorpe feebly, undecided whether to make after her, or let her go to her room alone and come to terms with the total disintegration of her world picture.

'I suppose we must give her time . . .' she murmured, not seeming aware of the irony of this remark.

'How very touchy she is,' remarked Grandma, hoping to trigger her son's repressed fury. 'I thought Daisy's offer most handsome. What a sweet and generous nature she has.'

Her strategy was sucessful. Within seconds Mr Bagthorpe was yelling, Daisy bawling, and the entire company into a fullscale furore. At its height Uncle Parker and Aunt Celia entered, having been unable to attract any attention by repeated ringing of the door bell. Aunt Celia immediately hurried to Daisy and clasped her tightly, wailing:

'Daisy, darling, why are you weeping?'

She repeated this query twice more, as if it were a refrain.

'Everybody's got to die, everybody has!' Daisy sobbed.

'Of course they have, my darling,' soothed her parent. 'Never send to know for whom the bell tolls – it tolls for thee!'

'Hell's *bells*!' yelled Mr Bagthorpe. 'Will you stop burbling about *bells*, for God's sake!'

Most people there heartily wished that bells were tolling, in earnest – for Daisy.

'Are you mad, Celia? That child has just pulled the king pin from under every expectation I ever had. She has at a stroke reduced us all to eternal penury!'

He carried on yelling for some time in this vein, and talked a lot about lawsuits, and making claims for loss of expectations. Much of this was inaudible, however, because of strong competition for the floor from most others present. Aunt Celia was screaming about gold and dross and corruption, Uncle Parker was warning Mr Bagthorpe off his family, Grandma was talking about *her* will, Daisy bawling and Mrs Bagthorpe vainly trying to scream out advice from Stella Bright.

'It was like *The Fall of the House of Usher*,' Mrs Fosdyke later told her cronies in The Fiddler's Arms. 'Only worse. The row they was making, it's a wonder it didn't bring the roof in. There's no wonder that cat was out of its wits with fright.'

The cat referred to, the putative Thomas the Second, was not in fact introduced until the furore had been raging for a full ten minutes. No one had till then noticed that Uncle Parker was driving home some of his points by emphatic rappings of a large wicker basket, which could hardly have been reassuring to its occupant. It was Daisy, disengaging herself from her mother's protective embrace, whose eye first fell on it.

'The pussy!' she shrieked delightedly, her mood undergoing an abrupt change. 'That's the pussy!'

Everyone stopped shouting at once and all eyes were now riveted on the basket. In the silence there was a faint mewing and scratching. Mr Bagthorpe, his cup full, lurched off. His mouth was working, but nothing was coming out. A moment later the door of his study banged.

'Nasty Grook!' Daisy squealed after him. 'Daddy, Mummy, get the pussy out!'

The Bagthorpes watched numbly as Uncle Parker undid the catch. Daisy ran over and peered inside.

'Oooh, it's lovely!' she squeaked. '*I* want to give it to Grandma Bag!'

'Take care that it does not scratch or bite,' Aunt Celia told her anxiously.

The rest blanched. Daisy reached into the basket and scrabbled about before capturing its occupant. The kitten was bright ginger. Its dangling legs were tipped by claws unsheathed and sharp, its eyes were staring and wild. It was writhing frantically to escape Daisy's tight clutch.

She went over to Grandma.

'*Here* you are, Grandma Bag!' she cried, and plonked it directly in her lap.

'Oooeeech!' screamed Grandma, and the cat sprang in two bounds on to the dresser, where it arched and spat, fur stiffly on end. The Bagthorpes stared aghast, their worst fears apparently realized. Not so Daisy.

'Oh *Grandma*!' she squealed. 'You've frightened him! Poor little pussy. Look at his little legs all shaking!'

Grandma did not obey this instruction. She was currently more interested in her own limbs than those of the second Thomas. She was cautiously sliding up her frock to inspect the state of the damage. When she glimpsed the blood and the torn stockings, she let out a faint cry and dropped the hem.

'Mother, dear, are you all right?' inquired Mrs Bagthorpe anxiously.

'I should like some brandy,' Grandma replied faintly.

As Mrs Bagthorpe hurried off in search of this commodity, Grandma slowly and incredulously turned her gaze back towards her assailant. Now, the whole point about the original Thomas was that while he had spat at, scratched and bit indiscriminately and without provocation almost everyone within a considerable radius, he had made Grandma herself a notable exception to his attentions. Possibly, as Mr Bagthorpe pointed out, he had recognized in her a kindred spirit. He had actually lain in her lap and allowed her to stroke him and had even sometimes, she claimed, purred.

Grandma, clearly, had hoped and expected that the second Thomas would show exactly the same loathsome proclivities. Instead, here he was arched and spitting, his wild eyes fixed rivetingly on herself (it being she who had screamed). It was a case, as Mr Bagthorpe later pointed out with delight, of the biter bit.

Daisy then trotted forward.

'Poor pussy!' she said. 'You come to me.'

'Daisy!' moaned her mother protestingly.

Daisy's hands and face were already within scratching and biting range. The kitten, astonishingly, relaxed. Daisy's chubby fingers went under his chin, making little scrabbling movements. She then lifted him, unprotestingly, into her arms.

'He was frightened, poor little kit,' she told everyone. 'He likes me, don't you, little Tommy?'

This seemed indisputable. The Bagthorpes were disappointed by the unexpected development. Up to this juncture, it had seemed possible that Grandma would reject the animal out of hand. If, however, the cat liked Daisy, she would certainly be inclined to review the matter.

What happened next, therefore, was in the nature of a miracle. Great Aunt Lucy entered, leading Wung Foo.

Instantly Grandma and the kitten bristled. No one had expected to see the old lady reappear so soon after Daisy's ruthless estimate of her life expectancy. It had even seemed to them on the cards that she would never appear again.

'I think you had better take your animal out,' Grandma told Aunt Lucy, taking the offensive.

'And why is that?' inquired Aunt Lucy coolly.

'Because you would not wish, presumably, to see its eyes scratched out,' Grandma told her.

'Wung Foo is not afraid of cats,' replied the other. 'Perhaps you should remove *your* animal from the room.'

The Bagthorpes watched this interchange with keen attention. It seemed likely that what the pair of them were working up to was a kind of cockfight. The Bagthorpes were always interested in anything of a competitive nature, and were most of them already mentally improvising a system of scoring.

An impasse having now been reached, Grandma made a move to develop the situation.

'Put the cat down, Daisy,' she ordered. 'It cannot be comfortable being held so tightly.'

The Peke was straining at its leash and puffing and snorting. Jack felt that it more or less deserved to be attacked by Thomas the Second. Daisy, reluctantly, made to lower the kitten to the floor. At this, to the amazement of everyone, it began to whimper plaintively, and scrabble desperately to retain its hold on Daisy's pinafore.

'The animal is clearly terrified,' said Great Aunt Lucy smugly. 'Pray do not put it down, or it will be bitten. Why, might I ask,' she went on, addressing herself to Grandma, 'have you elected to have a cat of that colour? It is quite horrid.'

Jack held his breath.

'The animal does not belong to me,' replied

Grandma, without turning a hair. 'It belongs to Daisy, and is, I think, a very attractive shade.'

There was a moment's silence while this appalling falsehood sank in, and then a moderate babble set up. Its main contributors were Aunt Celia, who had always turned down her daughter's impassioned pleas for a pussy on the grounds that cats clawed out people's eyes, and Daisy herself, made ecstatic by this generosity on Grandma's part. She loosed her hold on the kitten in order to embrace Grandma, Aunt Lucy let go of Wung Foo's lead, and next minute the recently averted confrontation was taking place. It was not strictly a confrontation, in that the last thing Thomas the Second appeared to desire was to confront Wung Foo. And had Daisy released her hold on her newly acquired pet, and allowed it to jump to safety, little damage would have been done.

In the event, a great deal of damage was done. Altogether three people were bitten – Daisy herself, with her stranglehold on the kitten, Aunt Celia, attempting to intervene, and Mr Bagthorpe, who had come striding in from his study to find out what was going on. Jack could not help feeling that it was very bad luck for his father to be bitten, and Mr Bagthorpe himself certainly thought so.

'There is no justice under the sun,' he declared, nursing his bleeding shin.

Grandma disagreed.

'You are always talking about poetic justice,' she

told him, 'and now you are experiencing it. You have no just cause for complaint.'

Mr Bagthorpe did a lot of very noisy complaining, both at the time, and afterwards. Despite the fact that it was Wung Foo who had bitten him, it was Uncle Parker, Daisy and Grandma to whom he allocated all blame. He acted as if it had been they who had bitten him.

All in all, it was a relief when Uncle Parker with his family, and Mrs Bagthorpe with her husband, drove off to the hospital in Aysham for tetanus shots.

Grandma was on the whole pleased with the way things had gone.

'That animal of yours is not so silly as it looks,' she told Great Aunt Lucy. 'Though it certainly showed lack of discrimination in biting darling Daisy, who has a natural empathy with all living creatures, great and small.'

This was news to the rest of the Bagthorpes. The only living – as opposed to dead – creatures with whom Daisy had in their experience demonstrated any affinity, was maggots.

'Shall we be waiting breakfast until Henry returns from the hospital?' inquired Aunt Lucy, ignoring this criticism. 'Darling Wung Foo and I are now ready for our kippers.'

8

To say that the situation at Unicorn House was now volatile would be to badly understate the matter. Almost every member of the household felt him-or herself to be near the verge of breakdown – except, of course, Grandma and Daisy. Even Jack was beginning to feel edgy, mainly because of the strain of preventing a meeting between Zero and Wung Foo.

'It's undermining his confidence, being shut away half the time,' Jack thought. 'He's in solitary confinement, and that always affects people.'

He seemed to remember having read somewhere that people frequently lost all sense of identity during solitary confinement. This Zero could not afford to risk. His sense of identity was never strong at best. Jack tried to counter the effects of Zero's imprisonment by taking him for long walks during which he did a good deal of patting and praising. Mr Bagthorpe, however, soon put a stop to this.

'If you've got the energy to go twenty-mile hikes with that numb-skulled hound,' he told Jack, 'you've got the energy to dig. Get out there and dig.'

Mr Bagthorpe, once he had recovered from the

shock and humiliation of being bitten by Wung Foo, had surveyed the courses open to him and decided that to forge ahead with his Master Plan for Survival was the only realistic one. He no longer entertained any real hopes of a bequest from Great Aunt Lucy.

'That accursed daughter of Russell's has put paid to that,' he said. He no longer bothered to be particularly polite to his visiting relation, now that there was nothing to be gained by this.

Astonishingly enough, considering that nobody in the household cared either for herself or her dog, Great Aunt Lucy stayed on. This pleased nobody. The pair of them caused great inconvenience. For one thing, Daisy had returned with her kitten, and evidently intended to prolong her stay, too, as long as possible (during which time, of course, there was the ever-present danger that the two animals might meet again, and there be some more biting).

'Grandma Bag and me's going to train Little Tommy up,' she told everybody.

No one was reassured by this intelligence. The two of them spent hours holed up in Grandma's room along with Little Tommy, and were almost certainly, Mr Bagthorpe said, brainwashing him, and using every technique at their disposal to ensure that he turned out a veritable hell-cat.

'Though at least it will be living, long-term, with *that* lot,' he added, meaning Uncle Parker and Aunt Celia, 'and with any luck, will make their lives purgatory. *Mine*'s been purgatory long enough.'

His suspicions might well have been justified. Nobody knew for certain what the Unholy Alliance were up to during their training sessions, but Grandma, once Great Aunt Lucy was safely out of earshot, had certainly made no secret of her disgust at the showing put up by the kitten in its encounter with Wung Foo. It was this, indeed, that had prompted her to deny ownership. She wished for no association, she said, with anything so feeble.

'Milk and water creature!' she had exclaimed scornfully. 'Where is its spirit? Has it no fight? If only Thomas were still with me, in his great golden glory. No wishy-washy Pekingese would have been tolerated by him within his own house. He was an emperor among cats.'

The younger Bagthorpes felt that however intensive the training the kitten was now receiving from Grandma and Daisy, it would be in no position to drive Great Aunt Lucy and Wung Foo out of the house in the foreseeable future. Nobody wished to wait this long.

'We must think of a way to clear them out ourselves,' William told his gloomy siblings. 'I am sick of being polite, and sick of having to keep closing doors to keep those two horrible animals apart. And I am sick to death of the eternal smell of kippers. She has had breakfast four times in the last twenty-four hours.'

'And I'm sick of always digging just to show her I've got determination,' Rosie said. 'Either that, or having to cook her horrible kippers. If she went, we wouldn't have to look as if we'd got strength of character.'

'The mere fact that she has been reduced to partaking of her breakfast at such ever-shortening intervals would seem to indicate that she feels herself to be, to some extent, threatened,' mused Tess. 'Perhaps we could turn this to our advantage. Evidently she is not currently coping with Time as well as she likes.'

'All that stuff Daisy said to her about legs and wrinkles couldn't have helped,' Jack said. 'Good old Daisy. And that funeral. Why don't we get Daisy to have a lot more funerals?'

There had been a lull in Daisy's undertaking activities since the advent of Little Tommy.

'That,' William told him, 'is not a bad idea.'

'But what about corpses?' objected Rosie. 'We haven't got any corpses.'

They sat and pondered this incontrovertible truth. Corpses were not, they realized, easily come by, even at Unicorn House.

'Where's she been getting her corpses up to now?' Jack asked. 'Uncle Park said she'd had about two dozen funerals last week. She can't have found two dozen corpses. She must've been burying other things as well.'

'That chicken . . .' William murmured thoughtfully. 'That was dead meat, all right . . .'

'Dead meat!' Jack was struck by a thought. 'Chops and things – out of the deep freeze!'

They considered this proposition. Whether or not

Daisy would be moved to bury chops they were not certain. What they did know, was that once the supply of meat in the deep freeze was exhausted, Mr Bagthorpe had ruled that no more was to be purchased. Meat, therefore, was now at a premium. Thoughtful consideration was necessary. Things had to be weighed and balanced.

'What it amounts to,' William said, 'is whether a chop in the grave is worth two in the freezer.'

'Or vice versa,' Tess added.

'I think Daisy *could* bury chops,' Jack told the others. 'She's really dotty about burying things. I think we ought to egg her on.'

'A non-stop procession of funerals would certainly have a depressive effect on Aunt Lucy,' Tess said. 'What we could also do, is turn the conversation as much as possible to the subject of Time.'

This, too, was considered to be a sound proposition. Everyone undertook to do some rifling through books of poetry during spare moments, in search of apt quotations.

'And I'll have a quick scan through the hymn books,' William volunteered. 'Any thing about Time in them is usually pretty depressing.'

Jack and Rosie were deputed to catch Daisy during one of the rare moments when she was not in Grandma's room with Little Tommy, and make an effort to rekindle her apparently waning interest in funerals.

'Lay it on really thick,' William advised them. 'Say

you'll go to the funerals. Tell her I've got a big bell, and'll toll it for her, if she likes. Tell her anything. And don't call the chops chops.'

'Why?' Rosie asked. 'What shall we call them, then?'

'Call them "poor little dead lambs",' he told her. 'Or piglets, as the case may be.'

'Will she be burying *sausages*?' Jack could not see even Daisy looking on these in the light of deceased piglets, and shedding tears over them.

'Pork *chops*, idiot!' William said. 'And while you're digging, keep your eyes open for anything dead. Or any odd bones.' (Daisy, he knew, had a powerful attraction toward skeletons, and had once tried to engineer William into becoming one himself.

The younger Bagthorpes, then, scattered on their various missions, though these had to be dovetailed with their duties allotted by Mr Bagthorpe on his hell-bent career towards Self-Sufficiency. Currently, Tess was working on the salad section of the garden, Rosie acting as mate to William, who was converting the summer house to a hen house, and Jack just digging.

It was just after lunch (or supper, as Great Aunt Lucy preferred to call it) that Jack and Rosie managed to corner Daisy. They coaxed her into the sitting-room as she was on her way to fetch the kitten for an outing in the garden.

'I can't stop long,' she told them. 'Little Tommy mews when I'm not there.'

'The thing is, Daisy, we need your help,' Jack told her.

'What to do?' she asked. 'I'm not digging. I don't like digging. Except graves,' she added as an afterthought.

Rosie and Jack exchanged triumphant glances. Clearly Daisy was *not* out of her Intimations of Mortality Phase, and her undertaking urges were merely lying dormant.

'That's exactly what it is, Daisy,' Rosie told her. 'A grave. Poor little dead lamb.'

'Little dead lamb?' Daisy's eyes stretched. 'Where? Oh dear, poor little fing!'

Jack knew that the chop was going to prove something of an anticlimax for Daisy, who would be expecting something white and woolly, and accordingly chose his words carefully.

'It has been cut up, I'm afraid,' he told her.

'Oh *dear*!' squealed Daisy, aghast and enchanted at once. 'Oh, *poor* little fing! Oh, when shall we bury him?'

'As soon as you like,' Jack said. 'We'll come to the funeral as well, won't we, Rosie?'

'And Grandma Bag,' Daisy said happily. 'And will old Auntie Lucy come?'

'I shouldn't think so,' Rosie began, but Jack interrupted.

'That's a good idea. You ask her, Daisy.'

The more Great Aunt Lucy heard about Daisy's funerals, the better.

‘I’ll go and ask her.’ Daisy trotted to the door. ‘And I’ll tell Grandma Bag. You go and get the poor dead lamb. I never buried a lamb before. I’ll write him a lovely pome.’

From there on, things rapidly began to snowball. William had already abstracted several chops and other cuts of meat from the deep freeze, and these were defrosting in his room. He had enough potential corpses, he said, to keep Daisy going for days, if necessary.

‘Though the sooner Aunt Lucy clears off the better,’ he added. ‘I’d give anything for a lamb chop with mint sauce.’

They all would. Meals, on Mr Bagthorpe’s instructions, were becoming increasingly spartan. He too, it appeared, wished his elderly relative elsewhere.

Daisy invited Great Aunt Lucy to the funeral, but she strenuously declined.

‘She said I mustn’t *mention* poor dead fings.’ Daisy told the rest indignantly as they assembled for the funeral of the chop. ‘Silly old griffin!’

Daisy was, as had been anticipated, somewhat disappointed at the lack of resemblance of the chop to a real dead lamb, but soon perked up when she saw the increased number of mourners, and was informed that a bell would toll.

‘And I’ll take some photos,’ Rosie promised.

William had selected a suitable spot for the interment, in full view of Great Aunt Lucy’s window. She had gone up to her room for a doze because, she had informed them all at lunch, the full moon was now imminent. Mrs Fosdyke had a prolonged fit of choking when she heard this.

'I shall require some heavier curtains, Laura,' Great Aunt Lucy had continued. 'The present ones are quite inadequate. The rays of the moon will pass straight through them. I am already beginning to be affected by them.'

Mrs Bagthorpe had looked quite desperate at this, and Jack longed to tell her that her fears were groundless, because the old lady would almost certainly have left before the full moon.

Aunt Lucy was wakened, as had been intended, by the loud tolling of William's bell, and Jack, glancing up, saw her inadequate curtains move, and caught a glimpse of her face.

The funeral went swimmingly. Daisy, once she had accepted the fact that her corpse was dismembered, acted as bereaved as she ever had. A further funeral took place several hours later, and she wept at that, too.

'Poor dead piglet, poor dead piglet!' she sobbed as the pork chop was laid in its shallow grave. 'Dusters to dusters, ashes to ashes!'

The younger Bagthorpes themselves found that they, too, were enjoying the proceedings, though they sometimes had difficulty in disguising their giggles as sobs, and Tess was in fact reproved for this on one occasion.

'You *never* laugh at funerals,' Daisy told her severely.

'You *cry*. Jus' try to fink of the poor dead lamb. How would *you* like to be a poor dead lamb?'

A relentless procession of chops, then, made their way to the grave, and a curious assortment of headstones sprang up in the part of the garden designated as the graveyard. Daisy was running out of things large enough for her to write her epitaphs on, so had now adopted the policy of selecting articles for their ornamental value, and then attaching her poems on sheets of paper either cellotaped or pinned on. There was a cross formed by a ruler and silver spoon taped together, a brass candlestick, a pair of cast iron Punch and Judy doorstops and a large Staffordshire figure which, Daisy said, reminded her of an angel.

She was increasingly exercised in the composition of suitable epitaphs, because all her corpses at present fell into only two categories.

'I'm getting *bored* writing pomes jus' about lambs and piglets,' she said, as she attached her latest composition to Mr Bagthorpe's shooting stick. 'I wish I could bury something different. For ever and ever amen.'

The epitaph read:

All the lams are dying
All the lams are ded
Evryone is crying
Cos the lams has gone to bed.
Forever and evver.
1629–1842

This seemed to Jack to have a more than usually final ring to it. Daisy's boredom threshold was notoriously low. He intensified his search for something more out of the way for her to work on. In the meantime, William told her that one of the chops was a cow, and another a giraffe, it being unlikely that Daisy would see through this fraud.

The other prong of the campaign to drive Great Aunt Lucy away was also going extremely well. When the younger Bagthorpes were hatching up their scheme to steer conversation whenever possible to the subject of Time, they were not aware that Grandma had privately decided on exactly the same line of action herself. She had already a considerable repertoire of gloomy quotes that she would come up with when she was feeling low.

Like as the waves make towards the pebbled shore
So do our minutes hasten to their end

was one of her favourites, and she was also fond of telling everybody:

Time, like an ever-rolling stream,
Bears all its sons away.

Mealtimes, then, became extremely morbid occasions, what with the insipidity of the menus, most people wearing black because of the imminence of yet another funeral, and the lugubrious nature of the conversation. When even Rosie started coming out with things like:

> But at my back I always hear
> *Time's* wingèd chariot hurrying near

and

> Gather ye rosebuds while ye may,
> Old *Time* is still a-flying,

with particular emphasis on the word Time, Mr Bagthorpe cottoned on to what was happening. He did nothing to prevent it, however, and even stopped his wife from doing so.

'It'll do 'em good, ferreting round for all those quotations,' he told her. 'They have read more Shakespeare in the last two days than in the rest of their lives put together. They are rounding off their education. It is an ill wind, Laura – try to look at it like that.'

'I do think it is all rather unfair on the poor old lady,' she told him.

'Bilge,' returned Mr Bagthorpe. 'Poor nothing. If she's got a Bee in her Bonnet about Time, it's our duty to smoke it out, not pander to it.'

When Mrs Bagthorpe pointed out that a reluctance to accept the idea of mortality was not strictly a Bee in the Bonnet, but a fairly common human frailty, he replied that he did not agree. No life could be properly lived except in the full consciousness of eventual death, he said, and furthermore, some people even welcomed the prospect, as he did himself, at times.

'And if eating kippers at all the hours God sends is not a Bee in the Bonnet, you tell me what is,' he said. 'William had better get on to that Anonymous fellow from Grimsby and get him to catch further supplies. The North Sea will soon be bled dry of kippers.'

'But she may genuinely *believe* there is no such thing as Time,' Mrs Bagthorpe persisted. 'I really think she does. I think we should give her the benefit of the doubt.'

Mr Bagthorpe was not in the habit of giving anyone the benefit of the doubt, and he was not about to start now.

'If she genuinely does not believe in Time,' he replied, 'then the only logical thing for her to do is to clear off to where there *isn't* any – namely, eternity.'

Great Aunt Lucy was, in fact, about to clear off. She shuffled, however, not off this mortal coil, but off out of the Bagthorpe household and into hospital. This calamity was brought about entirely by herself, and nobody, Mrs Bagthorpe said, was likely to be cut out of her will on account of it.

'If, indeed, any of us still figure in it,' she added worriedly. 'I do think you have all tormented the old lady dreadfully.'

'Rubbish, Laura,' Grandma told her with asperity.

'She enjoyed every moment of her stay. She aggravated every one of us, and enjoyed doing so. I could tell.'

She probably could. When it came to aggravating people, Grandma could teach most people a few things – and certainly Great Aunt Lucy, who was not even in the same league.

9

The immediate cause of Great Aunt Lucy's being admitted to the Nightingale Ward of Aysham General Hospital was a broken leg, but the real reason, she later claimed, was the quality of the lining of the curtains in her room. This did not at once emerge, as the old lady was understandably shocked and rambling after her injury, but when the true facts came to light, Mrs Bagthorpe was quite distraught. Her deep breathing failed. She went, temporarily, into being a failed Stella Bright.

'I should have *listened*!' she wailed, to an audience more fascinated by her derangement than by what she was actually saying. 'She *knew* that the rays of the moon were affecting her, and I dismissed it all as idle superstition!'

'It *was* idle superstition,' her husband told her. 'Pull yourself together, Laura. If the sanity of mankind hinged upon the utilization of super-quality curtain linings, the race would have become extinct at the palaeolithic era. No cave, so far as I know, made use of such a product.'

'They used animal hides,' Rosie told him. 'Animal hides are a lot thicker than *any* curtain, even velvet.'

'Be quiet,' he told her, irritated by the realization that a pertinent point had been made. 'Your mother is in no mood for that kind of trivial talk. Lucy had an outsized Bee in her Bonnet, and is paying the price. We must all hope that she will emerge from the experience a little older and wiser.'

'Older, anyway,' William put in, 'though she'll never admit it.'

The amazing thing was that Mr Bagthorpe's hopes were eventually realized. Great Aunt Lucy did emerge (though not for three weeks) considerably wiser. She emerged, in fact, converted to a belief in Time. What brought about this miraculous change was not breaking her leg, *per se*, but her stay in hospital. The manner of her accident had indisputably been brought about by her strenuous belief in the sinister influence of the moon's rays. She had been roaming about the house at dead of night in search of kippers, in order to convince both Time and the moon that it was breakfasttime, when she had tripped against a sack of mushrooms, and fallen. (Normally, bags of mushrooms would not have been lying around on the landing, but Mr Bagthorpe had heard that a great saving could be made by raising these fungi in a large bag of suitably compounded compost, and had accordingly invested in one.)

The rest of the household were woken by Aunt Lucy's screams and the barking of Wung Foo. They emerged from their rooms bleary-eyed and bad-tempered, to find out what was going on. When they did find out, sympathy for Aunt Lucy was scant.

'Why, Lucy, in the name of all that is wonderful, did you not switch on the *light*?' demanded Mr Bagthorpe.

The patient was in no mood for cross-examination, though one was inevitably to take place later, in hospital, to the intense interest of the rest of the ward. It later transpired, however, that not turning on lights was part of her strategy to fool Time. She maintained that if lights were turned on, then Time would *know* it was night, and she had accordingly tried to sneak past Time with a small torch. This had failed to pick out the bag of mushrooms.

Great Aunt Lucy had already established a minor reputation for eccentricity by the time the Bagthorpes went to visit her the following day (though the hospital was not yet acquainted with the full range of Bees in her Bonnet). The ward sister had been able to make little of Aunt Lucy's description of how the accident occurred. She asked the Bagthorpes to give her the real facts.

'People simply do not fall over sacks of mushrooms on landings in the middle of the night,' she said.

'At our place they do,' Mr Bagthorpe told her. 'How long is she going to be in here?'

'It is for the doctors to say, of course,' replied the sister. 'But I should imagine for several weeks – especially at her age. And perhaps you could tell me, incidentally, what her age is? She doesn't appear to know, and became quite agitated when we pressed her.'

'She would,' Mr Bagthorpe told her. 'If you've got her for a month, you'll find out how agitated she gets, all right. And for all our sakes, try to get her sorted out, will you? She's eighty-seven.'

'May we see her now?' inquired Mrs Bagthorpe.

'There is rather a large number of you,' the sister said dubiously.

'Look,' said Mr Bagthorpe, 'we do not have the time, and nor can we afford the petrol, to pay daily visits here for the next few weeks. We are trying to Survive. We will take our full quota of visiting time for the week now, please.'

With this he marched past her and the rest of the family trailed after him. Great Aunt Lucy was halfway down the ward, propped up on pillows and with a hooped cage over her legs. Nobody else had visitors (it was not, in fact, visiting time, simply a time convenient to Mr Bagthorpe) and all eyes followed the procession with interest.

'It's not visiting time, is it?' asked the woman in the next bed to Aunt Lucy.

'There is no such thing as Time,' Aunt Lucy told her coldly. 'Kindly do not refer to it again in my presence. Ah, there you are, Henry and Laura! Why did you put a sack of mushrooms on the landing where I was almost certain to fall over it?'

'If the light had been switched on, you would have seen it,' Henry told her. 'And you should have been in bed, asleep, the same as anybody else not roving abroad in search of kippers.'

'It was breakfasttime,' Aunt Lucy asserted obstinately. 'You do not switch on lights at breakfasttime.'

The listeners in the surrounding beds, having all observed Great Aunt Lucy's entry into the ward at two a.m., raised eyebrows at one another. They had also witnessed her refusal of breakfast.

'I have no wish for a poached egg,' she had informed a bewildered orderly. 'I am not in the babit of consuming poached eggs at lunchtime. I should like a lamb chop please, lightly grilled, and mint sauce.'

In the end, the orderly had fetched the ward sister, who gave it as her opinion that Aunt Lucy was still under the effect of the anaesthetic.

'She will be right as rain by lunchtime,' she forecast optimistically.

Daisy, who had never been in a hospital (except as an outpatient), had pleaded to be brought along too. Her reasons for this had nothing to do with a wish to comfort her Great Aunt, and everything to do with her current preoccupation with mortality.

'We might even see some *skelingtons*,' she confided hopefully to Rosie. 'And there'll be people all cut up.'

She was very interested in the ward, and trotted up and down it. The inmates, enchanted by her cherubic appearance, and unaware that Daisy was in search of a skelington or, failing that, a corpse, made much of her. Before long Daisy was relaying to a fascinated audience details of life as lived by the Bagthorpes.

'I been having funerals,' she told them. 'Every day. And I been burying poor little dead lambs and giraffes. And I know all the proper words to say, and I say "dusters to dusters and ashes to ashes for ever and ever amen". And Grandma Bag helps me, but she's not here because she don't like old Auntie Lucy. She thinks she's a nasty Grook.'

Meanwhile, at Aunt Lucy's bedside, a furore was gradually gathering momentum, and the patients were torn between listening to that and hearing more from Daisy. The nurses began to hover anxiously, wondering whether or not to put the Bagthorpes out, and if so, how on earth to set about this.

Mr Bagthorpe was beginning to shout. The subject of Wung Foo's accommodation during his owner's stay in hospital had been broached. It was she herself who brought it up.

'Where is darling Wung Foo?' she inquired. 'I hope that you have remembered to bring his little bowl?'

'But, Lucy dear, one cannot keep a dog in hospital,' Mrs Bagthorpe said.

'Why not?' she demanded. 'There seem to me to be a good number of people here who would be able to exercise him for me. The rest of the time he can stay on my bed.'

'We will take every care of him,' Mrs Bagthorpe promised.

'We will what?' It was at this point that Mr

Bagthorpe began to run out of control. 'We already have in the house the most numb-brained, non-productive hound that ever went on four legs, but at least it does not feed on kippers at all hours of the day and night, and nor has it, to date, bit. That Peke of yours bit me, Lucy, and nobody can go around expecting hands that get bitten to go around feeding the mouth that bit them.'

He was becoming incoherent. Also, of course, it was not his hand that had been bitten, but his shin. His wife was not herself anxious to have custody of Wung Foo for any length of time. If he bit Mrs Fosdyke, she would leave for ever.

Mrs Fosdyke was already becoming restive about the new dietary arrangements, and had made no effort to conceal her satisfaction on hearing that Great Aunt Lucy was no longer at Unicorn House.

'Hospital's where she belongs, leg broke or not,' she had declared. 'She ain't fit to be loose. Weeks it'll be before we get that horrible smell of kippers out the furnishings. I thought fish bones was meant to *make* brains, not turn 'em.'

She had soliloquised thus at some length, though nobody, of course, paid any attention, because they were all arguing with their mouths full, as was customary at Bagthorpe mealtimes.

Mrs Bagthorpe now, however, timidly put in her own oar.

'I think, Lucy dear, that Wung Foo will be much happier in proper kennels,' she said diplomatically.

'Pekingese are such delicate creatures, and need much sensitive handling.'

'Which will *not* be forthcoming at our place,' Mr Bagthorpe supplied unnecessarily. 'If it stopped there, it'd probably have a nervous breakdown. I certainly should. It will go to the kennels, and you, Lucy, will foot the bill.'

Aunt Lucy was not going to give in this easily, and was about to embark on a thoroughgoing row when a diversion occurred in the shape of an elderly lady at the far end of the ward rising from her pillows, waving her arms wildly, and screaming for a nurse.

'Take her away!' she screeched, meaning, apparently Daisy. 'I won't listen, I won't!'

She covered her ears with her hands, and a contingent of nurses moved rapidly down to her end of the ward.

'What is the matter?' they asked. 'What has she done?'

What Daisy had been doing soon became clear. Abandoning with disappointment her fruitless search for skelingtons and corpses, she had turned her attention to the patients themselves. Some of them, she thought hopefully, might become corpses quite soon, and she could put in an offer for the undertaking.

She had therefore been systematically working down the row of beds, making a critical appraisal of the life expectancy of their occupants. She was to some extent handicapped in this by being unable to see the length of their lower limbs, and was accordingly asking each lady, 'Is your legs long or short?' before making her diagnoses.

The ladies in the ward had been held in a state of hypnotized fascination, until one of their number had started screaming. The sort of things Daisy was saying no one present (and many of them were mothers and grandmothers) had ever heard from the lips of one so young. And they had no idea, of course, of her background, or that she was currently in a Phase of Intimations of Mortality. She was saying things like,

'Ooooh, look at *your* hair! It's all grey. And you've got a lot of wrinkles as well, specially on your neck. I fink you might die quite soon, really soon. Is your legs long or short?'

She made her speculations in so matter-of-fact a way that her subjects actually felt that she might know something about the matter, and those among them with grey hair and wrinkles were quite frightened.

When Daisy's part in the screaming episode was established, she in turn became extremely unhappy, and sobbed bitterly. Aunt Celia was not there to protect her, and Mr Bagthorpe, abandoning his row with Great Aunt Lucy, pitched into her on a scale never before known. Jack found himself feeeling sorry for her. He did not pretend to understand the way Daisy's mind worked, he thought it possible that nobody ever would understand this, but he felt certain that however cataclysmic the effect she so often had on those about her, it was quite unintentional. Daisy did not really have any vice in her, it was just that she liked experimenting – with fire and water, for instance – and that she became bored when she was not occupied. Jack had been impressed by the way Daisy had been shedding real tears over her recent victims (including the chops). He thought this showed an essential softness of heart for which people were not apt to give her credit – with the exception of Rosie, who herself deputized for Aunt Celia by attacking Mr Bagthorpe.

'You're a nasty Grook, just like Daisy says!' she shrieked at him. 'You don't care tuppence when things die and get buried! Daisy's really sweet the way she sobs and cries and has funerals and writes on their tombstones! If you don't look out, I shan't cry when *you're* dead!'

All this bandying about of words like tombstones and funerals, and at a pitch more suited to a music hall than a hospital ward, was becoming too much. One of the younger nurses panicked and telephoned for the matron. She had heard that this august person was a battleaxe when roused, and thought that she, if anybody, would be able to quieten and evict the Bagthorpes.

She was mistaken about this, because Mr Bagthorpe knew nothing of hospital hierarchies, and did not at first even know that she *was* the matron. He thought she was a stout, elderly nurse in a different uniform from the rest. Even when he had been made to understand who she was, matters were improved for nobody but Daisy, from whom he immediately turned his attention to pitch into the matron instead.

Mr Bagthorpe detested bureaucracy and authority in any form, even at the best of times, and of course believed that he was in his present plight as a direct result of the activities of these nebulous enemies. So far he had not confronted anybody, even his bank manager, about this, and the luckless matron made a convenient whipping boy.

'I would not at this moment be in the throes of a desperate fight for Survival,' he told this bewildered lady, 'if it were not for the System. You are a part of the System. You do not run this hospital – *I* do. You, madam, are a servant of the State. I am for ever paying out vast sums of money left and right in taxation for the maintenance of this kind of benighted institution.'

Mr Bagthorpe often did not know when he was mistiming his tirades. A ward full of semi-hysterical patients and frantic nurses do not wish for an exposition on taxation. They wish for order to be restored, for peace and quiet.

The scene ended in a way that was less than dignified. The same resourceful nurse who had called the matron reassessed the situation and sent for two porters. Their burly and belligerent appearance caused Mr Bagthorpe's tirade to tail off in mid-sentence.

'I am leaving,' he announced, 'and I shall not be back. You, Lucy, should try to take advantage of the next few weeks to get your ideas sorted out. Put your house in order.'

He stamped out followed by the rest of the Bagthorpes and all eyes in the ward. Most of the patients were left feeling distinctly limp after this visit, and Mrs Fosdyke later received a first-hand account of it from one of her cronies, Mrs Pye, who was in there to have some ingrowing toenails removed. She had been one of the luckless ladies with grey hair and wrinkles, and Daisy had firmly placed her in the category of being in early need of burial. Mrs Pye was much upset by this, despite repeated assurances from the sister and nurses that people do not die of ingrowing toenails.

'Them Bagthorpes you work for certainly is a bunch of lunatics,' she told Mrs Fosdyke after her discharge. 'Them nurses was dishing out tranquillizers like sweets. You never in your life could imagine the racketing they set up in that ward.'

Mrs Fosdyke denied this. She could imagine it, she said, clearly. Only that day Mrs Fosdyke had received further indications of the seriousness of the Scheme for Survival and was considering, not for the first time, giving her notice.

'You never heard such mad twaddle in your life,' she told Mrs Pye. 'That beautiful summer house – there's all the deck-chairs and parasols stuck in my outhouse, and wire netting all over everywhere. And the food they're eating you'd never believe. It's all right for them that's been bankrupted, and *got* to Survive, but what about them that hasn't?'

Her own health, she maintained, was probably

being damaged (she took a large number of her meals at Unicorn House) by all the lettuce and rhubarb and beetroot. She had a cousin, Kitty, who had died of an overdose of vitamings, she said, and she had no wish to go the same way herself.

10

The Bagthorpes now really began to feel that they were, as Mr Bagthorpe maintained, ranged up against the whole world. More accurately, they felt that the whole world was ranged up against *them*. They were used to a moderate degree of unpopularity. People who are brilliant and, what is worse, constantly boast about this, seldom attract warm and friendly feelings from other people. But the Bagthorpes did, however surprisingly, have several friends, with the exception of Mr Bagthorpe, who had none. He was accordingly less affected by this chilling-off in relationships.

Anyone friendly with the Bagthorpes knew, naturally, that they were not quite as others. Some people found them quite entertaining, and liked hearing about their fires and floods, and so forth. But the friendship of these people was now being tested. A lot of the young Bagthorpes' friends were accustomed to coming up to Unicorn House for meals. These were always well worth coming for. People would walk or cycle for miles to catch a slice of Mrs Fosdyke's apricot cream gateau, or one of her stuffed eggs. Having partaken of these, they would then circulate rhapsodic descriptions of the experience to acquaintances, and regular visitors were therefore more in the nature of an unofficial Gourmet Society than bona fide lovers and admirers of the Bagthorpes themselves.

It was, then, the falling off of standards of cuisine, rather than the Bagthorpes' Plan for Survival *per se* that was responsible for the rapid decline in their social life. Nobody, as William bitterly pointed out (his latest girlfriend having become cool) is going to walk even fifty yards for lukewarm beetroot salad, followed by gooseberry fool made with half milk and half water. The Bagthorpes were themselves beginning to lose their appetites, and most of them were losing weight.

'*I* shall be bankrupt soon!' wailed Rosie. (Her savings were being rapidly depleted by frequent visits to the village shop for supplementary rations.) 'It's not fair! Children aren't supposed to have to buy their own food. Their fathers are supposed to feed them. I bet there's a law against it!'

The idea of taking legal action against Mr Bagthorpe was actually seriously considered. The younger Bagthorpes were quite prepared to do this in principle. There was, however, one insurmountable deterrent. The Bagthorpes had had a good deal of adverse publicity during the preceding year, some of it reaching the national press and television networks. A court case brought against a father by his own offspring would only invite further unwelcome headlines.

'And just think how that ghastly Luke and Esther'd

gloat,' said Rosie glumly. 'The only reason they're jealous of us is because we've got Fozzy's cooking, and they only have lettuce and nuts. If they knew *we* get lettuce as well, think how they'd *smirk*!'

The truth of this was patent and incontrovertible, and the idea of instigating litigation against their father was reluctantly abandoned. The young Bagthorpes, however, were not of the stuff of which martyrs are made. They did not suffer setbacks with stoicism. If circumstances did not suit them, they made all-out efforts to change them. If there was no way Mr Bagthorpe could be coaxed or coerced out of his current obsession, then their only course, they decided, was to enter into it equally wholeheartedly themselves.

'There is no question of becoming immortal,' Tess wisely pointed out, 'if one is not even able to achieve Survival.'

They accordingly dropped their frenzied pursuit of immortality, and channelled all their considerable energies into Survival. By and large they were temporarily united in this. Unfortunately, however, there very soon occurred a major rift as a result of certain events later in the day of the Bagthorpes' visit to hospital.

Daisy, upset by her unsympathetic treatment there, set about consoling herself by holding another couple of funerals on her return. Nobody but Rosie and Grandma was interested in assisting her in these, however, because now that Great Aunt Lucy was out of the way, everybody else had lost their motivation. Only William, surprisingly, complied.

'There's still a couple of lamb chops left,' he said. 'Might as well tell her they're a lion cub and a panda, and let her bury 'em. It'll keep her out of the way.'

The others did not care one way or the other, and said she could bury them if she liked, but they wanted no part in the funeral arrangements. Nobody even saw the processions, but the ceremonies had evidently been a great success.

'I never buried a baby lion before,' Daisy told everybody happily at tea-time. 'And lion rhymes with dying, so the pome was easy.' (Daisy made extensive use of poetic licence. Jack later saw the tombstone of the purported panda, and it read: Here there is a pore ded panda, pekked to deth by goosy ganda.)

Nobody encouraged this line of conversation, and the matter of the funerals was dropped until the following morning, when it was raised again with a vengeance. Daisy, it appeared, did not just bury her remains and then forget them. She visited their graves to inspect them and sometimes change the flowers. And on this particular occasion she went further. Although she so frequently made use of the phrase 'dusters to dusters and ashes to ashes', she had recently been much exercised by the question of whether her corpses actually *were* metamorphosed in this way, and if so, how long it took. Were the assortment of toffee tins and chocolate boxes used as coffins and recently interred, actually now containing dusters and ashes, she wondered? Her curiosity had reached such a pitch that, being Daisy, she had no alternative but to satisfy it. She had decided to exhume one of yesterday's fatalities first, and then, if the results were disappointing, go back to an earlier corpse, Rosie's hamster, and take a look at that. In the event, her experiment was shortlived.

Daisy was an incurably early riser, and the whole household was therefore woken by her shrieks. She ran first, naturally, to Grandma's room, and most other people assembled there to see what was happening. No one but Rosie, and possibly Mrs Bagthorpe, much cared what had happened to Daisy. They simply, being Bagthorpes, found a furore, of whatever kind, irresistible.

It was some time before Grandma, still half awake and befuddled, could elicit from her protégée what was causing her present distress. Daisy was sobbing uncontrollably, and only odd words and phrases were intelligible.

'Gone for ever and ever amen!' she wailed. And 'Nuffing, now, not even dusters and ashes and anyfing! Poor fings, poor fings!'

The baffled Bagthorpes little by little pieced together some kind of picture. The gist of what was being said seemed, incredibly, to be that some of Daisy's most recent victims had been exhumed during the night.

'The child is raving,' said Mr Bagthorpe decisively. 'That blasted Peke is fifteen miles away by now, thank God.'

'Hush!' cried Grandma. 'Daisy is distressed beyond all measure!'

'We're *all* distressed beyond all measure,' he told her unrepentantly, 'as, indeed, we can count upon being, whenever that unholy infant is in the vicinity. We are to take it, then, that there is a grave-robber at large?'

'Certainly there is,' replied Grandma. 'Daisy's word is her bond. I shall put on my wrap and go instantly to investigate.'

'There is no need for that, Mother,' interposed Mrs Bagthorpe. 'The dew may have been quite heavy. Jack will go, won't you, dear?'

Jack went. He stared in amazement at the soil-speckled toffee tin that had held the remains of the fraudulent lion cub. It was empty.

'She could've forgotten to put the chop in,' he thought, though without conviction. Daisy was nothing if not thorough. Jack seemed to remember that Daisy was enclosing her chops in plastic bags, and *then* placing them in their various coffins. He also, now he came to think of it, seemed to remember that this had been at William's suggestion. William, indeed, had been uncharacteristically helpful over the whole business of chop-burying, especially considering his views about Daisy, which were frequently aired, and unflattering to a degree.

'It will be more hygienic, Daisy,' he had said on this occasion, obligingly proffering a polythene bag.

'Oh, fank you, William!' Daisy had squealed. 'What's hygienic?'

'It's something everybody needs to be,' he told her, 'alive or dead.'

Daisy, while by no means a conformist, nor even particularly hygienic, had been happy to observe this formality. It had been an extra little ritual for her to enjoy, putting the chops carefully into their polythene bags before enclosing them in their tins and boxes.

On impulse, Jack stirred with his foot the loose soil of the adjacent grave, that of the panda. He could see the pattern of the tin lid showing through (Daisy's graves were all very shallow). He hesitated. It *did* seem sacrilege, of a sort.

'It's only a *chop*,' he told himself.

He knelt and scrabbled with his fingers and easily lifted out the tin. He opened it. It was empty. He set off back for the house still carrying it. It would be evidence, he thought, that Daisy was telling the truth, if nothing else. Though he thought he had now put two and two together.

He had. When the true story emerged it was like, as Mr Bagthorpe observed, something straight out of Dracula.

'We are embarked on a full-scale tilt into the macabre,' he declared, 'and I shudder to think how this family might end up. What in the name of the devil have we spawned?'

'Only *William*,' Rosie protested. 'Greedy thing!'

'It was not greed,' corrected her father. 'It was nothing like so simple as that. It was sheer, blind, carnivorous craving. It was a primitive blood lust.'

Jack thought Mr Bagthorpe was exaggerating, in that William had not killed the chops, merely eaten them. He guessed, rightly, that his father was chagrined that he had not thought of this idea first.

'He consumed them at midnight,' Mr Bagthorpe continued, 'at dead of night he conducted this grisly post morten. I suspect that he did not even use a knife and fork. I suspect that he held them in his fingers and tore at the flesh. Did you, by any chance, devour them raw?'

'I grilled them,' William replied. 'And I had mint sauce with the lamb ones. They're the best thing I've had for days. I ate every single chop she buried, if you want to know.'

He was not at all repentant, and refused to allow that there was anything Satanic, or even macabre, about his actions.

'The chops had merely been laid in the cool earth rather than a fridge,' he said, 'as they would have been before fridges were invented. You are just jealous because you didn't think of it yourselves.'

They were, of course, almost to a man, with the exception of Mrs Bagthorpe, Daisy, and Grandma, the latter secure in her possession of a Fortnum and Mason hamper. Rosie would dearly have liked a grilled chop, but certainly not at the expense of hurting Daisy's feelings.

'Poor little Daisy – you never thought of *her*!' she shrieked at William.

'I did not,' he assented. 'I never gave her a second's thought. I put the graves back how they were, and if she hadn't gone poking around she'd never have known. It's *her* that's morbid.'

'It's not! It's not! She cried and cried and cried. She thinks that all the things she's buried have vanished into thin air for ever and ever, and now she's really upset!'

'What she was probably looking for,' William continued, 'was maggots.'

'She wasn't then! She thinks things turn to dusters and ashes, and I think it's really sweet! And—'

'I think we are going round in circles,' Mr Bagthorpe intervened. 'You know, don't you' – addressing himself to William – 'that your grandmother is talking of cutting you out of her will? I should have thought that a high price to pay for a couple of clandestine chops.'

'And Daisy's going to train Little Tommy up to scratch you,' Rosie put in, '*and* bite you. And it'll serve you right!'

Grandma and Daisy had certainly been holed up in the former's room once the initial furore died down. Grandma had been extremely scathing prior to her withdrawal.

'You have betrayed at a stroke the innocent dreams of a little child,' she told William. 'That is the eighth, and the most heinous, of the Seven Deadly Sins. You should wear sack-cloth and ashes for the rest of your days.'

Her Old Testament line and the unfortunate reference to ashes made no impression at all on William, and served only to heighten Daisy's hysteria.

'I fought fings turned to dusters and ashes,' she sobbed. 'And now they don't, and I'm not having funerals any more. I hate funerals!'

'Of course you do not, dear child,' Grandma told her. 'And of *course* things turn to dusters and ashes, if they are not interfered with. We shall hold many more lovely funerals, and put this whole sordid business behind us.'

'I'm going to tell Arry Awk!' Daisy wailed, unsoothed.

At this all present, including Grandma, stiffened. If the exhumation of the chops had brought about the resurrection of Arry Awk, who had been conspicuous by his absence of late, then things were taking a more dangerous turn. He was, they well knew, the most malignant and slippery member of the Unholy Alliance. Despite his invisibility to the eyes of anyone but Daisy, he certainly knew how to make his presence felt. He also enabled Daisy and Grandma to perpetrate whatever atrocities they chose, and then disclaim all responsibility by blaming them all on the tireless Arry Awk.

'Arry Awk is the Archetypal Can-carrier of all time,' Mr Bagthorpe would declare. 'I should know. I am one myself.'

'If Arry Awk is again among us,' he now said, 'we must look to ourselves. We are already beset with cannibalism (meaning, presumably, William) and saboteurs (meaning Daisy and Grandma). Now we have a hell-raising entity who will strike at any time, from all sides. Mayhem will break loose.'

A profound silence followed this statement. It was broken by the rattling of the doorknob that heralded the arrival of Mrs Fosdyke. The Bagthorpes tried to rally themselves into some kind of appearance of normality, but failed signally.

'Morning!' Mrs Fosdyke kept shooting suspicious looks at them as she whipped about donning her overall and fur-edged slippers. The Bagthorpes, in their strenuous effort to look normal, in fact appeared less so than usual.

Grandma rose.

'Come, Daisy,' she said. 'We will leave others to explain to Mrs Fosdyke the grisly proceedings of the past few days. She may wish to consider seriously whether or not she wishes to be attached to such a household.'

Having made this intentionally inflammatory speech she withdrew, taking Daisy with her.

'What's been going on, then?' demanded Mrs Fosdyke flatly.

'Nothing,' replied the young Bagthorpes in unison.

Unlovable as Mrs Fosdyke was, she could at least do more with rhubarb and beetroot than any of themselves. She had even produced a moderately acceptable soup with the latter.

'What's on for today, then?' Mrs Fosdyke asked. 'It's never lettuce and onions again?'

'I had rather thought a salad at lunch,' Mrs Bagthorpe said apologetically. 'And then this evening, I thought an omelette?'

'An omelette?' Rosie echoed. '*One* omelette, between us all?'

'Don't be an idiot,' William told her. 'Have you forgotten? The hens are coming today.'

'My chickens!' she exclaimed joyously. 'Hurrah! I'm going to give them all names, and call them, and I'm going to fill my apron with corn, and they'll all come running to me!'

'I should not become too involved with them, Rosie dear,' advised Mrs Bagthorpe, worried by this speech. 'They are not to be pets, remember, but productive members of the ménage. They are coming for a *purpose*.'

Rosie had clearly overlooked the undoubted fact that these hens, having produced their eggs, would almost certainly end up in a casserole. (Given that they were able to bypass Daisy.)

'I've thought of lots of names already,' she continued happily, appearing not to have heard what her mother had said. 'Biddy and Cluck and Speckles and Blackie. But I'll wait till I see their faces before I decide, so's they'll have names to really suit them.'

Mr Bagthorpe rose.

'Cease your prattling,' he told Rosie. 'Those hens are here to lay eggs, not to feature in a Walt Disney film. And you, William, get on to that prophet fellow in Grimsby and see if you can't get him to catch some kippers. We're clean out of them. Tell him to let his everlasting Alien Intelligence get on with it by itself, and get catching some kippers.'

'You don't catch kippers,' William told him.

Mr Bagthorpe stared at him.

'Shoot them perhaps?' he inquired sarcastically.

'There are no kippers in the sea,' William said.

'Look,' said Mr Bagthorpe, 'I may not be the Brain of Britain, but I do happen to know that the North Sea is full of kippers, and that Grimsby is the place where they pull 'em all in.'

William, who was in no mood to explain to his father the processes whereby a herring becomes a kipper, himself rose.

'I am glad you reminded me of the Brain of Britain,' he said. 'It's on tonight. I'm going to have one last shot at blacking the wavelength.'

'Do you really think you should, dear?' Mrs Bagthorpe was anxious about this. She genuinely believed that her elder son was capable of plunging Britain into total silence on the Radio Two network, and was fearful of the repercussions of this action.

'Just leave it to me, Mother,' William told her loftily. 'No need to get in a stew.'

He went out.

'Stew!' came Mrs Fosdyke's disillusioned voice. 'That'll be the day . . .'

11

The day the hens arrived was an active one even by Bagthorpian standards. It was lucky that Mrs Fosdyke was not there to witness most of the happenings. She was dismissed after lunch by Mr Bagthorpe.

'Take the afternoon off,' he told her. 'I shall need the kitchen.'

'Why is that, dear?' inquired his wife nervously.

'I am going to brew beer,' he announced.

'But, Henry,' she protested, 'you do not know how to brew beer.'

'It's easy,' he told her. 'Any fool could do it. I'm going to make eight gallons. And I may as well tell you I'm going to make rhubarb wine as well.'

'I do not consider wine and beer to be essential to Survival,' Tess told him. There was currently precious little sweetness and light in her own life, and she did not see why there should be in his. 'They are luxury commodities.'

'Bilge,' said Mr Bagthorpe. 'They are life-enhancing, and, as such, part of Survival.'

The rest of the family thought the logic of this shaky, but did not trouble to say so. If Mr Bagthorpe said he was going to brew beer and wine, then he would do it.

'It is to be hoped, Henry, that you do not blow up the house in the process,' Grandma now remarked.

Grandma counted as lost all time not spent either conducting a row or planning how to stage one. She was on this occasion rewarded by the expression on Mrs Fosdyke's face, which was one of undiluted horror.

'Blow up?' she echoed. 'My kitchen?'

'I shall blow nothing up,' Mr Bagthorpe stated with a confidence shared by no one else there present.

'I have certainly read in the press of cases of severe injuries inflicted in the process of amateur winemaking,' Grandma continued. 'And you, Henry, are nothing if not an amateur. You are scarcely able to brew a pot of tea without incident.'

'If my kitchen blows up,' Mrs Fosdyke said, 'there'll be no point my coming here any longer, if you'll excuse me saying, Mrs Bagthorpe.'

'Oh really, Mrs Fosdyke,' Mrs Bagthorpe protested. 'There is absolutely no question of such a thing happening.'

Mrs Fosdyke was little comforted by this assurance, knowing, as she did, that her employer was an incurable optimist – as, indeed, she needed to be as head of so accident-prone a ménage.

'That's what you said about the dining-room,' Mrs Fosdyke reminded her. 'You said history never repeated itself, and it did. History's always repeating itself round here.'

'I think it would be prudent if we were all to vacate the house while the brewing is in process,' Grandma said. 'Though if my memory serves me correctly, the explosions do not tend to take place during the actual brewing, but at a later date, and quite without warning.'

'That's marvellous, that is!' William said. 'We're already bags of nerves and skin and bone from all the muck we've been eating, and now we're told we're sitting on an active volcano. That is just about all we needed.'

'You are being silly, William,' his mother told him. 'Think, Rosie, your hens will be here at any moment!'

This transparent attempt to steer conversation away from the subject of explosions within earshot of Mrs Fosdyke met with total failure. Daisy had so far taken no part in the conversation, but now, having assessed the situation, made her own contribution to the general jumpiness of the company.

'If the house blowed up,' she remarked pensively, 'everybody could be dead. And if everybody was dead, just *fink* how many funerals I could have!'

Nobody but Daisy herself wished to think about any such contingency, even Grandma. The latter, however, thought this was a promising line along which conversation could be steered.

'Certainly you could, Daisy,' she said. 'Though you

and I must ourselves beware that we are not victims. Perhaps we should take our meals in my room.'

Grandma's Fortnum and Mason hamper was up there, anyway, as a precaution against pilfering by her ravening and unscrupulous relatives, and Daisy herself was still quite chubby, having come in for a good share of the delicacies.

'I'm off!' Mrs Fosdyke was by now thoroughly disgusted. 'And it's to be hoped when I some in tomorrow I'll find my kitchen as I left it!'

This sounded like a threat. She slammed out.

'Those that can't stand the heat should get out of the kitchen!' Mr Bagthorpe said delightedly. 'And that applies to the lot of you!'

They scattered willingly enough. William was supposed to be putting the last touches to the hen-run, and dealing with its occupants on their arrival. Instead, he sneaked back up to his room for a final desperate bid to jam one of the BBC's radio networks. He accordingly was later held responsible for much of the pandemonium that ensued, though in fact very many people were to blame, including Mr Bagthorpe himself.

Mr Bagthorpe started brewing his beer, and then remembered that he had heard somewhere that if extra sugar is added, the resulting mixture will be much more potent. He understandably felt that he would be in frequent future need of such a brew, but found no sugar in the pantry.

'You go and get some,' he told Rosie, who was

hanging around outside, for the arrival of her chickens. She protested strongly at this, but there was no one else within call (or if there were, they were lying low) and she was despatched none the less.

No sooner had she gone than the chickens arrived. Mr Bagthorpe was reading a book about edible berries, and did not wish to be interrupted.

'Just bang 'em down there,' he told the man. 'We'll sort 'em out later.'

'You'll 'ave to pay a deposit on the cages,' the man told him. 'Returnable when you send 'em back.'

With ill grace Mr Bagthorpe forked out the deposit and returned to his book. Not many people who brew beer sit reading books at the same time. They stir continuously, as advised in the recipe. Mr Bagthorpe, however, in common with his offspring, had a very low boredom threshold. He was not the kind of man to stand round stirring over a low heat. He had never, in fact, followed a recipe in his life, and hated to be given instructions of any kind. He tended to rely on inspiration. Accordingly, he turned the hot plate up full, and left the beer to its own devices.

He was so engrossed in his book that he did not notice Daisy's passage through the kitchen, nor hear her reception of the hens. She was enchanted by these, but very upset to see them in cages.

'Poor little hens!' she said to them. 'It's not fair to be in cages. You should stretch your wings and fly away like the eleven swans.'

For Daisy, to think was to act. The catches of the

cages were simple to unfasten, even for her small fingers. The hens wandered out on to the drive, and started pecking at the gravel. This in itself would not have mattered if two further developments had not followed closely. The first was that Jack appeared on the scene, followed by Zero, and the second was that Mr Bagthorpe's beer boiled over.

Zero had never seen hens before. He never did much chasing of cats or rabbits. The only things he had ever been interested in chasing had been squirrels. Jack later said that he thought hens were squirrel-shaped, and Zero had become confused by the likeness, but no one else could see this.

'If that infernal hound cannot distinguish a hen from a squirrel,' Mr Bagthorpe fulminated, 'then you should get some shears and lop some of that matted fur from over its eyes. *I* couldn't see under fur like that. Nobody could.'

For whatever reasons, then, Zero became very excited and started to chase the hens. The effects of this were very gratifying, and Zero rapidly became delirious, hardly knowing which way to turn next. The hens scampered frantically hither and thither and one or two of them managed to get back in their cages. Three of them, running in convoy, ran straight through the open kitchen door, pursued by Zero. This was at the precise moment that Mr Bagthorpe's beer boiled over.

All hell then broke loose. Zero, barking wildly, was still chasing the hysterical hens. He bounded straight into Mr Bagthorpe, who skidded in some spilt beer and went headlong. He lay there yelling and cursing, and Jack vainly tried to catch Zero, and the beer went on boiling. Two of the hens then flew up, one on to the table, where it knocked over a half-full bottle of wine and a jug of marigolds. The other hopped from a chair to the dresser, where it ran up and down flapping and squarking and soon dislodged, inevitably, the replica of the replica of Thomas. The crash was spectacular. It was, Mr Bagthorpe later said, the only good thing to have come out of the whole débâcle. Grandma, having given much thought to the positioning of this dubious ornament, had finally opted not for the place of honour in her own room, but for the dresser.

'Where we can all enjoy it,' she said.

Most people were surprised by this, but not so Mr Bagthorpe.

'Mother knows full well,' he declared, 'that the sight of that repellent ginger pot will put us all off our food. She has deliberately, and with diabolical intent, chosen the place where it will cause most suffering.'

He had even threatened to knock it off himself once or twice, and was certainly inclined to congratulate the hen responsible for its destruction.

This, however, was the only congratulation to be made by anybody to anybody, and for hours after the incident recriminations were flying on a scale never before known. Insults were exchanged, characters denigrated and voices had to be raised to an almost supersonic level in order to be heard at all. Every single person in the household was in a passion for one reason or another.

Grandma was fuming about the fall of her pot Thomas, and accused Mr Bagthorpe of deliberately engineering the whole thing, quite overlooking the undoubted fact that it had been Daisy, and not he, who had set the hens free. Even after this had been pointed out she persisted in her accusation.

'If you had done the humane thing,' she shrieked, 'and taken those hens straight to their run, none of this would ever have happened. Of *course* Daisy freed the birds from those barbaric cages. She cannot endure the sight of suffering, and is a lover of all creatures great and small. I am proud of her, and I am utterly ashamed of you, my own son, who stood callously by, brewing intoxicating liquor, while a little innocent child strove to redress wrong!'

She made Mr Bagthorpe sound like the villain of a Victorian melodrama. She was, of course, secure in the knowledge that she had the backing of most of the family, though they were less elaborate in their phrasing.

'If you hadn't sent me for that stupid sugar I'd've been there!' Rosie screamed. 'They're *my* chickens, and now you've frightened them, and they might not lay any eggs now for ever and ever!'

'Amen,' added Daisy automatically, but no one heard this.

The issue of the chickens' future egg output was

not at the time considered vital by anyone but Rosie herself.

'To *hell* with eggs!' Mr Bagthorpe yelled. 'What about my beer?'

Mr Bagthorpe's beer, or what remained of it, was going, patently, to be undrinkable. If it tasted anything like it smelled, it was probably poisonous. The smell of burnt sugar and yeast is not a pleasant one, and William actually volunteered the opinion that it was sniffing this that had sent Zero and the hens out of their minds.

'It's enough to make anyone blow their mind,' he said, pinching his nostrils. 'Pooh!'

There was blackened beer all over the stove, and when the obnoxious brew was seized and poured down the sink by Mrs Bagthorpe there was discovered to be a solid crust of burned yeast and sugar on the bottom of the pan. This was the inevitable result of Mr Bagthorpe's lack of conscientiousness in the matter of stirring.

'How shall we remove it?' she wailed. 'Oh – it is Mrs Fosdyke's best jam pan. Whatever will she say?'

Mr Bagthorpe consigned Mrs Fosdyke to Hades with the same fine disregard he had shown the eggs, and announced his intention of brewing again, immediately.

'If I do not, I shall lose my nerve,' he asserted.

During the stunned lull produced by this announcement Tess, who had not been missed in the general pandemonium, entered, herself in a state of near-hysteria. So distraught was she, that she actually used words of few syllables, like ordinary people. She was graphic to an unprecedented degree.

'Get your beastly hens off my patch!' she screamed at Rosie. 'You get them off this minute! All my plants! All my plants – they'll be dead of shock, every one of them. Go on! Go on, I tell you!'

Here she stamped her foot. The Bagthorpes were impressed by this uncharacteristic performance, though no one had the least idea what she was talking about.

'You haven't *got* any plants!' Rosie screeched back. 'You leave my hens alone! You only *sowed* them yesterday!'

Jack himself thought that Tess was over-reacting, and it was some time before the reason for her outburst became clear. She had lately, they were vaguely aware, been much caught up in the paranormal. She had been reading, for instance, a good deal of Lyall Watson. From this she had become drawn to several theories, all of them described by Mr Bagthorpe, who was a fine one to talk, as half-baked. One of these theories was about the sensitivity of plants, and how they reacted to what went on around them. From all accounts, seeds were a good deal more sensitive than the Bagthorpes themselves.

Her day-old seeds, Tess maintained, as well as those germinating after being sown a week previously, had been subjected to the 'threat to well being' principle. She insisted on describing in detail certain experiments in which plants had been tortured, by having their leaves dipped into a cup of hot coffee, for instance. These plants had all been wired up to a lie detector, to measure their emotional reactions, and at the mere touch of the scalding liquid, she said, their tracings had risen dramatically. Not only that, but apparently somebody had only to *think* about harming plants, and they would pick this up by telepathy, and react similarly. It was this that was called the 'threat to well being' syndrome. (Plants also cared deeply about shrimps, it emerged. When this experimenter had dropped live shrimps one by one into a pan of boiling water, one particular rubber plant had fainted each time.)

Nobody believed a word of any of this, least of all Mr Bagthorpe, who had little time for other people's half-baked theories. He said that if there were really such a thing as the 'threat to well being' principle, then the Bagthorpe line would have become extinct long since.

'Everything that ever happens around here is a threat to well-being,' he said.

'*You're* always talking about vibrations,' Tess told him, with perfect truth. 'And if you can pick up vibrations, so can plants!'

Mr Bagthorpe replied that if all this were true, then it was self-evident that the immediate environs of Unicorn House would be totally devoid of plant life. They would be not so much a garden as a desert.

'Even a cactus could not survive on the vibrations emanating from this house,' he declared. 'And Fozzy's herb garden would sure as hell be flat on its back.'

Jack thought he had a point here, but not so Tess.

'Whether or not you wish to admit it,' she told her father, 'we are all part of the Cosmic Mind. Every violent thought you have is reverberating through the entire Universe.'

This was a considerable prospect. If it were true, Jack thought, it was a poor look-out for the Universe.

The long day wore on, with people finally abandoning their verbal onslaughts and scattering to repair the damage done and put themselves together again. It took Rosie and William a good three hours to capture all the roaming hens. At one time, it seemed that it might be a good three weeks, until they hit upon the expedient of using the now redundant strawberry net.

Daisy and Grandma retreated to the latter's room, and Jack took Zero to *his* room so that he would not become excited by the squirrel-shaped hens still loose in the garden. He then set off alone to the village, on Mr Bagthorpe's instructions, to purchase further supplies of sugar. Tess disappeared, presumably to talk soothingly to her shocked seeds.

Mr Bagthorpe relentlessly went on brewing beer. He used the second-best jam pan, while Mrs Bagthorpe energetically scraped and scoured the burnt one. She had just completed this labour by the time Mr

Bagthorpe had all his ingredients tipped into his pan, and Jack returned with the sugar.

'There!' he exclaimed with satisfaction. 'That's broken the back of it. Keep stirring it, Laura, will you? I have just had this shattering idea, and wish to note it down before it has gone for ever. Inspiration in this house dissolves like foam upon the deep.'

With these words he made his exit, leaving his spouse, her brow deeply furrowed, stirring hard with one hand and holding the book of brewing recipes in the other. After a time, tiring of this tedious exercise, she switched on the wireless, for light relief.

What she heard could in no way be described as light, nor did it give her any relief.

'It is the point at which it would be impossible for a body to get any colder, that is, at which it is totally devoid of heat. This is estimated at about – 273° Centigrade.'

Mrs Bagthorpe herself froze considerably at the sound of this piping, familiar voice.

'Absolutely right!' came the voice of the quizmaster. 'That is the exact definition of absolute zero, and you, Luke Bagthorpe, are winner, by one point, of the semi-final round of this Young Brain of Britain Contest, and will go forward to the final next month.'

Numbly, Mrs Bagthorpe turned off the radio. At Unicorn House, rock bottom, if not absolute zero, had now been reached.

12

Much of the blame for Luke's success in his semi-final was cast upon Mr Bagthorpe himself. It was he who had given Zero his name.

'If there was anything less than zero, that hound would be it,' he had stated (wrongly, of course).' But there isn't, so we'll settle for that.'

If Zero had not been given that particular name, the young Bagthorpes argued, then Luke would not have been moved to look up the definition of absolute zero, and would have lost this vital point. Also, had they not themselves been occupied repairing the ravages caused directly or indirectly by Mr Bagthorpe's ill-starred beer brewing, they would have been able to transmit wrong answers to Luke by sending out powerful thought waves, they said. Nobody but Tess herself actually believed this, it merely suited their purposes to say that they did.

Tess told them privately that they had better believe it, and that they had better practise the sending out of these thought waves if Luke was to be foiled. Some of them actually did, on the quiet, Jack himself included. He found the practice difficult, however, because it did not matter how powerfully he *thought* he was thinking, there seemed no way of measuring how far these thoughts were in fact travelling. He persevered mainly because he genuinely thought this would be a useful power to cultivate, and because he was impressed by the total conviction with which his elder sister was pursuing her theories.

One thing Tess was doing was talking to her plants. She was also playing music to them. She took, without permission, every portable radio and tape recorder in the house, and had these positioned at strategic intervals in her vegetable garden. Sometimes, of course, it rained, and William, whose equipment had been very expensive, and paid for out of his own pocket, did so much shouting in the vicinity of her vegetables that it must certainly have negated any therapeutic effects the music might have been having. Tess, doubtless realizing this, redoubled her efforts. She would turn all the available radios on to Radio Three, which offered a diet of classical music all day, interspersed with the occasional highbrow talk given in measured and cultivated tones. There was nothing on Radio Three that could upset any seedling, however young.

Tess developed extended theories of her own, such as, for instance, that courgettes responded better to Mozart and Haydn than to Beethoven. Lettuce, she maintained, had a partiality for Handel, while tomatoes stood up and fruited for Wagner. There was no way anybody could either prove or disprove these theories, but most people admitted to themselves, if not publicly, that Tess did seem to have green fingers.

'You have probably always had green fingers,' her father told her, on one occasion when she was boasting of this herself. 'Your trouble is that your fingers have been forever monkeying about twiddling oboe keys, instead of getting to grips with Nature, as they should have been.'

As it turned out, Tess's delight in her saladings and vegetables was to be short-lived. As the seedlings waxed and flourished on their regime of classical music and kind words, Tess began to compare their appearance with that shown on the seed packets from which they had been sown.

'*Lettuce*?' she was to be heard dubiously murmuring, and 'Surely this leaf formation is at odds with that depicted here?'

Nobody took much notice of this initially, but as her unease mounted, several of them were requested to come and themselves compare the pictures on the seed packets with the actualities sprouting among the canned music. Jack was asked to inspect the lettuce, and admitted that he did not recognize it as such. He had a fair idea of what lettuce should look like, with or without the aid of a seed packet.

'The funny thing is,' he told her, '*some* of them look like lettuce. Those bigger ones at the end do, and even one or two of these little ones. Perhaps they're a kind of variegated lettuce.'

'Don't be an idiot!' Tess told him. 'The ones at this end I sowed exactly a week later, as one is supposed to do, to ensure a regular supply. And they came out of exactly the same packet as the first ones. Do these look like radish to you?'

'Pull one up,' Jack advised. 'See if it's got pink at the bottom.'

Tess did so. The experiment was inconclusive.

'It's too early,' she said. 'They wouldn't be pink anyway, at this stage. It's the *tops* that are wrong.'

Mrs Bagthorpe was finally called in for an opinion. She tripped happily down the path to the mixed strains of the Mozart Horn Concerto No. 3 in E flat major, and the *Siegfried Idyll.*

'How perfectly splendidly you are doing, Tess,' she told her daughter. 'How straight you have kept your rows, and how marvellously healthy all your plants look. Do you know, I think you may even begin to add Gardening as a String to your Bow.'

Tess ignored her mother's effusion.

'These,' she said without ceremony, pointing to the putative lettuce. 'Are they lettuce?'

Mrs Bagthorpe looked slightly troubled. Although she pottered about a good deal in the flower garden, and was something of an authority on clematis and Old English roses, she had heretofore met salad only when it reached her kitchen. She peered closer, and her brow cleared. She was on home territory, it seemed, after all.

'Why, no, dear!' she cried. 'See – these are pansies,

and these antirrhinums – and those, see, are certainly night-scented stock. The paler green ones I am not so sure about . . .'

'They're lettuce!' Tess snapped. 'And the others are *what*?'

Mrs Bagthorpe repeated her diagnosis with confidence.

'I have some night-scented stock at exactly the same stage myself,' she said (she was defying her husband's instructions to grow only what was edible). Daisy sowed them for me only last week. It may even be that *she* has green fingers, too.'

'Daisy? Daisy?' Tess's voice was on an ascending scale. 'If that pernicious, meddling, undisciplined—'

Jack tugged at her sleeve.

'Don't you think we ought to move away where the plants can't hear?' he asked. He had the feeling that harsh words were about to be spoken – as indeed, they were. The kind of words used must have reverberated through the Cosmic Mind like anything.

Where the Bagthorpes had gone wrong was in assuming that Daisy could be in only one Phase at a time. It had simply not occurred to them that they might overlap. Thus Daisy, while currently in a predominately Intimations of Mortality Phase, was none the less still dabbling in Reconciling the Seemingly Disparate – and, for all anyone knew, in pyromania. When Mr Bagthorpe learnt this he became frantic.

'My God!' he yelled. 'Get the matches rounded up,

quick! All I need is for this place to go up in flames to *know* I'm in hell!'

The full extent of Daisy's crime emerged only gradually, though the effects of it were with them for a long time to come. To start with, apparently, all she had done was take a pinch of one kind of seed and drop it into a different packet. Given Daisy's tendency to extremes, however, this had soon begun to pall. It seemed altogether too tame. She had begun, it seemed, to feel like doing something more drastic.

'I wanted to be a witch and mix a spell!' she sobbed to the stony-faced Bagthorpes.

'Witch is right!' gritted Mr Bagthorpe. 'Didn't I tell you? Exorcism – two exorcisms!'

Daisy's next act, then, had been to trot back to the house and find a receptacle that bore some resemblance to a witch's cauldron. The nearest she could come to this was a valuable black Wedgwood bowl (later found in pieces behind the potting shed). Into this she had tipped the contents of every seed packet she could lay her hands on. These had included cabbage, sunflowers, asters, carrots, night-scented stock, lettuce, radish, marigolds, lobelia, alyssum, beetroot and nasturtium. Nobody ever discovered what the exact mix had been. The flowerbeds of Unicorn House presented a unique spectacle during the coming months, with lettuce nestling among the roses and herbaceous borders of a variety that could never before have been seen anywhere. Grandma said that it was original, and that she liked it, and that Daisy's policy should be adopted every year.

'We might even present it at the Chelsea Flower Show,' she said.

While the row about Daisy's spellmaking was going on it had occurred to Jack (who rarely took part in rows) that now, perhaps, with the vegetable garden sprouting inedible produce, Mr Bagthorpe might finally decide to abandon his Scheme for Survival.

Not so. People were now made to fill any spare moments on their knees in the vegetable garden, comparing seedlings with pictures on packets. This was work of astonishing tedium, and strained everybody's eyes.

Jack was glad when one morning Mr Bagthorpe dispatched him into Aysham with instructions to buy, beg, borrow or steal a book about how to milk goats, this information not being given in any of the library books William had fetched earlier.

'And don't come back without one,' he told Jack. 'We must get our goat.'

As it happened, Grandpa was driving into Aysham to purchase further supplies of angling gear. He had been sent fishing so often of late that his equipment was wearing out. The two of them drove in together, and held a companionable conversation. When Grandpa was away from Unicorn House he seemed able to hear much better than when in the thick of things.

'I was wondering if I ought to call in and see

Great Aunt Lucy,' Jack told him. 'I bet she'd like a visitor.'

He had in fact been instructed to do this by his siblings.

'She is our last ditch,' William said. 'If this goes on much longer we shall all drop dead of malnutrition.'

'Yourself, presumably, rather later than the rest of us,' Tess told him coldly, alluding to the exhumed chops.

'Please, Jack, be really nice to her,' Rosie pleaded. Her chickens were a disappointment to her. They did not behave at all like the birds of the forest in Walt Disney's version of 'Snow White'. She had never really expected them to flutter about her head or perch cooing on her shoulders, but she had expected them to be more affectionate than they were. When she threw scraps they just ignored her and fought and pecked amongst themselves. Not one among them looked cosy and placid enough to be called Biddy. Rosie *had* given them names, but they never came when called, and so she found herself forgetting which was which. The only enjoyable part was picking out the eggs, still warm, from the nesting boxes. Even this she did not often get to do. Daisy liked doing it, and Rosie always let her because at least it wooed her away, temporarily, from Grandma and Little Tommy.

Mathematics was one of the Strings to Rosie's Bow, and she acquired a small notebook in which to keep a Record of eggs laid, with the intention of producing some kind of Statistics. Given Daisy's frequent visits to the hen house this was not easy. For one thing, Arry Awk dropped quite a lot of eggs, and did not own up unless he was caught out. For another, Daisy kept secretly burying eggs, in the hopes that they would hatch out. Nobody could convince her that this was impossible. She said that ostriches buried their eggs in the sand, and so hens ought to be able to bury theirs in the soil. ('They might even hatch out into *dragons*!' she said with satisfaction.) Given all this, Rosie's Statistics were clearly to be taken with a pinch of salt.

Rosie had given Jack six brown eggs as an offering to Great Aunt Lucy, though needless to say her motives for this were less than altruistic.

'Make sure she knows I grew them myself,' she told him. 'It'll show I've got strength of character.'

Tess sent a tin of talcum powder from the vast store she had accumulated during her Competition Entering days. Jack also smuggled a bunch of flowers, which was to be an offering from William himself, into Grandpa's car while Mr Bagthorpe was not looking. The latter, of course, had no idea of Jack's proposed visit.

Grandpa thought the idea of going to the hospital a good one.

'I will drive you there myself,' he told Jack, 'and will myself go and see how Lucy is. She is a very strange lady, and I am sorry for her.'

Jack fervently hoped that Grandpa would be wise

enough not to tell Grandma about this. 'She'd kill him,' he thought, but comforted himself with the realization that Grandpa could not have survived as long as he had, if he had not had some idea of how to handle Grandma. His being S.D. was part of his way of coping, Uncle Parker said.

Grandpa certainly seemed to hear all that passed during the visit to Great Aunt Lucy's sick bed.

Jack had been worried that the ward sister might not let them in. However, he himself was not even recognized, Mr Bagthorpe and Daisy having stolen most of the limelight on the previous occasion, and Grandpa, of course, had not even been there. The sister greeted them quite warmly (probably because Grandpa had such a nice face) and even told them about Great Aunt Lucy's previous visitors.

'She will be so pleased to see you!' she said. 'Some quite *dreadful* relatives came to see her when she was first admitted.'

'She is happy, I hope?' Grandpa asked, 'and her health is improving?'

'Oh, she's *enormously* better,' the sister assured him with pride. 'I think, though perhaps it is not for me to say, that her stay here is working wonders for her in every way. And she is getting on famously with her fellow-patients.'

This sounded so unlikely that Jack wondered fleetingly whether they were all talking about the same lady. His fears were short-lived. Great Aunt Lucy, still under her hooped cage, greeted them both with a smile. This was a real shock. Jack had not seen her smile before.

'How very kind of you to come, Alfred,' she told Grandpa, 'And you, too, William dear.'

'Jack, actually,' he told her.

'Of course. Do forgive me. I fear that I have in the past been very remiss in the matter of taking an interest in others, and hope to make up for this in the future.'

Jack boggled. Great Aunt Lucy, he knew, did not believe in either the past or the future. The old lady could surely not still be under the influence of an anaesthetic administered over a week previously?

'There is still time,' she continued, 'to make redress.'

She had actually now used the word Time. It was all quite incomprehensible. Jack made an effort to bring her back to reality as she knew it.

'Here are some flowers from William and me.' He proffered the bouquet. 'And here is some lovely flavoured talcum powder from Tess, and some brown eggs from Rosie. She laid them herself,' he added, remembering his instructions.

'How generous you all are!' she exclaimed. 'And new-laid eggs! I shall have one, lightly poached, for my breakfast each morning.'

The plot, so far as Jack was concerned, was now dense. Aunt Lucy was having her breakfast in the mornings. He stared at her for some kind of visible clue. His gaze fell on the pin fastening her bed jacket.

It was one of her brooch watches. It was showing the correct time.

'There is one thing, Lucy,' Grandpa was saying, 'you will not be troubled by wasps in here, I imagine. We are coming to the time of the year when they seem everywhere. I do everything I can to keep them down, of course, but one cannot exterminate a whole species single-handed, unfortunately.'

'When I am better, I shall help you, Alfred,' she promised. 'I shall not be sufficiently agile to swat them, as I could in my youth, but I can sit with an aerosol spray on my lap, and exterminate any that come within range.'

Grandpa took up this offer gratefully.

'You will remember, of course,' he told her, 'that cousin Cecil in Sevenoaks died of a wasp sting, and these things do run in families.'

'I suppose they do,' she agreed.

'I am convinced that that is the way I shall go myself,' he confided. 'Unless it be under the wheels of Russell's car.'

'Oh, I do hope not!' she exclaimed. She was, however, in no kind of a lather. Only a couple of weeks back she would have been in a considerable lather at such talk, and probably added wasps to the Bees in her Bonnet. Jack, still studying her, had the feeling that she was peaceful as never before.

'I am so happy here,' she told them. 'Each day has a pattern. Everything goes like clockwork.'

She then proceeded to outline the routine of the

hospital day. Each hour, each minute, was accounted for. At last, it seemed, the responsibility for Time had been taken out of Aunt Lucy's hands. She could lie back and leave it all up to other people.

'It is sheer heaven,' she said blissfully.

Mrs Bagthorpe, on a subsequent visit, learned from the ward sister the manner of Great Aunt Lucy's conversion. It was, it appeared, the sheer, relentless regularity of hospital routine, a routine that stops for no man, that had brought about the miracle. At first, Aunt Lucy had resisted strenuously. She had demanded meals at all hours, and kept on switching on her bed light each time it was turned off by the night nurse, and refused to have her pulse taken. Bees in Bonnets as vigorous as hers are not seen off without a struggle.

Hospital staff, however, have people where they want them. They have been trained to get patients organized. In the end, they always win. Great Aunt Lucy had been inexorably worn down. The first sign of this was when she meekly accepted kippers for breakfast, this being the first meal she had taken since her admission. From then on, she had succumbed with increasing happiness to every detail of the routine to which she was subjected. Now she was not even looking forward to her discharge.

'We will ensure that your life continues in a regular pattern,' Mrs Bagthorpe assured her. 'And once you have become accustomed to the rhythm, I am sure it will be with you for life.'

Mrs Bagthorpe really did have a gift for Positive Thinking. Anybody who could talk about life as lived at Unicorn House as either regular or rhythmic, had to be a Positive Thinker of titanic stature. They had to be the biggest Positive Thinker since Canute – or Icarus, even.

13

In view of the drastic turnabout in Aunt Lucy's world picture, Jack decided to confess to his father that he had been to the hospital. He had not, after all, been categorically forbidden to do so. He consulted his siblings first.

'Are you *sure*?' Rosie asked incredulously. 'She actually said *Time*?'

'Several times,' he assured her. 'She seemed to like saying it. And she even said she was glad she'd fallen over that sack of mushrooms. She said she would be grateful for all time.'

'Grateful?' interposed William quickly. This sounded promising. 'Well, make sure you tell Father that.'

Jack, then, passed on to Mr Bagthorpe the information about Great Aunt Lucy's conversion to Time, along with the manual on goat-keeping. Mr Bagthorpe was not comforted.

'Here!' he said, snatching the manual. 'Give me that! We have little time to tend Lucy's bees. We must get to immediate grips with the goat.' (This latter was an almost prophetic phrase, as it turned out.)

'But she really has changed, Father,' Jack persisted.

'She's gone all peaceful. And she's really grateful to us all, she says, and especially you for putting those mushrooms for her to trip over.'

'Look,' said Mr Bagthorpe, 'do not waste your time describing how Lucy feels to me. I have known her since before you were born. Here today, gone tomorrow – every benighted Bee in her Bonnet spins round in circles at the speed of light. Peaceful, you say. If you visit her again, she will probably attack you with a poker.'

Jack pointed out that hospitals do not have pokers, but Mr Bagthorpe dismissed this as a quibble.

'Poker – hatchet – what's the difference? You are missing entirely the point I am making. The point I am making is that the day Lucy thinks the same way two days running, will be the day pigs fly. Now get digging. And when I'm through with this book, *you* read it. When that goat gets here, it will want milking. Fast.'

Grandma was equally dismissive about Aunt Lucy's personality change.

'You do not surprise me in the least,' she remarked when she was told of it. 'Lucy has always struck me as quite unstable. I have always been profoundly grateful that she is no blood relation of mine.'

She looked pointedly at her son, who *was* a blood relation, and therefore, by inference, prey to the same instability.

'I fink Auntie Lucy's a silly old griffin anyway,' piped up Daisy.

'Of course she is, dear,' her grandmother assured her. 'That little child is more perceptive than any other single member of this household, including, I fear, yourself, Laura. Why do you not consult her about your Problems?'

'When that hell-raising infant is about,' Mr Bagthorpe said, before his wife had a chance to reply, 'Laura is so beset left and right by her own Problems that she rarely has time to attend to the others. That child is herself, so far as we are concerned, a Problem with a capital P the size of Purgatory. She is, to use the words of that half-baked theory of Tess's, a Threat to Survival. Burying chops, biting people's legs, mixing seeds, dropping eggs—'

'I di'n't!' Daisy squeaked indignantly, interrupting this catalogue. 'It's Arry Awk! I told you, di'n't I, Rosie? He's a bad boy, and *he* mixes seeds and drops eggs. He dropped *six* eggs, yesterday.'

'That,' said Mr Bagthorpe grimly, 'is tantamount to a confession. Keep the score, Rosie, and I'll get the cash off Russell.'

'Daddy don't care!' Daisy said, keeping her end up. 'Daddy's got lots and lots of money!'

This tactless statement must have hit home hard. Mr Bagthorpe, however, had only entered into the exchange with Daisy while temporarily off his guard, and now tightly compressed his lips and affected to read the cricket scores in his newspaper. (This *had* to be affectation. Mr Bagthorpe had only ever once attended a cricket match, and had hideously disgraced the whole family by triumphantly yelling 'Howzat?' every time a batsman, on whichever side, scored a run. In the end the umpire had come over and had a word with him. Mr Bagthorpe had maintained that he thought this expression a cricketing variant of 'Hurray!' or 'Huzzah!' This happened to be true, though you could see the umpire did not believe him. When, several balls later, a batsman was given out Leg Before Wicket, Mr Bagthorpe had stood up and yelled '*Now* who's shouting Howzat?' Soon after this Mrs Bagthorpe had claimed that she had a serious headache, and they left the ground.)

'There is more livestock arriving tomorrow, I understand,' remarked Grandma, who did not like to see a state of simmer die down.

'What's livestock, Grandma Bag?' asked Daisy, who had been told by her mother always to ask the meaning of words she did not understand.

'It is any creature that is alive, Daisy,' Grandma told her. 'Everything that lives and moves and creeps upon the earth.'

'Is maggots livestock?' Daisy asked.

'Naturally, dear,' Grandma replied, 'though I should prefer you not to dabble in these.' (She had herself been a victim of some of Daisy's previous maggots at the Family Reunion Party, and her memories of this event were painful.)

'It's not *me* that wants maggots, Grandma Bag,' Daisy said. 'It's Arry Awk. He ha'n't *got* no livestock, and he wants maggots.'

Nobody liked the sound of this much, but they were not seriously perturbed, inasmuch as they imagined that Daisy would have no way of procuring such livestock single-handed. Her previous ones had been raised in the airing cupboard by William, during the Germ Warfare on the Latter Day Saints.

'I should rest content with Little Tommy, dear,' advised Grandma, who did not know this. 'He is fast becoming a shining jewel of a cat, and requires your constant companionship. Why, dear, do we not hold another funeral, and bury Arry Awk?'

She had imagined this an inspired thought, and was not prepared for the violence of Daisy's reactions to it.

'He in't dead, he's not, he's not!' she squealed. 'He's my bestest friend in the whole world and he's *not* dead! And *he* han't got a wrinkly face and short legs. He's not *never* going to die, not till I do!'

Most present felt that the time for this double demise could not come too soon. Grandma, however, alarmed by the strength of the passions she had aroused, immediately tried to modify her position.

'Hush, dear,' she told her protégée. 'You have quite misunderstood me. I was not for a moment suggesting that Arry Awk was dead. I merely thought that he might enjoy attending his own funeral.'

Daisy's sobs abated, and you could see that she was attracted by this novel proposition.

'There are, after all,' Grandma continued cunningly, 'few people who can ever have done this. In fact, Arry Awk is the only person I have ever known of who *could* attend his own funeral. It would be an historic occasion.'

At this Mr Bagthorpe made a strangled noise and left the room.

'It's all hopeless,' William said gloomily. 'He doesn't even believe that Aunt Lucy talks about Time all the time and is eternally grateful to us. Can't we get him to go and see for himself?'

'I think that would be most unwise,' his mother said hastily. 'We must give him Time. He must be allowed to work through this obession with Survival.'

The Bagthorpes sat morbidly contemplating this prospect, and at that moment there came the sound of grinding gravel that meant Uncle Parker had arrived.

'It's Daddy, it's Daddy!' Daisy squealed. '*He* can come to Arry Awk's funeral as well. *Everybody* can,' she added generously. 'And even Uncle Bag, even if he is a nasty Grook!'

Uncle Parker breezed in, accompanied by Aunt Celia.

'Hello, all,' he greeted them. 'Still Surviving, I see?'

'Only just,' William told him.

Aunt Celia passionately embraced Daisy who, as usual, struggled to get free.

'Listen, listen!' she cried. 'We going to have a big funeral today and it's going to be Arry Awk's! And Grandma Bag says it'll be *hysterical*!'

'By Jove!' Uncle Parker was clearly impressed.

'Arry Awk, then, has finally kicked the bucket. I feared we should never see the day. Congratulations, Daisy – or rather, of course, condolences. Think, Laura, Henry and I will be able to reduce our Insurance Premiums which were, one is bound to admit, becoming crippling.'

'No no no!' shrieked Daisy infuriated that Arry Awk, just because he was going to have a funeral, should be presumed dead. 'He's *not* dead, he's not!'

'Really?' Uncle Parker was quite nonplussed. His daughter's Intimations of Mortality were apparently taking a devious turn. He was slightly shocked. 'We are going to bury him *alive*?'

Obviously he felt that even Arry Awk did not deserve this fate.

'No!' squealed Daisy. 'You're not *listening*! You tell him, Mummy! We're going to have a funeral for Arry Awk and he's going to *come* to it!'

Aunt Celia instantly renewed her attempts to embrace Daisy. Evidently she alone perfectly understood the situation.

'It is wonderful!' she told everybody. 'The symbolism of the ceremony is almost too deep for words. We are to witness the Phoenix rising from the ashes!'

'Will it be a cremation, then?' Jack asked. He, for one, devoutly hoped that it would not. This could mean that Daisy would then be in *three* Phases at once, which was a mind-blowing prospect.

'So literal,' murmured Aunt Celia, meaning Jack. 'How rare and precious it is to see poetry in a little child. I am constantly being reminded of how I have, in Daisy, a being quite unique.'

There was nothing in this last statement with which anybody could quarrel, and nobody did.

'Even Little Tommy can come,' Daisy was now burbling. 'You come and see my little pussy now, Mummy and Daddy. He's getting bigger and bigger and got *ever* so long claws.'

Aunt Celia allowed herself to be led off to view what sounded like an ominously developing Little Tommy. Uncle Parker remained.

'I'll take a look at him later,' he promised Daisy. 'Little beggar!' he added, as the door closed behind the pair.

'I may as well tell you,' he continued, 'that the real object of our visit is to persuade Daisy to return home.'

There was at this intelligence a great sigh of relief from everybody except Grandma and Rosie.

'The truth of the matter is,' he told them, 'that her mother is pining for her. She could stop here for ever, so far as I am concerned, but you know how Celia is. She's also a touch concerned, to put it bluntly, that if Daisy stops much longer amongst you lot, she'll get all the poetry knocked out of her.'

'We are certainly all getting a lot knocked out of *us*,' William told him, as Mr Bagthorpe himself would have, had he been present.

'The point being,' Uncle Parker said, 'that Daisy has got herself pretty well dug in here, latterly. And is also considerably attached to her grandmother – as who can blame her?' He here gallantly saluted Grandma, who ignored him. 'An inducement is therefore called for. And so, what with one thing and another, and all of you on a diet of beetroot and whatever, we thought of holding a Banquet.'

The Bagthorpes were rendered quite blank by this.

'We are calling it a Banquet,' Uncle Parker told them, seeing their surprise, 'partly because it will indeed be a Banquet, with every gastronomic delicacy in or out of season, and partly because Celia has now become irremediably nervous at the very sound of the word party.'

Given the long Bagthorpe history of making a clean sweep of party tables and usually burning out their locality to boot, this was hardly surprising. The Bagthorpes, however, were still not clear what exactly was being mooted.

'Do you mean a homecoming party for Daisy?' Rosie asked.

'That,' he replied, 'is precisely it.'

'At your house?' she asked incredulously. 'At *The Knoll*?'

'Where else?' he returned.

'But what about Aunt Celia?' Jack asked. 'What about her vibrations and things?'

Aunt Celia shared with Mr Bagthorpe an immovable conviction that people gave off vibrations. Given the kind of unsettled childhood they had probably had with Grandma, this was not perhaps surprising. Mr Bagthorpe's main obsession was with his study. He was very funny about whom he would let in, and had once even stopped the vicar entering. He was so frightened of the effect Mrs Fosdyke would have on the vibrations in there, that he actually hoovered and dusted it himself. He said this was because there were important papers that must not be disturbed, but his family knew what the real reason was. It was probable that Mrs Fosdyke did as well. Mr Bagthorpe by and large discouraged all visitors from Unicorn House by dint of shouting and general want of hospitable behaviour.

He did not, however, place an embargo on visits from the Parkers. Aunt Celia's vibrations, he claimed, were so wishy-washy as to be virtually non-existent, and Uncle Parker's so superficial as to be likewise. The main reason he let them come, however (he did not, after all, underestimate the power of *Daisy's* vibrations) was that he and Uncle Parker carried on this long-standing feud. They would conduct frequent and protracted rows, and Mr Bagthorpe usually made notes afterwards, and used some of the dialogue in his television scripts. Uncle Parker had once threatened to sue him over this, on the grounds that anything he, Uncle Parker, might say was copyright.

Aunt Celia's obsession with vibrations was of a different order from that of her brother. She was affected by *everybody's* vibrations, though she did, as

Mr Bagthorpe once sardonically pointed out, seem to have a remarkable immunity to those of her unholy daughter. Aunt Celia had then replied that he was confusing vibrations with charisma, which shone out from Daisy, she claimed, like a halo.

Aunt Celia spent a lot of time writing poetry and throwing pots, or else thinking about these activities. She would spend hours just gazing at things. Uncle Parker let her because he loved her to distraction. He protected her as far as possible from the rest of the world's vibrations, but she was so easily upset that she would often have to lie for hours in a darkened room after hearing a harsh word spoken.

The Bagthorpes, then, had not for years crossed the threshold of The Knoll, apart from the odd occasion when Mr Bagthorpe had gone storming up there uninvited, having just thought of a scoring shot in whatever was the current battle of words. Uncle Parker had told them that they could not be invited there because of the threat it would present to his wife's sanity.

'Your combined vibrations,' he had said, 'are, you will concede, formidable. I do not necessarily say malignant – but formidable.'

Nobody cared much whether they visited The Knoll or not, and so the absence of invitations to do so had never given the Bagthorpes much pause, and the present summons was naturally something of a shock.

'This really is most kind of you, Russell,' Mrs

Bagthorpe now said. 'How exciting it sounds – a Banquet!'

Here Mrs Fosdyke was heard to snort. She was probably trying to convey her conviction that the disasters attending a Bagthorpe Party were in direct proportion to its ambitiousness. At this rate, a Banquet could easily involve fatalities – of which there had been none so far. (Banquets were quite frequently featured in her Friday night Dracula films, and had therefore already become associated in her mind with dismemberment and much blood.)

'How many courses does a Banquet have?' inquired William with interest. 'Don't we keep eating courses till we're cramful, and then make ourselves sick to make room for more?'

'Something like that,' Uncle Parker agreed. 'Though I hope you'll all have the grace to be sick out of the sight of Celia.'

'Will there be a boar's head?' Rosie wanted to know.

At this, Mrs Fosdyke again snorted. She considered herself the best producer of party fare in the country, if not the world, but had never to date even considered a boar's head. She had only a confused notion of what it was.

'Anyone'd think,' she told Mesdames Pye and Bates in the Fiddler's Arms that night, 'that that lot'd never ate in their lives. The food I've given 'em! I've done 'em enough stuffed eggs in my time to build the Eiffel Tower with, and the gateaux I've done'd stretch to

Land's End. Boar's head! I reckon I've *seen* some of them, at least, I think I 'ave, on them 'orrible banquets on Dracula, and I reckon they're 'orrible great enormous things with snouts and jelly all over and oranges in their mouths instead of teeth.'

Her cronies shuddered sympathetically at this description.

'Whatever next!' exclaimed Mrs Pye. This was a purely rhetorical remark, but Mrs Fosdyke went inexorably on to *tell* them whatever next.

'They was all *ordering* that Mr Parker what they wanted, as if they was a bunch of cannibals. All fancy foreign stuff it sounded and talking about syllabubs and venison and spits – oh, you can't imagine!'

'And will that wife of his do all that?' inquired Mrs Bates incredulously. She had often heard Mrs Fosdyke's assessment of Aunt Celia, which was, by and large, that she was 'only half there'.

'*Her?*' echoed Mrs Fosdyke. 'She could no more stick an orange in a pig's mouth than she could fly! One of them vegitinarians – I *told* you – never hardly touches anything but lettuce.'

She went on to tell them what she had heard Uncle Parker explaining to the Bagthorpes, which was that, as Aunt Celia was so highly strung and easily unhinged at the sight and smell of strong meat, a firm of London caterers was being called in to make all the necessary culinary arrangements. He had then, realizing that Mrs Fosdyke was within earshot, and that her sensibilities might be bruised by hearing all this, gone on to invite herself to attend, in a supervisory capacity.

'Keep an eye on things, you know,' he told her. He had a fair grasp of psychology (he needed to have) and knew how to butter Mrs Fosdyke up. 'And to tell you the truth, the one thing I really hanker for is a supply of your remarkable stuffed eggs. Could teach that lot a thing or two!'

'Shall you go, then?' asked Mrs Fosdyke's friends eagerly.

'Oooh, I should, Glad,' urged Mrs Pye. 'They say it's like Buckingham Palace inside.'

Who 'they' were was not clear, given Uncle Parker's reluctance to let people and their vibrations over the threshold of The Knoll. To Mrs Fosdyke, the Parker residence sounded very little like Buckingham Palace. She well knew that Daisy Parker was allowed to write her thoughts on the walls, and had started several fires there during her Pyromaniac Phase. It seemed unlikely that the royal children had ever been granted these prerogatives. But Mesdames Pye and Bates were dedicated inspectors of the interiors of other people's houses, even if they sometimes had to settle for second-hand accounts rather than a personal inventory. They might have acquired some information from somewhere.

Mrs Fosdyke allowed her friends to urge her acceptance for a little longer, and then assented with a show of reluctance.

'S'pose I might as well,' she told them. 'If all that

foreign stuff ain't fit to eat they can always fall back on my stuffed eggs.' (Mrs Fosdyke really did have an unconscious gift for prophecy. She had not meant this last statement literally at all.)

Next day, then, Mrs Fosdyke indicated her willingness to attend the Homecoming Banquet at The Knoll, with the proviso that there should be no candles and no crackers.

'A Banquet by its very nature does not have crackers,' Mrs Bagthorpe assured her. 'And as the evenings are still light, there will be no need of candles. I am sure the occasion will pass off beautifully. We are all so looking forward to it.'

They were – even Mr Bagthorpe, though he would not admit to it.

'It is like Russell,' he declared, 'to take a sledgehammer to crack a nut. Surely to God he could have rehabilitated his daughter without this kind of a masquerade. I may or I may not go. It will depend whether I feel I can face such rich and unwholesome food after a taste of nutrition as it should be.'

He had been given an outline of the proposed courses of the Banquet, and was very dismissive about them.

'We shall all be furred up for weeks afterwards,' he said. 'Menus of that order are totally out of date. They were drawn up when people knew nothing of cholesterol and polysaturated fat and vitamins.'

Mr Bagthorpe, of course, *still* knew very little about

these matters, but he was not the man to let this stop his delivering a lecture about them. Mr Bagthorpe could deliver a lecture about anything, given one or two half truths.

14

The funeral of Arry Awk took place that afternoon with due pomp and ceremony. It had been postponed from the previous day with the arrangement of this pomp and ceremony in mind. Most people attended in the end, optimistically imagining that this was a finale, the *pièce de résistance* to mark the end of Daisy's Phase of Intimations of Mortality. Even Uncle Parker went. You never knew, he said, Arry Awk might accidentally fall into his own grave, and that he would not want to miss.

In the event, he was not far short of the truth. To begin with, things went smoothly enough. Daisy trotted round her procession inspecting its members and making sure everyone was wearing some black and carrying a floral tribute. She herself was bearing a bunch of flowers and foliage almost as big as herself, tied with pink ribbon and having a card attached that read 'Goodby Arry Awk my bestest frend in the hole world for evver and evver amen'. She had also appropriated her most original monument to date, in the shape of a giant glass jar of green bubble bath which would serve, she said, to remind

Arry Awk of his lovely flood. His epitaph she had already composed in private, and intended to attach it with ribbon to the neck of the jar at the end of the ceremony.

She had insisted that Arry Awk be buried away from what was by now known as the Highgate Cemetery end of the garden. She was probably dimly aware that, even in death, Arry Awk was something on his own.

'It is as though,' crooned Aunt Celia dotingly, 'the darling child has unconsciously recognized the need for a Poet's Corner.'

Mr Bagthorpe elected, predictably, to give the funeral a miss, even though Daisy had magnanimously said he could attend. William, too, was absent, there being no possibility of later disinterring Arry Awk and having *him* with mint sauce. He was not even prepared to toll the bell, so Rosie volunteered for this duty. Unfortunately, she had not acquired the knack of tolling a handbell, and the resulting sound was more like a summons to school dinner than a solemn call to mourning. The vibrations of this clanging got on everybody's nerves in the end, with the astonishing exception of Aunt Celia, who, one would have imagined, would have been the first to clap her hands over her ears.

'No man is an island entire unto himself,' she was heard to murmur. And 'Never send to know for whom the bell tolls, it tolls for thee.'

She was presumably somewhere so far off on her

own that she was not even hearing the vibrations, let alone feeling them.

The spot Daisy had selected for the laying to rest of the imaginary remains of Arry Awk was at the edge of the shrubbery, near a flowering rhododendron. (This imaginary side of things was very confusing to everybody except Daisy herself, and her mother. So far as the Bagthorpes were concerned, Arry Awk had always been imaginary and invisible, and it was weird the way Daisy seemed to think he was imaginarily in the empty toffee tin, but actually in pride of place in the procession at her side.)

'Come on, Arry Awk,' she said, instituting the proceedings, 'you jus' walk along with me. Walk in slow steps, and don't talk – jus' sing.'

The cortège set off, wailing in a dirge-like way. Daisy had said they could all sing anything they liked, so long as it was sad. Simultaneously and mercifully the bell stopped tolling, as Rosie dropped it in favour of her high-speed camera. She kept darting about ahead of the procession and filming. She had obtained permission for this seemingly disrespectful behaviour from Daisy.

'All historical funerals have photos taken of them,' she had told her. 'It'll make this funeral immortal.'

The others had heard this, and became even more confused by immortality being added to an already inextricable mixture of what was invisible, imaginary and real. The result of this was that hardly anybody among the mourners had any clear conception of what they were supposed to be burying.

They wound their way slowly to Poet's Corner and then halted, still singing, while Daisy got down to business with her trowel. Jack found himself, all at once, understanding what Rosie saw in her. She was so serious – almost dedicated – in whatever she was doing. He cast his eye over the other mourners, almost daring them to giggle. No one as yet showed any signs of doing so, nor were they to do so later.

'There!' Daisy stood up and surveyed her hole with satisfaction. 'You can stop singing now.'

This they obediently and thankfully did.

'This is the funeral of Arry Awk that Arry Awk has come to,' Daisy announced. 'It is a hysterical funeral. There will never be another, not for ever and ever amen.'

She looked about her fellow-mourners for corroboration of this, and they all nodded and assumed appropriate expressions of awe and solemnity.

'There is no need for anybody to cry,' Daisy then told them, 'because Arry Awk i'n't dead. He's here, i'n't you, Arry Awk?' She paused. Then, 'Yes, he is,' she confirmed. 'I will now put him in his coffin. He choosed it himself.'

She picked up the polythene bag and the toffee tin and went through the motions of placing something inside. Her audience all craned forward to see what it was, and for a fleeting moment Jack almost expected to catch a glimpse of Arry Awk himself. He was disappointed. What was actually standing proxy for this invisible person was some kind of blue plastic troll out of a cornflake packet.

Daisy held the tin aloft in her usual manner.

'Oh dear oh dear!' she cried. 'Poor Arry Awk! No more floods and no more eggs! Gone to heaven for ever and ever amen!'

This was all very baffling – and not only in Daisy's confident assignment of her friend to heaven. The Bagthorpes had only a moment ago been instructed that any outward show of grief would be misplaced, yet here was Daisy herself giving every sign of getting into her usual stride, and acting very bereaved indeed. She seemed to have forgotten that Arry Awk was there at her side, witnessing the whole thing. As Jack watched, her face crumpled and tears began to roll down her cheeks.

'Poor little fing!' She was sobbing in earnest now, as she placed the toffee tin into her newly dug hole. 'Oh, dusters to dusters, ashes to ashes! Oh dear, oh dear – Mummy, Mummy, I want him back!'

Aunt Celia, herself weeping, cried:

'No, darling, no! He is not dead, but sleeps!'

'He's dead, he's dead!' wailed Daisy.

Her grief was so real that everyone present began to feel affected – even Grandma, who had always been jealous of Arry Awk's place in Daisy's affections, and would have been only too happy to see him dead.

Daisy was now scattering forlorn little fistfuls of earth on to her tin.

'Oh Arry, Arry,' she sobbed, her face besmirched with soil and tears. 'Don't leave me, Arry! Oh dear – dusters to dusters!'

Uncle Parker, impressed by the way things were going, ventured to put his oar in. He patted his daughter gently on the back.

'Look, Daisy,' he said, 'it's not too late. Fish him out again, why don't you?'

It must have cost him some effort to make this suggestion, because Arry Awk had always been a source of great trouble and expense to him.

'I can't, I can't!' screamed Daisy. 'He's dead! Oh, I wish I never done it! Darling little Arry Awk!'

Grandma, not wishing to appear deficient in feeling, but quite misjudging the depth of Daisy's despair, said:

'It's *always* a shame when somebody dies, Daisy. But you will soon have a new friend – and you have Little Tommy, remember.'

'I don't want Little Tommy,' Daisy screamed passionately, 'I want my Arry Awk back!'

'Don't cry, Daisy,' Jack said. 'Have you forgotten, Arry Awk is *with* you.'

'He i'n't, he i'n't,' she wailed. 'He's just gone down to ashes in that tin!'

The complicated metaphysics of the whole business had evidently become too much for her too, for she no longer seemed to understand it. She had on this occasion, as Mr Bagthorpe later unsympathetically observed, bitten off more than she could chew.

'Anybody who can go around burying people who are dead and alive at the same time has to *expect* to get tied up in knots,' he declared. 'Even Shakespeare never did that, and there's no reason why *she* should expect to get away with it. At least Shakespeare's ghosts were *dead*, for God's sake. Her whole diabolical creation has now ricocheted back on her. It is neither more nor less than poetic justice.'

It was in fact much later on that Mr Bagthorpe made this speech, because at the time when Arry Awk's funeral broke up in disarray, he was occupied in wrestling with a goat, and in no position to utter anything much more than expletives.

How the funeral finally broke up was with Daisy flinging down her floral tribute and fleeing, still sobbing bitterly. Aunt Celia instantly went after her, and the rest of them were left standing there awkwardly, uncertain of what their next move should be.

'Poor old Daisy,' said Jack at last.

'Perhaps it is all for the best,' said Mrs Bagthorpe weakly. (She had never received a Problem relating to Resurrection.)

'D'you think he *is* dead?' asked Rosie nervously. 'Had we better put our flowers on, or not?'

She had gone to some trouble to create a circular wreath, using wire clothes-hangers, beech twigs and roses.

'Better pop 'em on the hole,' Uncle Parker advised. 'Might cheer her up a bit when she sees 'em.'

This they all did, feeling much sadder than they

had anticipated. Jack put the bath-salts jar at the head of the grave and propped Daisy's own floral tribute against it. As he did so, he spotted a crumpled piece of Grandma's lavender-scented notepaper. It was Daisy's special epitaph:

Only me knows Arry Awk
Only me can here him tawk.
I luv him and he luvs me
And hes as bad as bad can be.
Frinstance won day Arry Awk
Broke sum dums with a nife and fawk.
He had a flood and broke sum eggs
And he mixed up sedes wiv his twinkling legs.
Arry Awks my bestest frend
For evver and evver til the end
Amen.

Jack thought it clear from this composition that Daisy had not in fact contemplated losing Arry Awk in arranging his burial. There was no ring of finality about it – rather the opposite – and, significantly, no date. He himself thought Arry Awk sounded an attractive and lively character from this description, though he supposed that the twinkling legs attributed to him by Daisy were more or less poetic licence, there being few usable rhymes for 'eggs'. He carefully attached this eulogy to the neck of the bath-salts jar and followed the others, all of whom had already left the graveside.

Having been immersed in perusing the epitaph, he had not really noticed all the yelling and screaming up to this juncture, but now he automatically hurried in its direction.

'It really is all Hail and Farewell,' he thought.

So it turned out to be. Farewell Arry Awk was overlapping with Hail Jemima – this being the name already chosen in advance by Rosie for the Bagthorpe goat.

Mr Bagthorpe alone had been there to greet this addition to the livestock. William had his earphones on at the time, and so could not hear his yells and come to his assistance – even had he been inclined to do so.

Mr Bagthorpe had no kind of rapport at all with four-legged creatures. (He did not even have a marked rapport with *two*-legged ones.) His reception of the goat had been, then, initially lukewarm. He had been somewhat nervous of the animal, having heard about goats butting, and eating everything in sight. He did not, however, wish to lose face in the eyes of the delivery man, so he did not tether the goat at a distance and beat a hasty retreat, but held on to the end of its rope in what he thought to be a nonchalant and manly way.

'I'll soon settle it down,' he told the delivery man. 'I've got a way with animals.'

What he intended was to hold on to the rope just so long as he was in view of the retreating van, and *then* tether the goat and beat a hasty retreat. Unfortunately, he left this too late. It was probably the noisy revving of the van, and the spinning of its wheels on the gravel, that upset the goat. Or it might, of course, have been Mr Bagthorpe's vibrations. In either case, the goat had become, so he averred, berserk. He went on to compare his own struggles with those of St George with the dragon.

'The only difference being that I shan't get a knighthood,' he added bitterly. 'There's no way I shall ever get a knighthood.'

When he was reminded that the George in question was a Saint and not a Sir, be became even more bitter, especially as he had been caught out.

'There is no way I shall ever get canonized, either,' he said, 'though I should be. I am a martyr, of the first water. I am the Archetypal Can-carrier of all time. St George can never have carried so many cans as I have.'

And so on and so forth. He was all the time tending his wounds, and allowing his wife to put the odd dab of antiseptic cream on his grazes, though he doubted, he said, whether these would afford any protection against possible rabies. Mrs Fosdyke wanted to put butter on all the bruises, but he would not let her. He said he considered this suggestion morbid.

'I need neither anointing nor embalming, as yet,' he told her coldly.

He was being particularly frigid toward her, partly because she had witnessed his humiliation by Jemima, and partly because she had not herself come to his aid.

He had caught the occasional glimpse of her pop-eyed face during his protracted wrestling with the goat.

'She is yellow to the core,' he told his family after her departure. 'So much for loyalty. "Thy tooth be just as keen although it be not seen as benefits forgot," and all that. "Thy breath be not so rude as man's ingratitude."'

Jack thought this confused quote more than usually inept, in as much as Mr Bagthorpe had never, ever, so far as he knew, done anything to earn Mrs Fosdyke's gratitude. He even risked saying as much.

'And she might have been frightened, as well,' he added. 'And she's only little.'

Mr Bagthorpe then rounded on him.

'It is you,' he told him through clenched teeth, 'who will be milking that hellish thing. If you think you can do better, do. When you are black and blue from head to foot, you might remember those words, and have the grace to blush.'

Rosie giggled.

'Black and blue and red all over,' she said.

'Very funny. Jack, go and fetch that manual.'

Mr Bagthorpe clearly could not wait for someone other than himself to get to grips with the goat.

'See what time of day it wants milking,' he ordered, 'and how many gallons we're supposed to get. You'll keep milking till we get our full quota.'

In fact the Bagthorpes were to get no milk at all from the misnamed Jemima, who was a billy-goat. Anyone with the slightest knowledge of animals might have queried at the time of delivery a female goat without udders. This was not the kind of detail Mr Bagthorpe ever noticed, and it was his careless dismissal of detail that had resulted in the delivery of a goat of the wrong sex. He had been curt to a degree to the man on the other end of the line when ordering the animal.

Mr Bagthorpe was not in the habit of ordering goats. When the breeder started asking all kinds of questions about breed and other technicalities, Mr Bagthorpe had cut him off short, fearing that any further discussion would result in his revealing his own ignorance.

'Long-horned, short-haired – what's the difference?' he had said brusquely. 'Wednesday afternoon, please, without fail' – and slammed down the telephone.

Mr Bagthorpe really was his own worst enemy. If he had talked politely to the goat-breeder, he would at least have ended up with an animal of the right sex, of whatever breed. In the event, his rudeness was such that the man, who had the impression from something Mr Bagthorpe had said earlier in the conversation that it was a nanny-goat he was after, deliberately sent a billy. It was, after all, a very human reaction.

When the mistake was discovered, Mr Bagthorpe tried to bluster his way out of it.

'We'll eat it,' he said. 'We'll fatten it up on the spare grass and then eat it. Robinson Crusoe did it all the time. So did Ulysses. It will see us through the winter. We can use its blubber to make candles.'

The billy-goat did not meet this fate. Daisy came upon him while everyone else was in the house yelling or wailing. She had managed to elude her mother and was hiding in the shrubbery to grieve privately over her lost friend. There, through her tears, she saw, within inches of her own, the mild yellow eyes of the goat. (He had finally got his rope tangled round a shrub, and Mr Bagthorpe had managed to secure it with a hasty knot before lurching back to the house.)

Daisy's eyes blinked rapidly. *The Three Billy Goats Gruff* had always been one of her favourite stories. She used to make Uncle Parker keep reading it, in the hope that one day the troll *would* eat somebody. This was not because she had anything against billy-goats, simply that she liked to hear about bloodbaths.

'Oooh!' she gasped. Her sobs abated. She stared at the goat and he stared unwinkingly back.

'You're a Billy Goat Gruff!' she exclaimed with awe. 'You got yellow eyes and a little tufty beard and horns jus' like in the book!'

The goat chewed thoughtfully.

'There i'n't no *troll*, is there?' she asked, looking fearfully about her. Daisy liked to witness bloodbaths, not participate in them.

'I sink p'raps we better go, case there is,' she told him. Her chubby fingers fumbled with the knot. In the end she managed to loosen it, and carefully unravelled the rest of the rope.

'C'm'on, Billy Goat Gruff,' she told him, and led him out of the shrubbery, over the lawns, and right into the mêlée in the Bagthorpe kitchen.

This was a stunning entrance. No one felt more stunned than Mr Bagthorpe himself. It was, moreover, hideously embarrassing. Here was the creature recently delineated by himself as voracious, cunning and even rabid, being led by a four-year-old like a lamb to the slaughter. The goat gazed mildly about him and took an exploratory chew at some rush matting. Mrs Fosdyke pressed herself right back against her sink. She had seen with her own eyes the other side of the goat's nature. She kept her eyes fixed on it, so that if it turned its gaze on herself, she could stare it out, as she had heard you were supposed to do with lions and pythons and so on.

'Oh Daisy, darling,' quavered Aunt Celia. 'Oh Russell – save her!'

'From what, dearest?' he asked. She was swaying slightly. He supported her, because if things became too much for her she would escape from them by fainting.

'Isn't he lovely?' Daisy inquired of the benumbed Bagthorpes. She patted his head and he curled his tongue and looked pleased.

Grandma was the first to recover herself.

'Darling Daisy has tamed the ravening beast,' she observed. 'The wolf is lying down with the lamb.'

'Which,' gritted her son, rising to the bait, 'being which?'

15

Daisy was allowed to keep the goat, of course. Aunt Celia averred that it had been sent by Providence, in Daisy's darkest hour of need, tying it in with the Ancient Mariner in some incomprehensible way. She made what was, for her, a very long speech about it.

'He is the Phoenix who has risen from the ashes of Arry Awk,' she crooned. 'From henceforth, he will be Daisy's guide and mentor. He will protect her from all ills, as the lion protected the gentle Una.'

This hopelessly mixed-up assessment of what was, to all other eyes, a particularly destructive member of a breed noted for its destructiveness, irritated everybody, and most of all Mr Bagthorpe.

'Protect hell!' he shouted. 'That goat just damn near killed me, Celia. And the minute it gets itself together, it'll try killing again. Get it straight out of here. You owe me seventy pounds, Russell. You realize, don't you, that it'll probably kill your benighted daughter? You may, of course, think it cheap at the price.'

Daisy herself had no such misgivings, and was caressing her new pet non-stop.

'What a picture!' sighed Aunt Celia, in no way,

now that her first shock was overcome, alarmed by her offspring's newfound affinity.

Grandma in turn became infuriated, not least because she was already experiencing powerful feelings of jealousy. She had expected Daisy to draw even closer to herself following the demise of Arry Awk, and now here she was, within the hour, showing every sign of becoming besotted with a goat.

'Picture!' she snorted. 'Are you deranged, Celia? The scene reminds me of nothing so much as Titania fondling Bottom with his ass's head. The child is bewitched. She has become possessed. Look at the creature's evil yellow eyes!'

'They *i'n't* evil!' Daisy now squeaked, having come to sufficiently to overhear this speech. 'Don't you *say* that, Grandma Bag! They're all lovely and yellow like bananas like in the book and I'm going to call him Billy Goat Gruff.'

'But, Daisy,' said Grandma, 'what about Little Tommy? Goats, I believe, particularly detest cats. What if the goat were to harm him?'

'I don't care!' Daisy answered. 'I like Billy Goat Gruff best. *You* can have Little Tommy. You keep him, Grandma Bag.'

The rest of the Bagthorpes paled at this offer.

'Certainly I think you should keep the cat, Mother,' Uncle Parker now smoothly interposed. 'He was, after all, intended as an offering to yourself from Daisy.'

'You keep out of this,' Mr Bagthorpe told him tersely.

Grandma, seeing her son's mounting fury, came to an instant decision.

'Very well, Daisy dear,' she replied, 'I shall keep the kitten. He has, after all, been responding well to his training, and is by no means the milk and water creature he was on his arrival. Thank you, dear.'

'Now *everybody's* happy,' said Daisy contentedly. 'I got Billy Goat Gruff and Grandma's got Little Tommy.'

This was a totally inaccurate assessment of people's feelings. Nobody was happy, unless, perhaps, the speaker herself. Quite apart from the prospect of having to live out their lives along-side a malevolent and unpredictable ginger tom, the younger Bagthorpes were now coming to realize that if Daisy were to depart happily with her newly acquired pet, then Uncle Parker's planned inducement to rehabilitate her at The Knoll would no longer be necessary. The Banquet, presumably, would be off.

William, who felt this as keenly as anyone, took the unprecedented step of offering advice on child-rearing to his aunt and uncle. He tried to sound dispassionate and wise in doing so.

'If I may be allowed to offer a word of warning,' he said, 'I really think it inadvisable to allow Daisy to have the goat. Daisy has a very symbolic mind, and the symbolism of a goat is not good. Not for a young child.'

This was a fairly cunning ploy, Jack thought, given the stress Aunt Celia always placed on poetry and symbolism. It nevertheless failed.

'The creature will have only that symbolism with which Daisy herself invests it,' replied Aunt Celia obscurely. 'She is her own mythmaker.'

'Oh my God!' Mr Bagthorpe exclaimed. 'Look, are you getting that animal out of here, or aren't you? Any minute now it'll start trying to kill again. And what about that seventy pounds?'

Here another argument set up. Uncle Parker declared that he had no intention of paying Mr Bagthorpe the full price of the goat.

'We are taking it off your hands, Henry,' he told him. 'You are scared out of your wits by it, and would probably pay money to rid yourself of it. I shall, however, take a fair view of the matter, and will give you half the sum you paid. I will, of course, wish to see the invoice.'

A real row now developed. Mr Bagthorpe was yelling and blustering even more than usual, because he on no account wanted Uncle Parker to see the invoice, which was for only fifty pounds, plus a delivery charge of three pounds. He had anticipated that Uncle Parker would try to knock a tenner off what he himself had paid, and with what he had smugly imagined was true financial wizardry had come swiftly up with a sum that would ensure that he would emerge from the deal in pocket.

Everybody present (except Daisy) was on Uncle Parker's side, in that in nobody's view was seventy pounds a realistic price for so unprepossessing an animal. The younger Bagthorpes kept shouting out their own estimates, ranging from fifty pence (William) to fifty pounds (Jack, who had believed his father's story about paying seventy).

The unexpected, however – the miraculous, even – was always tending to happen in Bagthorpian lives, and so now did the seemingly impossible occur. Daisy, sufficiently aware of what was going on to realize that the future of her Billy Goat Gruff was at stake, put her own oar in. She came heavily down on the side of Mr Bagthorpe. This made history.

'Daddy, Daddy!' she squealed, rushing toward him and tugging her goat after. 'Give Uncle Bag that seventy pounds! Give it him! You're mean! You got lots and lots of money and I want my goat, I *want* him! Mummy, Mummy, make Daddy give it Uncle Bag!'

There followed a stunned silence.

'There you are, Russell,' said Mr Bagthorpe at length, 'even Daisy acknowledges the animal's worth.'

It was a measure of his gratitude that this was the first time, so far as anyone could remember, that Mr Bagthorpe had been able to bring himself to allude to Daisy by name.

It was Daisy's appeal to her mother, of course, that settled the matter. Aunt Celia turned imploringly towards her husband, and laid a hand on his arm.

'Russell, dearest,' she murmured. 'For my sake . . .'

The next minute Uncle Parker was meekly fishing for his wallet and the transaction had been completed. It really was amazing, Jack thought, that Uncle

Parker's Achilles Heel should be Aunt Celia. One honestly would have thought he was made of sterner stuff.

Mrs Fosdyke made no secret of her own disgust when later describing the scene in The Fiddler's Arms.

'That Mr Parker's the only one of that whole bunch that's a proper gentleman,' she told Mesdames Pye and Bates, 'and what he was about, marrying that half-baked wife of his, I'll never know. There he is – like putty in her hands. Seventy pound! I ask you – seventy pound!'

The others clucked disapprovingly over their stout.

'And you never *saw* such a tussle as there was with that animal when it came! Saw it all, I did, from the window, and I swear to heaven I thought Mr Bagthorpe'd've got killed. Not that it wouldn't have served him right, but you don't expect goats to go round killing people. Nice headline *that*'d've made in the newspapers!' (Even Mrs Fosdyke, moving as she did only on the periphery of the Bagthorpes' lives, was becoming sensitive about headlines.)

'Anyhow,' she continued with satisfaction, 'it'll make an even better headline when that goat kills that Daisy. Which it will, sure as eggs. And at least their surname's Parker, and people won't go connecting it up with me, unless I tell 'em.'

'What about that banquit, Glad?' inquired Mrs Bates. 'Off now, is it?'

'On,' returned Mrs Fosdyke fatalistically. 'On. Said

they'd done all the bookings now, and o' course all them children was clamouring terrible about the food. Then that Daisy said she wanted a party for that goat of hers, and that did it, o' course. That poor Mr Parker. However he came to be mixed up with that bunch of lunatics, is—'

'And what about that old woman in hospital?' asked Mrs Pye, interrupting this all too familiar line of speculation. 'Her that got us all tranquillized?'

'Don't *ask* me,' begged Mrs Fosdyke, none the less going on to reply. 'They ain't *told* me anything, but I've got a 'orrible feeling she's getting better. And I've got a 'orrible feeling she's even madder. There's some of 'em been to visit 'er – Mr Bagthorpe senior 'as, *and* Mrs Bagthorpe – junior, o' course – and from what *I* can make out, she's started believing in Time all over again! Now! What do you make of *that*?'

Her audience shook their heads, indicating that they could make nothing whatever of this heretical turnabout.

'Would you believe!' murmured Mrs Bates. 'Believes in *Time*!'

'It'll be for the worse,' said Mrs Fosdyke darkly. 'You mark my words.'

'Well, anyhow, Glad, you've got that Daisy out the 'ouse,' Mrs Bates told her friend encouragingly. 'You try and look on the bright side.'

It was not in Mrs Fosdyke's nature to look on the bright side, and even the departure of Daisy had not been as straighforward as it might have been. There had been certain mysterious arrangements to be made, hints of dark secrets.

'You got to wait while I get fings ready,' she told her parents, once the purchase of the goat had been made. 'I got to go in the garden and I got to go up to Grandma's room and I got some fings to do yet. Come on, Billy Goat Gruff!'

She went out into the garden with a submissive Billy Goat Gruff in tow. It was hard at that moment for anybody but Mrs Fosdyke and Mr Bagthorpe to believe that his nature was anything but soft to the point of soppiness.

The latter, realizing this, said:

'If she's not back in five minutes, you'd better send out a search-party, Russell. Even man-eating tigers stop for a breather sometimes.'

This remark was made partly to justify his own earlier tirade about the animal's behaviour, and partly with the intention of sending Aunt Celia into a full-scale flap. It failed signally on both counts.

'We are all aware, Henry, that you have no affinity whatever with animals,' Grandma told him coldly, 'unlike Daisy, who is a child of nature.'

'Even the birds of the forest would fly to her bidding,' cooed Aunt Celia, making her daughter sound like St Francis of Assisi, to whom, the rest well knew, Daisy bore not even a passing resemblance.

A fairly heated debate about Daisy's character then began, interrupted only by the return of its subject, beaming happily.

'Everyfing's all right,' she announced contentedly.

They all assumed, mistakenly as it turned out, that she had been making a final tour of Highgate Cemetery, or paying her last respects to Arry Awk.

'Now I got to go up to Grandma Bag's room,' she told them. 'Come on, Billy Goat Gruff!'

'But really, Daisy dear,' protested Mrs Bagthorpe weakly, 'I really do not think that the goat should be taken upstairs.'

'You see, Russell?' said Mr Bagthorpe delightedly. 'You see now what you'll be sharing hearth and home with for the next God knows how many years? It is a young animal, and I have read somewhere, I think, that the life expectancy of a goat is somewhere in the region of forty years. It will see you all into your graves, and sooner rather than later, I should guess.'

'Unless, of course, it gets run over in the drive,' William said.

Uncle Parker was well and truly caught in the cross-fire. It was wonderful how the Bagthorpes so often managed to manipulate their own disasters to encompass other people. Uncle Parker kept up his cool front, but was very unhappy. He had forked out seventy pounds for a goat for whom, on sight, he had felt instant distaste, and it now did indeed appear that this animal was to be as inseparable from Daisy as Arry Awk had been. This would make life uncomfortable, almost certainly smelly, and possibly even more expensive than it had been during Arry Awk's regime.

Mr Bagthorpe's good humour, on the other hand,

was increasing by the moment. He had rid himself of the goat at a handsome profit, secured Daisy's simultaneous departure and was definitely one up on his old adversary. Characteristically, he could not resist rubbing salt in the wound.

'Let the child take the animal upstairs,' he told his wife. 'Let's find out if it's house-trained, eh, Russell?'

Daisy and the goat trotted out, followed by Grandma. Those in the kitchen could hear scuffling as the goat's hoofs slid on the rugs on the polished floor in the hall. 'It's to be 'oped it's not scratching up my parquet,' Mrs Fosdyke said to Mrs Bagthorpe, almost threateningly.

'It is indeed, Mrs Fosdyke,' said Mr Bagthorpe, forestalling his wife's reply and making this one of the rare occasions when he actually entered into any kind of direct conversation with Mrs Fosdyke. 'Fair acreage of parquet yourself, haven't you, Russell?'

'Though not 'im that 'as to polish it, I daresay,' said Mrs Fosdyke sourly.

'Indeed no! There you have a point!' Mr Bagthorpe exclaimed, seizing the opportunity to inflame matters further. 'Will your own housekeeper be inclined to take to the animal, Russell? Or up and leave, d'you think? There can hardly be any small print in her contract relating to a goat – house-trained or otherwise.'

'Oh dear,' said Aunt Celia faintly.

Mr Bagthorpe, satisfied, sank back into his chair. The best way to get at Uncle Parker was through Aunt Celia, who was less equipped to do her own housework than most ladies. Her fingers were long and white and tapering – though they did sometimes arrange flowers. At The Knoll, household duties of a more mundane nature were performed by a personage called Mrs Bend, who lived not in Passingham, but a nearby village. She came in every day on a bicycle, come hell or high water, which would seem to indicate that she was made of fairly strong stuff – as, indeed, she needed to be. What with Daisy's writing on walls and setting fire to things in corners and experimenting with water, life at The Knoll, as often as not, *was* hell and high water.

It could not, Mr Bagthorpe further reflected, be easy for this Mrs Bend to get on to Celia's wavelength. Nobody found it easy – or possible, even. Housekeepers generally like their employers to be recognizably of this world, and Mr Bagthorpe knew that Mrs Fosdyke, for instance, would not long tolerate an employer who was always gliding about with her eyes glazed, throwing pots or lying in a darkened room. That Mrs Bend did tolerate all this was a further indication that she was a lady who was not easily thrown.

Most people, on the other hand, have a breaking point. Mrs Bend's, he gleefully told himself, could well turn out to be the goat. He found himself speaking his thoughts out loud.

'They'll chew anything, of course, goats. They say they can go for months without food, as such. They'll manage on things like rugs and upholstery and curtains, and such. Water, that's the only thing you need give 'em.'

'You're overdoing it, Father,' William said. 'We get the message.'

He was afraid that if his father needled Uncle Parker beyond endurance, the Banquet could yet be cancelled.

At this point Daisy and the goat reappeared, followed by Grandma, the latter looking pleased.

'The animal is *not* house-trained,' she informed the company. 'We discovered this on the landing.'

Had the discovery been made in her own room she would, presumably, have looked less pleased. Mrs Fosdyke let out an exclamation of disgust. There was nothing in the small print of *her* contract, either, about goats.

'I'll be off now, Mrs Bagthorpe,' she said, whipping off her overall. 'Dental appointment, you'll remember' – scooting over towards her coat at a rate fast even by her own standards. The door had banged behind her within the minute.

'I said goodbye to Little Tommy,' Daisy said, 'and Grandma gived me this pretty box to put fings in.'

'Lovely, darling!' cooed Aunt Celia.

'It is not to be a parting present,' Grandma told her. 'Darling Daisy and I shall keep in close touch. I have promised to report to her daily on the progress of the kitten, and have also undertaken to come over from time to time and assist her with the training of the goat.'

'Good idea, Mother!' exclaimed Mr Bagthorpe heartily.

Grandma's influence on the goat could not be anything but bad. The goat's behaviour would spiral downwards at the speed of light.

At this moment the telephone rang and Jack went to answer it. He quickly reappeared.

'For you,' he told his mother. 'Hospital.'

Everyone's worst fears were confirmed on Mrs Bagthorpe's return a minute later.

'Great Aunt Lucy is to be discharged tomorrow,' she told everyone. 'The sister says she is much rested, and quite ready to go home.'

'Then they'd better put her in an ambulance and *send* her home,' said Mr Bagthorpe, his mood undergoing an abrupt change at this reminder of his own problems. 'She need not imagine that *I* am driving all the way to Torquay.'

'But – when I say *home*, dear, I mean *here*,' Mrs Bagthorpe faltered. She had meant to prepare her husband for this eventuality, but had never quite seemed to find the right moment to do so. 'She will require some attention for a while to come.'

'Look, Laura,' said her husband, 'the last place anybody can look for any attention of any kind is in this godforsaken household. And at the moment, some of us are still sane. A few more days of kippers at the full moon and buttered scones at dawn, and we shall *all* require hospitalization.'

'But, Henry dear, I told you. Lucy now believes in Time. She believes in it *implicitly*.'

'So you say,' he returned. 'Even if it is true, this

news is of no comfort to me whatever. Nobody round here *knows* Lucy like I know her. People with Bees buzzing around in their Bonnets like her don't change their spots overnight. If, as you maintain, she *does* believe in Time, she will not be believing in it like any common or garden mortal. She will have spun round a full one hundred and eighty degrees, like any damn politician.'

'Which is to say?' Mrs Bagthorpe was now rather cool. Every now and again she found her husband's exaggerations intensely trying.

'Which is to say,' continued Mr Bagthorpe, 'that she will now be working to the clock like any bolshy trade unionist. She will have armed herself with a stop-watch. She will have carved the day up into segments. She will want everything done spot on, to the nearest fraction of a second. We shall all be regimented out of our minds. She will probably insist on bells being rung, like in the navy. You'll see.'

There was a pause.

'The Sister did say something about . . .' Mrs Bagthorpe's voice trailed off.

'About *what*, Laura?' Mr Bagthorpe demanded.

'Oh dear – about being sure to pick her up at eleven o'clock *sharp* . . .'

Mr Bagthorpe groaned.

16

Mr Bagthorpe's prophecies about Great Aunt Lucy turned out to be almost uncannily accurate.

Nearly everybody heard, with misgivings, her first words on arrival at Unicorn House. The hall clock was just striking noon. She held up a hand, forestalling Mrs Bagthorpe's effusive welcome.

'Ah!' she exclaimed. 'The stroke of twelve!'

She heard the chimes out, and made everyone else do the same, before saying with satisfaction, 'There is something so *rounded* about the stroke of twelve, I always feel. Don't you?'

Nobody knew what to say to this, except Grandma.

'I find it a quite undistinguished hour,' she said. 'So far as I am concerned, one hour is much the same as another. Are you sure you are quite recovered, Lucy? You are still pale – though that may be, of course, the shade of your powder.'

Great Aunt Lucy did not hear any of this because she was fishing, with the hand that was not holding her stick, into her pocket.

'Ah!' She drew out a large and ancient timepiece. This she consulted, and instantly exclaimed:

'But the clock is wrong! There are still two minutes before twelve!'

'You are mistaken, Lucy,' said Grandma calmly 'That clock was a wedding present from myself to Henry and Laura, and keeps perfect time. It has never lost a minute in eighteen years.'

'But my own timepiece is accurate to within fractions of a second!' Great Aunt Lucy was already becoming agitated, the Bees were buzzing ominously. 'I have had it overhauled by a master clockmaker. Quickly, turn on the wireless! We must check!'

'Jack, switch on the portable in the kitchen,' his mother told him.

'I can't,' he said. 'All the radios are in the garden, remember, playing Radio Three to Tess's seeds.'

He knew this for a fact. He would not part with his own transistor from Mondays to Fridays until he had heard Terry Wogan. When he had taken it out that morning, just after ten, the vegetable garden had already been in full concert, with radios and tape recorders everywhere. He remembered glancing over to the meadow beyond, with its giant oak and beech trees, and wondering how they had got to be that size without the benefit of music? He had actually voiced this thought to Tess, who had said witheringly:

'Yes, and look how long it's taken them! Centuries! My own seedlings are already through, within the week.'

Jack thought the analogy between radishes and oaks an unfair one, but did not say so. He rarely entered into argument with any of his siblings, because they were so much cleverer than he.

At this point Mr Bagthorpe, surprisingly, ordered, 'You go and get that transistor and put it back where it belongs. This benighted country could be overrun by Martians, and we'd never know, for all the news we ever get to hear these days.'

Jack went. His father really was very difficult to understand. Mr Bagthorpe hardly ever listened to or read the news. He did not care for it, he said. Even Jack could see that he got politicians hopelessly mixed up and was always confusing Presidents of different countries, and even the countries themselves.

Jack would not have been so surprised by his father's apparent change of heart had he been present in the car during the drive back from hospital. Great Aunt Lucy had been so genuinely effusive in her thanks to Mr Bagthorpe for restoring her belief in Time that he had been impressed despite himself.

'Just think, Henry, if you had not placed that bag of mushrooms for me to trip over, none of this would ever have happened!'

'That's true, I suppose,' he agreed.

'And I shall be eternally grateful, Henry,' she continued. 'I shall never forget who was the instrument of my newfound happiness.'

All this sounded very promising. Mr Bagthorpe had every reason to be wary of any apparent changes of heart in this particular relative, but she had, he reflected, already been converted to Time for nearly three weeks. This phase was apparently ticking over very nicely. And given her obvious gratitude to himself, it now seemed that he could again be in with a chance in the inheritance stakes. It would do no harm, he decided, to humour her for the remainder of her stay.

None the less, he was to find this as trying as did the rest of the family. His aunt's conversation was tedious to a degree, being confined almost entirely to time checks, and there were frequent altercations with Grandma, whose own sense of Time now seemed to have slipped badly. She was late for every meal, and on one occasion almost succeeded in destroying at a single blow Aunt Lucy's newly discovered confidence in Time. She telephoned the Speaking Clock, with the wireless beside her giving a time check, and triumphantly reported that either the BBC or the GPO was three seconds out.

Whether or not this was true nobody knew. The immediate outcome was that Great Aunt Lucy herself took to telephoning the Speaking Clock on the hour, with the wireless beside her. Every now and then she would ring *between* hours, to catch it off guard, as it were. Mr Bagthorpe was enraged by this practice, and laid the blame for it squarely at Grandma's door.

'When that telephone bill arrives,' he told her, 'you will foot it. And you may even find yourself paying for my having a nervous breakdown. It now feels to me as if there are many more than twenty-four hours in a day. My whole body and brain rhythms have been overturned. I am suffering from chronic jet lag.'

The rest of the Bagthorpes were irritated by Great Aunt Lucy, but not beyond endurance. They comforted themselves with the prospect of the Parker Banquet on the horizon, this to be followed by the departure of their guest to Torquay (where she would doubtless embark on the life-long work of having all her haywire timepieces thoroughly overhauled and tested).

Tess was the sole member of the family really interested in Great Aunt Lucy's revised world view. The only trouble was, she was constantly trying to make the old lady revert to her former stance.

'There *is* no such thing as Time,' she insisted. A lot of the books she was currently reading advanced this theory. Jack sometimes worried about her. The experiments she was making were becoming increasingly bizarre. She had recently, for instance, mounted in a corner of her salad patch an experiment involving cardboard pyramids, razor blades and dead mice. Any razor left under a pyramid shape would sharpen itself automatically, she claimed. The dead mouse under the cardboard pyramid would not decay, she said, whereas the one under an ordinary empty carton certainly would.

'In a week's time I shall remove the coverings and we shall see,' she told everybody. 'The pyramid shape has extraordinary powers, as the ancient Egyptians were well aware.'

'So if we all built ourselves pyramid-shaped houses and stopped inside them all our lives, we'd all be immortal, I suppose?' inquired William sarcastically.

'Very probably,' she replied coolly. 'If, of course, there was any such thing as Time.'

There really did seem every danger of Tess exchanging Strings to her Bow for Bees in her Bonnet.

When the day of the Banquet arrived, the younger Bagthorpes, at least, prepared themselves in a state of pleasurable anticipation. They all put on their best things, and Grandma and Great Aunt Lucy were so bejewelled and ornamented in the effort to outdo one another that they would have appeared overdressed even at a Coronation. Mrs Fosdyke had on her best turquoise crimplene and bore two covered baskets containing quantities of stuffed eggs. She was, though she would not have admitted this, pleased at the prospect of overseeing a firm of London caterers, and even allowed Grandpa to sample a couple of eggs in advance. These, judging by his reactions, were well up to standard.

The first hint of a cloud on the horizon came when Grandma requested Jack to go up to her room and fetch the cat basket.

'Cat basket?' repeated Mr Bagthorpe sharply, overhearing this. 'Why in the devil's name do we require a cat basket?'

'Because there is no question of a Banquet without the presence of Thomas the Second,' she replied.

(She had ceased to refer to the kitten as Little Tommy immediately after his change in ownership, understandably feeling that this title did not command respect.)

'If that cat goes,' her son told her, 'then I don't.'

'That is entirely up to you, Henry,' she told him calmly. 'He received a specific invitation this morning from Daisy herself. As this Banquet is in her honour, I would not dream of disappointing her.'

Mrs Bagthorpe here smoothly interposed in an effort to extract her husband from a seeming impasse without loss of face.

'Do hurry up and fetch the basket, Jack. It shall travel in my car. Father, Mother, Jack and Rosie – you will travel with myself.'

At this Mr Bagthorpe stamped out muttering, followed by his own allocation of passengers, and the confrontation was thus resolved. Jack himself could not help feeling that the respite was only temporary. Judging by the hissings and scratchings from inside the basket he went to fetch, Thomas the Second had been trained up with great effectiveness. Also, he alone, besides Great Aunt Lucy, knew that a similar basket, containing the formidable Wung Foo, was already reposing on the back seat of Mr Bagthorpe's car. He had been given a pound note for putting it there.

When the Bagthorpes arrived at The Knoll they saw at a glance that the Banquet was going to be a thoroughgoing affair. Already parked in front of the house were two vans and a Rolls Royce, which turned out to be the property of the head chef. Mr Bagthorpe did not at the time know this, and leapt to the conclusion that the Rolls was a recent acquisition of Uncle Parker's, left in this prominent position with the express intention of impressing and infuriating himself. He did not fail to respond.

'My God!' he exclaimed in disgust, climbing out of his own battered estate. 'Look at that, will you! A parasite on society and – if ever there is a bloody revolution in this country, it will be that gin-swigging tailor's dummy and his like that bring it on. He spends his entire life . . .'

On he raved, giving Jack the opportunity to carry Wung Foo's basket into The Knoll unobserved. Daisy was already hopping up and down at the door. She was got up in what looked to Jack like a Miss Muffet fancy-dress costume, and was leading Billy Goat Gruff by a matching silk ribbon with a large bow at the neck.

'Zack, Zack!' she squealed. 'Ooooh, it's going to be—'

'Later, Daisy,' Jack told her. 'You look smashing. Where can I hide this?'

Daisy, who was a born conspirator or nothing, pointed to a panelled door, and Jack swiftly opened it and deposited the basket with relief. He had only an instant to register that the room seemed to be somebody's study, and thought how fortunate it was that it was not his father's.

* * *

Aunt Celia and Uncle Parker were now approaching, the former attired in a dress that, even to Jack's uninterested eye, was clearly a replica of Daisy's – or vice versa, of course. Uncle Parker, he noted, looked more or less as usual, in a pale-green suit with matching waistcoat.

'Hello, there!' he greeted Jack. 'And by Jove, Grandma, what a get up! Welcome to The Knoll. And to yourself, Lucy. How are you?'

He was sufficiently tactful not to comment on Great Aunt Lucy's attire, too, but Jack was already beginning to feel uneasily that the whole set-up had a nursery tale feel of unreality, what with Aunt Celia and Daisy got up as Miss Muffet or Little Bo Peep, and the two elder ladies looking as if, as well as rings on their fingers, they might well have bells on their toes.

Mr Bagthorpe, still under the misapprehension that Uncle Parker was the owner of a brand new Rolls, brushed straight past him and demanded of his sister:

'Where shall I put this accursed cat?'

'I'll take it, Father,' said Jack swiftly and with what at the time he imagined to be great cunning. He took the basket from his father's grasp and, quickly opening and shutting the same door as before, gave a sigh of relief.

'That's them out of the way,' he thought.

Such was the babble and general air of hospitality and goodwill in the hall, that one would have imagined Aunt Celia to have been nominated hostess of the season. She seemed quite to have forgotten her dread of intrusive vibrations in general and those of the Bagthorpes in particular. If anything, Jack thought, she was overdoing it. There was certainly no need to embrace Mr Bagthorpe, and it was clear from the latter's expression that he thought the same.

As few people were acquainted with the layout of The Knoll after so many years of absence, they all hung around in the hall waiting to be shown elsewhere.

'Shall I be getting along to the kitchen?' inquired Mrs Fosdyke loudly at length. 'If you'll be so good as to show me where?'

'Ah, Mrs Fosdyke!' Uncle Parker bowed gallantly. 'I shall myself take your incomparable stuffed eggs through, and you, I hope, will join us in the drawing-room for champagne.'

They all found themselves in a large room with French windows opening on to the garden and one burnt-out corner. Jack, once in, nipped out again, intending to accost Uncle Parker on his return from the kitchen and apprise him of the presence of Wung Foo and Thomas the Second. Uncle Parker, however, returned at speed, and clearly had his own problems.

'Got to keep Fozzy out of there, if we can,' he whispered loudly in passing. 'Old Bend's just about had enough as it is, with that damn goat. I'll get cracking with the champagne.'

This he duly did, with a vengeance, though the younger Bagthorpes were impatient of what seemed to them an unnecessary postponement of the real business – the Banquet.

'The present, Daddy, the present!' Jack heard Daisy squeal above the general hubbub.

He did not much like the sound of this. Surely Uncle Parker had not already commissioned a replica of the replica of the original replica of Thomas the First? He hoped not, if only because this would certainly remind Grandma of the live Thomas, and this in turn would remind Great Aunt Lucy of Wung Foo, and there might be some gruesome snowballing of events that would finish the Banquet before it even got started, and leave half the company in need of tetanus shots.

As it happened, Grandma was not to be the recipient. Uncle Parker, after first calling for silence (and obtaining it only with difficulty) made a short speech.

'We are all aware,' he began, 'that this Banquet is in honour of Daisy.'

'An' Billy Goat Gruff!' squealed that infant.

'Precisely,' he nodded. 'But it is also, we feel, fitting that we celebrate the recovery of dear Aunt Lucy, and her first visit to our home.'

He here bowed to that lady, and both Grandma and Mr Bagthorpe assumed expressions of extreme displeasure. The former, of course, was jealous. The latter was already beginning to scent a plot laid by the Parkers with the intent of attracting a sizeable slice of Great Aunt Lucy's fortune in their direction.

'Celia and I have learned of your conversion to

Time,' he went on, 'and rejoice in it. We congratulate you upon it. We were therefore determined that you should not leave without what is the oldest and most accurate timepiece known to man. If every clock in the world stopped tomorrow, if the BBC blew up and the GPO got its lines tangled for once and all, you, dear Aunt Lucy, would nevertheless be not a whit worse off.'

'As long as the sun shines, dearest,' murmured Aunt Celia, but nobody really heard this because Uncle Parker now, with a sweeping movement, removed a drape from an object that had been standing unnoticed by the French doors. It was a stone sundial.

Instant silence fell. All the Bagthorpes knew a master stroke when they saw one.

In the end Great Aunt Lucy herself advanced slowly, like a somnambulist.

'Time by the sun is yours for ever, Lucy,' Uncle Parker told her.

'By the sun, and by the moon!' she exclaimed in awestruck tones.

'And by the moon,' affirmed Uncle Parker. Jack had not thought of this. Could a sundial be also a moondial, he wondered? He noticed that his father's hands were clenching and unclenching ominously, and that Grandma was already drawing herself up in the way she did when about to pronounce.

Uncle Parker had also evidently sensed that the occasion would rapidly deteriorate, and was prepared for this.

'And now – the Banquet!' he announced. He strode forward, pulled at a rope, and a pair of green velvet curtains swept back to reveal what looked at first sight like a jungle.

'I have garlanded the banquet hall with flowers!' cried Aunt Celia ecstatically – and unnecessarily.

She certainly had. The scene now before them would have left the Tropical House at Kew, as Mr Bagthorpe later observed, standing. Especially as this well-known place does not have boars with apples in their mouths poking out of the greenery and mounds of pineapples, or a string quartet.

At a signal from Uncle Parker – carefully timed to fall between the gasp of astonishment from the assembly and the hubbub that would inevitably ensue if given the chance – a gay Mozart air struck up from somewhere among a clump of potted palms in the far corner of the room. This, it later turned out, had been the inspiration of Aunt Celia, who, having once embarked on playing the role of hostess, had evidently been taken over by it hook, line and sinker.

The Bagthorpes advanced, boggling. The board before them was groaning beyond even their wildest dreams, and was the more exotic for seeming to be sited in a tropical rain forest. Had cockatoos been perched on the chandeliers they would scarcely have seemed inappropriate. Mrs Fosdyke, herself a caterer of no mean order, boggled more than anyone. She was unprepared not only for the overwhelming greenery aspect of things, but also for the presence of at least six waiters in tie and tails standing stiffly to attention.

'For all the world like a set of stuffed penguins in a jungle,' she later told her friends, with a fine disregard for geography. 'And four more of 'em fiddling and blowing in the corner like mad things. She's mad, that Mrs Parker, and haven't I always said so?'

At the time, however, she was too dazed and dosed with champagne to do more than take a seat at the place Uncle Parker had cunningly had laid for her. He thought it safer to have her in sight as a guest than out of sight sabotaging activities in the kitchen. He diplomatically signalled to a waiter bearing a large silver platter of Mrs Fosdyke's stuffed eggs, garnished lavishly with parsley. This was placed, with an expression of outstanding disdain on the face of its server, in a central position on the table.

The five other waiters then closed in, and the Banquet was underway. It began surprisingly well. The long-starved Bagthorpes fell upon the food with a will. Conversation was thin on the ground and there was virtually no lively interchange of views and opinions. A neutral observer would have formed the impression that the guests had been given five minutes in which to consume enough nutriment to last them for the next calendar month. The waiters themselves formed more or less this opinion, and as the meal progressed their lips curled the more. They were accustomed to the kind of people who pick at things, and push away their plates half empty.

No plate was likely to be left half empty at this gathering.

Unfortunately, Daisy herself was not hungry. She had had unlimited access to Grandma's Fortnum and Mason hamper during her stay at Unicorn House, and had fed well since her return. She began to find the spectacle of so many people stuffing themselves and paying no attention whatever to herself and Billy Goat Gruff, depressing. Her eye fell speculatively on the small covered tureen by her plate. She shook her head sadly.

'You got to stay on, lid,' she told it.

She cast around for something that would cheer her up, and almost at once remembered the two baskets she had seen Jack deposit in her father's study. Despite her seemingly careless reassignment of Little Tommy to Grandma, Daisy had become genuinely fond of him. It seemed a pity for him to miss the proceedings. She wound her goat's ribbon loosely around the back of her chair and trotted out, unnoticed by anybody.

Now Daisy had intended only to introduce the kitten into the party. She had no real reason to feel affection for Wung Foo, and indeed still bore the marks of his bite. She said later that it had been the sad little whimpering noises from his basket that had upset her.

For whatever reason, then, once she had loosed Little Tommy and given him a good cuddle, she turned her attention to the other basket.

'I better not mix them,' she thought wisely. 'I'll

put Little Tommy in the party, then I'll come and fetch the Pekey on his lead and take him to the old griffin.'

She accordingly went back to the hall and, half opening the dining-room door, slipped Tommy through. She then returned and opened Wung Foo's basket. By the time she saw her mistake it was too late. The Pekingese was out at a bound and through the door. Daisy gave chase, but Wung Foo was not even wearing a lead at which she could clutch.

'Oh dear!' she squealed – and lost her head.

The Bagthorpes never really knew what hit them. One minute they all had their heads down, feeding deliriously, the next the table was rocking, pots breaking on all sides and a jungle coming down about their ears. The people who did most yelling (and competition was keen) were the London caterers, who had not been conditioned to this kind of scene. Two of them witnessed the dislodging of the lid of Daisy's tureen, and saw the mass of writhing white maggots which had certainly been no part of the set menu. They became quite hysterical and ran straight out of the house, although not before one of them had been bitten by Wung Foo.

The goat, who had recently been kept on a fairly tight rein by his possessive owner, was now hell-bent on a field day. He reverted to form. Only Mr Bagthorpe had reason to be pleased about this. At least now the rest of his family had seen the animal in its killing mood. It charged indiscriminately at everything. If there had been a troll present, it would have charged at that.

Jack tore at the streamers of vine and ivy tangled about his head and looked wildly about for the three loose animals. This was not easy, because they were all moving very fast. By now, everybody was moving very fast.

When Mr Bagthorpe yelled, 'Out – all of you! Get the hell out of here!' Jack, for one, was inclined to obey. So, it seemed, was everybody else. The younger Bagthorpes made for the door after their father, leaving their mother to help Grandpa with Grandma, who was shrieking, 'Get him, Thomas, get him!' and carried on shrieking this even as she was bundled into the car.

As the cars simultaneously revved up Uncle Parker lurched out of the front door, a garland of roses and ivy draped over his right ear. He was yelling something, but nobody waited to hear what.

'Thank God we're out of that!' Mr Bagthorpe exclaimed fervently as he threw the car out of the drive in the direction of home.

Epilogue

Mr Bagthorpe's thankfulness was short-lived, as it turned out, because when they arrived home it was to find that most of the wine which he had finally succeeded in making had blown up in their absence. Some of it, indeed, was still in the process of blowing up. The floor, ceiling and walls of the kitchen were spattered with red and yellow juices, and broken glass was strewn everywhere. It was at this stage that the Bagthorpes realized that in their haste to retreat they had forgotten Mrs Fosdyke – last seen spread-eagled in a pile of her own stuffed eggs. (They had also forgotten Great Aunt Lucy, but did not notice this until later.)

Nobody dared enter the kitchen, because a wine jar blew up just as they were opening the door. Mrs Bagthorpe was quite distraught.

'How shall we ever use the kitchen again?' she cried. 'We dare not touch the bottles! They are as volatile as gelignite!'

'Henry must move them,' said Grandma. 'He would not heed a mother's warning, and must pay the price.'

'Or get the Explosives and Anti-bomb Squad in,' William suggested.

Mr Bagthorpe was by and large in favour of this, even though the suggestion had been made in a spirit of sarcasm. He was unwilling, however, to risk the attendant publicity. What they did in the end, then, was defuse the remaining bottles themselves. They did this by crouching behind the kitchen door and hurling bricks and stones at the jars and bottles. None of them was very good at aiming, and a good deal of Mrs Bagthorpe's blue Staffordshire pottery ended up in pieces. Mr Bagthorpe's wine, per bottle, had cost rather more than vintage champagne, William later worked out.

The exploding of the wine- and, as it later transpired, beer-bottles certainly sounded the knell of Self-Sufficiency. Even Mr Bagthorpe could now see that it would be cheaper to revert to being un-Self-Sufficient.

Once the bottles had been defused the Bagthorpes gingerly advanced into their shattered kitchen just as the telephone rang. Jack picked his way through the debris and answered it. The voice on the other end of the line was unmistakable. Jack listened numbly to the text-strewn effusion that followed. When at last the voice stopped, 'Jolly good,' Jack croaked, 'I'll tell the others' – and hung up. Luke had become Young Brain of Britain.

He did not, of course, tell the others. By tomorrow morning they would know anyway. They would read it in the newspaper. He returned to the kitchen.

'Wrong number,' he said, but nobody was listening.

'Let your grandmother in through the front door, Jack,' his mother told him. 'She cannot be expected to go through all this. She must need to rest.'

She did not, of course. Adrenalin was coursing through her veins as furiously as through anyone else's. At this point Tess, who had gone running straight off into the darkening garden once she had hurled her share of bricks, returned in a state of near-hysteria. She too had caught a glimpse of Daisy's tureen of maggots and had put two and two together. Daisy had dislodged her dead mouse experiment.

'I'll kill her!' she screamed.

Nobody attempted to dissuade her from this course of action, even Grandma, who had by now realized that Thomas, as well as Mrs Fosdyke and Great Aunt Lucy, had been abandoned at The Knoll. She was evidently not sufficiently confident of the effects of her intensive training to be sure that he had killed or severely maimed the other two animals at large, and her pride would not allow her to telephone and find out. (It later emerged that the only casualties had been human ones.)

When the dust finally settled all that had really happened was that the Bagthorpes returned to normal – or as normal as they would ever be. Self-Sufficiency was abandoned, hopes of a legacy from Great Aunt Lucy relinquished, and Mrs Fosdyke finally persuaded to return, once the kitchen had been redecorated.

Mr Bagthorpe and Uncle Parker each had sufficient ammunition to last them in their rows for months, if they spaced it out properly.

Jack himself was pleased with the long-term outcome of the final débacle. Of all the pets owned by the family, Zero alone had been absent and free from all blame. He had been guarding Jack's comics up in his room, even through all the exploding going on below. Even Mr Bagthorpe conceded his innocence.

'Numb-skulled and mutton-headed that hound may be,' he said, 'but at least he's not a killer' – which was the nearest he would ever come to paying Zero a compliment.

By Helen Cresswell

The Bagthorpe family is unforgettable. Eccentric, hilarious and disaster-prone, they never fail to make an ordinary idea a quite extraordinary event . . .

Book 1: ORDINARY JACK

Poor old Jack Bagthorpe. He lives in the shadow of his talented siblings. It's so hard to be ordinary when the rest of your family is utterly brilliant.

Only Uncle Parker truly understands. But could his madcap plan really help Jack to be brilliant too?

Book 2: ABSOLUTE ZERO

Uncle Parker has won a competition. The prize: a cruise to the Caribbean. Not to be outdone, the Bagthorpes enter every competition in sight . . .

The Prizes roll in – though none of them *quite* match up to Uncle Parker's. Only Zero beats all expectations. Has he really won a contest all of his own?

By Helen Cresswell

The Bagthorpe family is unforgettable. Eccentric, hilarious and disaster-prone, they never fail to make an ordinary idea a quite extraordinary event . . .

Book 3: BATHORPES UNLIMITED

Only the Bagthorpes could turn the burglary of their home into a public humiliation. Grandma is so distraught that she demands a family reunion!

But the arrival of their unbearably gifted cousins is sure to upstage the younger Bagthorpes. They must go one better. Even if it means attempting a world record . . .

Book 5: BAGTHORPES ABROAD

When their father announces he's taking them all on holiday abroad, the Bagthorpes are delighted. No one thinks to smell a rat . . .

But on arrival at their holiday home, the family comes down to earth with a bang. Patently the word 'abroad' has an unusual meaning for Mr Bagthorpe – as does the word *holiday* . . .

By Helen Cresswell

The Bagthorpe family is unforgettable. Eccentric, hilarious and disaster-prone, they never fail to make an ordinary idea a quite extraordinary event . . .

Book 6: BAGTHORPES HAUNTED

On holiday in Wales, Mr Bagthorpe is on a stubborn quest to find a ghost, and he's driven to desperate measures. The rest of the family are in despair.

The chaos continues with Daisy Parker's beloved goat, Billy Goat Gruff, which wreaks so much havoc that even Uncle Parker loses his cool – an *ominous* sign. Could this be the holiday from hell?

Book 7: BAGTHORPES LIBERATED

Life is simply not fair for the Bagthorpes. Having endured the worst holiday ever, they have returned home to find a tramp in their kitchen.

Mrs Bagthorpe is at the end of her tether with the whole of mankind, and believes it's high time she took a feminist stand. If only somebody would take her seriously . . .